Gibson's Legacy

Last Score Series

Book 1

K.L. Shandwick

Publisher: KL Shandwick

2nd Edition

Cover Design:Russell Cleary

Cover Photography: KL Shandwick

Editor: T.Bacher (Editor in Heels)

Format: Riane Holt

Beta readers, Emma Moorhead and Joanne Swinney.

Disclaimer: This book contains explicit, mature content and language and is intended for adults aged 18+.

The book content is a work of fiction and any resemblance to any persons alive or dead is purely coincidental, names, places, characters, band names and incidents are the product of the author's imagination or names of actual places or other references are intended to be used in descriptive terms to inject depth of relatable content for the enjoyment of the reader.

DEDICATION

For Pete, (my rock star) Russ & Kris and to Sarah Tree, who works tirelessly to promote my work. Also, for #TeamGibson and to rock stars everywhere for being my inspiration and muses. Thank you.

“Darling, my attitude is ‘fuck it’;
I’m doing everything with everyone.”
Freddie Mercury – 1979

CHAPTER 1

M3RCY ME

Chloe

Shaking my head at Ruby's antics I wandered slowly down the passageway at the back of the bar, on my way to the staff room. It had been a long, busy night and I couldn't wait to get out in the fresh air and away from the smell of stale beer, loud music and drunken students.

Pushing open the door, I headed into the staff restroom before gathering my stuff to leave for home. I was feeling pretty wiped out. Saturday nights were always hectic, especially when there was live music, but collecting glasses and replenishing bottles of beer was an easy, non-taxing way of making ends meet.

While I was washing my hands, I heard a low groan and what sounded like slapping noises coming from the communal area I had just walked through. Retracing my steps, I regretted it the instant I opened the door.

My heart stopped when I was faced with a sight which has always remained with me. Sometimes, things happen that are beyond anything you can comprehend, and that was one of those moments for me.

Halted in my tracks, I stood statue-like, arm in mid-air after smoothing my hair down. Staring open mouthed, my brain was completely blank of thoughts. I had no clever or grace-saving way of dealing with what I was seeing.

Gibson Barclay was sitting back, slouched down on the leather couch. His jeans were around his knees and he was going at it, hot and heavy, with a young blonde girl. Less than ten minutes since his gig ended and he was getting laid again.

Some people may not have been as affected like I was, by witnessing something like that, but there was something raw and degrading about what they were doing; having sex without being in a relationship. Hook up sex was the one thing that I knew I would just never understand.

Ugh, and I wondered if the guy ever thought about anything else. This wasn't the first time I'd seen one of Gibson's private performances. Another instance sprang to mind. Late one night in the bar parking lot he had a girl bent over on her belly, across the hood of his car.

Thankfully that time, I didn't see any flesh. Gibson's jeans were still on; it was just the rocking motions and loud screams of the girl he was taking, while the suspension on his car took quite a beating that gave the game away. There had actually been about a dozen incidents I'd happened upon altogether.

On this particular occasion, Blondie was sitting astride him, and it was obvious there had been no foreplay, because she still had her panties on and they'd just been yanked to the side. Plus, it was less than five minutes since I'd seen him in the bar talking to her after his gig.

Trying to step back quietly, the door hinge squeaked and Gibson pushed the girl's head down and pulled it into his neck to see who was there. Staring straight at me he continued what he was doing and never broke his stride.

Paralyzed by the sight of them in front of me doing that, blood rushed to my face and my heart beat accelerated instantly. Shock and embarrassment flooded my body and I couldn't decide what to do about being in such a confined space with them.

Smirking salaciously, Gibson continued to pound into her, lifting her on and off of him, but his eyes remained transfixed on me. No idea why my eyes flicked down to the business end, but they did, and damn Gibson was dishing out a pretty thick package to his lady.

Knowing he had been busted didn't deter him at all, and if anything, it fuelled his efforts, making him pound the girl faster from underneath with his butt hanging clear off the couch. From the noises she was making, I figured she was close. No one could make that amount of noise and fake it that badly, and she kept begging him to keep going.

Once I found my composure, I stepped back out of the room. Swallowing hard, I dropped my gaze to the floor closing the washroom door softly. I sagged against it, with a few feelings I knew I shouldn't have had about the guy.

Gibson Barclay was every inch sex on legs. If God intended on making a sexual being it would be him. Tall, mid-brown colored hair, stunning even features, grey eyes, tanned, toned… no, ripped – with the most lickable soft, golden skin.

The way he moved was downright mesmerizing. Really, I tried hard not to be attracted to guys like him, but there was just something about Gibson. There was something so alluring about him. He was a people magnet. For males and females.

I suppose you'd say he was a man's man, but women adored him, reputation and all. Everyone wanted to be near him, women wanted to touch him which was fine by Gibson, because he was seriously into women.

Moving away from the door, I went to sit in one of the stalls. "Lookin' For A Good Time" by Lady Antebellum was playing through the bar sound system and I shook my head and began to text Kace.

Stuck in the restroom because Gibson Barclay is in a compromising position out in the staff communal area.

Kace texted back.

I don't believe you, I want pictures!

Kace's text was like a punch to the center of my chest. Feeling incensed and disgusted, I wondered if all men were pigs when it came to sex. I had only ever been with Kace, and that was after we'd been together for two years. Kace had been very persistent about it, but I had been determined to hold off until it was the right time for me.

Deciding when to have sex had to be my decision; and as much as I loved Kace, no one was going to talk me into something I wasn't ready for. My beliefs were that it was a very intimate event, not just a fun thing to do. Despite Kace's pursuit, I had only felt ready and allowed him to take our relationship to that level a few weeks ago.

My busting in on Gibson and the girl, and seeing what they were doing, was totally mortifying for me. In my view, neither he nor the girl had any respect for themselves or their bodies. I doubt I would ever shame myself by doing something as crude or public as I had just inadvertently witnessed with them.

About ten minutes later, there was a soft rap on the door and I heard a creak as it was pushed open. Fera, one of the bar girls, came in and said, "Gibson asked me to come and tell you the coast was clear."

I couldn't believe the audacity of the guy, to leave me sitting in there and calmly leave. Filthy, selfish bastard. What made it worse was the look on Fera's face, because I could see she thought I was Gibson's 'lucky strike' of the night.

I was blushing furiously, that anyone could have

thought it had been me that was caught having sex with him. I was going to explain, but thought better of it. I didn't want to draw any more attention to the whole sorry episode.

Passing back through the bar on my way to leave, I felt like it was me doing the walk of shame. Entering the bar area, the first thing I saw was Gibson, his eyes connected with mine before I quickly dropped my gaze in the direction of the floor and rushed past him. Kace grabbed my arm. "Hey, what's the rush? Where are you going?"

Mumbling for him to let me go, I pulled my arm away and told him I'd see him at the car. I just wanted to be out of there so I headed out the door towards the parking lot. Kace came jogging along behind me. "Jesus Chloe, wait up. Where's the fire?" Spinning around, I snorted at him.

"Seriously? I texted you because I was stuck in the restroom while Gibson Barclay was hitting a home run in front of me, and your response was for me to take pictures?" Stomping to his truck still mad, I reached out and jerked the handle, but nothing happened. Kace's blasé attitude about my feelings made me too angry to realize that he had yet to unlock it.

Kace caught up to me and looked concerned. Taking my face in his hands, he dipped his knees to look into my eyes. "Babe, you weren't serious about that Gibson thing were you?" Seeing his ashen face made me realize that he had been joking in his text.

"Why would you think I'd make a joke about

something like that, Kace?" Searching his face, I was still angry that he had taken it so lightly. Kace realizing I was angry puffed out his cheeks, dropped his hands from my head and thrust them deep into his front pockets with his arms looking straight and awkward.

"Everyone jokes about how promiscuous he is, Chloe. It isn't like saying something like that would cause offense to most people. Gibson's slutty behavior is a standing joke around campus." I knew that but it wasn't helping me get my point across.

"Kace, this is *me*. I'm not everyone. And, if this is your idea of apologizing, just save it and take me home please, I've had enough disappointment about men for one evening." Glancing up at him again, I could see the penny had dropped and he knew how seeing that had affected me.

Looking remorsefully at me, Kace pulled me into his chest and kissed the top of my head. "Jeez, I'm sorry honey." In the two years we'd been together, this was the first time Kace hadn't read the situation right and there was no way I was about to let Gibson Barclay, or anyone like him, interfere with what we had as a couple.

Witnessing Gibson doing those things with those girls gave me feelings I didn't want to feel about him, and there was no point in thinking that way anyway. We were poles apart socially and in every other way for that matter.

Gibson was a babe magnet and I was plain Jane. Anyway, I was in love with Kace, so I accepted his invitation to spend the night at his place. He shared an apartment with Brody, my roommate Julie's boyfriend. Kace and Brody had full scholarships so they could afford to live off campus.

Gunfire was blaring from the television when Kace opened the apartment door. Julie was covering her eyes and there was some evil looking gangster staggering around with his arm hanging off on the TV screen. Brody turned and when he saw us pressed pause on the remote.

"Hey! We've been waiting for you, dude. Want to get some pizza?" Kace turned to look at me, and I wrinkled my nose up in disgust. It was after midnight and all I really wanted was a long soak in the tub and to cuddle up with my man.

Declining politely, Kace made our excuses and headed into his bedroom. Their apartment wasn't huge, but they had the luxury of a bathtub; which was in Kace's bathroom. Setting down my things on the green velour armchair, I went into the bathroom and turned the faucet on and began to fill the tub.

Wandering back to the bedroom, I crossed my arms over the front of my t-shirt, taking it by the hem and pulled it over my head, discarding it on the chair with the rest of my things. Kace was sitting on the bed looking at my tablet and setting up a playlist for us to listen to. "Rude" by Magic started playing.

Glancing up, he smirked playfully and rose from the bed. Swaying over to me, he slipped his arm around my bare waist and pulled me against him, still swaying from side to side with me. Instantly I felt my tension drain away. Being in his arms was calming and the firm way he held me gave me a warm feeling.

Stopping briefly, he pulled his t-shirt off and pulled me back against his chest. Skin to skin, apart from my bra. My hands automatically glided around his waist and up his smooth muscular back to rest on his shoulders.

Kace smiled down with affection at me and bent his head forward to brush his lips against mine. "I love you, Chloe," he whispered softly, pressing his lips against my closed mouth. I was about to kiss him back when he suddenly set me away from him. "Tub," he declared, patting my butt, leading me into the bathroom.

Bending to turn off the faucet and check the temperature, Kace snuck up behind me and I jumped, but he pulled me upright and against him. Sliding his hands around to the front of me he began to unbutton my jeans.

Opening the zipper, his strong hand slid down and inside my panties, his fingers teasing my now hard nub. Stroking it back and forth, his feet kicked mine further apart and his fingers began to stroke from my entrance up to my clit.

"Let's get you out of those jeans, honey. I want to see what I'm doing." He murmured sexily in my ear and then began tugging my jeans down my legs and over my knees. Once he had helped pull me free of them, he picked them up and dropped them over by the vanity unit.

Kace's eyes glanced appreciatively over me as I stood there in my black lace bra and panties. "Very pretty. I love that lingerie on you. Come over here." He motioned for me to stand beside him and turned me to face the full length mirror that was stuck on the back of the bathroom door.

Still behind me he began to kiss my neck and fondle my breasts from behind at the same time. What he was doing felt really good and as tired as I was, he was turning me on. My head rolled back to rest on his shoulder and he kissed my temple as his hands began to slid down my abdomen, one disappearing into my wet panties again.

Learning about my body and how to please me was Kace's aim and I was still a little hesitant when we made love, but he was patient and gentle, and I knew sex would get better as time went on. He had made me come with his mouth and his fingers, but I was yet to orgasm when he was inside me.

Unclipping my bra, Kace drew the straps down my arms and dropped it to the floor. Watching me in the mirror, he palmed my breasts. He was smiling at me and bent to kiss my neck again. Shivers ran down my spine and a soft moan of pleasure escaped from my throat.

Not sure when it happened but my mind drifted back to earlier in the evening. Gibson had been having sex with 'Blondie,' and I suddenly wondered how his hands would feel touching my breasts like Kace was doing. Thinking about that made me really excited and I began undulating my hips, matching the rhythm that Kace was setting against my clit.

Turning around to him, I placed my arms around his neck and pulled him to me in a fierce, hungry kiss. Before I knew what was happening Kace had pulled my panties down to my ankles and off one foot. I had unbuttoned his jeans, my fingers wrapping around his erect dick still inside his boxer briefs.

Everything seemed like a blur after that. Our hands all over each other; me, frantically tugging at his clothing stripping Kace naked, and my leg bent at the knee over his arm as he supported my weight.

Kace pushed himself inside me and I was shocked at both the urgency and the rough way he took me. Most of all, I was stunned at how turned on I was and I'm ashamed to say I wasn't thinking about him at all, I was imaging Gibson Barclay.

Flashbacks too many encounters I'd witnessed of him with various girls flashed like some kind of slideshow through my mind. When the final image of his thick length plunging in and out of the blonde girl earlier in the evening flashed through my mind, I was done.

Coming hard, my legs buckled and primal noises, I never knew I was capable of, tore from my throat. Kace pulled himself out of me and came over my butt, groaning loudly, "Ohh." Afterwards, he sagged against me, pulling me tightly to him and I felt the discomfort of his hot, sticky come between us. I closed my eyes feeling ashamed that I'd had an orgasm with Kace while thinking of another man.

Kace seemed delighted with himself thinking it

was his skill that had set me on fire and I was embarrassed when he commented that he had finally learned how to 'push my buttons'.

Once in the tub with him, I lay resting between Kace's legs. Dropping my head back against his chest, I closed my eyes. Glad that my back was to his front and thankful that I didn't have to face him for a while.

Reflecting on what had just happened I couldn't deny what thoughts of Gibson did to me, but wondered how I could find Gibson Barclay remotely appealing with his whorish behavior towards women.

CHAPTER 2

TOWELS

Chloe

Reluctantly, I began to prepare to go to work, and dreading the thought of facing Gibson after the night before. M3rCy were playing again that night. Hoping that with my short shift, I'd have done my work and left by the time they arrived. I wasn't on glass duty that night, just cleaning and replenishing the bar for the evening shift.

Placing my tablet on the side, I set the music on shuffle Nico and Vinz, "Am I Wrong," was playing and began to clear the counter top to clean and polish. Startled by the suddenness of a blinding flash of lightning, followed by a loud clap of thunder, I made my way to the window to look out.

Staring out at the heavy downpour, I was distracted from the mundane task I was doing. Relentless patterns tapped out on the window panes like beats of a rhythm of a tune. Life wasn't easy away from home, but I had learned to deal with most things since moving here.

Sweeping floors and washing beer stained, wine colored vinyl seating wasn't exactly what I thought college life was going to be about, but needs must are a reality and I was definitely in need. Learning the value of money was one of the compromises I'd made to come to college in California from Florida.

Staring out, I was pulled from my reverie by a commotion in the hallway which led from the bar to the car park out back. Before I could figure out what the noise was, Gibson Barclay and his rowdy band had invaded the bar.

Dripping wet, his hair plastered flat to his head, Gibson was the vision of male perfection. His wet t-shirt was clinging to every fabulous sculptured contour of his ripped torso. Satiny tanned skin was shining with a glow only cool rain seemed to give it. Thick lines of his tattoos were clearly visible through the thin, white, cotton material which had gone transparent and clung to his honed muscular frame.

"Any towels for a drowning man over here?" Drawing my gaze reluctantly up to meet his, my legs buckled and my heart raced at the shock of even interacting with him, that he had even noticed I was in the same room as him. Girls like me were invisible to guys like Gibson in normal circumstances.

Smiling sexily at me with his perfectly formed mouth and luscious lips as water droplets ran down his face and neck, he raised an eyebrow in question at me, waiting for me to respond to his request.

There was a glint in his eye that said he may

have very well begun to flirt with me. Silence hung in the air whilst I tried to assimilate what he had asked me. The effect he was having on me was incredibly distracting.

Glancing up at his face, I thought my imagination must have been playing tricks on me, but I had a weird feeling there was this… 'thing,' that happened between us. And, for a few seconds it seemed like we had shared a moment when our eyes connected, because his smile then stretched into his trademark roguish grin. That's when I felt it was definitely my fantasy messing with my mind.

Honestly? It could have been a fantasy interjecting in my real life interaction with him, but whatever it was, I was riveted to the spot. Hungry eyes feasted unreservedly on the sight before me, taking in every inch of the sexy manwhore that was Gibson Barclay.

Becoming conscious that I was dressed in my tatty, white tank-top and how plain and dowdy I was in comparison, I shifted awkwardly in front of him. Open mouthed and practically drooling, I drew my arm across my chest to hide my horrible worn down appearance.

There had been several occasions when I had been subjected to his 'less than discreet' womanizing and lewd behavior, but even after everything I'd seen and knew about his reputation, I still fantasized about him. I'd never felt a pull toward any other guy like I had with him.

Just being in the same room as him made me a

quivering, nervous mess, and I hated that a guy like him could have that weird sexual effect on me. Being in a long term relationship with Kace didn't seem to be a consideration, especially when I tried to imagine the kind of kinky stuff Gibson might get up to in the bedroom… or anywhere else for that matter.

The conversation I had with Ruby the night before was playing over in my mind. Once, when my girlfriends and I were having a slumber party, I admitted that I would have considered throwing over my relationship with Kace, my high school sweetheart and steady boyfriend, for one night with a guy like Gibson if he'd asked me.

Maybe I'd said that because I knew there was more chance of hell freezing over than any possibility of that happening. No matter what I knew about him, even with all the red flags that were everywhere in relation to him, I'd become sexually aroused while being touched by Kace, with Gibson on my mind.

"Did you hear me, darlin'?" Horrified at my own lack of composure and that I'd drifted off into my fantasy, I realized I'd been objectifying him while he was watching me. Catching the briefest glimpse of his wicked grin again, I dropped my gaze once more to the floor, nodded and headed off to the closet in the office, where spare towels were kept.

I was mortified at the way he could make me feel so unsophisticated, yet he was only a year older than me. I was dreading the thought of returning with the towels because that meant facing him again.

Luckily, Matt the owner of Beltz Bar, liked to shower during the long hours he kept, so there was always a good supply. Reaching up on tip toe, I began to pull five from the top shelf and as I was about to turn, I felt firm hands on either side of my hips with finger tips applying the slightest pressure into my flesh. "Whoa! Careful. Let me take those from you."

Gibson must have crept up on me, which heightened the effect of his touch on my body. Sharp pangs of electrical currents jolted deep in my core and my mouth went dry. Trying to swallow, I turned my head. I regretted it as soon as I realized his lips were only a couple of inches from mine. Damn he smelled incredible. Clean fresh laundry, mingled with a unique body smell in his wet clothing and fresh rain. Jeez the guy was so hot I could have scorched myself.

Releasing his grip, Gibson reached out to secure the pile of towels in his grasp, his hand brushing over my fingertips as he did so, sent tingles down my spine. Blushing, I passed them forward and quickly made space between us walking over to the open doorway

Touching me like that was a liberty, but everything Gibson did was one big liberty and he seemed to get away with it because of how he looked and his charismatic ways. Plenty of times, I'd seen him pull a 'lucky girl' from the audience and kiss her roughly during his band's performance. He definitely wasn't playing to the crowd either.

Sometimes Mick, his lead guitarist, had to pull him away from them to keep the gig on track.

Turning away to hide the fact that he'd unnerved me so much, I headed to the staff room to collect my jacket. Staying there in the bar a moment longer would have become even more awkward for me. Besides, the storm had passed and my shift was short so I didn't want to hang around longer than necessary.

Kace was waiting in the parking lot and was already opening the door of his truck for me. I climbed up into the cab, feeling guilty for having those unwelcome feelings about someone like Gibson, when I was lucky to have a fabulous boyfriend like Kace.

Smiling warmly, I leaned over and kissed Kace and tried to put as much passion into it as I could, partly because I loved him and partly to rid myself of the feelings that I'd just had when Gibson had touched me.

Entering the floor where my dorm room was, I heard music and smiled when I saw Julie dancing with her back to me. She was in her underwear and lost in the moment to "Poker Face" by Lady Gaga. Oblivious that I had walked in on her, she was twerking and trying to body pop, which made me shriek with laughter. Spinning around, she hid her body, then realizing it was me she lunged at me swiping my arm. "Jesus, you gave me the fright of my life."

Smirking wickedly at her, I responded, "I could

say the same. Look at you dancing around in your panties." Shaking her head, she leaned over and picked up a blue cotton t-shirt from the pile of clean laundry and pulled it down over her slender frame.

"What time are you meeting Kace?" Those words jolted me right back to the bar and M3rCy's upcoming performance. Unsure I would be able to sit through it, I swallowed hard twisting my mouth at Julie.

"I don't think I'm going to make it tonight. An assignment for my media class is proving more difficult than I thought." It was a bare faced lie. I could still feel the soft pressure of his hands on my hips from that briefest touch, but one that I was finding hard to shake.

Eventually, Julie wore me down because part of me was being irrational about that little encounter. Wishful thinking probably made me see more than there was, besides, I couldn't hide from him indefinitely. Once Julie talked me around I showered and changed to go out with them. There was no way around it anyway, I had to face him again sooner or later, Beltz Bar fed me.

Seeing Kace made my heart swell. After all this time he could still make my heart flutter. I'm sure the thing with Gibson was probably infatuation. Leaning back lazily against the front of his truck, his legs crossed at the ankles, Kace was engrossed in his cell phone. My stiletto heels clicked noisily as I approached and he looked in my direction.

Slowly, his pouting mouth stretched into a

beautiful, sexy smile, his eyes twinkling with mischief. "Well, hello there beautiful. How is my gorgeous girl tonight?" Smiling warmly as we walked towards each other, I licked my lips preparing for the kiss I knew we'd have as soon as we made contact. Strong, warm arms wrapped around me, one around my waist, one over the back of my shoulders as Kace pulled me into his chest.

"Great, and it just got a whole lot better." Grinning with pleasure, I glanced up at him, right before he bent and kissed me softly on the mouth. All my worries about Gibson and going back to the bar dispersed as soon as Kace and I were together.

I had started to think that my interlude with Gibson was all nonsense and I'd been ridiculous in my thinking that what happened was anything other than an innocent interaction. From my own perspective, I thought it was probably best for me to get this particular gig over with as it would be the first of many more times I'd have to be around him.

My friend Ruby and her boyfriend Dylan had already snagged a table for us. Unfortunately for me, it was right in front of the stage. Stupid that I should feel so shaken by what was probably a very innocent situation I had blown out of proportion.

Ruby stood up from her chair and edged her way around Dylan's legs to cuddle me. "Thank God you're here, I thought I was going to be stuck listening to these guys talking car parts like they were pornographic images. I mean who would have thought there were so many parts to an engine, it has been the only topic of conversation for the last twenty minutes?"

Ruby's face was a picture, her lips pursed and her eyes rolling. She always did look very dramatic. She had one of those really animated faces when she was explaining something. Smiling my understanding of how boring the guys got when they talked cars, I nodded towards the rest rooms for us to have a five minute catch up without the guys in earshot.

Kace saw someone he knew and excused himself from me as we were walking to the table. When I turned to see if he was coming he was at the bar talking to one of the girls in his lab class. Their discussion looked pretty intense.

Glancing over, he seemed to stop in his tracks and smile at me and I immediately relaxed. Turning back to the girl, he continued to talk to her, leaning in a little as if she couldn't hear what he was saying.

She looked frustrated with him whatever they were talking about, and although Ruby was talking to me, I was still watching them as we crossed the floor. I lost sight of them as we walked into the restroom.

"So, we have a 'close up and personal' of Gibson tonight, Chloe. Still got that hot fantasy going around in your head about him?" Feeling flustered, my heart started beating quickly because I was taken off guard by Ruby's remark about the disclosure I made at the slumber party. She was choosing this moment to throw it back at me. I began to blush and protest that it was all made up on the spur of the moment to shock her and the other girls there.

Ruby laughed loudly and shook her head. "No way, Chloe, we all saw your reaction when you were talking about him, honey. It wasn't as much about what you said about him, but more about *how* you said it."

Turning away from her to use the hand drier, I was glad of the noise it made because I needed a moment to collect my composure and leave a pause in the conversation. Protesting too much was much worse than letting it go.

Leaving the restroom, I wondered how I was going to get through the evening after the encounter with Gibson that morning and Ruby's comments. The night was only beginning. Desperate to shake off the lingering feelings that his brief touch had given me, I decided to focus completely on Kace during M3rCy's performance.

Not usually the most outgoing or demonstrative person, I surprised Kace by sitting on his lap when we got back to the table. I felt a bit embarrassed about my public display of affection but this was rewarded with a seductive smile on his part, and he slid his warm hand inside the back of my tight fitting red t-shirt, causing the hem to ride up my belly at the front.

Just as he did that, Gibson and the rest of M3rCy walked out on stage, his gaze immediately falling to my bare midriff. When he looked up again, he caught me watching him, watching me. Raising an eyebrow at me, he smirked suggestively then licked his bottom lip.

Looking away I squirmed uncomfortably on Kace's lap, which Kace read as a sexual overtone and pulled me tighter onto his growing erection by gripping my left hip, and positioning me more central on top of him.

For a moment I thought about having an imaginary migraine so that I could leave, but I knew I had to get over the stupid misplaced attraction I felt for a guy who treated women like sexual objects.

The conversations I'd heard previously from his band members was enough to turn me off. And, although I hadn't actually heard Gibson use the term, his band mates often talked about other bars they were going to as places where they got to sample 'fresh meat'.

Striking the first cord, Mick, the lead guitarist, dragged me out of my reverie and my eyes automatically followed the sound. Gibson was walking over to the mic wearing a tight fitting black t-shirt with a Harley Davidson motif on the front, tight fitting dark blue jeans and a pair of biker boots. Classical disheveled rock star attire.

Strong upper arms strained the short sleeves of his t-shirt and exposed his amazing bold tribal tattoo on one arm, and a clever bass guitar tattoo on the other. The guitar strings on this were inked like the stave on a music manuscript, with notes positioned along the strings or stave, and words written along the neck above which said, 'Heart strings can only truly be tugged by music'.

While wrapping his fingers around the

microphone he took from the stand, the introduction to a cover of "Just Like Heaven" by The Cure played. An instant hush fell as the room held their breath waiting for him to sing.

Choosing the line 'I'll run away with you,' he started staring straight at me and I was embarrassed by his attention. Gibson seemed to sense my discomfort and that only made him focus all the more on me.

Coming close to the edge of the stage, he made me his target female to sing to. That was a very normal occurrence for him; Gibson did that with every song. He generally singled out a female in the audience and sang in a way that made the girl feel it was just for her.

Averting my eyes from him, I looked in Ruby's direction and she was singing along but raised her eyebrow at me. Her questioning brow made me feel like I was being ridiculed by the both of them, so I looked at the floor. Rising off Kace's lap before the song ended, I excused myself to go to the restroom.

I was humiliated by what had happened and there was no way I could continue to sit there with the level of scrutiny I was under. Twice in twenty four hours I had been stuck in the same restroom, mortified by the selfish attitude of Gibson fucking Barclay.

CHAPTER 3

LUCKY GIRL

Chloe

Somehow, I managed to fumble my way through the rest of the night in the bar after Gibson's 'personal performance' aimed at me. It wasn't so bad when Julie and Brody arrived. She positioned a chair directly in front of my line of vision from the stage, and that gave me some respite from the scrutiny that Gibson had me under.

Ruby was the only one who seemed to notice what was going on with Gibson and as soon as we were alone she cornered me. "Oh. My. God. Chloe. Talk about eye fucking? It's a wonder he didn't whip his dick out and shove it down your throat. That performance between you both was smoldering hot! If you had seen your face, it was priceless. You were trying to give him an, I-couldn't-give-a-shit face, but what I was seeing was an uncomfortable, hot and horny reaction from you."

"Ruby! That's bullshit, why would I feel anything

for a guy like that when I'm lucky to have someone like Kace?" Ruby looked like she was considering my comparison for a moment then grinned.

"Gibson Barclay... experienced, seriously hot, highly sexed and well-oiled machine is why." She grinned wickedly at me. "Come on Chloe, there isn't one girl on campus that would turn that guy down if they were on his radar. Well, I definitely wouldn't."

Dropping my jaw, I questioned, "Even after what I told you about him yesterday?"

Laughing out loud, Ruby threw her head back before making eye contact with me again, widening her eyes at me. "Especially after what you told me yesterday. I'd love a guy to take me like that; with that amount of want that he just couldn't control himself and couldn't stop."

Shaking my head in disbelief I responded, "Ruby he wasn't doing that because he was being passionate about being with that girl, he was taking her like that because he didn't give a shit about what she wanted, or how she felt. Don't you understand the difference?"

Staring at me like I had just said something outrageous, she smirked. "I get it. Sex is still new to you, right? You're the one that has no idea about the difference. Sex isn't all hearts and butterflies, stolen glances and going to bed in the dark naked, Chloe. There are *all* different kinds of sex, fun sex, angry sex, make-up sex, hard and fast, slow and sweet, kinky, freaky, quiet, sneaky..."

Not wanting to listen to any more, I interjected.

"Alright, I get it. You think my inexperience is making me miss something? Let me think about that a moment." I pretended to reflect and tapped my lips with my forefinger and rolled my eyes high to my eyebrows, as if deep in thought, then gave her eye contact again.

"Umm, no way. It would make no difference to me, if I'd had ten guys and tons of sex. One thing I can assure you of is that Gibson Barclay would still not be a candidate for me to have sex with."

Smirking, Ruby rolled her eyes. "Okay. Have it your way Chloe, but at some point in your life you are going to regret making that remark and you'll have to eat your words on that one. I hope Kace is everything you ever dreamed of in bed, because my thinking is that there is something about Gibson's smile that says there is a lot more to him than people know."

Huffing out loudly, my thoughts were that she was being absurd. "Ruby, look at me. This is me. Chloe. Average build. Average height. Average student. Average. What would a guy like Gibson 'I can have any woman I want,' with his velvety soft southern twang that makes women swoon, see in someone like me, apart from an easy lay? Incidentally, he'd be way off with that, if he ever tried to pick on me."

Ruby was shaking her head and the disappointment on her face was a clear sign that she was fed up with me putting myself down. We'd had many conversations about how she thought I looked to other people. She felt I had some 'image issues', as she called them. And I felt I was being realistic.

"How many times do we have to have this conversation Chloe? Do you think you would have landed a guy like Kace if you weren't a stunningly gorgeous, sweet girl? Kace is one of those visual guys who needs to like what he sees to be interested. I've never known him to go out with anyone who wasn't beautiful, and before you, there was never anyone steady. You need to wise up about how you look, lady. Sure you don't get dressed up and wear make-up, but you have no need for that stuff. You are an extremely beautiful girl, Chloe. You need to start owning that."

Leaving the conversation hanging, I was too tired to argue any more. Gibson had messed with me enough, and the less I thought about him the better. Kace was waiting outside the restroom when we came out and I saw this as an opportunity not to go back to the bar.

"I'm beat honey, do you mind if we leave?"

Ruby raised her eyebrow at me and I nodded. Arranging to see each other on Wednesday she headed back to be with Dylan, while Kace and I headed home.

In the few short weeks since Ruby and I had arrived at college we were already growing apart. We had been so nervous about leaving each other behind that Ruby, Kace and I had all applied to the same university. We were stoked when all three of us got accepted.

Walking towards the car, we saw Gibson already getting into his car, with what looked like the red headed girl, Sian from my creative writing class getting in on the other side. Shaking my head, I was surprised at the sudden feeling of disappointment that seemed to grip me and squeeze at my heart.

Unsure whether I was disappointed with myself, or with Gibson, I asked Kace to take me home. There was no way I was having sex with Kace until I was back on track and had rid myself of the crazy thoughts I was having about Gibson. Kace looked disappointed when I said I wanted to stay on my own, especially after the way I was behaving during the gig, sitting on his lap and what he had probably thought that meant for later.

Shivering when I entered the dorm room, I found the window still open and the room smelling of damp night air and the smell of Julie. She wore Opium perfume, which had an overpowering scent, which seemed to cling to the fabric in the room long after she'd left.

Reaching up to close the window, I looked down when I noticed a car drawing up and the headlights go out. I almost fainted when I saw it was Gibson directly in front of my dorm. Sian was bringing him into her dorm room and I felt weirdly jealous and annoyed at her.

I had a tense knot in my stomach because it felt like there was nowhere I could escape to from him to let me bring my feelings back into check.

Preparing for bed, I pulled my tablet out and

searched for something to clear my head. Swiping it to shuffle, I had to smile when Bruno Mars, “Billionaire” blared out with such a catchy tune. I danced around while dressing for bed and tried to forget my feelings.

By the time the song was finished I felt a little less fragile about my feelings and thought about everything that had led to Kace, Ruby and I being there and her taking up with Dylan.

Choosing a college so far from home felt more secure in numbers and our little support network was already there because of our history together. Ruby knew Kace before I knew Kace and she read me very well. They had grown up together as next door neighbors. When I moved into their neighborhood at sixteen, Ruby had played matchmaker for Kace, who was too shy to ask me out on his own.

Times changed, and Kace grew up and by the time he was seventeen he was completely comfortable in his skin, and a cool, confident guy who had been dating me for over a year.

So we were all in the same place for our college adventure and making the transition from teenagers to adults together.

It took no time at all for Ruby to attach herself to a hot guy and she met Dylan the first day we moved onto campus. She had been trying to pull the stupidly awkward trunk she was insistent on bringing, and had cussed it upside down, while struggling to maneuver around it in her dorm room ever since.

Dylan, Ruby’s new guy wasn’t a student. He was

in a band, just like Gibson's, but Dylan was the strong silent type. As the drummer in his band, 4Tfy, he was only interested in making music and dealing with the business end of things for the band.

Taking his craft very seriously, Dylan was multi-talented and was accomplished in many percussion instruments, bass guitar, piano and violin. Studying for years at the renowned San Francisco Conservatory of Music he was classically trained.

Working as a percussionist in an orchestra for a year had helped Dylan decide that playing rock music was much more his scene. Once he met Zander, his best friend, and found a bass player for their band, they formed 4Tfy and never looked back.

So Ruby and Dylan just clicked and became an item by the first night we spent together, when Dylan was showing us around. As for Kace and me, like I said, Ruby played matchmaker, but I think we'd have found each other regardless. We had this amazing connection as soon as we met, and for the last two years of high school, we were inseparable and so in love with one another.

Guys used to give Kace hell for being pussy whipped, and my own friends fell over themselves to give him compliments for the romantic and thoughtful gestures he was always doing for me.

Kace's overt adoration in high school had made me the envy of all the girls in my year group. Mature and calm, everything a girl could have wished for, stunningly handsome, tall, charming and a warm approachable personality. In addition to those attributes, he was also super smart and athletically gifted.

We progressed through high school joined at the hip and had both applied and been accepted at UCLA with Ruby. Enrolled in the arts and media program, I was studying a combined degree in media imagery and digital arts, with a minor in creative writing, and Kace was studying sound engineering on a full science scholarship.

So that's how we'd found ourselves in California. I had been worried about being assigned to a dorm room with Julie, a student from Maryland. When I had found out Ruby and I weren't sharing a room, I initially freaked out, but eventually, I saw it as a good thing because I would have to push myself socially.

Once we were settled into college my priority was finding a job. Seeing a vacancy notice for Beltz Bar on the notice board on campus, I rang to set up an interview. Matt, the owner, told me that I looked much younger than eighteen. He gave me work, but it was cleaning rather than anything in service. To be honest he did me a favor. Those bar shifts would have played havoc with my unsocial study assignments I had been set.

Matt was a great guy, and only twenty three years old. His uncle had left the bar to him in his will. Matt decided to skip the whole college experience because he knew that running the bar and building his business up was what he really wanted at that point in his life.

Reflecting on everything to where I was at had

made me more settled. Reaching over I pulled up a playlist I used to relax to and fell asleep listening to it.

I woke early for my usual morning run. It was still dark outside but I liked running in the dark. The solitude of that time in the morning was usually really helpful for centering me and my thought processes.

Plugging my iPhone earphones in, I set off pounding the asphalt on campus. The smell of damp leaves and dewy grass at the side of the road was strong and all of my senses became heightened as my mind cleared of everything except music and setting my pace.

Three miles later I still had a mile to go to finish my usual circuit, when I saw someone running almost parallel to me, in the same direction as I was heading. Hairs at the back of my neck pricked in warning as the figure got closer and an uneasy feeling crept over me.

Usually, I felt safe on the route I had taken, but on that day, it was like I had a sixth sense as to someone being around that could be a danger to me. Glancing out of the side of my eye, I couldn't see his face. A dark hoodie covered his head and he was wearing jeans, not sweat pants or shorts as I would expect from someone out training.

Thankfully I was a ten thousand kilometer runner so I always had tons in reserve for a sprint finish. Without warning I took off in the direction of my dorm. With every step, lactic acid built up in my aching legs, making them feel like lead, but I didn't stop until I reached the door.

Fighting back panic, I punched in the entry code on the key pad and pulled the heavy door closed behind me. Leaning back against the wall, my chest heaved and I breathed loudly as I tried to recover from the oxygen deficit to my lungs and the adrenaline that was coursing through my body.

Looking out of the wire mesh window of the door, I saw the same dark shadow lurking by Gibson's car. He pushed back the hood as he walked under the bright street light. I was surprised to see that it was him.

Bending forward to look out, I watched as he placed his hands on the hood of his car and began stretching his legs; first one and then the other. Afterwards, he twisted his body first to the left then to the right.

Placing his hand over his shoulder, he grasped a fistful of material at the back of his sweatshirt and pulled it over his head and clear of his body. By default his t-shirt rode all the way up to his armpits.

Mesmerized by him I couldn't stop looking at the amazing contours of his pectoral and abdominal muscles through his thin, sweaty t-shirt. No doubt about it, I was definitely in lust with Gibson.

Still staring, I couldn't believe when he continued his strip routine and pulled his t-shirt over his head, wiping the sweat off his front, the back of his neck and finally his under arms. Watching the way the different muscle groups on his arms, back and torso moved as he opened the trunk of his car made my mouth dry. When he took out a clean t-shirt and covered up that fabulous body again, I sighed out loud at the loss of the visual I'd been enjoying.

Gibson closed his trunk slowly leaning hard on the top to close it. Walking to the driver's side he suddenly stopped and turned his head, staring directly at the door as if he knew I was watching him. Jerking back, I hid in the shadow of the stairwell that ran parallel to the doorway and stood there until I heard his engine start and he drove away.

Heading up to shower I wondered what he was doing out there on my route. He wasn't dressed to run. I was confused that someone like him, who seemed to live his life so chaotically, could have the discipline to take the time to look after his body.

Julie was up when I got back and Ruby was sitting on my bed waiting for me. "Jesus, Chloe, do you ever just slouch and stay in bed like the rest of us? I came up to ask you to come to breakfast at the crack of dawn, because I just got home, and you're already out there perfecting that fine ass of yours."

Smirking at her I grabbed a towel and wiped the beads of sweat from my face. "Maybe you should try it sometime, then you won't find that fine ass of yours has dropped some day." Julie burst out laughing and shook her head in amusement and wandered over to me.

"So, now that you've run off all those calories, you can put them back by taking us to breakfast. If I recall it's your turn to pay so get your ass in the shower ma'am and let's get down to Benny's, I'm starving." Julie smiled and whipped the towel away from me then flicked it at my legs as I jumped away from her and headed for the shower.

After dressing we headed to Benny's, a local student haunt that did the most amazing breakfast deals on pancakes, patties and eggs. Benny's contribution to students' emotional well-being was to a student's physical health deficit. Heart attack on a plate was the way he described it, but if I had to choose a way of dying, there were a lot worse ways than eating Benny's delicious student special. Besides it was a weekly treat for us because the meal plan food at college sucked.

Julie splattered maple syrup in copious amounts on her pancakes and licked her fingers as she set the dispenser down. "So, I hear that 4Tfy is taking over the regular spot at Beltz from now on." My ears pricked and she had my attention immediately.

Ruby looked excited, her eyes opening wide. "Yes! Isn't it fabulous? Dylan and the guys are really excited about it." I was desperate to ask why M3rCy were no longer playing there, but after Ruby's remarks about Gibson I didn't feel I could. So I sat there almost in pain, waiting to hear whether either of them were going to drop it into the conversation.

"Pity because it looks like you missed your chance for that hard and fast sex, Chloe." Ruby's words drew me out of my trance and back to the conversation.

"Huh?" Confused that I'd missed something and not quite taking in what she was saying, I stared at Ruby blankly.

"Gibson Barclay. You know... manwhore extraordinaire, Gibson. Come-fuck-with-me-after-my-gig, Gibson. Come on Chloe, the guy who was eye-fucking you in front of a couple of hundred people last night." Julie's mouth hung and she turned to me raising her eyebrows.

"Okay, so what the hell did I miss arriving late last night? Gibson Barclay hit on you? You lucky bitch! What were you doing for him to notice you?"

Embarrassed by their attention, I shrugged my shoulders, swallowed hard and gave Julie a solid stare. "I don't know what she's talking about. All he did was his usual stunt of picking a female to sing to. I guess pickings were pretty slim last night, is all." Shaking her head, Ruby cut into her pancakes and stuffed a huge mouthful of them and her eggs into her mouth.

"Have it your way, Chloe, but I think horny Gibson had begun to have the hots for you. Pity he's shipping out. Anyway, I guess loyalty would have made me root for Kace, and you're such a good girl, I'm sure nothing would have come of it."

CHAPTER 4

GETTING IT OFF THE GROUND

Gibson

Waking with a start to the urgent, loud sound of bony knuckles banging on my wooden door, I flung back the comforter and bounced off the bed. Yelling at my bandmate, Lennox, who was determined to help me lose my rental deposit for causing damage or get me evicted for noise disturbance.

"Fuck! You need to quit behaving like this, dude. I was asleep not fucking dead. At least, waking the dead is what I think you were aiming at with that incessant hammering. You're a fucking drummer Len, have you no respect for your knuckles you idiot? What happens if you injure your hands?"

Lennox stared back at me for a second, sniffed, scratched his balls and walked in and made straight for the fridge door. "I'd been knocking for a good five minutes before you decided to let me in. What the fuck was I supposed to think? I knew you were home. Your car is in the lot out back."

Lennox reached into the fridge and pulled out the carton of orange juice that was in there. Smirking, I waited for him to take a swig.

"What the fuck, Gibson…?" Orange juice came spewing out of his mouth, splattered onto the black granite countertop and down the front of his taut white V neck t-shirt. Lennox's contorted face was a deep puce color; his tongue hung limply out of his mouth.

A smug smile curved my lips, that particular carton had been in there for ages. Serves him right for not using a glass. Beginning to retch, Lennox leaned over the faucet and began cupping water in his hand and rinsing his mouth out.

Chuckling heartily, I couldn't help but think of it as ample payback for the way he'd just woke me up. "Jesus… that was fucking disgusting, dude. You might have warned me it was off."

Ignoring his comment I began to speak, "So, what's so urgent you have to drag me up at the butt crack of dawn, Len?" Shaking my head and running my hands back and forth through my hair, I back and sat heavily on the bed and he followed me. I leaned back, supporting my head on my elbow. I bent my knee up to place my foot flat on the bed the other still on the floor and waited for him to answer me.

Walking over in my direction, he threw himself down lazily on the chair, and stretched a leg over the arm. The over familiar way he regarded my apartment used to bug me, but not anymore. Lennox was like a big brother to me.

Meeting him purely by chance, Lennox West had changed my life. Smiling appreciatively, he had approached me after hearing me play on the demonstration drum kit in a local music store. Striking a conversation he'd asked if I did anything else, and when I said I played the guitar and sang a bit, he asked if I wanted to try out for his new band. Initially, I had wanted to play the drums but that was his instrument.

After hearing me sing "Sex On Fire" by Kings of Leon as one of my audition numbers, he then asked me to sing "Superheroes" by The Script. When I finished, he'd offered me a trial as lead singer. Ever since Lennox, me and the rest of the band have been water tight.

That Saturday was almost two years ago, high school dropout and now at nineteen I was a full time musician in our band M3rcy, and earning a decent living by playing in bars around town and in some of the adjoining cities.

Lennox squinted at me and smirked in his dick-sure manner, the one that always managed to piss me off. "Remember that scout that came to see us in Culver City that one time?"

Of course I did, that was a huge deal; a scout from a record company sitting in on one of our bar gigs. We were ecstatic that he wanted to talk to us afterwards and kind of built up our hopes that he was going to do something amazing, like whisk us all off to his personal New York recording studio and help us hit the big time.

"Not ready." When the scout, Syd had uttered those words back then, I'd been devastated. My heart sunk down to the pit of my stomach. Being rejected like that was a major body blow to my nineteen year old ego. Shrugging off that painful memory, I stared back at Lennox without acknowledging he'd spoken, then saw his face break into a huge grin.

"Well... guess what? Six months later and he's coming back. So get your ass into some kegs and let's get down to Beltz to practice. The rest of the guys are meeting us there."

I didn't need to be told twice and was ready to go in less than fifteen minutes. Just as we arrived at the bar parking lot, there was a massive clap of thunder and the sky was lit brightly by lightning. Rain lashed heavily from the sky and grabbing my guitar, I ran for cover behind Lennox. Simon and Mick came running at us from the other direction, all of us arriving at the bar door at the same time.

By the time I got inside I was soaked to the skin and began shaking the cool rain from my hair. When I glanced across the bar, she was there. Chloe I think they called her. Sweet and innocent looking girl she was and she didn't seem like the other girls at all.

Something strange happened to me when I looked at her, which was too difficult to explain, but every time I got with a girl she never failed to show up in the wrong place at just the right time.

My fault really, I was so pumped after performing and I openly admit, at nineteen I was addicted to sex and was ready to have it anytime, anywhere. Performing and sex were my lethal combination as far as my self-control was concerned.

The previous night's encounter was the worst. Seeing Chloe walk out of the restroom almost crucified me and I nearly threw the girl that was bouncing on my dick off me.

In a split second I figured she hated me after what she'd seen anyway, and as I'd already been caught, I may as well finish. Angry feelings about spoiling any chance of knowing her made me more aggressive in how I was taking that blonde girl. I never did get her name.

Then again, I never got any of their names. That wasn't how the groupies that hung around me worked. All they were interested in was fucking a musician with a big dick.

It was hard to shake the look Chloe gave me that night. Staring at me like she did is something that will be embedded in my brain forever.

The disdain on her face told me she hated me and everything I was about. I couldn't blame her really. As young as I was, I'd been around a lot of women but until that point, no female has ever looked at me with disgust the way she had.

Standing still, she was staring out the window and watching the rain streaming down. It was clear her mind was somewhere else. Nico and Vinz, "Am I Wrong," was playing on her tablet playlist. She turned to look at us and she looked amazing. Then I realized she was taking in my soaked appearance, so

I said the first thing that came to mind. "Any towels for a drowning man over here?"

Being a lead singer in a band I was used to being objectified, but I wasn't used to this weird feeling about her looking at me. I watched her eyes tick over my wet clothing. Chloe was obviously thinking about what she was looking at.

Biting her lip, she looked up and I couldn't help but smile at her. Raising my eyebrow, I waited for her to speak and when she didn't, I almost flirted because I wanted to make her feel at ease around me. She had only ever seen me at my worst, some of my behavior on stage and with those girls.

Damn, when her eyes connected with mine she stared. I could see the pink tinge of pleasure clouding her eyes. She was enjoying what she was looking at, and there was this... moment, a fleeting connection between us. Not used to these silences I'd smirked because I was self-conscious.

"Did you hear me, babe?" I grinned because she just gave a vacant stare that said she didn't know what to do. Then I saw that I'd embarrassed her. Blushing she dropped her head, nodded and scurried off in the direction of the office.

Thinking I'd upset her, I followed her down to Matt's office. Chloe was stretching up into a cupboard to pull down a pile of towels. She was wobbling on her tiptoes, so I reached and caught her by her hips to steady her.

Shit! Her body felt tiny and delicate in my hands and when I pressed my fingertips into her flesh a little I could feel the bones of her pelvis through her jeans. Chloe might have been cleaning but damn, she smelled awesome. Her light fragrance and maybe some pear shampoo in her gorgeous, shoulder length blonde hair were quite an aphrodisiac. Not sure, but whatever it was, I remembered thinking that if I made it to the big time, I wanted shares in that smell.

Looking over her shoulder, her hot minty breath fanned across my face, and our mouths were only a couple of inches apart. My eyes flicked to her lips and her tongue licked between them, before she closed her mouth and massaged her lips back and forth.

Looking back into her eyes, they were like this mysterious inky blue color and I knew right then I could easily get lost in them. Dropping my hands, I sighed out loud and tried to do the right thing.

Strange situation for me, I'd never been that close to any woman's mouth and not able to kiss it before. And although kissing someone wasn't enough to make me hard anymore, my dick was straining in my pants from our little interaction and I hadn't even gone that far.

"Shall I take those for you?" Reaching over her hand, I took a hold of the towels. Chloe was still staring back at me like she was in shock and didn't respond, so I grasped them a little tighter. When she realized she was still standing there with me, her cheeks blushed and she almost shoved the pile at me and made her way to the open doorway.

Briefly meeting my gaze once again, she turned

on her heel and disappeared down the corridor. I'd had some shitty reactions from people in my life, but I have to say, of all of them, something in the way that Chloe looked at me, was the only one that had ever had a negative impact.

As I sauntered slowly towards the staff room at the end of the hall, she suddenly reappeared, turned towards the fire exit and pushed the door open, allowing it to bang shut behind her again.

Staring at the door for a second, I shook my head. Fuck her. No way was a stupid girl going to mess with my life. No matter how hot I thought she was. Needing a distraction, Lennox appeared at the end of the corridor.

"When you've finished bagging the hot cleaner, we've got the performance of our lives in a few hours. Keep your dick in your pants and take your frustration to your throat, your singing has more of an edge when you haven't been laid."

Singing shook me of my funk and as well as our own material, we chose a couple of covers to perform for the set that night to show our versatility, The Maine's "Everything I Ask For" and thinking about Chloe, the song that came to mind was by Train, "Angel in Jeans."

Taking a deep breath, I suddenly realized how much I wanted Syd to like us this time. Another rejection would have tipped the scales for me with the band. I was hungry for fame and some money to get my life to the next phase, and if that meant I needed to move on from the guys to do it, then I would.

Still only nineteen, people often took me for several years older. Maybe it was what I'd been exposed to in my childhood and being with the band, but I never really related to kids my own age and often hung out with the cool guys much older than me.

Playing the drums and guitar in various groups, I had been accepted by them as an equal and no one seemed to notice my tender years. One of the reasons I became promiscuous from the age of sixteen I suppose. Girls were attracted to musicians and no one seemed to think of me as too young. Maybe, the way I was so comfortable and open about sex as well, due to my mom's not so subtle profession as a hooker.

Playing gigs and being around her and her colleagues exposed me to so much pussy that by the time I wasn't a minor any more, I had experienced most sexual scenarios.

Knocking on the edge of the bar drew my attention in the direction of the noise. Syd Jones, the scout was early to the party. Thinking he was going to show up at the gig, he'd caught us out by turning up several hours early.

"Hey guys sorry, but I'm on my way back to New York this afternoon for an important meeting, but I didn't want to let you down. So if you can do your set now for me I can fit you in."

Mick gave a quick what-the-hell look at Lennox and Simon's eyes widened at me in a subtle panic.

Lennox put his sticks down and eased himself around his drums. "Hey Syd, glad to see you, we're ready. Thank you for coming. Okay, guys, let's do this."

Len slapped my back on the way over to the stage set, nodded at Mick, and pointed at Simon, our bass player, to start the intro with Mick while he slid back behind the drums.

For the following ten minutes I sang for my life, imagining the crowd was there spurring us on and not just the same two regulars who were actually there. Vocals I never knew I was capable of impressed even me, as I gave my all to the guy that held my future in his hands.

We'd sung two original numbers and were half way through the second of our two covers when Syd looked at his watch and held his hand up. Panic gripped at my throat like a tightening hand, and I almost spoke up to tell him he couldn't possibly have made up his mind based on what we'd done.

Syd stood up, shoved his hands deep into his pockets and sauntered towards the small stage with his head down, deep in thought. Suddenly, he jerked his head up and looked me right in the eye.

"Alright, I liked you six months ago, but you weren't ready." He put his hand up to stop anyone from protesting and continued, "Now, I know some of you were pissed when I said that, but I didn't get where I am today by signing half assed bands."

Drawing breath I was about to argue our cause, when I felt a hand on my shoulder silencing me. Lennox stood tight to my side and held my wrist behind my back. Squeezing it, he was telling me this moment was not the time to let my impetuous nature take the lead.

Syd turned a chair around back to front and slung his leg over it, sitting himself down and leaning his elbows on the back of the chair.

"Right. I think this band is definitely ready now. Even the young one here." Syd pointed his nicotine stained finger at me. My initial thought was, *fuck you*, but then it sunk in. Syd Jones from Zuul Records was going to sign us.

Trying to behave in a professional manner until Syd left was fucking difficult from there on out. Inside my head was buzzing with the conversation he had just had with us; about the where, when, how, and who was going to take care of this and that. By the time he left my head was ready to explode, and time had gone so quickly that we were only fifteen minutes away from gig time.

Holding our breaths, we all watched him weave his way through the tables and disappear through the door. Lennox spun around to look at me and punched the air, while Mick ran at me, jumped up and wrapped his legs around my waist. Simon was still staring at the door as if Syd was going to reappear any minute and shout, only kidding. He didn't, and he wasn't kidding. It was the real deal.

CHAPTER 5

TAKING IT IN

Gibson

Scanning the room as I walked onto the small raised stage at Beltz, the first person I noticed was her. Right in front of me was Chloe. Strange that I had never noticed her anywhere else, except for all those times when one of us seemed to be in the wrong place and the wrong situation; for her anyway.

I would have taken responsibility for that, but there were a few times when my sexual encounters should have been private and unseen from other females as far as I was concerned. Places like in my own car, the male restroom and down in the bar cellar. Not places I'd have expected to be interrupted by another girl, but she had anyway.

Seeing her sitting on a guy's lap, I wasn't surprised she was already taken. Strange but I definitely felt disappointed about that. Actually, if I'm honest, I felt pissed about it. When I thought more about it, it was probably for the best though, because I doubted she was the kind that would ever be with a guy like me, after seeing me with all those other girls anyway.

Besides, I was getting out of town and I had no chance with that one anyway, she was way too innocent and proper to hook up with anyone, especially me.

Seeing her sitting in the guy's lap, like it was going to be some kind of deterrent for me to have fun with her, was never going to work. If the All-American boy even was her guy. From what I saw of how he acted around the feisty brunette at the bar earlier, I had my doubts.

As soon as I laid eyes on her I was transfixed by her little diamond piercing just above her belly button. Her waistline was slim and she was showing an incredible toned, tanned section of skin that was so fucking tantalizing.

I watched his hand gliding back and forth, All-American boy was stroking her back and I was fucking envious he was getting to touch her so intimately.

When I looked up for her reaction I was hit with that stunning pair of inky blue, lust filled eyes staring back at me. With a wicked smirk, I raised my eyebrow playfully, and licked my bottom lip, which was suddenly very dry.

Wandering over to the mic stand slowly while Mick was playing the intro to our first number, I gripped the mic taking it off the stand. Chloe's eyes widened and continued to stare into mine and I couldn't help but smirk wickedly at her.

There was a definite attraction stirring inside her, even if she would never have admitted it. Not one ever to pass up an opportunity with a girl, I decided to keep flirting with her. Fuck the challenge of the guy she was sitting on.

Staring back at her intensely, I could see that she was unnerved by my attention. The way her gaze always dropped to the floor when I looked at her as I sang, told me she had no idea how beautiful she was, and there was just something about it that got me.

Chloe wiggled on the guy's lap and he took the opportunity to maximize that by pulling her ass closer to his groin. Exactly what I'd have done in his circumstances, and I bet he was busting out of his pants with the feel of her on him. I know I was just from watching her.

I didn't think she was being horny though, because remembering how awkward she was when I spoke to her earlier, it was probably because I was making her uncomfortable. Shame I didn't have more morals because I was the one that should have been uncomfortable; the girl had caught me hooking up so many times it was unnatural.

Obviously I pushed it too far and she couldn't take what I was doing anymore, so she rose up off her guy, and then leaned in and spoke close to his ear, giving me a prime view of her ample perfect cleavage. Straightening up she began weaving her way to the back of the bar and out of sight. *Damn*.

When she did that it kinda threw me off for a couple of songs, but I figured there was no use in crying over spilt milk and tried to focus on a girl I'd fucked a couple times before to take my mind off her. Plus I knew she'd be willing to do whatever I wanted when the gig was done.

Second to last song was when Chloe reappeared, moving gracefully back to her group, tucking a blonde lock of hair behind her ear in a very feminine manner, she sat down on a chair that time. Another couple had joined their group by the time she came back.

A short dark haired girl had positioned her seat exactly in line with where Chloe's seat was, blocking her from my sight as soon as she sat down. Feeling kinda weird about how she reacted, I became annoyed with myself because I figured I'd been targeting someone who was clearly struggling with who she was, and perhaps, sexually quite innocent. That didn't sit well with me so I knew I had to drop it and move on.

Strangely enough, after that, I didn't really feel like hooking up that night and I left the bar alone to head home. Walking to the car, I could see Sian, the girl I'd bagged a couple of times, sitting on the hood of my car.

Her short skirt rode up, showing her white panties even in the low light of the car lot, and she was smiling seductively at me.

Once when Simon was moping after breaking up with a girl, Lennox had told him the best way to get a girl out of your head was, 'to find yourself another piece of pussy and hit it hard'. So with that in mind, Sian became my fuck-it-and-forget-it ride for the night.

Breaking my own rule, I went back to her dorm, which was very unusual for me. Normally, I bagged the girls close to the venue we were playing, mainly because for one, I wasn't interested in knowing anything about them, and two, not spending the night meant there was no awkward morning after conversations to struggle past.

However, this was my last gig in town because we'd accepted a resident spot on a tour with another band before Zuul got their act together, so I figured there was no harm in fucking on an actual bed and having a shower afterwards, just for a change of pace.

Pulling on my jeans, I checked my phone for the time. 5:30 a.m. I was wide awake and fucking restless, despite a marathon kink session courtesy of Sian, who lay dead to the world and completely sated. Damn, the girl actually purred at times during the night, which was so fucking hot. I liked that one a lot, and knew her name because she wasn't clingy. I definitely wasn't the only one tapping that.

Closing her dorm room door softly, I made my way out of the building. Breathing deeply, I felt more relaxed when the fresh air hit me. Fall is great for running. Cool breeze to keep you on pace, and the air seemed to cleanse my lungs. My lungs were the body parts that kept a roof over my head, you can't sing if your lungs aren't on form.

Unlocking my car I grabbed a grey hoodie and pulled it over my head. Running was something I took seriously. It kept me fit, cleared my thoughts and regulated my temperament.

People thought it weird that I never slept much. All the time I was in school, I was familiar with the term ADHD; Attention Deficit Hyperactivity Disorder. I was never sure why they didn't just get it over with and name it, 'I can't control this fucking kid syndrome.'

Everyone talked about strategies and coping mechanisms and shit like that to me. Who the fuck knows what kid understands they have ADHD and what that means at the age of seven or even eleven years old? Hell I'm still struggling with what it actually means now. No one ever sat down and spoke *with* me about it, just *at* me. If they had asked me, I'd have told them that when it all got too much for me and my head was buzzing, to take me outside and let me run.

Reaching back into my jacket pocket, I pulled out my blue tooth and clipped it on my ear. Swiping my phone, I pulled the app up to my playlists and chose my running one. I began to run, not caring that I was in my jeans and the shoes I was wearing weren't what I would normally run in.

'The Boss' Bruce Springsteen began to belt out, "Born to Run", it was fucking perfect to set my pace. It was such an old classic tune with an amazing arrangement. In my mind I was transported to a visual of their official video that accompanies it on YouTube, wishing our band was able to replicate that sound of the seventies.

Listening to music and running to the beat of a good tune was like the best drugs money could buy for rewiring my brain. Focusing on my breathing, counting beats and listening to the music was multitasking my brain could cope with.

ADHD meant my mind usually felt like someone had asked me to work out a simultaneous math equation, listen to the most intricate composition by a classical composer and identify the instruments, whilst someone talked over the top of everything. Nothing registered for me to process.

Three miles later I became aware of a girl running along in front of me, and it occurred to me that it wasn't the smartest thing to do, following a lone female running before dawn. My stride was naturally much longer because I was taller and my pace meant before long I was coming up alongside her. Glancing to the side, I realized it was Chloe. She was pounding the ground; stride for stride in time with me and I shortened my stride to match hers. I was about to speak when suddenly, she took off like a bat out of hell and left me stunned at the acceleration she had in her little legs. *Damn.*

There was no way I was going after her to explain, I'd obviously done enough damage and scared her by running alongside her in the dark. Slowing my pace, I made sure she was gone before I headed back to my car. Stretching out afterwards, my body ached but it was a good feeling.

Sweat ran down my back, in fact, my whole body was saturated in sweat but my head was clear, and in a way, I was glad I didn't have to be around Chloe again, because there was something about her that affected me and I couldn't fathom it.

Life as I knew it was about to change, and I also knew it was up to me to take the opportunity that was being thrown my way, because it was a one-time deal and I sure as hell wasn't going to get another one.

Stripping out of my sweat stained hoodie and t-shirt I went to the trunk and took out a fresh one. I always kept fresh clothing in the trunk because I hated being sweaty after gigs. As I was pulling the t-shirt down, I had a weird feeling like I was being watched.

Glancing over to the dorm door I was parked in front of, there was a shadow of a person that disappeared as soon as I looked over. I thought it was probably just someone passing the doorway inside. Turning, I got in my car and started driving home.

Later when I was standing in the shower, I got to thinking about the way Chloe had looked at me when she was taking the towels out of the closet and I wished I'd just fucking kissed her. Closing my eyes, I could still see her eyes as clear as day. I washed the sweat off my body as the shower beat down hard on me and I tried again to shake the uneasy feelings I had about Chloe who had managed to get my attention and yet had never spoken a word to me.

Once I had gotten into bed, my mind was trying to dart back to that one little moment in Matt's office, and just the thought of that look in her eyes gave me a semi hard-on. Then I got to thinking, that maybe it was just the thought of leaving, and the unknown road ahead of me that was causing me to have all these fucked up feelings that were going on inside.

Turning on my side, I pulled the comforter up to my neck and tucked it under my chin – finally I'd felt ready to sleep for a few hours. Smiling, I contented myself with the thought that life was finally going to change for me.

GIBSON'S LIFE: FIVE YEARS LATER

CHAPTER 6

HIT IT

Gibson

Adrenaline pumped through my veins as my heart squeezed in a rapid, excited rhythm. The bass beats were vibrating up through the soles of my feet and the roaring crowd was fuelling me to take the gig to another level.

Our rock music was blaring as I strode down the runway jutting out of the stage and into the audience. Sweat was blinding me, my clothes were saturated and rivulets ran down my forehead and stung my eyes. My hands were so soaked. I was hardly able to grip the neck of my guitar as I pounced forward and scissor jumped high above the crowd below me, raising it in the air.

More roars and cheers of appreciation swelled from the already frantic crowd, who bumped shoulders and swayed in unison to the number one song that started the whole, crazy-trip-infested life, I had found myself in.

Awesome, Gibson! A female voice broke through the crowd on a momentary music silence between the end of the first verse and the bridge as a black lacy thong landed at my feet. Looking down in the direction of the voice, I saw a frenzied female fan, currently being dragged backwards and away from the stage by her sweater.

One of the security guys was desperately trying to place his arms under hers, as another wrestled with her and tried to lift her legs off the floor to prevent her from getting to me.

Feisty little thing she seemed to be as well; her dark brown hair was whipping back and forth as her head turned from side to side, arms flailing everywhere, and she did that 'going limp' thing with her body, that makes it almost impossible for someone to get a hold and lift their dead weight up.

Determination showed on her face, and her teeth were biting into her bottom lip as she attempted to free herself from their grasp. There was something about her eyes that made my mind dart back for a nanosecond. Placing those eyes to a look someone gave me when our eyes connected for that briefest moment. Chloe. Her eyes reminded me of Chloe.

Sniggering into the mic, I shook my head slightly. I couldn't help but see the funny side of how someone could lose all of their dignity like that, especially when I was the reason. That girl was just another random female who wanted to touch me.

Then again, from her appearance and wildcat

behavior, I would have probably loved a ten minute interlude with that one. She looked like she would have put some effort in if I'd have hooked up with her.

Glancing back at the mass of faces staring up at me, it was exhilarating and kinda freaky to think that we'd risen to the level of stardom we had in just a few short years. What a buzz it gave me, every time I stood looking out from the stage to all those fans and saw faces staring up at me, with a multitude of expressions, from joy to angst; depending on whether it was a ballad or a rock tune I was delivering in my performance.

I was humbled by the amazing crowd that night, by the way they all seemed totally invested in our music. And all of our original material. Hearing people humming along to our tune was crazy. For me, one of the weirdest experiences was on a rare occasion where I had been in a store and our music started playing. A couple of times I've heard an intro and almost burst into song too, forgetting where I was for a moment.

Whenever and wherever we performed, the venues were always full to capacity. Playing a gig to 12,500 people in a place like Wembley Arena seemed quite intimate, especially with some of the festivals we'd headlined at in the UK, such as V Festival and Glastonbury.

Still buzzing after the last note had been struck and the last beat of the drum sounded out from the massive amplifiers, I headed off from the blackened out stage toward the stark, bare clear bulb lighting to the stage right.

Grabbing the white towel the aid gave me, I wiped it swiftly and vigorously over my head, catching beads of sweat, and drew it around my neck. Taking a fresh towel, I pulled it down my face, catching the sweat from my brow that was running down and into my eyes. The cool, comforting toweling soothed the discomfort I felt from being so overheated.

Reaching over my shoulder with my hand, I bunched my t-shirt in my fist and pulled it over my head to rid myself of the sweat soaked feel of the clammy material against my body. As I drew my head up my eyes came level with a beautiful little blonde piece of ass standing right in front of me.

Adults can make their own choices right? That was my philosophy anyway. Those that condemned me… well I thought they were really just pissed because they were jealous they weren't getting enough. No excuses from me about what I liked or what kind of man I was. I had just turned twenty four years old and I lived my life how I'd wanted since I'd left home at seventeen.

Growing up with a mother who earned her living by being an escort, she and her friends had been very open… about sex. My mom was a classy looking chick so she got some great gigs, which kept us warm and fed after my piece of shit musician father ran off with an eighteen year old after a gig that he never even bothered to come home from.

I was ten years old at the time and my mom had no choice, we were a day away from homeless when she took a job with a guy that offered her big bucks and a safe, protective environment for me. I wanted for nothing materially and as music was my thing, had some of the best teachers money could buy.

Lesley Paul Barclay, my father, turned up when I was sixteen. My mom passed suddenly at the age of forty three of an unknown cause, and he took me to live with him for a year. By the time I was seventeen no one was paying any attention to what I was about. He gave up trying to 'master' me and just pretty much let me do my own thing after that.

No doubts about it, I was a shit of a kid. Never been able to sit down and pay attention, driving most folks to distraction. Constantly fidgeting or bouncing on my toes, which made my knees bounce. I must have spent close to half my school years outside of the principal's office for 'defying,' many a teacher's demands for me to sit still.

They really didn't get it. Labeling me with ADHD meant a big red dot beside my name on the register, yet the first thing they would say at parent/teacher consultations to my mom was, "Gibson is a very bright young man, he just doesn't pay attention." Not one of them saw the irony in that statement and choosing that moment to forget the deficit, hyperactivity and disorder parts of that particular diagnosis.

Staring back at the girl in front of me, her jaw was hanging as her eyes perused me at leisure, her tongue tantalizing me as she licked back and forth on her bottom lip. Standing speechless staring and, more importantly, blushing because she knew she'd been busted doing it.

My one and only thought was, *so you are the one with the golden ticket to suck my dick today?* Shitty right? Well, to be honest, I didn't give a fuck what anyone thought about me anymore. Everything I did was public news.

Even my sex life was up for grabs frequently, with tabloid newspapers paying the women I slept with for stories of paternity claims that were time consuming and unfounded and to share my bedroom secrets. My one saving grace was that no one had ever said I wasn't a great lay.

What could I have said? The fact was, I was a manwhore, I'd been brought up around sex and it was always pushed at me as normal and healthy when they talked about sexual appetites. Plus, women loved to have sex with me. And they'd all said the same thing. I was fucking amazing at it. Sex and rock music is what I lived for, although not necessarily in that order.

Hands invaded my body space and ran up and across my pectorals, my head dropping to see what she was doing. She glided her palms around and under my arms, until they stopped on both scapula bones on my back.

Stroking me, she smiled suggestively and continued to trail downwards toward my ass, and by the time I made eye contact with her, she was so close her hot panting breaths were fanning over my face.

Groupies had no shame. Then again, I was so fucking wired after the gig, I needed something to bring me down, and an easy fuck meant I didn't have to be charming or polite to anyone. This girl knew the score and she was begging for it.

Gripping her hair, I tugged her head back, tilting her face up to look at me. I stared at her to make sure she was paying attention to what was happening. Dropping my head down, I took her mouth in a demanding and hungry kiss.

Feeling her legs buckle from under her, I caught her and slung my arm under hers and around her waist, pulling her hard against my naked, sweaty torso. She whimpered and sighed deeply at my action. I shook my head, she was gone even though I smelled musty from the effort on stage and was still dripping with sweat. I remember thinking that she must have been desperate to want to do anything with me like that and was going to be one of those girls that came at the drop of a hat.

Crazy, the effect rock musicians had on women. They seemed to lose all their inhibitions and I've yet to meet one that wasn't impressed by me being in a band. Setting the girl straight on her feet, I placed my hands under her armpits and lifted her up.

As soon as I did that, her legs wrapped around my waist and she wiggled her pussy against my belly. The short skater dress she was wearing was loose enough for her damp, lacy thong to make contact with my skin.

Sliding my hands under her dress, I felt two perfectly peachy ass cheeks. They felt silky smooth, warm and just the right size in the palms of my hands. Crushing my lips on hers again, my tongue penetrated her mouth in deep exploration.

Turning, I walked with her in the direction of the dark corridor at the back of the stage for some privacy. Simon called out, "Ten minutes Gib, no more, you hear?"

Overhead, I could hear lighting technicians starting the tear-down, but that was soon forgotten when I turned and shoved my reward roughly against the wall. My wandering hands slid around her; one under her leg to support her better with one arm, the other, teasing the thong to the side, while my thumb traced from her clitoris all the way down her slit.

Soft, throaty moans escaped her mouth with even softer gasps. Her body sagged against mine as I held her up against the wall. Her arms were around my neck, while her fingers wove their way in and out of my hair in time to the stroking I was doing below. Leaning back to look at her, she smiled and for the first time I really took in what she looked like.

Even in the dimness of our position, I could see she was an extremely attractive girl. Huge big, brown eyes, long, silky blonde hair and from what I could feel, a tight little body. Most important of all, she was very game for whatever was next.

Kissing me hungrily again, she made her move to

take things to the next level. Sliding her hand down my back, she brought it around and in between us, then suddenly it was dipping inside the waistband of my jeans and teasing at my hard, swollen dick.

Urgently, she wrapped her small, cool fingers around my aching shaft and moaned softly again into my mouth as my fingers penetrated her warm wet pussy. Taking my fingers away, I stepped back to free myself and dropped her legs to the floor, removing her hand from my shaft.

Sensual smiles and hooded eyes told me we were far from done. Staring at me briefly, she smirked naughtily, before dropping to her knees on the floor in front of me and reaching for the fly of my jeans.

Firmly rubbing across my erect dick with the flat of her hand made me desperate for more. Already pumped from the gig, my heart raced and my dick was desperate to penetrate her. Less than a minute from when we were against the wall, my hard swollen dick was in her mouth.

Unable to wait until she fully opened my jeans, she had whipped my dick out around the unbuttoned flaps of material, and was working me like a pro. Staring up at me all seductively she grinned between sucks and licks. She had great blow job lips and I remember thinking she had nice teeth.

Actually, she was hot but to be honest, I wasn't in the mood for being playful towards her. My feelings were more about hard and fast. Fuck her and forget her, really. No pretenses about playing nice, she knew what that interlude was between us, and I was more than happy to oblige her.

Taking her by her hair again, I made a messy pony tail and took control. "Open your mouth," I commanded. Positioning her head at an angle just right for my height, I began to fuck her mouth, my dick hitting the back of her throat.

Experience told me this was nothing new to her. She didn't even have a gag reflex. Only the noise of her gurgling and her watery eyes made me aware that she needed a little restraint on my part.

Amazing oral skills she had acquired when I let her take charge. Sucking and stroking my dick just right and I could feel myself grow and thicken as she worked me. "Play with yourself." My demand was met with instant obedience, her hand sliding under her dress without breaking the rhythm and pace she'd set for herself.

"Are you wet?" Nodding she continued to suck and stroke my dick. "Are you ready for me?" Nodding again, I pulled my dick out of her mouth. "Get up and turn around." I ordered, and without hesitation, she was leaning against the wall, her chest resting against her forearms, offering up her ass to me, turning her head to look over her shoulder at me.

My hands fell to the hem of her dress and I bunched it up pushing it high on her back to give me access to her I pushed my jeans down my legs. Pushing her forward by her upper back to arch her, I kicked her feet apart to give her a better center of gravity, knowing that with my hard and fast, she was going to need all the help she could get to stay upright.

String thongs are a mystery to me. Why the fuck women wear them is beyond me. There is no way you could tell me it doesn't hurt to wear one of those. Constantly rubbing against their asshole, it must be fucking irritating. Reaching forward, I ripped that shit clean off her and then she was ready for me.

Licking my fingers before I felt between her legs again, she was a hot slick mess down there. Completely open and waiting for me. Reaching behind me, I pulled out a silver foil pack and wrapped myself before leaning forward and drawing my sheathed, swollen dick down her slit, and without ceremony, sunk myself deep inside her

A loud groan of pleasure tore from her throat, and after two gentle thrusts, I rode her deep and hard. Smirking when she came for the first time at around the tenth pound, I could see she was going to be exhausted in the next ten minutes.

Lennox turned up just as she was coming for the second time and I glanced over when I heard him approach. I grinning wickedly when he laughed, and shook his head at me, and turned to walk back in the direction he'd just come from.

Damn, she was a screamer as well. Actually, she was not so much of a screamer than a 'pained wailer.' Kind of on par with the noises that cats make when they mate. It was fucking off putting so I just rode her as fast as I had to in order to get myself off and to get the fuck away from her. Talk about a passion killer!

As soon as I came, I pulled out of her, thanked her and walked briskly away without looking back. There were no awkward after moments after a fuck like that. When I caught up with my band Lennox turned and spoke, in a matter of fact manner, that the venue organizers were ready for the meet and greet 'VIP winner's party,' from the radio stations.

Nodding at the guys, I grinned again and made a quick trip to the rest room to make myself decent and pull on a fresh t-shirt. Everyone was gone by the time I came out apart from Charlotte, my PA, who walked beside me hugging that ugly blue organizer she has. Opening the door to enter, I pasted on my best smile and with the first face I saw, became Gibson Barclay, lead singer of M3rcy. Public property.

CHAPTER 7

BREAKING FREE

Chloe

Crap! I need to get the hell out of here. Blood trickled down my cheek as I stared at my red rimmed eyes on my tear stained face in the bathroom mirror. My puffy, bruised bottom lip oozed clear serum from the swelling. I looked disfigured.

Lifting my shirt to inspect myself more closely, I could see there was already fresh bruising forming over my ribs, right beside the old green and yellow bruises that were fading from last week. Reality finally dawned on me that I couldn't allow him to abuse me anymore.

God only knows what had brought out the beast in him on that night. Everything about that moment had been meticulously planned and delivered with precision, to ensure it was just the way he liked it, but it seemed that nothing I did for him back then was the right thing.

I wasn't able to pinpoint exactly when that shift

happened, but we definitely reached a watershed moment at some point. Once it had, nothing I did pleased him. How in hell we arrived at that point I have no idea. Kace used to idolize me, yet there came a point where I had been terrified to speak and he was reacting negatively to anything I had done.

Staring at myself; confusion clearly written on the face staring back at me in the mirror, I hardly recognized the reflection in the mirror as me. Timid and petrified. Alien feelings to the strong girl I once had been.

Although my appearance used to make people think I was younger than I was and I wasn't that confident in myself, I was usually the most outspoken person amongst my friends about domestic violence.

Who would have thought that I, Chloe Jenner, would have become a victim of something so degrading? Yet, within a couple of years of leaving college, I was a broken wreck of a woman, terrified of my high school sweetheart.

Kace and I were inseparable during our college years, and he couldn't see past me. I loved him deeply. Our friends weren't so lucky. Ruby had split with her long term boyfriend, Dylan, the last year of college when Dylan's band got signed and he was caught on camera having more than one clandestine relationship.

Julie and Brody were still a couple, but Julie wasn't happy, Brody was living a very single guy's lifestyle, in that he golfed, played football and baseball and always seemed to be taking road trips with his football buddies.

Kace and I were a popular couple, and we had our little clique group of couples we hung out with. As a couple we were inseparable except when he had to go off on science trips as part of his degree, and when he took a summer job working in a recording studio in Sacramento.

Graduating summa cum laude, Kace and I had naturally progressed to moving in together straight after college ended; he'd even proposed to me at our graduation party. It came as a bit of a shock because I'd still felt too young to get married.

I loved Kace with all my heart; and at that time, I couldn't imagine my world without him in it, so I said yes. Refusing to get married straight away, we had moved back to Florida and I had opted for a long engagement. Mainly because I knew I wanted to do visual imagery for large productions and to work on either film or live events.

This was the only thing that Kace and I disagreed on, because realizing that dream may have meant moving state to make it happen. As fortune would have it, we had a pretty big venue for music events less than twenty minutes from where we lived and I managed to land a job as a digital image designer for them.

The buzz of working in a concert venue and the bustling pace of live performances had me in my element. I had loved being a part of that scene.

Most of the bands that played there had their

own set production teams, but occasionally there were some that were more about their music than the technical stuff so that's where we kicked in, and even if I do say so myself, I was pretty good at the visual stuff.

Kace was happy for me at first, but with the unsocial hours of a career such as that, it wasn't long before he began to get pretty fed up with me not being around when he finished work. Being a much sought after sound engineer in a recording studio, Kace didn't exactly keep regular hours either.

So what started as bickering slowly became emotionally charged, heated exchanges between us, to the point where I constantly dreaded the subject of work coming up, because after a few months there was always conflict around me having the career I had studied hard for. I don't even know when it happened, but Kace became more and more dismissive and depreciative of me.

Arguments about my work gradually became personal attacks about me as a partner and eventually about not being the woman I should be in his eyes. Eventually, Kace had chipped away at my self-esteem so much that he eroded my confidence in my own abilities, either in my work, or as someone worthy of a guy like him.

Becoming controlling and angry, Kace grabbed me by the throat one night and told me he was glad he hadn't married me, but still expected me to be a loving partner and have sex with him whenever he decided to be intimate with me.

Our whole relationship shifted again when he stopped coming home at the usual time saying he had to stay late at work, until eventually, he was just blatant about going for drinks with the guys and girls he worked with at the recording studios.

So the mental abuse continued, but the physical violence was a slow burner. However, two months later it happened again. Kace came home drunk one night and forced himself on me when I refused to have sex with him.

Extremely aggressive towards me, Kace seemed to develop an intolerance of anything to do with me and seemed to hate everything I did. The spite he then levelled toward me was frightening.

Ultimately, my decision had been to completely submit my body to him and let him have sex, rather than to put up a fight. I wasn't submitting to him out of trust but out of fear of what might have happened if I refused, and if I just lay there the whole ordeal was over much quicker.

Bruising my neck when he bit me on the last occasion gave me feelings on another level of degradation. Feeling low and dirty at the hands of my own partner had my stomach churning over with nerves, but I sucked it all up and waited for him to go to work the next day before I let my feelings out.

Once he had left for work, I scrubbed my skin for hours. My own focus on my work wasn't on form and it had suffered because of what was happening at home. Eventually, by mutual agreement, I had to resign my post.

Being stuck home was the worst thing that could've happened to me. At twenty two years old, I had become a master at concealing my bruises from my friends and family. I also discovered how good an actress I was in the presence of them.

I knew instantly the first time he had an affair, because he came home with a huge bouquet of flowers, and I saw glimmers of the old Kace in his attentive, complimentary behavior. The guilty look and the sudden attention he paid me spoke volumes.

Devastated by his treatment of me, I had felt even lower both in my mood and my self-esteem. Kace had me feeling so unattractive I had begun to have skewed thoughts that he deserved to be with women who could be more attentive towards him.

When he knew I knew about her, he projected his anger onto me, telling me I didn't care enough about him when I could let him do that. This was the first time he really lost it and hit me.

One hard slap across my face was all it took to change my life completely. Our loving relationship was gone forever. Mistrust and fear had taken over and his domineering and manipulative behavior came to the fore.

Kace threatened that if I ever told anyone he'd hit me, he'd tell them it happened under extreme provocation, when he had found out about my affairs. That kept me scared because I knew that Kace always held the room captivated when he spoke, so I knew he was very clever and capable of convincing people that his life was so awful, that by the time he was done spinning his story they would have been lining up to give him a medal for staying with me.

I couldn't have risked that happening. There was no way I wanted to be put in the position of defending myself, especially to my parents, they idolized me. So, I said nothing and the mental abuse continued, but the physical violence was on hold again.

To be honest, I was thankful for Kace's affairs because when he was with those women, he wasn't at home beating on me. Although I was repulsed one morning when he'd come home smelling of sex, perfume and liquor and had tried to climb on top of me.

That was the one time I fought back and paid dearly for it. He hit me so hard, I was dizzy and sick. I read up on it and found that from the force of his hit on my head when I struck wall, I knew I had a concussion.

Stuck in hell. That was how I felt, and I couldn't see any way out of the horrible life I had fallen into. Kace's mind games had messed with my head to such an extent, I was scared to be around him, but even more frightened to be without him.

However, that all changed the day of my twenty fourth birthday. For almost two years I had suffered the life he was dealing me, when the letter threw me a life line.

Collecting the mail from the letterbox at our apartment block, there was a rare letter for me.

Apart from the two birthday cards from Ruby and my parents, there was a crisp, white, expensive looking, watermarked business envelope addressed to me.

Correspondence by mail by anyone toward me was a rarity with me being a stay at home partner and completely reliant on Kace for everything. So when I saw the expensive looking envelope with the lawyer's stamp on the back I was anxious to know what it was about.

Pushing my fingernail under the seal, I ripped it open while I headed in the direction of the elevator and back to the condo. Expensive watermarked paper with gold embossed lettering stated that it was from Sherman, Braun and Partners, Attorneys at Law, Will & Probate specialists and it showed an address in New York. Bunching my brows, I frowned, wondering what in the hell a law firm was doing writing to me.

Dear Ms. Jenner,
We are writing to inform you that as of the 20th April 2014, you are now in control of the trust fund set up in your name by George Alexander Jenner, on 13th May 1991. Please contact Mr. Francis Sherman at the above address at your earliest convenience to claim control of said trust and complete the necessary transfer of title deeds for property in your trust. If you have any questions regarding this correspondence please do not hesitate to contact me during office hours. I look forward to hearing from you.
Yours faithfully

Francis Sherman, P.A.

My legs buckled as I grabbed a hold of the mail box to steady myself. After reading the letter for the sixth time, I pulled out my cell to call the number. I was trembling and my heart was almost beating out of my chest, because I so needed this letter to be true.

My fingers were shaking so badly I could hardly punch in the number. As the line connected, adrenaline coursed through my body at such speed that it made my heart pound even faster than the effect of the letter and I had a metallic taste of shock in my mouth.

After several minutes of speaking with the fast talking New York lawyer, Mr. Sherman, I learned that I was the owner of a small apartment in New York and I had a trust fund of eight hundred thousand dollars. Everything he had said sounded incredulous.

My dad's father, my grandfather, had left my parents a house worth two hundred thousand dollars and about eighty thousand in cash, but there was no mention of me in his will that I was aware of. I was only a baby when he died.

Ringing my dad to check if this was true, my heart fell to the pit of my stomach when he told me he knew nothing about any apartment, or other money belonging to my grandfather. So I called Mr. Sherman back and asked him to talk to my dad, because I had begun to think the whole thing was a hoax.

When my dad called me back, I heard the smile

and excitement in his voice. "It's true, honey. I spoke with your attorney and he's Frank Sherman you're granddad's friend. He wasn't able to tell me about the trust before due to client privilege, but as you gave permission, he told me that the apartment had been rented out for all this time and maintained by the trust fund. Until recently it had a life-long friend of your grandfather's living in it, but he died and as soon as he did your trust fund was to be released to you. Mr. Dunn died last month, so the lawyers had twenty eight days grace to wrap up his affairs and free it up to pass on to you."

Stunned, my dad was as stumped as I was about my inheritance. He had no idea my grandfather had this amount of money stashed anywhere. My next request to my dad should have sounded strange, but I asked my dad not to tell anyone, until I had my head clear about what this meant to me.

Twenty four hours later, when Kace had gone to work, I met with Mr. Sherman at a local hotel. Coincidently he was flying to Florida on vacation hence the speed of our meeting. "For twenty odd years I've wondered what you looked like. You have a lot of your grandmother in you; she was a very beautiful woman as well."

Explaining that he was also a personal friend of my grandparents, and one of my grandfather's closest, Mr. Sherman told me the title deeds were held in his name as trustee, so the transfer would be simple. We both signed in the presence of two notaries that Mr. Sherman had lined up as witnesses, and he faxed it back to his office for them to handle.

"Your grandfather knew he was dying and his one regret in life was not living long enough to get to know you. The apartment paperwork will be completed in due course, but there is no reason why you can't have the keys now, Chloe. You are free to do whatever you wish with it. If you intend to sell you'll have to wait for the transfer of the title deeds to be recorded. Under the terms of the trust I am permitted to transfer one tenth of the trust today and the rest will be freed to you in seven to ten working days after signing. As you have signed all the necessary paperwork and provided me with your bank account details, my office will transfer $80,000 to your account this afternoon. As previously discussed the $800,000 is your net worth after taxes."

When he handed me the keys to my apartment, I wrapped my fingers around them and all my pent up emotions almost choked me. Not because this was a connection to my dead grandfather, but because I had just been handed a life line. Swallowing nervously, I placed the keys safely into my pocket.

A plan to escape had been forming in my mind ever since I'd been given the news and I knew I had to leave Kace and claim my life back. I was frightened about how to do that, but no matter how scary that felt to me or how lacking in confidence I felt, I knew that my life depended on it.

CHAPTER 8

COWARD

Chloe

After I met with Mr. Sherman, I went to see my parents. Finally telling them what had been happening to me. I was feeling embarrassed and ashamed about telling them, worried as well, because I thought my dad would go ballistic and I just wanted to get away.

I hadn't seen them face to face for a couple of weeks and both of my parents were devastated when they saw my bruised face. My heart pounded in my chest and ached because I knew I was hurting them when I told them about Kace and even more when they realized it wasn't a one-off event.

Tears streamed down my mom's face as I told them the only way forward would be to get as far away from him as possible, but my dad was furious and wanted me to stay with them and to go to the police.

That made me panic as well because the thought

of going through something like a trial on top of everything I had already faced felt like too much to deal with.

Eventually, once we had finished talking and my dad saw the state I was in; he very reluctantly came around to my way of thinking. I could simply disappear and live my life in safety fourteen hundred miles away. Kace would have no idea about the apartment or the money, so would never suspect where I had gone.

I could have gone to stay at a hotel and not gone back at all, maybe I just wasn't thinking straight or maybe I just knew how Kace was always one step ahead and would find me before I could get away.

One thing I knew was that if I was going to leave, it had to be impulsively or I would talk myself out of it. My mom nearly fainted when I made the decision to leave the next day. I had somewhere to live and enough money to do just that; the rest I'd figure out as I went along.

So I went home for the last night and as frightened as I was I knew it would give me closure. I could see my parents were frightened for me but I'd lived with it for the past year another night of survival I could manage.

To cover my tracks, Flight SB 11 was booked by my dad's secretary by the time I left my parents and I was flying to New York the following day, but meanwhile I had to try to contain my nerves and disguise my apprehension from Kace.

Initially, I was thinking of just walking away,

leaving everything, and just closing the door, but he didn't deserve to be left any pleasant memories of me.

My dad sent his secretary to collect my stuff so that it would be long gone before I was. Pamela rang the doorbell and was visibly shocked when I opened the door. Knowing that I hadn't done as well with the concealer as I thought I had when I saw her reaction to what I looked like, my hand immediately rose to hide the bruising. Obviously, the only person I'd been fooling was myself.

Taking my case, she asked me if she could do anything. Smiling at her genuine concern for me, I reassured her that I was fine and after that day, I would never have to endure anything at the hands of Kace again. Squeezing my hand, she kissed my cheek hugged me tightly and left wishing me luck. I had a feeling I already had that.

Quickly cleaning the house, I made Kace's favorite dinner and was determined to have the element of surprise about leaving, but for all my efforts he never arrived home to eat it. Eventually, he came home a little after midnight, and I pretended to be asleep. He didn't wake me, just climbed into bed and fell into a deep sleep, snoring heavily. I thanked God for the mercy he'd shown me on my last night with him.

Cruel hands gripped my forearm and shoulder and woke me abruptly. I went from sound asleep to a heightened state of awareness. My heart was thudding in my chest and my nerves jangling in anticipation of what he might do next, and then he started shoving me out of the bed.

"Get me coffee, I don't know why I still have you around. You're a lazy, fat, ugly bitch." Kace growled and pushed me harder. Catching my fall on the floor with my hand, I managed to right myself and stood up straight, turning to look at him. Kace's face was contorted in a sneer, and if I'd had any last minute misplaced guilt about what I was going to do, it disappeared right at that moment.

Saying nothing, I walked purposely from the bedroom and padded into the kitchen to do exactly what he told me. I really couldn't have faced it if he had hit me again on my last day. "God, woman will you look at your face, why do you make me so mad?" Kace was standing at the kitchen counter.

Panicked that he was paying attention to me again, I worried that if I answered him with something that didn't meet with his approval, I might have been on the other end of a beating again. "I'm really sorry, Kace, it's my fault. I am going to try harder to make you happy. Tell me what to do baby and I'll do it," I cooed and lied through my teeth.

With less than an hour left in that miserable hell hole, I would have done anything I needed to do to survive until he left for work, then I could close the door on the whole sorry chapter of living with him.

Kace stared at me, his eyes narrowing suspiciously, and my heart almost stopped. "What are you being so agreeable about?" Fighting with my body not to tense up, I swallowed quietly and tried to paste on a passive, innocent face.

"It's just that I've been thinking a lot since yesterday. And you're right, Kace, I need to do better. You work so hard for us and I need to be more in tune with your needs." Glancing at the clock, I was thankful that he was running tight on time and wouldn't be hanging around this morning.

"Oh, God, is that the time? Do you want to get in the shower and I'll organize your clothes and breakfast, honey?" Turning to glance at the clock he muttered to himself, before he headed to the bathroom without answering me.

Forty five minutes and I knew he'd be out of the door and I'd never have to set eyes on him again. Making his favorite pancakes and bacon, toast and coffee, I then carefully laid out his suit, shirt and tie on the bed for him.

When he came back to the kitchen fully dressed, I couldn't help but think how handsome he was, and a flashback came to mind of the first time I saw him. Kace was a great looking guy, but that didn't matter anymore, he was ugly on the inside.

All during breakfast he never spoke, then surprised me by telling me to make dinner for us, and that he was coming back to spend tonight at home with me.

Shrugging himself into his jacket, he was about to leave and suddenly he put his arm around my waist. Almost flinching, I fought my body's reaction to his touch and allowed myself to meld into him.

Unexpectedly, he crushed his mouth on mine in

what was the first passionate kiss in about a year. I have to admit, I did kiss him back, but not for the reason he might have thought. I was kissing Kace and my old life as I knew it goodbye.

Staring at his back from the window as he walked along the sidewalk, initially I felt numb. Then something inside me still managed to prick my conscience and there was a fleeting thought of feeling sad for him.

However, Kace was a head turner, and I saw a couple of girls glance back at him with awe at his handsome appearance and perfect body, immaculately wrapped in a suit. That's when I knew he'd be fine.

Flashbacks ran through my mind again, of that beautiful face twisted in anger, his strong hands grabbing and shaking me in the terrifying way he did, made any feelings of guilt melt away.

Appropriate feelings began to surface within me. Hate and shame being the main ones, as I watched him get smaller the further away he got from home. I hated him for the way he'd treated me.

Feelings of self-loathing and shame were fighting for the upper hand in my brain, for staying after that first slap and allowing the abuse to escalate. I'd been in a long term relationship with a partner who subjected me to domestic violence.

Watching his figure get smaller through the window, I was thinking that it was the last time I would ever see him. Seven years, and all the firsts we'd ever done together and what we had meant to each other was dead. Our life together was going to be closed off when he took those final steps and turned the corner at the end of the street.

When he finally disappeared out of sight, I exhaled heavily and realized I'd been holding my breath. My forehead leaned heavily on the window pane, my breath misting the glass and the feeling of anxiousness suddenly dissipated.

Turning to face into the room, my body sagged and my knees gave way as I sank to the floor. There were no tears for the life I was leaving behind. All I felt was a deep rooted anxiety, a need to escape, and if I was going to do it, the right moment had just arrived and I had finally found the courage to do it.

There wasn't really much I wanted to take of my old life with me, but I wasn't leaving it for him to pour over like some shrine, and possibly gain more attention for himself in all of this. One picture that was special to the both of us was the one of our friend her graduation and who we rarely saw anymore, Ruby.

Ruby had moved to New York to work as a Speech and Drama tutor at the famous AMDA: American Music and Dramatic Academy there. Studying acting and taking classes since she was a child, her hobby had helped her excel in her college life.

Head and shoulders above her peers, she was snapped up straight out of college to teach in New York City. I was glad that she had no idea what Kace had become, because I knew she'd have challenged him or shouted it to anyone who would listen, and I'd have had repercussions from that from Kace.

Apart from personal pictures, sneaking a couple pictures off the wall in the hallway and replacing them with others was my biggest challenge. The pieces were of digital artwork I did after leaving college and were central to my portfolio. I needed them to help me market myself when I got back into the job market. I knew that if Kace suspected I was plotting he'd have found out because I'm a bad liar.

Kace had noticed. They were the only things he couldn't miss. Commenting as soon as he'd walked through the door the night before I left about their absence, I'd played them off, by telling him that there wasn't much use in having them displayed any more, since I wasn't doing that work and it didn't fit in with our future of me staying at home.

I had replaced them with a few paintings he'd bought when we visited a street display of local artists at Vero Beach one day. Kace smiled and told me that he was glad I had seen sense about trying to work when I should be home taking care of him.

Calling for a cab to take me to the bus station, and from the bus station I took a bus to the mall. From there I took yet another cab to the airport. I knew Kace was smart and would check the buses and the local cab companies, and I was determined to cover my tracks so that he'd never find me again.

In the cab, the driver asked me if I minded the radio being on and shaking my head, I almost burst into tears when "Mr. Know It All" by Kelly Clarkson came on. That little sign gave me the boost I needed to know I was doing the right thing.

When the cab pulled up in the red zone in Orlando International Airport, I paid the driver and stepped onto the drop zone sidewalk. He handed me my small red suitcase with a smile.

It was a beautiful day and the sun was shining, and for the first time in a long time, I felt excited and hopeful about my future. I just hoped that after a year out, I hadn't left it too long to be competitive in my choice of career.

Walking through the main concourse at Orlando International Airport I went to meet my parents who drove separately because I was so paranoid that Kace would find out and follow them. He was so controlling and hyper-vigilant stalking my every movement from home that I somehow felt he knew about everything and was just waiting to pounce.

My eyes scanned over the plastic booths and tables before settling on my mom's stunning red, curly hair. She was in her early fifties, but was still elegant and beautiful. She could easily have passed for her late thirties.

Dad's hair was a shock of blonde, like mine. They were a truly stunning couple when they were younger, but even with age, they still managed to stand out in any room, especially when they were together.

Rising out of his seat, my dad strode across and hugged me tightly. "Geez, your face is still bruised, bastard. I wish you'd let me tell him I know what he's been doing."

Panicked by that, I cut my father off. "Please dad, let me go. It's the best way for me to deal with this." Nodding, yes, I could see the conflict in his eyes. It was hard for him not to follow his instinct to protect his little girl.

Looking desperately sad, her bottom lip quivering, my mom stood and hugged me tightly. "We're going to miss you, honey." She had tears in her red rimmed eyes and tissues in her hand. Smiling affectionately at her, I fought back my own tears as I took her tissue and carefully wiped two small smudges of mascara under her left eye.

"Mom, I'll probably see you more now, than I have for the past two years, I was never allowed to see you guys without Kace being with me. Although I can't come to see you, there is nothing stopping you from coming to New York to shop whenever you want." I winked at her.

I could see the penny drop that she had never realized that he'd kept me from seeing them. I suppose it was easy because we didn't have family events as such. "He really stopped you?" She whispered. I nodded and both my mom and dad's eyes closed simultaneously as they digested this.

"Okay, Kace O'Neill is a mute subject from this day forward. You have no idea where I am." If the police get a missing person's report, I'll contact them and tell them I don't want to be found. That way you guys are completely clear of Kace and any stunts he might think of to trick you into telling him where I am.

Waiting to board the plane, I was a nervous wreck, checking the Duty Free shop entrance where everyone who was coming to the gate had to walk through after passing the security station. In my mind I was thinking of all of things Kace may do to get at me. Only when I got on the plane did I think I'd be able to sit back and relax.

CHAPTER 9

FLYING NORTH

Chloe

Herded onto the United Airlines flight to Newark Airport, I found and settled into my seat. I didn't relax because my eyes were trained on the cabin door watching for Kace, still not really believing what I was doing.

Reality struck when I saw the cabin crew put their thumbs up, and the captain announce the cabin doors were closed and we were preparing for takeoff. Sinking further into my seat, I closed my eyes as the last few passengers loaded luggage in the overhead compartments.

Aware that someone had sat down next to me, I didn't bother opening my eyes, all I needed to know was it wasn't Kace. I had been living at my wit's end for the past few days and I was exhausted.

Passing out before takeoff because my body had been running on adrenaline for the past few days, I never even felt us taxi or climb to the required altitude. When I woke, the first thing I was aware of was a dull droning noise, which I realized was the airplane's air conditioning and the engine. The second thing was that there appeared to be something heavy on my shoulder.

Weird thing was, that it had become the norm for me to be hypersensitive to touch and hyper aware, yet I had slept soundly and felt no fear at being touched by the stranger leaning against me.

Opening my eyes, I turned my head, to see the handsome face of a really good looking guy who had apparently fallen asleep on me. I'd never seen him before and I should have been freaked out after what I had been through with Kace, but I knew that not all men were like him and it was important for me to resist that feeling and not judging everyone by the actions of one person.

I was envious of the stranger who was obviously so secure and relaxed that he could fall into that deep of a sleep. It was hard, but leaving him sleeping on my shoulder was therapeutic and kind of comforting.

A member of the cabin crew came by, doing her rounds with drinks. Her name was Sue, according to the name badge on her smart blue uniform. Giggling at my sleeping man when she passed me the Coke I'd asked for, she asked if she should leave something for my partner.

Turning my head to look down at the sleeping head on my shoulder, I told her she could probably have told me more about him from looking at the seating log, than I knew of him.

Eyes widened in shock as she registered that we weren't together. Whispering in a husky tone, she offered to wake him. As she was doing this, he grunted and began to wake up. As he tilted his head upward his face was inches from mine, then it was funny when I saw his reaction as he realized his head was resting on some random woman next to him. Although, looking at him I probably wasn't the first random woman he'd woken up to. He really was that good looking with his dark muzzy hair and hint of beard, huge sexy brown eyes, kind of Julio Iglesias to look at.

Shooting upright, he straightened his back and ran his hand through his hair before he turned his head back to face me again. "Shit, sorry, I had no idea I was doing that." He looked completely perturbed by his behavior, and was pointing at my shoulder where his head had been resting.

Sue and I began to laugh. This wasn't the kind of response I would have expected from a confident, self-assured guy. Relief registered on his face once he knew I was okay with it, but he looked sheepishly at me.

"I'm very sorry about that, I don't usually sleep with random women." Laughing harder at him only made him even more flustered, to the point where I felt sorry for him. It wasn't often hot guys were genuinely embarrassed by their behavior and his vulnerability made me warm to him instantly.

I reassured him I was fine and Sue poured him

an orange juice. Sipping the drink he observed me over the rim of the clear plastic glass and smirked bashfully. "Sorry, again, that was embarrassing."

Smiling warmly, it dawned on me that it was the first time in a long time I felt myself smile. "At least I know my left shoulder is comfortable enough for someone to sleep on." My smile became a grin and his lips curved into a smile back at me.

"Chloe," I said, sticking my hand out for him to shake. "I feel I should at least introduce myself, since you've slept with me already." My jaw hung at my mistake and he almost choked on his drink, and laughed heartily. "Damn, I walked straight into that one, huh?"

He chuckled as he slipped his hand in mine and gave me a strong handshake. "Gavin."

Effortless chatter followed and Gavin told me he only lived about five blocks from the general area where I was going to be living. He was very easy to talk to and made me feel relaxed about being on the flight. I found out that he was an electrician in a theatre on Broadway and that his parents had retired to Cocoa Beach about three years ago, where he visits them bi-annually.

Gavin gestured at my face, "Did you have a run-in with a cupboard or something?" I could see from his reaction that my own had wiped the smile off his face. Feeling brave and determined not to lie for Kace anymore, I took a deep breath.

So, Gavin got what he wasn't expecting. I told him the truth, surprising myself by pouring a lot out about my life with Kace and he sat quietly listening and paying attention to what was being said with a dark expression and his jaw twitching.

"What a fucking coward." He shook his head softly. "And for the record Chloe, you are a very beautiful woman, and I'm glad you got away from him. Now you've shared all of that with me, I'm guessing you don't have many friends in New York." I smiled shyly at him and immediately thought there was no way I was getting into another relationship with anyone. That didn't mean I wouldn't like him as a friend when I got settle though.

"Even if I did, I can never have enough friends, Gavin." I hesitated, wondering how to phrase this next part. "But, I need to tell you, I am only interested in those that don't want any more than I can give. It will be a long time before I am ready to trust a man in a relationship, except in a purely platonic way."

Gavin smiled warmly and pulled a packet of Juicy Fruit chewing gum from his jacket pocket. Shaking them from the small packet he asked, "Want one?" I smiled back and took a piece.

"Thank you, I've not had this for years."

Smiling bashfully he said, "I love it! It's so underestimated though. Beats spearmint and peppermint flavors hands down." He chuckled at his little sales pitch for a second before his face became serious.

"Chloe, I was in a relationship for a long time too. My girl left me for a geeky guy with a huge inheritance. My parents tell me I had a lucky escape with that. For about a year I didn't believe them, I couldn't see past the girl. When my parents moved to Cocoa Beach from Boston, I took it as my chance for a clean break and moved to New York." He gave me a half smile. "So, apart from the physical stuff, I can relate to your situation a little."

Tapping his fingers nervously on the pulled down tray, his eyes flicked to mine again. "Would you take my number... just in case you need anything? I'd hate to think you were out there and had no one to call. You don't have to give me yours. I'd just feel happier knowing that there was someone you could rely on if you needed help."

I smiled at Gavin, "I'd like that thanks, but I won't give you mine if you don't mind, I'm changing it anyway. Can I call you when I'm ready to deal with friends? I just feel I need to take stock for a while, you know?"

Gavin looked completely comfortable with my admission. "Sure, Chloe, whatever you need, and when you're ready for work, call me and I'll see if there's anything that you might want to go after." I felt that Gavin was a really genuine guy, he really did just want to help, but after the mind games of Kace I was wary.

Gavin told me that he shared an apartment with Ed, a theatre production guy. Ed had advertised on a board in the theatre staff canteen for a roommate and Gavin moved in two weeks later. Gavin also told me that Ed has since moved to a more senior role at another theatre.

He asked Sue for a pen when she passed. He scribbled on a napkin and passed it to me. "This has my address, the telephone number of the theatre I work at, and my cell. Keep it safe. Add my numbers to your cell. Gavin Dawkins is my full name. I'd like you to call, not because I have designs on you, but because I think you could use someone to trust."

We left the plane together and Gavin asked if I wanted a lift to my apartment block. I really didn't feel that confident about letting anyone know where I lived although he knew the general area, but I said no. Gavin told me he understood and surprised me when he pulled me into a hug before he released me just as suddenly and walked away.

"Call me when you're ready, Chloe," he said when his head turned back to look at me. I nodded and stood watching him disappear into the crowd in the direction of the airport parking.

Standing in line waiting for the cab, a range of emotions washed over me. Fear, relief, anxiety, excitement as well as sadness and loss ran through my mind. Each new emotion affected my body by making my heart race, or making it feel heavy and heartbroken until I was standing in public, fighting back tears.

I was terrified and resolute at the same time. There had been no other way but to break free. I even felt sorry for Kace, that he'd come home and find me gone. I felt like such a bad person for leaving him wondering what had happened to me.

The cab driver was a fast talking New Yorker, and his conversation distracted me from my thoughts and made me concentrate on where I was headed. I hadn't seen it yet, but according to Gavin, my apartment was in a nice neighborhood, and relatively safe. Gavin didn't know that wouldn't mean much to me, because we'd lived in a great neighborhood with a very low crime rate in Florida. Yet, the safest place for me was anywhere away from there.

The contrast of the fast moving pace where everyone seemed to be in a hurry felt overwhelming to me as I stared out of the yellow cab window. Craning my neck to look up at the buildings, it was impossible to see the tops of most of them up close.

The apartment was on the Upper East Side of New York. A wealthy area but the block itself was an older one and less affluent looking than the plush new skyscrapers surrounding it. Still, it had a doorman and central keypad entry, so at least no one could walk in off the street without being noticed. I loved the fact he didn't take me at face value either and asked for my ID and checked his information sheet. All those things served to reassure me that I was safe.

My apartment was on the eleventh floor and to the front and had a decent view. The thing I noticed the most about it was it was really quiet. I didn't care what I could see on the outside, it was how safe I could be on the inside that mattered.

Once inside, I leaned against the door, closed my

eyes and became overwhelmed by all the emotions I had suppressed for the last couple of days. Relieved and thankful for my second chance, but at the same time, I was still grieving for the life I could have had with Kace, before all the bad things started happening.

I sat in the sparsely furnished apartment which was now my sanctuary, and looked around. Acknowledging this to myself of how thankful I was to my grandfather for this gift, because I felt that my inheritance was more than money. It was a lifesaver.

There were a few pieces of antique furniture, such as an old writing bureau made of yew wood, highly polished and a little incongruent to the apartment, which I fell in love with on sight, and a massive old pine chest of drawers in the master bedroom.

They were obviously my grandpa's, from knowing his taste in furniture at his place in Florida, as the place was otherwise unfurnished I could see I was going to have to make the place my own faster than I'd expected.

I loved the open space of the apartment. It only had two bedrooms, but it felt very spacious, with its tall ceilings, large, picture windows, and beautiful old highly polished, oak wooden floors. The place just needed some tender loving care and it would look fabulous in no time.

My mum was so resourceful and had managed to find a bed and a sectional couch in a consignment store which she had delivered. The building's service manager had helped them to install it for me. There were built in appliances in the kitchen, which were a little dated, but seemed to be functional.

All I needed right then was food. My cell started ringing as soon as I switched it on. Kace's ID flashed and I froze, sitting petrified for a moment. Even here in New York, he could still affect me like that.

Beads of sweat broke out onto my forehead and nose and my palms became clammy. Dry mouthed I felt adrenaline coursing through my body, making me feel like I needed to get up to run and hide.

Cutting the call off, I rang my parents to tell them that I had arrived and was safe. As soon as I spoke to them, my dad told me that Kace had already rung them looking for me and he had played dumb. I felt bad that I'd left them to deal with this and told them so.

My dad's response was that if he didn't leave them alone they would probably move too. My parents didn't need to worry about money and my dad works from home, so I guess that would probably be an option for them at some point anyway.

When I finished my call, I switched my cell off and that was the last time I ever used it. I had made a note of the contacts I wanted to keep. There were only two numbers on the list, Ruby who was here in New York, and my friend Carla, who was currently living in Marbella, Spain. They were the only two people apart from my parents that I trusted not to give in to Kace's charming ways.

Taking my suitcase, I heaved it onto the bed. The fabric was straining under the tightly packed clothing my mom had squeezed in. Unzipping it, I threw the top open. Pulling out another sweater, I stuck my arms in the sleeves and pulled it over my head. It was the end of April, but there were still very cool days in New York, this was one of them.

Once I was wrapped up against the cold, I made my way down to the street. I had no clue where to buy anything or where I needed to go, so I did what every tourist would do and flagged a yellow cab driver to help me out.

Hank, the cab driver, was a retired policeman so I'd seen him as safe. He took me around the entire afternoon for a fixed fare of $250. We agreed on the fare when I told him there was a lot I had to achieve, and rather than leave the meter running, he suggested it might be cheaper to do it that way.

A wealth of knowledge about New York, Hank had a great sense of humor and made sure I knew everything I needed to know about all the things I wanted to do. He even came into Walmart in New Jersey and helped choose pots and pans, flat and silverware, a new phone, a TV, sheets and a comforter set.

CHAPTER 10

NESTING

Chloe

By the time I got home I had achieved far more than I'd expected. Hank was a lifesaver, he'd helped me back and forth with all the stuff I had purchased and before he left he advised me that there were a lot of con men in New York. Hank gave me is card and said if I needed anything to call him.

Chuckling, I attached Hank's number to Gavin's which was already stuck to the 'I heart Paris' magnet that had been left on the fridge door. Ironically, I'd been in New York for less than six hours and two guys had given me their cell numbers. Kace would have had a breakdown if he'd known about that.

Opening the box of my new iPhone, I plugged the charger in to the socket and headed to the kitchen to get the fried chicken I'd brought home to save me cooking.

Unpacking the flatware, I placed them all in the

dishwaher, bar one, to run a cycle before storing them in the cupboard. Washing the single plate, I dried it with a new dishtowel and placed the chicken on it. Taking a can of soda from the box of twenty four I had also bought – my dinner was now ready.

I had just taken my first bite when my new cell phone began to ring. Fear gripped me, a stunned feeling hitting my chest as my eyes flicked to the screen on the phone. I stared at it for a split second before I remembered that I had a new number which had no connection with my past life.

Padding over to answer it, I had the idea it could be the phone company I'd taken the contract out with. Swiping the screen to answer, a rich deep voice boomed out at me. "Toby, dude, are we meeting up or what?"

Clearing my throat I squeaked, "Umm, Toby?"

"Oh, sorry honey, could you put Toby on the line? Where the hell is he anyway?" I breathed in deeply, and exhaled.

"I'm sorry you have the wrong number." I was about to end the call, and the voice spoke back to me again.

"What number did I dial?" I raised my eyebrow.

"You have a smart phone in front of you, don't you?"

An infectious chuckle came back at me, "You think if I ask this piece of shit, it's smart enough to answer me?"

I smiled at his humor, "No, but you could read the last number dialed."

He snickered down the phone. "Damn, I just showed my stupid gene there, huh?"

Smiling at his funny self-deprecating comment, I could feel myself physically relaxing. "Don't worry, your secret is safe with me. After all, I have no clue who you are." There was hesitancy, and wrong number guy came back again.

"This is true. I kinda like that idea. It means that you couldn't pick me out in a line-up of stupid guys." I smirked because he was amusing.

"Unless, you spoke and said something equally as dense, then I'd have a fighting chance of that," I quipped and giggled back. There was silence for a while and I thought I had offended him, but what the hell, he didn't know me. "Anyway, stupid-gene-wrong-number guy, I'm afraid you'll have to dial again. I sure hope Toby's coming after all this."

He chuckled, "Yeah, well hot-sounding-good-sense-of-humor girl, I'd better chase him down. Sorry to disturb you." I meant to say no problem but I said, "Anytime," then screwed my face up at the phone thinking, *WTF?* Again there was a small silence.

Expecting him to hang up, I was surprised when he answered back again. "Huh? Hmm... well, maybe I'll just have to test that comment out sometime." Beginning to chuckle, he had a smile in his voice. "Nice call forward, darlin', have a good day." I don't know why but just calling me darlin' lifted my spirit.

Still smiling, I walked back to the couch and sat down slowly, still staring at the cell. He was the only number logged in my received calls list, my first call of my new life, and it wasn't a bad start at all.

After dinner, I dug into my bags of purchases and began to give my new home some character. Some duck egg blue scatter cushions I'd bought were thrown onto the large sectional, and I lit a couple of small table lamps. The effect of these items warmed the room immediately.

While running a bath, I made up my bed, standing back with my arms folded to admire the cream and gold bedding. It looked rich and inviting, and I couldn't wait to be snuggled down in it, even if I hadn't washed the linen first. I was exhausted, both mentally and physically.

Intending on soaking in the bath, I lay back but soon felt my eyes drooping as I enjoyed the simple tranquility it offered me. I and nodded off and when I woke the water was freezing. I got out and dried. No use in escaping the clutches of Kace, only to drown in a bath fourteen hundred miles away on the same day.

I pulled on a blue figure hugging tank top and pajama shorts, making a mental note to get some warmer clothing, then snuggled down with the duvet pulled up to my chin. As soon as I was in the silent darkness of the room, tears fell softly down my face.

I owed it to myself to grieve properly for the life I had lost before I could begin to build a new one. After this though, I promised I wouldn't shed any more tears for Kace.

When I woke, it was with a start and I could hear my cell ringing all the way down the hall in the sitting room. I wasn't in a hurry to answer it though, because I hadn't given it out to anyone, so it would probably be the cell phone company this time with something to do with the contract. I swept the duvet back and slid out of my bed when it became obvious whoever it was wasn't giving up.

Picking up my cell, I swiped to answer. "Toby?" I huffed. "Nope." I was tired and didn't expand my conversation. "Shit, I've done it again, huh? I'm sorry darlin' did I wake you?"

Feeling in a sarcastic mood I answered. "Hell no, I always wander around my apartment in the middle of the night, answering random phone calls."

"Ouch. And there I was thinking I had this hot babe that I could call at any time and tell her all about my day." As soon as he'd said it, I thought it could actually be fun, talking to a guy without him knowing where I was.

Controlling my interaction with a man on the phone without any commitment, maybe I could cope with this. More alert now, I asked, "Is that what you want to do? Talk to some random female about your life, and kind of hear what I have to say about it, but don't judge me kind of relationship?"

Snickering, I could hear the humor in his voice, "That'd be a first, someone not judging me. It sounds like an excellent plan, are you game?"

Not hesitating I found myself saying, "Sure, I'm up for that, as long as I can do the same." Suddenly, I was feeling kind of excited about talking to a mysterious anonymous guy on the line.

"Do I get a name?" At that point I hesitated and almost gave him a false one.

"Chloe." I swallowed hard because the way I was feeling even someone knowing my first name sounded like too much.

After I said it, I was met by a moment of silence, which I broke by asking if I could have his. "Oh, yeah, sorry. Paul... my name is Paul." His voice was flat as if he was distracted by something then he came back more focused. "Hey, Chloe. Pleased to meet you... on the phone," he said playfully with the smile back in his voice.

Chatting about nothing in particular for another couple of minutes, but it was the way he spoke to me. Like I mattered. He had an amazingly smooth tone to his voice and the way we conversed was easy. Paul concluded the call because he remembered he was calling his friend and we concluded the call. I hung up and padded barefoot back to bed and fell asleep thinking about my mystery caller. The rest of the evening was uneventful, but as I climbed into bed my mind drifted back to the call. It had been a while since I'd had a normal conversation with another guy around my age.

Later, a low vibrating noise broke into my sleep. My cell on the nightstand was slowly moving towards me across the glass making a soft clinking sound which added to the annoyance of the ringing. In my sleepy state, I'd forgotten where I was and fear instantly flooded my body. I'd been waking with those feelings for about a year.

Once I remembered where I was, my racing heartbeat began to slow until I had the thought and wondered if my parents were okay. Squinting over at the cell, I swiped to answer anyway.

"Toby! That was ace!" Paul's wired voice shouted down the line at me and it was weird how I recognized it.

"Paul if we're going to do this, it needs to be when I'm awake." I mumbled into the phone, before pulling it down from my ear to glance at the screen, still trying to focus on the time display.

When I put it back to my ear again I heard some shuffling in the background before he said, "Jeez, did I do it again? I stretched again, and then yawned and exhaled heavily into the phone.

"I don't know who you intended on calling Paul, but you got me instead." I croaked.

"Oh geez, sorry darlin'. I didn't realize I hadn't dialed the correct number. I'm going to have to store this under Chloe so that I don't wake you again."

Smiling sleepily, I wondered if this call was an accident and replied, "You've made my day… or night. I'd really appreciate it if you did, I just changed my number and I'd hate to do it again."

Paul snickered into the phone, "Gotcha, don't piss Chloe off when she's just woken up." Saying our goodbyes again, I swiped the cell phone on silent and went back to sleep.

For the next couple of days I heard nothing from Paul and I figured that I'd probably never hear from him again. I spent my time fixing the apartment up and working on my portfolio. As I did I thought there was no way I could have had any type of career with Kace's level of control on me. And with all his connections and his skills at finding out things I was afraid he'd track me down. As soon as I'd thought of that, my mind went back to how interfering and difficult he was about me.

Just thinking an incident when I'd been introduce to a new collegue at work and Kace's behavior toward me afterward made me feel sick. Derek and I were discussing some aspects of the project we'd just been assigned that day and wandered over to the coffee shop across the road for refreshments. It hadn't occurred to me to mention that to Kace. He'd somehow found out about it and confronted me.

The black eye he gave me had meant a week off work and I hadn't even known the guy's last name. As for poor Derek, Kace went to his wife and told her he had designs on me, and told her to tell him, to stay away from his girl.

Shaking myself out of that memory, I was positive that my life could only get better. Being left a hefty sum of money I was able to think about how I could have a career and stay safe. And that led me to think about indulging in my other passion–creative writing. The idea of writing a book excited me, and I could afford to stay home for a year. Thinking maybe the isolation would do me good after the ordeal I had been through. Switching on my mellow music playlist I had made on Spotify I began to research what I could find to write about.

CHAPTER 11

PLAYFUL BANTER

Chloe

Engrossed in what I was doing, I almost missed the call. My phone was vibrating on the end table. I became vaguely conscious of it while I was listening to "Somebody That I Used To Know" by Goyte. My one caller's number flashed on the screen.

Answering the call, my heart squeezed when I heard him say my name, "Hey, Chloe."

The familiarity in Paul's voice seemed to nag at me. Smiling at the use of my name, I asked, "You meant to call me and not Toby?" Something in his voice made me tingle, he had a great voice, and reminded me of another voice that brought back feelings of a something and nothing encounter I'd once had when I was at college.

"Sure I did. Your voice is way sexier than Toby's and I can't flirt with him." Between his low, velvety-rich Southern accent and his comment, I was rendered speechless for a moment before trying to continue the conversation. *He sounds like Gibson Barclay.*

My heart skipped a beat when I thought about Gibson, "So...?" I asked, leaving the question open as to why Paul was calling.

"So," he mimicked back playfully and began chuckling. I froze for a second because I wasn't used to anyone flirting with me. Then I thought the poor guy had no idea what I'd been through.

"Where are you?" It had only just occurred to me that he may not be in New York and could be anywhere.

"I'm in Arizona right now, you?" I wasn't sure about telling him where I was, but he was just some guy on the end of the phone, he couldn't find me. "New York."

"I'm a few hours behind you. Sorry I woke you up at that ungodly hour, darlin'. Toby is in LA and in the same time zone as me."

Thinking he'd rung to apologize for waking me, I started to say that it was an easy mistake to make when he said, "So who's going first?"

"Going first for what?"

I could hear the playful tone in his voice as he replied, "Well, we could have phone sex, but I think I'd kinda like to get to know you first, if that's okay with you... I'm messing with you of course, I meant going first to talk about our day."

Maybe it was the reference 'our day', but God knows what got into me after that, but I'd pretended to sound disappointed. "Oh, so you're kidding about the phone sex, hmm, pity. Right, talking about our day it is then."

Paul didn't miss a beat, coming back at me saying, "Maybe once we're a little more familiar we'll get to that. I NEVER put out on the first phone date." He started to chuckle again and it was quite infectious but I kept my cool.

Wanting to put him in his place, I flirted back, even though my cheeks were heated and my vagina had clenched from what he'd just said. "Hmm, you think you're capable of that… phone sex huh?"

He was really laughing down the line by then and cooed, "Oh darlin', you have no idea what I'm capable of. I've been known to make girls come just talking to them."

A female voice came and murmured something to him and he briefly covered the phone saying, "Two seconds," before he turned his attention back to me. "Well, Chloe it looks like you are going to have to hold that thought on the day's events. I had a great time talking to you, but I have to be somewhere in a few minutes, so I need to go and make another call to Toby."

Honestly? I was glad that the call ended there, because I doubted whether I could have continued to keep that level of flirting up with him. What could I have said in response to his comment about his voice anyway?

Calling Ruby, I left her a message because it was still early and I was guessing she must have still been asleep. I took a shower, it was great to have the time just relax and rejuvenate my body for a while... When I came back there were three new text messages, two from Ruby and one from Paul so I opened it.

Paul: Sorry Chloe, that was so wrong of me. It won't happen again.

I was weirdly disappointed by the whole thing and got back into bed. Tossing and turning, I got to thinking about Paul. His voice had caused me to think of Gibson Barclay. Their accents were the same. When I got to thinking about him – my fantasy about spending a night with Gibson – it all flooded back and I fell asleep with memories of my college days and that one brief, up close and personal moment I had with him.

When I woke it was daylight, and glancing at the clock it was 10am. I sat bolt upright in bed, I hadn't slept that long since I was in college. Lifting my cell from the night stand, I turned it on. There were four missed calls and two texts.

Ruby had tried to call me, and then texted.

Can't wait to see you, Friday, Andaz Restaurant, 5th Ave, 7pm. Squeeeee!!!

Excited at the prospect of seeing Ruby again, I only hoped I wouldn't become emotional about everything that had happened with Kace when I did.

I decided to be proactive about trying to write and visited the library that morning. Doing some research for writing a love story, I came out with an assortment of books to sharpen my mind before I got started. Grabbing a sandwich, I made my way to Central Park with my lunch. Being in the apartment all the time, I was beginning to miss the outdoors.

Sitting down on the grass, I began stuffing my face with the delicious ham on rye bread and I popped my earphones in to listen to music. The phone was synchronized to my Spotify playlists, "Waiting for Superman" by Daughtry was playing. I loved the idea of having my favorite music while eating alfresco.

Less than five minutes into my playlist, my cell rang. Seeing it was Paul, I held my breath and my heartbeat fluttered at the fact he was continuing to call me. Unsure of what to say after the earlier call, I almost let it ring out. Feeling nervous and embarrassed about the interaction we'd had, and not sure whether I could talk normally after his comment about making girls come by talking to them.

Not trusting my own judgment because of how Kace had messed with my head, I tried to dig deep to find the old Chloe. The old me had a quiet confidence, but I was principled and hadn't a lot of sexual experience. None outside of Kace really, apart from a couple of boys I had kissed as a young teen.

However, I wouldn't have shied away from someone who had said something which made me feel uncomfortable. And really, there was only one person who had managed to make me feel the need to turn and run, and he became a world famous rock star. So my reputation on that score was still intact, as far as I was concerned.

Smirking, and confident the guy calling me would never know me outside of a phone call, I pinched my nose and decided to answer. "This is Toby's wrong number messaging service, how may I help you."

Rich spontaneous laughter boomed down the line at me. "Ha! Very funny." Something about the way his voice came across sounding relaxed and familiar made my heart skip a beat.

Smiling into my cell, I felt slightly weird that a guy I had never met could make me feel this engaged. Finding it very strange that I felt good about myself and that someone I didn't know could have an effect like that on me. I loved the rich deep tone of his voice, it was warm and there was something familiar in it. "Hey, Paul. How's it hanging?"

My jaw hung silently in disbelief as soon as my words were out. Where the hell had that phrase come from? I had no idea, and to say it to him after the last conversation was... well an epic fail on my part. Paul coughed and sputtered, like he'd been drinking something and gave me another belly laugh, trying to get himself under control.

"God, Chloe, that's too fucking funny, oops sorry, my bad, I didn't mean to swear." Continuing to chuckle, he asked, "Where are you?" I smiled looking at the spacious wide area around me.

"Umm, in prison... where else do you think I'd get all this time to answer Toby's wrong numbers? What the hell does this guy do anyhow?" My question was met with a silence that seemed a little odd, and then I heard him clear his voice.

"Ah, well... not very much if you ask me."

I exhaled and smiled again, "Thought so, he's too busy taking phone calls to work."

"So..." Paul said, changing the subject.

"So," I answered back playfully.

"Where are you? I mean... where are you, really?" Suspicion took over and I became cagey again.

"New York." Paul snickered down the line at me.

"I know... you told me that. I mean where are you and what are you doing?"

Swallowing noisily, I wasn't sure whether to tell him I was in Central Park because that would pinpoint me, but it was a big park so I answered. "I'm in the park." My voice sounded wary.

"I thought I could hear ducks, or are they geese?" Good guess, Paul. Grinning, I looked at the beautiful birds out on the lake. "Both."

"So, Paul... was there a reason for this call, or did you just want to hear my voice?"

"Well there was a reason, and yes that's it, actually." Confused, I asked him to clarify what he meant. "I did call because I wanted to hear your voice, and well... to apologize for my pretty stupid off-the-cuff remark to you the last time about phone sex... and to tell you that I'm sorry."

Smiling, I was glad he sounded so remorseful about it. It said a lot about him as a person. And, even though he'd apologized in a text, he wasn't beyond repeating that to me. While I was thinking he spoke again.

"Tell me something about Chloe. Anything."

Frozen by his request, I wasn't sure I was ready to share anything about my life, but like I thought before, the guy was on the phone and would never know me in real life. Besides not all men were like Kace. "So, this random guy rings me and it's a wrong number right? And he admits to a stupid gene, and then proves it 'cause he calls me again, so anyway..." Paul cut me off.

"Okay, I got it. I'll go first. I understand you're nervous, but we're on the phone so it's safe, right? I mean no one is going to get mauled or anything, and there will be no awkward end of night date thing going on, we're just two people talking."

Raising my brow I asked, "So you have nothing better to do than talk to some woman that's a wrong number?"

Chuckling softly he said, "You're getting the idea, and no I don't. Not right at this minute. And, to be honest, I can't think of anything better to do than to talk to you." It was a nice statement so I decided to play along.

"Smooth answer Paul. Hmm... let me see then, okay... my best friend is called Ruby." Chuckling at my disclosure, he mirrored back.

"My best friend is called... Toby." I could hear

the smile in his voice and it made me smile in return, liking his slight tease at me.

"Tell me something else," he coaxed, his voice encouraging me. Twisting my lips, I thought about that.

"I'm unemployed." He immediately came back sounding concerned.

"Do you have money to eat and live and shit?" Taken aback by his sudden concern, I had to offer some reassurance.

"Sure, I have plenty to keep me going for a long while."

I heard him exhale heavily. "Well, that's good. What do you do?"

The questions were becoming personal. "Ah, that would be question three and you're now two behind." Clucking his tongue at me, Paul thought about what to share with me next.

"I have a dog and a car."

Giggling at his odd choices to share, I asked playfully, "Is that in order of importance Paul?"

Laughing again, he said, "That's three times you've said my name. Does that mean you're my friend now? Not waiting for a response, he quickly interjected, "Your turn."

Smirking wickedly into my cell, I mirrored him back. "I have no car and no dog."

"Enough questions for today?" Paul asked, sensing my closed answers as an indication I wasn't ready to share anything else. I nodded and said yes, but liked the 'for today' part. Strange how I felt a little pang of regret that our call was coming to an end, but I definitely hadn't trusted anyone with anything that was worth knowing about me, except Gavin at that point.

"Yeah, my driver will be picking me up soon." Paul's voice sounded surprised. "Your driver?"

Smiling, I clarified. "Yeah, I'm not rich or anything, he's my taxi driver and he'll be here soon, so I need to get going, I have some errands to run. Nice talking to you, Paul."

Hearing him breathe in deeply, he asked, "So, are we friends now? If so, maybe you could add my name to my number on your phone?" Pausing he added, "Call forward friends?" I could agree to that.

"Okay Paul, and thanks for the chat." I touched the red call end button and dropped the cell in my bag. Still smiling as I stood up and cleared the crumbs from my pants, I made my way to the entrance where I had agreed to meet Hank. He was waiting for me and it felt good, even though he was only a taxi driver, he was someone I could depend on for the moment.

Falling into the calm lifestyle I was carving out, I had Hank drop me off at the library. After gathering some research, I went home and started to plot a chart of ideas for a book. I became so lost in it that I nearly forgot to eat until I couldn't ignore my rumbling stomach.

Taking sandwiches and soup to bed, I tried again to watch a movie on my laptop but I fell asleep. My mind playing catch up after more than a year of abuse and living on my nerves.

It wasn't until the following evening, around 11:30 pm that Paul contacted me again, this time by text.

> ***Has anyone told you that you have the sexiest voice ever?***

Pretty sure that he'd texted me by accident; I reacted strangely, feeling more than a pang of jealousy at the woman who should have received that message instead of me. Shaking off that feeling I told myself I was being absurd, the guy on the phone wasn't really interested, I was just someone he was passing the time with.

Besides, he could look like Quasimodo from the 'Hunch Back of Notre Dame,' although he had the voice of Gibson Barclay.

Sighing, I leaned over to my nightstand and swiped the screen of my tablet. Finding the app to my music, I found the song I was looking for. As soon as the music intro started, I lay back and closed my eyes. "Inches From Paradise," the song that made M3rCy superstars, filled the room and my imagination wandered back to the time when Gibson looked into my eyes – in my mind we had shared a moment.

The words were amazing and although the credits said that he wrote the song, the manwhore I had known about then wouldn't have been capable of the feelings behind those words in that song.

Unspoken moment, in a thunderstorm, a

moment remembered, that still keeps me warm, I'll never forget that sweet soulful look, a chance of a stolen kiss that I never took.

Living my life without regrets, until the moment our lips almost met, and then you were gone, but the fresh smell of rain still makes me wonder, where you are now and if for that second you'd felt the same.

Unlike the rest of his songs, this one had an element that clicked with me. Lyrics of a love song, instead of his usual rock songs full of metaphors for fucking women, drinking and broken fucked up relationships. This song had a different, slower tempo, sad sounding melody and softer music. Not a rock ballad per se.

All I knew was that I connected with it, and I never thought I'd ever hear myself say that I had something in common with Gibson Barclay, but I did. It was the song that saved my life and kept me sane. When life was terrible, I'd put it on and lie flat on the floor with my arms stretched out to the side and imagine myself floating whilst it played. Those few moments of escape were everything to me.

CHAPTER 12

SHE HUNG UP

Gibson

Crazy I know, but she sounded like a great girl. I loved her voice too. There was a sweet way with her. And damn, she hung up on me! I snickered to myself. That's got to be a first… ever. Doubt she'd do that if she knew who I really was. Actually, that was a really arrogant thought. She may even hate my music and what I did.

Didn't think I'd ever really meet a woman that just wanted me for me. Maybe that's why I wanted to talk to her so much. I was getting a kick out of talking to someone who sounded so normal without all the adulation shit that I usually got. She was bright and funny and didn't want anything from me. So, I was getting a real buzz out of my mystery wrong number. Realizing I was smiling, I shook my head.

I'd never been so thankful to anyone for doing something wrong before. Toby's PA gave me his new number incorrectly, so it was a pure fluke. But Chloe, there was just something about her. She had a cute way of talking, not to mention a sexy laugh, but there was something in her voice that made me feel that something was wrong. I really liked talking to her, she was very real. Not like those plastic girls that were always hanging around in droves, wiggling their asses at me and asking me to sign their tits.

Man. Why did girls do that? What the fuck? Why anyone would want to screw a rock star with the reputations that fly around about us is beyond me. At first, when I hit it big I was like a kid in a candy store, trying everyone, not knowing which type of girl to go for next.

Nowadays sex only happens if I'm in a good mood, there is good conversation, the sexual chemistry is there between us, and I've had a fair amount to drink. Drinking made me feel horny so I tried not to do much of that either since I realized.

I wasn't proud of the girls I'd been with, and although it was just physical, I always tried to be honest with them and make sure they knew up front that there was never going to be anything more than that moment with me.

So that was why I was really thankful to Toby's PA for her fuck up. Looking at the number I kept calling, I admitted to myself I'd been calling it on purpose since after the first time.

Chloe was a girl I knew nothing about, but she'd become a welcome distraction from the crazy life I led every day. I had no idea what it was about her or what she looked like, or what her life was like. She just sounded like an upbeat girl with a great personality. Suddenly I wondered if she had a partner. I hoped not, because I hadn't wanted to create drama by calling her.

Somehow I figured she must have been involved with someone, a girl like her. Then I thought I should have been more thoughtful about that, asking personal questions. It had never occurred to me that her partner may be around. Hell, maybe she was married. I thought I needed to ask her those questions. I knew I couldn't go around hijacking someone else's relationship because I didn't have one.

What the hell was I thinking? I needed to be more careful. It was a fucking wrong number. Yet, there I was deliberately calling her. Hooked. When I was doing shit like this I recognized it was definitely time for a break in my schedule. How did my mind suddenly get filled with a girl I knew nothing about and had called by accident? Thing was, she was a smidge of normality, a tiny strand tied into a normal existence I knew nothing about.

When I mentioned Chloe to Toby, he'd thought it was hysterical. The thought of someone else continually getting his calls really appealed to him. "Poor woman," he groaned before laughing his ass off. Toby hated his phone because it never stopped ringing.

He stupidly kept the same number for years on his phone and constantly complained about old friends who suddenly were down on their luck and looking for a handout. I'd been telling him to get a set up like mine.

Everyone rang Charlotte, my PA, and the cell I have, I use to call out on. It's blocked from accepting incoming calls unless I punch that particular number into an accepted callers list, but I can get text messages on it. Besides only a very few have my number.

Actually, there are eleven now; if I include Chloe.

Chloe's the first normal 'non friend' person I had spoken to on the phone in years. She had no idea who I was or what I was, and that fact drew to me to her like a camel to water. Talking to her gave me a few moments of escapism from my mad world.

Calling Toby after talking to Chloe, I'd tried to sound upbeat. "Hey dude, wazzup?" Toby sounded upbeat as usual. No idea where he got his energy levels from.

"Just calling to tell you we're definitely going to be in LA next week."

Toby's voice came back rushed and animated, "Great, I can't wait to see you, bro. Are you staying here? How long do you have?"

I smiled because I couldn't wait to see him. "Gig Friday; then two nights and we're off to Rio on Monday." Walking across the room, I lifted my iPad off the chair and sat down and leaned back into it.

"Fucking ace! We're here until Friday so we're definitely partying when you get here."

I grinned widely and felt pretty stoked about that because Toby Francis and I only saw each other a few times a year due to our crazy schedules. We hadn't seen each other since last February and it was April now. Fourteen months since the last time and it was the longest time apart we'd ever had.

We spoke on the phone almost daily, or tried to, depending on the time zones we were in. If we hadn't talked we emailed. In this business, the normal and mundane things such as, talking to your friends, was so damned important.

What are the chances of two kids from the same town, who are best friends, becoming worldwide rock stars for different bands? It must be a wild number, but it happened to us. Toby and I had kept each other sane through everything. It could be so easy to lose touch with reality in this game, with people wanting to kiss our asses, or ride them every minute of every day.

Toby's lucky that he has Jill, but he's not that great at staying faithful to her. She seemed to accept it as part of the deal. I couldn't understand it at all. Toby loved her and told me the groupies were just sex, but I didn't think I could do that to any girl if I had someone I truly loved.

I knew how I'd have felt if it were me and my partner slept around. Toby's problem, as I saw it, was what made him like he was. His problem was that Jill accepted it. She was very faithful, and Toby knew she would never do that to him. It kind of made her a door mat and he didn't respect her that much for it.

Seeing how it hurt Jill, I tried to tell him about it. But I must admit; the girl was in an impossible situation with women throwing themselves at Toby. He needed to keep his dick in his pants or let Jill go. She was a fabulous girl and she deserved much better.

Soft knocking on my door preceded Charlotte poking her head into my study. "Transport's outside, you all set?" I nodded and stood up, swiping the iPad closed and made my way to the blacked out SUV waiting in the driveway to head to the venue.

My band was already there. They were rehearsing with a new keyboard player that morning. Keyboards were a recent addition to our music, but I liked the sounds on the new album. The keyboard helped to make our sound evolve into a sound that's more current. I played the piano but I needed someone other than me because of the composition of the music I was writing. And with me already singing and playing guitar it was necessary to get someone full time.

I'd been on the crazy ride of fame and music for just over eight years. The whole deal used to be exciting and I felt thankful every day that God had chosen me to give pleasure to people through music. After all this time though, my thoughts about that were a little bit jaded.

I still loved to make music and perform, but I hated the world that went with it; the travelling, the creepy people I had to meet, the ass kissing that went on with the business, and most of all, the expectations of people when they made demands on me and my personal time.

When I walked into the hall and heard the music that I wrote playing loudly, the sound reverberating throughout the auditorium, it immediately gave me a buzz. The lyrics immediately sprang to mind and I automatically started to mutter them to myself. Singing is second nature to me and I was so conditioned that I sometimes went into automatic pilot. I've even done it in stores when I've heard the intro to one of my songs.

My band is a bit different from Toby's, because in his group 'Gametes', everyone was famous. In mine, the band was more of a backing band with me as the main man. I'd written all the lyrics and most of the music. Occasionally, some clever guitar riffs came from Mick, but Lennox the drummer was an incredible percussionist.

Like I said before, Lennox was like a brother and he was a bit of a player as well. He was mainly responsible for me having a sex life at all lately. He was the hard party animal in the band, that invariably dragged me along with him, sometimes to parties we weren't even invited to. It was usually because he was chasing some piece of ass at the time.

We ran through the set and discussed the changes for a while. After they'd all been confirmed, I went into the dressing room to chat privately with Lennox. I knew I needed a break from the heavy schedule we had been punishing ourselves with over the past two years.

Two hundred and eighty nine days on the road

in the last year with no let up. Charlotte interrupted us five times during our chat with various management executive demands. There were also pictures, CD covers and programs to sign.

By the time we were due to perform, I'd spoken to more people I'd never met in my life, than anyone I knew. I'd been slapped on the back and had my hand shaken so much, it was a wonder I was still standing. It was actually a wonder I could still play my guitar, my hand was so tired.

Walking towards the stage, I stared at one of the roadies, who was playing air guitar to the cover being played by our opening band who were just finishing, "I Bet You Look Good On The Dance Floor" by Artic Monkeys.

When he saw me he looked embarrassed at being caught. Smirking, I nodded. "Keep it up; if Mick's ever sick, I'll bear you in mind as his understudy." Winking at him, he relaxed and grinned sheepishly at me.

Seconds before we started our set, I looked over at the other guys in the band and briefly wished I was one of them. They got to make music and were largely left alone. They didn't have to give a shit about all the stuff that went with it. Thousands of people had paid to see me and I felt worn out. Maybe once I'd had a break from this whole crazy lifestyle I'd come back fresher and revitalized.

As soon I walked on stage though, the funk I was in disappeared. That was where I felt most at home, completely relaxed and confident. It didn't matter that there were twenty thousand people out there in front of me. They had come because they liked what I did, so there was no stress involved. I could do my job and make them happy, then hopefully I could leave and go where I lay my head for the night. Pity the buzz of happiness I felt on stage disappeared as soon as I walked back off afterward.

Leaving to go to my own space straight after a gig was wishful thinking. There are always prize winners and suits to please, and I am smart enough to know that if I want to keep doing this, I have to give them their pound of flesh. I don't mind the meet and greet and the fans. These people are the reason I'm doing what I do, so I smile and stay charming until the last fan disappears, and afterwards, I can be myself.

After years of these sessions, TV and radio interviews, along with music magazine exclusives, there was only maybe one or two original questions a year for me to answer. The rest are the usual ones about who a particular song is about, and what was I thinking when I wrote it.

I also felt sorry for the fans that were so excited to meet me that they passed out right in front of me. I could never imagine another human being that I'd met having that kind of effect on me. I liked their enthusiasm for the work I did though, it gave me pleasure to know that one of my songs somehow brightened their day.

Finally having five minutes to myself I took a shower. Less than two minutes into it, the seamless glass door opened and Tori stood there grinning, buck naked, her eyes dropping to my dick. "Room for one more, Gibson?"

I was impulsive and weak when it came to fucking women. The guys in the band knew that. But as I stood there looking at Tori, I was thinking about Chloe and my dick stayed limp. I stood my ground thinking; *so what she can look.*

Smirking sexily, with one eyebrow raised, she tried to slip in beside me but I pushed her back. I'm sure she thought she was clever because she then reached for my cock like it was hers to play with. My anger rose at her nerve and I pushed her away again, telling her no. This didn't seem to deter her as she dropped to her knees behind me and bit my ass. The sharp sting I felt burned like fuck.

Twisting my torso, I tried to get her off of me, but she wasn't going anywhere. Her eyes staring up at me; still intent on sucking the fuck out of my left cheek. Managing to get my finger inside her mouth at the side, I broke the suction and pushed her away roaring, "What the fuck." Tori gave me a smug smile and when she did that, all bets were off–I had to teach her a lesson.

Reaching out with my right hand, I grabbed her by her hair, winding it around my hand, and pushed her against the shower wall with my body. A whoosh of air escaped her lungs as her body connected with the tiles. Grabbing her arms, I held them by the wrists, one pulled across her body and both pulled down to the left.

Still holding her by the hair, I bent my head and bit her on the right side of her neck, not in a playful way domineering. Determined to show her from the start that I was not going to be dominated by any woman, no matter how much she wanted me to think she had balls.

This wasn't about lust; this was about teaching her not to fuck with me. If she was going to be around us, I had to make it clear to her that there was no way she was going to control me or my band with her pussy or she'd keep coming at me.

Spinning her around, I pressed her front to the wall, pulled her hips back and kicked her legs apart. She was excited but there was no way I was fucking someone who was trying to control me. "You still want me to continue or you want to walk away?" I asked.

"Do your worst," she goaded in return.

Reaching around with my front to her back, I pulled her head back so that she was looking at me while I grabbed her throat and kept her in place. Sliding my hand down her flat belly into her jeans and found her wet, swollen pussy. I tucked two fingers inside of her and finger fucked her fast and roughly from behind, she lost all control but was smiling and moaning. Coming quickly her legs buckled as she trembled in a full body orgasm and screamed out a raw throaty sound that told me she'd definitely think again before she tried to fuck with me like that.

"That's a warning. You don't fuck with me or my

band. If you want to stay you better understand that. I'm Gibson Barclay your boss, not your new fuck buddy."

By the time I got back to the hotel it was 3:00 am. I was exhausted and felt like my world was upside down. I felt bad for calling someone who obviously needed company like me on one hand and doing that to Tori on the other. My world felt fucked up. What I'd done was fucking stupid but necessary in the crazy rock music environment we lived in. There were no blurred lines as far as she was concerned now. I knew I was nearing a crossroads with fame, because the highlight of anyone's life would be to do what I did a couple of hours ago and have everyone scream out their name. Yet for me, it was when I dialed a wrong number, heard Chloe's laugh, but most of all, when she'd hung up on me.

I stepped into the bathroom and turned on the shower faucet, then went back to my bedroom to put my cell on the nightstand. By the time I went back to the bathroom it was thick with steam. Steam is great for my vocal cords so as I walked into the shower, I breathed in deeply with my back to the showerhead. First time I felt I'd needed two showers in one night once Tori had invaded the first one. My shoulders were taking the strong force of the spray and it felt incredible. The water's force was like small needles pricking into my skin as the jets beat down on me. Rivulets of water ran down my body, carrying the sweat from my work and washing it away. I should have been at another after party, but that night I had told them I felt sick.

Hearing my cell ring, I stepped out of the shower and wrapped a towel around my waist before padding back to the room. Unfortunately I missed the call. When I saw it was Toby I called him back.

Toby answered and the noise of the madhouse he lived in, which was always full of people, was immediately apparent. It struck me how differently we viewed things. Maybe once in a while I'd have the band over and a few other friends that were in the same town to party a little.

Not Toby, he was ready to party from the minute his eyes opened in the morning and I was more of a 'night spent with close friends' kind of guy.

I'm not saying I'm downbeat by any stretch of the imagination, I just prefer things low key. I do know how to party, but I just feel that doing it every day takes the shine out of it. So, I prefer to do it in moderation, rather than party hard like Toby does.

We talked for about fifteen minutes, arranging our time together in more detail, catching up with family stuff and shared anecdotes of our tours. I was definitely looking forward to seeing him again. Toby had managed to wrangle a clear day for us both to surf and do water sports and I couldn't wait to do that with him.

I got into bed and lay with my arms behind my head staring at the ceiling. My mind drifted and I wondered what I might be doing in five years, because if I was still living at the crazy pace I was in now, then maybe it would be time for a career change. I'd be almost thirty years old then, and I definitely didn't want to be living out of a suitcase.

People looking in on my life must have thought I had it all, but I really didn't. Sure I had money and fame and the excess that it brings if I chose to go down that route, but at times it was a soul destroying and extremely lonely life being surrounded by strangers.

No one ever asked me how I was feeling or what I really thought. Everything was at a superficial level or about business decisions. That was probably because I was surrounded by people that made a living out of me making a living. Turning on my side, I punched my pillow and exhaled deeply and hoped I felt better about things again soon.

CHAPTER 13

DINNER

Chloe

After five days in New York I had begun to a feel a small glimmer of my old personality coming back. I was a long way from the girl I was in college, and still jumped at the sound of a raised voice, but with each day I was becoming stronger.

For the first few days in New York, flashbacks of things that had happened with Kace played over and over in my mind. It didn't take much to trigger them – a smell, a sound, nothing and everything brought back those memories and I was sure that some of those memories would never leave me.

Then I had started to wonder how he had reacted when he realized I was gone? What was he telling people about me? Dad told me not to give it a second thought. He said if Kace even tried to ruin my reputation there, he'd find a way of dealing with that.

Meeting Ruby later that day had been on my

mind and I wondered exactly how much to tell her about what had been happening to me.

All she knew was that she couldn't tell Kace where I was and she had promised not to tell him that I'd been in touch with her until I had explained. Ruby had warned me, "It had better be good." She was loyal to Kace and had been friends with him since they were kids.

With each day that had passed, I was gaining a little more confidence and I just had to keep telling myself that not all men were abusive. Stabbing my spoon into the cereal bowl, I was lost in thought, when my cell began to ring and brought me out of my daydream.

A smile played on my lips when I saw it was Paul. "Hey, isn't this becoming bit of a habit?"

Paul snickered down the line at me. "Well, good morning, Chloe. Is that a good thing... this ... habit? I'm told I'm like Krispy Kreme donuts; no one can ever get enough of me."

Surprised by his response, I smiled and felt my belly flutter inside. His response was totally unexpected. After a short pause Paul continued to talk. "I felt I should call you to say hi because I kind of ran out on you yesterday. You've been really gracious with me when I've tried to talk to Toby. And you called me Paul, so that makes us friends right? Besides, if I call you, I know you'll insult me, and that's just how I like it."

Smiling widely, I chuckled softly, "You like it? So, you're a sadist then? Another piece of the puzzle just slotted right in." Paul laughed, but stopped abruptly.

"What's that you're listening to?" I had my favorite band's song playing on my tablet on the desk beside me.

"Well, it's my favorite album, 'Crushed Dreams,' by M3rCy, Do you know it? This track "Inches From Paradise"... I hesitated then thought, no I'm just going to say it out loud, "It got me through some pretty tough times in the past."

There was silence at the other end. "Paul? Are you still there?" I thought I heard him gulp like he'd swallowed something and then his voice came back low and soft.

"Yeah. Sorry I was distracted there for a second. So you like Gibson Barclay?"

Snickering, I knew exactly what he was thinking – what most men thought about women who liked Gibson Barclay. No doubt about it, Gibson was the sexiest man on the planet and I bet there were only the odd few women in the world that hadn't fantasized about him.

"You think I'm just another swooning girl with a crush on a hot looking rock star, right? Not the case. I've kind of followed his music since I heard him in a bar when I was in college at UCLA. He used to play a regular spot at the bar I worked in, and I got to like the band. Don't get me wrong, I love his music, but I dislike the manwhore ways of Gibson Barclay. And let me tell you, all those stories out there are true. He was like that *before* he was famous."

Paul coughed, then chuckled and he must have

been bored with me talking about Gibson because he concluded the call shortly after I said that. "Sorry, multitasking here Chloe. I'm getting ready to go to a meeting." Immediately, I felt stupid going on and on about my taste in music and Gibson Barclay, and holding him up.

"Sorry, I'm keeping you back. I got carried away. Music is one of my passions, I love singing, but I play the guitar very badly."

"Hold that thought Chloe. I love passion," Paul said, playfully with a smile in his voice. "Gotta go now but would you mind me calling you back later and continuing where we left off? I want to know more about your music tastes, it's a passion of mine as well. I'd love to chat a bit longer about it with you, but I've got to run right now."

Hesitating again, I said, "You're going to chance calling back even if it means your ears being assaulted with Gibson?" I teased.

"Yeah, I definitely need to call you back and hear the end of that story, would that be okay? I mean there is no Mr. Chloe, who's going to take a contract out on me or anything if I call, is there?"

His question stopped me in my tracks. Kace hated men talking to me after we started to live together. It then dawned on me that I could speak to whoever I chose to now that he wasn't around. "No. No Mr. Chloe, Paul." I said smiling warmly, relief clear in my voice.

A woman's voice spoke to him in the background again and he covered the phone and mumbled back. For the second time I heard the same, "Sorry, my ride's here, I need to run. No doubt we'll finish this conversation another time." Paul hung up and I was left staring at my phone. I figured the woman wasn't his girl because he never seemed hesitant on the phone to me whenever she spoke to him.

Shaking my head, I tried to take myself back to work. Studying my researched articles and book excerpts, I began to write the storyboard for my book. Between Google and Wiki I was clued up on lots of stuff, but I wasn't too sure how far to stretch my genre. Was it going to be a straightforward love story or did I have the necessary skills to make it a more complex one?

Also, did I have the confidence to write sexy love scenes? If so, how many… how explicit should they be? Each time I answered a question, I asked myself another ten. It was dawning on me that writing a book was going to be much more complicated than I imagined.

Making myself comfortable after all my hard work, I dug into my oversized Gucci bag, the one luxury I had allowed myself from my inheritance, and pulled out my Kindle. I hadn't used it since I sat in the airport lounge.

Curling up on the sofa, I began to read where I had left off. I was reading *Interview with a Master,* by Jason Luke, an erotica novel. Since I had begun to work on my own book, I 'didn't just read it, I studied his work and how he had written the story. There was no study of the story itself really, it flowed beautifully.

My eyes scanned the pages, ticking over the text I was reading, and I wondered if I would ever be able to write anything like that? Could I hold the reader in the palm of my hand? What could I write and would I make it engaging and exciting for the reader?

My knowledge of sex would probably fit comfortably on a postcard if I were to write about my own experiences. I was assuming that what Kace and I did was very 'vanilla,' because neither Kace, nor I had too much of an imagination in the bedroom.

Hell, Jason Luke could even make a spatula from the kitchen drawer sound like the most exciting 'love toy' ever. Blushing at the guilty pleasure I was indulging in, I became absorbed in the story. Already, I was becoming aware of the level of description that would be expected of me, if I wrote a love story in that genre.

Sex sells, but I knew I'd want it to be credible and organic to the story. And, I wouldn't be able to leave readers wondering what came next by having a hot scene, which ended with the couple beginning to strip, and then writing about sunsets and crashing waves on a shoreline like some books do.

Those soft romantic books appealed to some, but I was definitely not the type of girl that could write those flowery type of novels. Deciding to write was one thing, but having commitment to the story was high on my agenda. If that meant writing about it in raw terms for the readers to feel the emotions of the scene, then that's what I decided I would do.

At five in the evening I finished reading the book and realized that I'd been engrossed in it for two and a half hours. Rushing around, I began to make myself ready for my night out with Ruby.

As usual, Hank was available to take me to the restaurant and pick me up afterward. He should have worked for the New York Tourist Board. The guy was a source of information, knowing all about the restaurant, even who the chef was. Hank told me the place had great reviews and that he'd eaten there once before on his brother's fiftieth birthday.

I heard Ruby's familiar squeals of delight before I saw her. She had recognized me and was shrieking my name loudly when she caught sight of me. "Chloe Jenner! Well look at you. You're a sight for sore eyes."

Well, I was definitely a sight by then, because the entire restaurant had turned to see who Chloe Jenner was. Not really caring who was looking, I flung my arms around her neck and we hugged from side to side in a tight embrace. My throat closed and I could feel my emotions threaten to overcome me.

Time flew quickly when Ruby and I got together; it was like the previous year and a half just melted away. Shaking her head in disbelief, she was having a hard time absorbing what Kace had turned into, and feeling guilty because she was the one that helped us become a couple.

Sitting with tears welling in her eyes, she swore that Kace would never know she knew about everything that had happened. Ruby knew if she told Kace about our discussion, he'd figure out where to find me.

After dinner she tried to invite me to go clubbing with her and her friends, but she accepted that I needed a bit more time before I was ready and confident to go out and have fun.

"Chloe, I know we've not been close in the past couple of years with living in separate states and everything, but trust me, I love you, and I'm going to do everything I can to help you put what happened with Kace firmly behind you." She hugged me tightly and tears began to flow down my cheeks as I languished in the warmth coming from that hug.

Feeling really touched by what she said, I wanted to lighten the mood. I told her about my new phone and the calls from Paul. When I mentioned he sounded like Gibson Barclay she became the old 'animated Ruby' I knew and loved.

"Oh. My. God. Do you remember that? Gibson Barclay, eye fucking you that night in Beltz? Jeez, that guy was so fucking stunning. And, what about now? I can't believe how massive a star he's become. Actually, I can. The guy could sing... and what a showman."

Ruby fanned herself with her hands and squirmed in her seat. "Even if he couldn't sing, I bet he'd have been able to fuck his way into the A-list of the rich and famous." Ruby winked wickedly at me and I felt heat rising to my cheeks while I was chuckling at her antics.

Looking away when she was scrutinizing my reaction to talking about him, my glance fell to my hands in my lap. "Jesus, there you go again, Chloe. You're thinking he'd never look at you, right? Well let me tell you lady, he most definitely did. I figure if it had been just the two of you there, he'd have thrown you over that table and eaten you alive."

Smiling, I almost joined in and said, I wish, but choked it back. Smirking wickedly, she waggled her eyebrows at me, which made the two of us burst out laughing.

"Ruby, I missed you so much, but you're crazy, you know that, right?"

Smiling back at me, she warned me sternly, "Seriously Chloe, talk to that guy Paul, but no last names and no addresses or personal details about age and schools and stuff, because you can be tracked, and don't agree to meet him either. People go missing like that."

Rolling my eyes, I twisted my lips, "Geez, Ruby he's just a wrong number, he's not Al Capone," I teased back shaking my head again and glancing at her dramatically serious expression.

Hank picked us up and Ruby was insistent he took me home before dropping her at the club. Driving along we passed a sign that had a massive poster of M3rCy, and I sighed heavily. "Damn, don't you wish you had lived out your fantasy with that guy, Chloe?"

Pursing my lips, I remembered that I had imagined that Kace was him once. Allowing myself to nod, she smirked wickedly and nudged me, then shrieked, "See! I knew you were hot for him."

Heat flushed my cheeks and I smirked back. "What can I say?" I was determined not to grin but it hadn't worked. It never worked.

Ruby huffed and snorted. "Are you for real, Chloe? Sexual tension was in abundance between you two that last night he played at Beltz. Believe me, you weren't trying to connect with him, but you couldn't deny he was making you horny. I believe you took desperate measures when you disappeared into the restrooms because of the way he was making you feel. I saw it Chloe… that smoldering passion that would have ignited if you had only given him the signal."

"That's not how it was, Ruby. Gibson Barclay was a terrible flirt and he'd screw anything with a pulse, plus… he could see he was embarrassing me. That wicked streak in him decided to torment me that night. Plenty of women fell for that crap, we saw him groom unsuspecting females for his own ends every time he played."

Ruby was grinning and I looked puzzled, "What is it?"

Shaking her head she burst out laughing, "You so would now huh? Pity, that particular gate has long since been closed." We both sighed at the same time and she nudged my side with her elbow. "Damn one night. Was that too much to ask for?"

They dropped me off at the apartment building and I waved goodnight, watching the red tail lights of

Hank's yellow cab being swallowed up with the constant flow of heavy traffic in the dark, before turning and going inside.

On the way up to the elevator I admitted to myself if it were possible to turn back time, maybe I would have liked to have been a little more reckless with my love life in college. Just that once.

CHAPTER 14

THE WINNER

Chloe

Sliding my key into the lock on the door, I was just about to enter my apartment when my cell started ringing. Opening the door, I rolled my eyes, expecting that Ruby was calling to tell me something she had forgotten. However, when I glanced at the screen the caller ID registered that it was Paul.

"Hmm, twice in one day, either you're stalking Toby or you're stalking me, which is it?"

Chuckling, he spoke with a smile in his voice, "Damn girl, I didn't even get to draw breath there." I grinned, feeling strangely relaxed by his familiar voice, "So?" I could hear the smile in that one word when he said it to me.

"So?" I mirrored back. Laughing softly at his humorous tone, "You rang me, remember?"

Snickering at me, his breathing was forced. "I did indeed," he stated flatly and seemed pleased with himself.

Grinning widely, my heart raced and I tried to control my breathing. I was enjoying this playful exchange. "And?"

Paul huffed out a breath, pretending to be curt with me. "Umm… weren't you telling me about the album you were playing, and that you said it didn't make you hot for the guy or something like that?"

I was amazed by his answer. Paul had been as good as his word. He really had called me back to continue our earlier conversation. "That wasn't what I said. You really want to hear about my music preferences?" The surprise in my voice said it all.

"It's late, but I figured if you were out, you may be home by now, but that it wasn't late enough for you to be in bed yet… I mean it's Friday night. No one goes to bed before 11:00 pm do they?"

My eyes widened again, surprised that he'd bothered on a Friday night. "You really *did* call to finish the conversation?" Chuckling softly again, he came back at me with the same humorous, rich tone.

"Absolutely, you think I'd be able to sleep tonight if I hadn't heard the end of your story?" I became conscious that I smiled a lot when he spoke to me. There was something about Paul that just seemed to set me at ease. And I enjoyed our little conversations.

"Okay, well… where did we get up to?" I asked, testing whether he had actually wanted to finish that particular topic.

"The guy… what's his name, and college." Paul prompted, recapping badly.

"Yeah, Gibson Barclay, he's actually a very talented guy. I *love* his music, and he's a very clever lyricist," I concluded, thinking we were done.

Paul hummed down the line, "Hmm, he is? So this guy... you said he was at college with you? Does he know you?" Shaking my head no, even though I knew that Paul couldn't see me, I answered.

"No, I don't think he went to my college, and no I've never really met him as such." My mind went back to him staring into my eyes and that look he had given me, and the electrical pulse that clenched between my legs that soaked my panties when he had.

Clearing my throat I continued, "I just saw him play in the bar a lot. He's an amazingly effortless musician." What I really wanted to say was he was an incredibly sexy guy and when he sang it tore up all my rules about bad boys and never wanting to have wild sex on a one-time basis. What I actually said was, "It isn't about the guy... it's his music that attracts me. I mean I wouldn't buy an album just to drool over the cover or anything."

Paul chuckled heartily. "Good to know you're more principled than that about music."

"See, that's the thing about guys. They don't think women can appreciate music the way they can." In my comeback I had sounded frustrated because I thought he was dismissing my opinion.

"Don't we?" He asked.

I nodded my head and began to explain, "No, most guys think all women are into are sweet romantic songs or morbid country and western stuff loaded with emotion." Paul remained silent for a minute, before speaking again.

"So, can I ask you a personal question?"

A warning light went on in my head and a flash back to Ruby's face in the restaurant, telling me to be careful about disclosing personal stuff. "Well, that depends what it is," I stated honestly.

"This song you told me about. "Inches From Parlor Side" or whatever..."

"Inches From Paradise," I interjected, rolling my eyes as I corrected his attempt.

"You mind me asking? How it helped you?"

Snickering sarcastically into my cell, I was feeling brave but not that brave. "Not sure you wouldn't be opening a can of worms with that question," I stated flatly, thinking it would close the subject down before it got started.

"Would you tell me if I gave you the can opener?"

I wondered if I could pour my heart out to yet another stranger. Telling Gavin on the plane had been therapeutic. But if I was honest I was scared that if I told Paul, he may have felt I was so fucked up, he wouldn't call back. And I was fast becoming dependent on our little chats.

"Are you still there?" His voice sounded tender, encouraging.

"Yeah, I am. I'm not sure I'm ready to share what's behind it." Paul sounded like he was in the bathroom because I could hear the faucet running and what sounded like a toothbrush clinking in a glass.

"Listen, I'm just going to brush my teeth and get into bed. Let's meet back here in five minutes and it will give you a few minutes to think about whether you want me to know, then I'll call you back. If you decide not to share, we'll just talk about something else or we can play the twenty questions game. I haven't done anything that stupid in years and my stupid gene needs an airing again." Paul snickered softly into the phone.

"That is, unless we should just wrap it up for the night and I can let you get some sleep. I'm really stupid because I'm just assuming there's no hot guy in your apartment right now. Although... if there was, I wouldn't have gotten this far into our conversation." He teased playfully again.

"No, definitely no hot guy here," I said with a slightly grating tone. Kace was hot to look at, but after what happened to me, I didn't care what someone looked like, it was how they made me feel. Kace had made me feel depressed and worthless.

"Brushing my teeth and getting into bed with you sounds great." As soon as the words came out I was kicking myself again. I felt stupid as I hadn't meant it to sound flirty, but it must have. "I mean, lying in bed with you talking sounds good." We both snickered at my double faux pas again.

"Yeah? Hmm... one step at a time, I don't sleep with women for the first few phone dates darlin'." Making light of my mistake, Paul teased me, and I felt grateful for his understanding. I ended the call before I could put my foot in it any further.

Wandering into the bathroom to brush my teeth, I was still feeling a little embarrassed. Slipping my tank top and pajama bottoms on, I climbed into my big snug bed with a glass of red wine and felt butterflies in my belly as I waited for Paul to call back.

More significantly, no man had asked what I thought about something in a while and I realized how important it had become, that he wanted my opinion. Even if it was only about Gibson Barclay and music.

Fifteen minutes later he still hadn't rung back and I thought maybe he'd found something better to do or I had put him off. Switching off my bedside light, I plumped my pillow and settled down for the night feeling more than a little disappointed. Drifting off to sleep, I was startled awake when my cell rang again.

As I answered the phone, I knew there wouldn't be the same connection as earlier. Obviously, my insecurities made me feel unsure about talking to him, especially when I considered how let down I had felt when someone I didn't know, who had said they would ring back, hadn't been prompt enough.

"Sorry, got side tracked." Paul said curtly, "You were saying?" I really didn't want to go there about Kace by then. The moment between us had gone.

"Well, the song thing? Sorry, if you don't mind, I don't want to talk about that right now, is that okay?"

Sounding reassuring, he said, "Sure, whatever you want darlin'," then quickly changed the subject and asked if we should play twenty questions.

From that moment on, the way Paul was able to read my moods during our calls was amazing, considering we knew very little about each other. Our calls went from small two minute conversations to long drawn out ones about anything that was on his mind or sometimes we just talked about music and movies. During those times we shared tiny snippets of information and built this great connection, which the both of us could manage.

Something that began to become noticeable was his dependability for ringing in the morning or late at night every day. I began to check the clock to ensure I showered and took care of my chores outside of those times.

Patterns of contact between us began to emerge. One thing was clear, I had never rung him. Paul worked odd hours and worked as part of a team. I was partly enjoying the fact I didn't know exactly what he did, it added a little more to the mystery of the whole thing for me.

Five weeks after our first call my cell rang at a time when I would have expected Paul to call. Answering, I was surprised to hear it was the telephone company, telling me I had won a competition to see M3rCy in concert. And, I was going to meet the band and have dinner with them.

Actually, the prize was for four people to fly to

LA to see M3rCy in concert and hang out with the band for the weekend. I wondered how Gibson felt about hanging out with random people who've won a competition on his days off.

Hearing the clipped tones of the brash New York accent telling me the details of my prize, I interrupted to explain that I hadn't entered any competition.

I was thinking it was either a hoax call or a mistake, until she explained that the entrants were automatically entered if they had purchased a new phone deal and handset, within a two month period that the competition had been running. Suddenly, the prize was a genuine win.

Excitement buzzed through my body, jolting my heart and making it thump hard within my chest from the shock of excitement. I could hardly work the phone keypad to text Ruby to tell her my fabulous news because my hands were shaking so much.

Ruby was the phone to me as soon as I told her the prize. She screamed so loud I jumped with fright at her sudden outburst. "OH. MY. GOD. You are going to come face to face with Gibson Barclay, Chloe. How do you feel about that after all this time?"

Face to face was the part I was trying to get my head around. As soon as the operator had told me we were meeting them and spending the day with them, I wasn't sure I'd be able to deal with that particular scenario at all.

What the hell would I find to talk about with Gibson Barclay for a whole weekend, I wondered? Worse than that, I'd probably be having flashbacks to scenes I'd witnessed of him with various women, most of them in very compromising positions.

Ruby knew me well. "And you can stop thinking you can't do it. I know you too well, Chloe Jenner. You think you'll freak out at the sight of him right?"

Truly? I had no idea what I'd do, but my saving grace was that he'd never remember me anyway.

Mumbling, I asked Ruby who else to take. Then I remembered Gavin from the plane. "Oh! Got it. I'll ring Gavin and his roommate." Talking fast and animatedly I told her about my flight with him to New York. Once I had finished my call with her, I padded barefoot into the kitchen and pulled Gavin's number from the fridge door magnet.

"Hey, I was hoping I'd hear from you again. You've been in my thoughts a few times. I've been wondering how you were fairing here in the 'Big Apple' all by yourself. Are you able to meet me for lunch later?"

Smiling at the way Gavin just fell right into conversation with me like I was an old friend swayed my decision. I agreed to meet him at a local delicatessen which had a fabulous coffee house at the back.

Expecting to see Gavin waiting, I was a little tense that he wasn't there when I arrived. I was even more apprehensive when he turned up with another guy, who looked pretty similar to an actor who was in tons of movies; but his name escaped me.

Eddie or Ed as Gavin called him, was a production manager at Madison Square Gardens, which was probably the biggest indoor venue for music in New York.

He was hilarious and had the measure of Gavin. Poor guy couldn't get anything past him. Explaining the reason for my call, Ed stood up, ran his hand through his hair and said, "Get the fuck out of here. You're joking right?"

Puzzled, I turned to look at Gavin who was grinning widely at Ed and chuckling at Ed's mouth that was mouthing words but was silent by then. "What am I missing here? Is someone going to fill me in?"

Gavin grinned again and filled me in. "We were discussing this at breakfast this morning. Ed was complaining that he sees tons of live bands a year, but has never seen M3rCy; his favorite band by the way. Every time they have played New York it's been at MetLife in Jersey which seats three times as many people as Madison Square Gardens.

"Well this isn't the New York gig. This is at The Staples Center, in Los Angeles," I corrected realizing I hadn't included that part. All I had told them was that I had won four tickets to see M3rCy and hang out with the band. I'd neglected to tell them that we were being flown to LA for the weekend as well.

Once I had finished filling them in on the details, I thought that Eddie was going to have a coronary.

"Fuck, Gavin… did that plane you were on land

at the end of a fucking rainbow? This is incredible. Not only do you meet a stunningly hot chick who's just run away from her guy, she's hit the fucking jackpot with tickets to see my favorite band. We are going right?" Turning to Gavin briefly for his reaction, he didn't wait for it but instead turned toward to me and said, "Well fuck him, I'm in whatever he's doing."

Smirking, Gavin rubbed his eyes with his thumb and forefinger and turned his attention to me. Biting back a grin, he nodded his head from side to side as if deliberating. "Yeah, if it's alright with Chloe. We'd love to come. Well, I would, I think Ed here is still on the fence." Giggling at the way he was being playful with Ed, I felt I'd done the right thing in asking them to come with us.

We discussed meeting the following evening for dinner, so that Ruby could meet the guys. The concert was still a week away, but I didn't want her to feel awkward with them. Having dinner would hopefully break the ice, and I had a feeling that she and Eddie would hit it off when they met.

CHAPTER 15

STUPID DECISIONS

Gibson

Fuck me! It's her. Oh. My. God. Chloe. The girl from Beltz Bar. Closing my eyes, her image flooded my mind, and I remembered the beautiful girl with the watchful stare. Of course her sweet, soft voice was like music to my ears. An honest voice, but there was a hint of sadness and I wondered what had happened to her.

I felt elated when she answered the phone and then my heart sunk like a stone, when I heard her talk about me like the manwhore that I was. That wasn't easy. Strike that. The way she spoke about me was fucking hard to listen to. Normally, I couldn't give a shit what anyone thought, but oddly, for some reason that girl affected me.

Five years and my old reputation was still embedded in her brain, just like the image of her staring at me was in mine. Nothing I could do about that. Initially, I was going to call her out, and tell her that I knew who she was. Tell her that I had noticed her watching me all those times, but I was enjoying our little chats until she said that stuff about me.

I'd never run from controversy before, but she kinda got to me with her comments, so instead of finishing the call, I left her hanging mid conversation by telling her I had to go do something else.

There had never been a previous occasion when I choked because someone cast aspersions on the way I lead my life. As far as I saw it, it was my life not theirs and if they wanted to live in their 'grey colored world', pretending they were happy, that was up to them – not me. If I wanted something out of life I took it.

Chloe said she thought I was hot. Well ditto, the girl was fucking gorgeous. Curvy but slender, great ass in jeans, perky braless tits in her little white tank top and toned arms. Silky sun kissed blonde hair and a golden glow about her. A *sexy* girl. And, what was even more of a turn on was the fact that she had no idea just how appealing she was.

Beyond hot, Chloe was a sizzling piece of ass, and I never got near her. Pity, every time I noticed her I was kinda busy with another female. The first time I noticed her was when I was bouncing a hot redheaded groupie on my dick in the alleyway at the back of Beltz Bar.

Vague cloudy memories of the girl I was fucking at the time; how she looked, red hair, other than that there was nothing memorable about her, except maybe the way she screamed when her pussy clenched tightly and she came again and again within that last couple of minutes before we were interrupted.

Actually there was nothing cloudy about Chloe, I noticed her straight away, when she had pushed open the emergency exit. The noise of the heavy metal door sprung back and she stood completely still, by the look on her face she had no idea what to do next.

Stepping back and uncoupling myself from the girl I had been getting jiggy with, I stood her on her feet and I stared past her at Chloe for a split second. What was I supposed to say? Sorry you saw that? Sorry, but you shouldn't have been looking? Want to join in? Hell, I didn't know, so I just kinda smirked and felt pretty shitty that she had to see me being so raw like that.

So, I dropped my head, zipped up my fly and buckled my belt before walking back along the alleyway, leaving them both still standing there.

It was great that she followed our music, shame my reputation followed with that as well. I was feeling pretty pissed, because even after five years she still affected me and I hadn't been able to shake off that look she gave me.

Hearing how she spoke about me affected me in a way I'd never expected. Her words squeezed at my heart in my chest, because I knew that there was nothing I could do to erase what she'd seen, not once but several times.

Standing, I walked over to the window and laid

my forehead on the cold window pane. Stunned, I couldn't think for about a minute, then an idea began to flow that I had to pursue. Calling Charlotte, I told her I needed a private investigator to find out Chloe's surname and I wanted to know the phone company she had her phone through.

I figured it couldn't be that hard because I knew exactly what day she had bought her phone, she'd told me I was her first call. I had gathered from later conversations she'd come to New York City around the same day. So there were a couple of leads for him to work with.

Then I remembered she was at UCLA in 2009 and worked at Beltz's Bar. One call to Matt, the owner, and I'd have her name in no time.

Fifteen minutes later, my heart was hammering rapidly in my chest with excitement and I knew Chloe was Chloe Jenner. My Chloe. Matt was cagey about giving me any other information, but I told him that she had 'connected' with me recently, and was coming to LA to see our gig. I pretended to him that I didn't want to look a complete shit by not knowing her name and I'd begged him for her details.

Matt got the wrong idea and thought I had tapped her and to be frank I never set him straight on that, so he told me her surname and that she'd gone back to Florida after her time at college was over. He seemed to think she was living with the same tool I had seen her with in the bar, so I wondered where he fitted into the picture I was building.

Four hours later and I had an address for her. The private investigator Charlotte employed was one we had used often for various reasons I won't go into. So I had Chloe's address, the fact that she'd come into money and had moved from the apartment she had shared with Kace O'Neill.

Something that the investigator found suggested that she didn't want to be found. I didn't get bogged down with the details of that, but asked that he help her cover her tracks better, if it had only taken him four hours to find her. I'd had to leave it like that at that point because I had to go to work.

Appearing on stage that night, my mind was elsewhere. My brain was ticking over all the facts he'd given me, and because I had them and my impulsive nature was desperate to do something about that. I usually made things happen for myself.

Looking out at the audience, I had a flashback to the night I watched a girl being dragged away by security. I knew there was something about her eyes, and it suddenly came to me, they were similar to Chloe's.

According to the investigator there was no guy on the scene, and that snippet of information made me want to go after her. Like I said, I made things happen for myself.

Chloe had a low opinion of me, and like I said before, I couldn't make her 'unsee' all the stuff she'd had access to about me and the other women a few years ago, but she had only observed the boy in me then.

Putting our heads together, we came up with the idea that Chloe had won a competition to see M3rCy. Trying to be clever, we decided that it would be for her and three friends. I knew the band would be happy to entertain a few girls with me.

All that was left was to get the telephone company on board. Again, that was simple because they were one of the sponsors on our tour, so they were more than happy to play along. The only issue I had was that Tori, our temporary keyboard player had set her sights on me, always touching me and trying to flirt, and I was aware of how dangerous she could be if she decided to meddle in any plan I had about Chloe.

Nervously, I waited for feedback and continued with my day, knowing I'd have to squeeze someone by the balls if there wasn't a positive result from our concocted plan to get Chloe to the show in LA. It had to be that gig, because that was the only time I had a weekend off.

Fuck Toby and water sports. I was thinking of something much more energetic than surfing, and with a bigger plus on the satisfaction, relief, and relaxation side. Toby and I could still find time to get with each other, even if we stayed up all night.

Coming off the stage, Charlotte handed me a piece of paper, which pissed me off, because she got paid to read and inform. "So?" Furrowing my brow, I waited for her to spell out the verdict.

Smiling widely, Charlotte handed me a towel to wipe the sweat off my brow and smirked, "Yup, she bought it. A week from Friday, 16th at Staples." Grabbing Charlotte by the back of her head I pulled her in and landed a kiss on her lips.

"Good girl. One of these days I'm gonna fuck you if you keep getting results like that for me."

Charlotte rolled her eyes, "In your dreams Gibson. My wife wouldn't be too impressed with that."

Snickering, I was quick to retort. "Oh honey, she'd be impressed. Tell her you're both welcome, I'll extend the invitation. I'm a fan of a double pussy ride every now and again."

Charlotte's jaw dropped and she shook her head. "You'll have to stay a fan and the same rules apply to me as they do for you on this tour. You can look but you don't get to touch."

Biting back a grin, I replied trying desperately not to laugh. "You know I don't do rules, but I'll take you up on watching. Thanks for that invitation, should I firm that arrangement with you or Wendy?"

Charlotte began to walk away and looked over her shoulder. "I'm not even going to dignify that with an answer, Gibson."

Chuckling I called after her. "So... I should ask Wendy then... got it!"

Lennox came over and bumped my shoulder with his. "Are you pissing off the hired help again?"

Grinning at Lennox, I bent closer and said, "Remember that smoking hot cleaner from Beltz's Bar I wanted to tap all those years ago? Well guess what? She's coming to the gig in LA next week."

Lennox stared at me, looking at me as if I was insane. "How the hell did you figure that out?"

Explaining to him about the random wrong number and it being hers, Lennox thought it was too incredulous to be the truth. Basically telling me I was talking bullshit. When I explained I'd been talking to her for weeks after Toby's PA gave me the wrong number, he shook his head in disbelief.

"I know right? The truth is stranger than fiction. What are the fucking odds of that happening? For the second time in my life there are two wild numbers for things that were coincidental. Toby and I becoming famous from the same place, and now a girl I'd shared the same air as, five years ago, getting a new phone and me being given her number."

Once Lennox was filled in on the whole deal, he was skeptical. "You know she'll blow you off or you'll have the usual ten minute fuck-and-forget-her session right? Nothing is going to be different from any other time. You've just put this one on a pedestal because you didn't get to tap her at the time when you played in the bar."

Closing my eyes and drawing her image out of my mind, as soon as I reflected on those eyes I knew that nothing Lennox could say would sway my judgment about her. "Nah, dude. This one is different. Can't say how, can't say why, but she's definitely had my balls in a vice since I first saw her."

At the end of the gig, I was persuaded to follow the guys to the strip club they were heading to. I already knew it was going to be a bad idea, but I went along with them anyway. Something about women swinging half naked around a long shiny steel pole always set my heart racing.

Not sure if it was because I hadn't got laid for three days – my longest dry spell in weeks, or the alcohol I allowed myself in celebration at finding Chloe, but I was wired.

Two bottles of scotch in forty five minutes between four of us and I was more than up for a hot session with one of those thong wearing, braless wonders, wrapping their legs around that pole and hanging from them like they were defying gravity.

"Hey, Gibson, are you as good as they say you are?" Glancing bleary eyed to my left, there was a tiny skinny girl of about five feet, with massive brown eyes, dark hair and the biggest set of natural tits that were made for her frame without her falling over.

She stood there in her red sparkly thong and matching strappy roman style shoes with what looked like glass six inch stiletto heels. I smirked but before I could speak, she was wiggling her ass on my dick to the music, which was some slow, shitty blues song I'd never heard before.

Turning, she slid one leg between mine all the way up my legs until her knee was rubbing hard against my vaguely interested dick at the seam of my jeans. Her hands were weaving their way in and out of my hair until they gradually slid down the front of my t-shirt and rubbed firmly over my semi-interested length.

She bent forward as she turned away from me

again, and my eyes registered her smooth, firm ass. My hands obviously didn't believe my eyes because both palms began to stroke the crest of her ass cheeks.

Lennox pushed her away and leaned in to talk into my ear. "Not here, Gib, that wouldn't be a smart move."

Staring up at him and trying to focus, I knew he was right, but when someone told me no, it made me all the more pissed and determined. "Fuck off, Lennox, I can do what I like, I've no one to answer to, so leave me alone."

Looking out for me was one thing, advising me was another, especially when I was drunk. Standing up, I took the girl by the hand and I knew he was right, even I wasn't stupid enough to fuck her in a room full of horny guys and strippers. A video would have been viral within minutes. "Private room, now."

Smirking wickedly with those hooded eyes that promised me a great time, she led me out to the back of the stage. Dressing room mirrors surrounded by light bulbs, smudged with make-up and the smell of cheap perfume and hairspray was kinda seductive for the mood I was in.

Kiran or Kelly-Anne or some shit like that her name was. I hardly ever pay attention to names, and anyway, I wasn't listening when she said it, because she was at the business end, unbuckling my belt and lowering the fly zipper of my jeans down.

Pushing me back on the seat she put her hand down inside her thong and started to massage herself. Between her doing that and the alcohol, I was more than willing to do whatever she wanted.

So, when I saw her grabbing some cord that was holding back the heavy velvet drapes that would shield us from the stage area and letting it drop to give us the privacy I needed, I sat back and let whatever was coming next happen.

CHAPTER 16

SWALLOWING HARD

Chloe

I woke with a start. My cell was ringing and my eyes squinted to focus on the clock on the nightstand. It was only 4:00am Taking my phone off the table I answered the call without looking to see who was calling. Muffled sounds and deep throaty groans came down the line at me.

At first I thought someone was hurt but it soon became apparent someone's phone had rung mine by accident and I jumped out of bed. Then, when I heard a female voice grind out, "Oh, sweet Jesus, YES! Right there... right there, don't stop... harder," followed by more soft moans and another exclamation, "Damn! That feels sooo fucking good, baby. You're very good at this, honey I love your big dick." Blushing, I realized the woman on the phone was having sex and had no idea I was listening.

Hearing a low throaty groan and the sound of a

male voice humming in appreciation, I was mortified. He huskily whispered, "Fuck... me." After that, I figured I'd heard enough. Bad enough I had listened for as long as I had. The session seemed to have intensified during the time I was listening and I heard a shift in positioning as the female moans got nearer to the phone.

Pressing the call end button, I placed the phone back on the nightstand with an unwelcome pulsing feeling in my pussy. I had known the call was turning me on and I felt guilty that some random people should have had that effect on me.

Climbing back into bed I drew my legs up towards my chest and curled into a ball. Suddenly I was missing the warm feelings I used to have when Kace made love to me. Tears rolled down my face and even though I'd never want to be with him in that way again, I missed the contact and warmth I had felt from being in a man's arms.

Waking up with the sun streaming across my bed through a small gap in the drapes, I turned my head away from the light, feeling sluggish and exhausted after crying myself to sleep. Rolling over, I slowly kicked the comforter aside and got out of bed. The clock read 8:00 am and my cell began to ring on the night stand.

Picking it up, I saw it was Paul calling and an excited, happy feeling grew inside of me. Smiling warmly, I answered the phone. "Good morning." I was aiming for a cheerful greeting but my voice sounded croaky. I looked at the phone to check the time and realized last night's call had been from is phone. A pang of jealousy ran through me, but I didn't really know him so it was none of my business.

A slurry voice answered back. "Heyyy, darlin', I just wanted to call you to say goodnight." From the sound of his voice, he was pretty drunk.

"Oh, hi. Sounds to me like someone has been celebrating, have you been drinking Paul?" Waiting a few seconds for him to reply, there was a slight delay then he snickered into the phone and exhaled heavily.

"Umm, I guess so," he replied sheepishly and I could hear a melancholy in his voice, but the overall tone was different, sad, and kind of lonely. When he didn't offer anything else in conversation, I thought I should suggest he take care of himself, but I was worried about him being so drunk and alone. Picking at my pajama shorts, I wondered what I could do to help him.

"Is there someone there with you, Paul? Does anyone live with you that can help you? You really should drink some water before lying down." Sitting back down on the bed, the mattress dipped under me and I tucked my hair behind my ear, trying to think of what else to suggest. Had I known him, I'd have gone over there and taken care of him.

"No one here but me darlin', I always sleep alone… unless you want to try to change that about me." My eyes rolled to the top of my head, unsure of how to answer that, given the fact he sounded a little down, so I decided to tease him to lift his mood.

I hated moping drunk people.

"Sure, lay the phone next to your head on the other pillow and I'll talk to you until you go to sleep. How does that sound?" I was pleased with myself for thinking of something that I could actually do which may have kept him safe and in a place where he wouldn't fall down and hurt himself.

"You want to lie in my bed? Fuck. That sounds like an excellent plan. Chloe my darlin', I'd love you to lie next to me. Do I get to be buck naked?" Paul's humorous tone made me think he was joking.

"Of course, Paul tonight you get whatever you want." As soon as I said it, I kind of cringed, because that was like giving a drunk man a loaded gun to play with.

"Oh, sweet Chloe I get to be whatever I want, huh darlin'? Sure you don't want to change your mind about that? I mean, before I ruin our beautiful friendship?" The challenge in Paul's voice excited me and I thought this call of all of the calls we'd had, would be the most open one I'd probably ever have with him.

"Doubt there is anything you can say that would affect that Paul, besides we don't have any awkward after date conversations do we?" I teased, throwing back a line he'd said to me right at the beginning of our phone calls.

"Hang on." Paul began to grunt and at first I imagined he was feeling sick but then I heard what sounded like a buckle being undone. "Just getting naked for you." His voice was different and further away and I realized he had put me on speaker phone. Another few grunts and I heard him moving and the phone being moved with him.

Exhaling heavily, he cleared his throat and spoke gruffly, "Alright seems you have me at a disadvantage here." Puzzled, my brow furrowed and I thought he must mean with him being drunk and me being sober until he spoke again. "Well, you know what I'm wearing. So... are you going to tell me what you're wearing?"

Blushing I thought that most respectable girls would conclude the call on a drunk guy asking that, especially after what I'd heard earlier, but it was a phone call with someone who I'd never know in real life, and I was so lonely that I made a snap decision to throw caution to the wind and let myself have that one indulgence with a stranger that Ruby kept going on about, in the safety of my own bedroom.

Squeezing my eyes tightly shut, I said, "A little sky blue tank top and pajama shorts." My jaw hung in amazement that I had been bold enough to play along with him. I just prayed he was one of those drunks that remembered nothing the next day.

"Oh girl, seriously?" He ground out gruffly. "Are you braless?"

Swallowing hard, I nodded, before squeaking out, "Yes."

"Am I allowed to hold your breasts in the palms of my hands?" He said seductively, his tone an octave lower and I heard him shift again.

Pursing my lips to stop my nervous giggle, "Is

that what you want to do?" I asked, prolonging the agony for him.

"So, let me clear this up with you. Am I asking permission for everything I want to do, or am I going to take charge and tell you what we're going to do."

Swallowing noisily, I felt my pussy clench in delight at his suggestion of taking charge. "I already said whatever you want. So, I guess it's your call." Shaking my head silently in disbelief, my mouth in a silent 'O' that I was having this conversation at all.

Hearing Paul moving again, I figured he was getting more comfortable. "Where are you?" he suddenly asked.

"Sitting on the edge of my bed."

"No you're not, you are in mine. Lie down beside me," he commanded.

If Kace had said that I'd have had to do it. With Paul I had a choice. So I went with my moment of madness, crawled on my bed and lay down. I told him I was lying down.

"Good. Now take your shorts off. Leave the tank. I want that to stay on, one of my pleasures in life is staring at a girl in a tiny tank top with perky tits. Call it a particular kink of mine. Now, tell me what I'm looking at." His tone was masterful and abrupt.

Again my eyes rose to the top of my head and wondered what he meant by looking at, but before anything came to mind he prompted me. "Describe your pussy I need to know what I'm playing with."

Another gulp, then I swallowed hard, wondering if I could really go through with talking about myself in such intimate terms. "Do it! Tell me. Don't think about it, just tell me," Paul ordered, his voice sounding persuasive.

"Well..." I giggled, "My pussy is neat." It was the best I could think of and he started chuckling heartily at me.

"Chloe, lesson one, men do *not* want to fuck a neat pussy. Make me want you. Tell me why I'd want your pussy over anyone else's."

Smirking, I thought his comment was too funny, but I wasn't sure I'd be able to do what he asked. "You need help for descriptive words? Alright, is it small, big, plump, slim, swollen? What are the lips like, outer, inner, color, odor, texture, smell, wet? Come on Chloe, use your imagination," Paul barked impatiently.

Without thinking I said, "My pussy is small, waxed, closed lips that form a clean seam, no extra skin, the lips inside are small and crumbled – like the petals of a flower. Right now, my clitoris is hard and swollen and from the hood to the end of my entrance is about one and a half inches. My pussy feels warm and is wet, because I guess this is turning me on. My inner creases are dark cerise in color and when I open my inner lips the entrance is very pink. Is that what you mean?" I concluded nervously and sounding timid.

"Damn, Chloe! And you've never done this before, right?" Paul was chuckling again and I decided to put him in his place.

"So, you have me at a disadvantage, Paul. You

know what my pussy looks like it's only fair you tell me about your dick." Biting my bottom lip, I was amazed that I was doing something so risky with someone I didn't know, but more than that I was so turned on by what was happening between us, I wasn't interested in being embarrassed from that point on.

Paul chuckled again. "Ah, well. Hmm... alright here goes. My dick is thick, straight, about five inches asleep and nine when I'm hard and the girth expands quite a bit when it gets into action. It's circumcised and I have an Apa through the slit, it's not too veiny and attached to some pretty hefty balls. And I guess the whole package is soft, shaved and velvety to the touch." When he finished describing himself, I could hear him swallow heavily, he then continued in a voice that was laced with lust. "And right now, my dick is standing proud at the full nine. Guess that's because it wants to sink balls deep into the pussy you just described to me."

Dumbstruck, I had never been so turned on in my life as I was at that moment. What he had described to me was so hot, and I felt deeply frustrated that I couldn't reach out and touch it. I was glad when he spoke again, because I had no clue what else there was to say about it.

"Now, we know what it looks like, but... how does it taste?" Prompting me to answer him, I said what I was thinking, honestly answering him.

"I don't know. I've never tasted myself." Covering my face with my hand, I felt mortified again to be talking to him about that part.

"Are you telling me that no one has ever gone down on you and then kissed you? Are you fucking serious Chloe? You're not a virgin are you?" Suddenly I felt embarrassed talking about my past with him.

"Sorry, no."

"Sorry, no? You're not a virgin, or you weren't serious about tasting yourself?" He sounded agitated and it made me wary again, but I felt this was something I needed to do so I answered.

"No I'm not a virgin and yes I was serious, I don't know how I taste."

"Well fuck, DO IT! I want to know how you taste. Take your right hand and place two fingers into your pussy." The way he said it was very authoritative and I immediately wanted to comply with his demand.

Taking two fingers I ran them up and down my wet, swollen pussy and couldn't believe how horny I felt by how he was handling me on the phone.

"Describe what you are feeling." Another command quickly followed the last one he had just given me.

"Soft, hot, wet, silky, slippery, slithery, puffy, open, sticky, tickly, tempting... you mean that?" Not sure exactly what words would be the best to describe what I was feeling, I just rhymed all the things running through my mind and I was beginning to get carried away.

"Whoa. Fuck Chloe, slow it down. You'll have me coming like a horny teenager if you keep up that pace." Clearing his throat, he chuckled again. "The flood gates kinda opened there for you, huh?"

Feeling embarrassed again, I gave a slight cough, and swallowed audibly. "Sorry, but I don't know what you want from me." I began to sit up because I was losing confidence again.

Paul spoke in a softer tone. "You know what I want? I want you to stick your fore and middle fingers into your pussy and coat them in your juices. Push them deep inside and then I want you to suck them. And I want to hear you sucking them."

In his husky, seductive voice, Paul's sexy tone was low and it broke slightly at the end of the sentence. Hearing the desire in his voice was damned hot. It was obvious he was enjoying thinking about me doing that and it was making his mouth dry. Paul was completely invested and turned on with what we were doing, so I lay back again.

"Talk to me, tell me what you are doing and what you feel." Biting my bottom lip again, I said, "Sliding my fingers down either side of my inner labia. It feels warm and wet, slippery and it's coated in my sticky juices. I can feel them running down my seam onto my butt. My entrance feels open, ready to receive my fingers."

Paul groaned and it was a guttural sound. "Fuck."

Smiling at his reaction, I was glad I had found the courage to continue. "I'm pushing my fingers inside and it feels, squidgy and tight and warm, and doing this is making my nipples tingle and my heart beat faster."

Paul interjected after clearing his throat, in a voice so low and gravelly that it didn't sound like him at all. "Fuck me! Are you sure you've never done this before?"

"No. I haven't," I stated flatly, stopping with my fingers still deep in my pussy. "Should I continue?"

"Chloe I'd hunt you down and kill you if you didn't." Even with his playful tone delivering those words I had frozen for a second. "Are you okay?" Paul's voice sounded concerned and I sensed he was aware I had stopped abruptly.

"Sure, I replied, trying to sound more confident than I was.

"Then take your fingers out gently and put them in your mouth. God, I wish I was there to put my mouth over one of your nipples and suck hard when you did that." Doing as he asked, I put my fingers tentatively into my mouth. "Suck, Chloe. What do you taste and smell like, tell me." In an urgent voice laced with frustration, Paul was sounding quite desperate.

Pulling my fingers out of my mouth, I rubbed one back and forth on my lip then tested it with the tip of my tongue. "Sweet, kinda faint body wash smell, but the taste is like really watery jello." It was the best I could come up with.

"Fucking perfect. My favorite flavor."

When Paul said those words, my pussy pulsed with excitement. The reaction my body was having from my hormones and the eroticism of tasting myself was unlike any other I had felt. Not to mention Paul's commanding words. It almost felt that what we were doing was not enough.

CHAPTER 17

STEAM

Chloe

I could hear soft shuffling noises as Paul moved around, his breathing sounded shaky and uneven and the rawness in that sound made me sigh deeply.

"You're gone on this, huh? Me as well. Dick is as stiff as a fucking dead man and nowhere to sink it into. Can't say I've had time for this before. And I never knew it could be so fucking hot. So this is a first for the both of us, darlin'." Paul's voice was still slightly slurry.

Clearing his throat again, Paul grunted and from the whoosh of air escaping his lungs I figured he had laid down flat on his back. The sound of his grunt made me feel as horny as hell.

"So, now I know what you're wearing, what your pussy tastes and smells like and you did say anything I wanted right, Chloe?"

Talking to me in an unashamed, raw, sexy tone about things that made me blush crimson gave me shocking electrical pulses of pleasure around my body, as his words set my hormones into chaos. Feelings I'd suppressed at the hands of Kace came flooding back, making me feel desperate, with a heightened level of arousal that I never knew existed before.

I bit my lip as I lay naked from the waist down. I was excited and wondering what Paul was going to tell me to do next, and hardly believing that I was actually doing something so naughty and scandalous. Paul was a stranger and my best friend in the world at that moment. In reality, he was the only person who called me almost daily just to connect with me.

I knew this was crazy, out of character behavior, but I lay waiting, holding my breath for him to take me to the next level. While I did, there was an ache in my chest and my heart squeezed with a pang of sadness, that I would never know the man who wanted to take the time to speak to me, in my safe but lonely world.

"So, I guess the next thing would be for me to satisfy you and for you to come for me." Quiet and still, I sat shaking my head, feeling so needy for anything he wanted to offer, but inhibited enough to think I couldn't go through with him telling me to make myself come while he was listening and telling me what to do. And I wondered what he would say if I said no.

"Place your pillows at the head of the bed and lean back on them, then put one under your ass so it is slightly raised." Speaking in a soft and gentle velvety tone, he was so seductive that I didn't want to argue and quickly did what he told me. "Tell me when you are sitting comfortably."

Plumping the pillows, I sat semi recumbent on the bed, crossed my legs at the ankles and answered, "I am."

"Tell me how you are sitting." Paul's tone sounded soft and encouraging, and there was a quietly confident air in his words.

"I'm sitting with my legs stretched out crossed at the ankles and laying back on the pillows like you told me."

"Alright Chloe, here is what you are going to do. I want you to slide down, uncross your legs and open them. Put the pillow under your ass like I told you. When you've done that you are going to take a picture of your pussy for me."

It was one thing to describe it, quite another to take and send a picture. What would I feel like, talking to him again after that? Would we even speak after what we were doing? What if he posted it somewhere? I could deny it; unless he was recording us talking of course, but it was still something else to send a picture that intimate to someone, especially a stranger.

Paul's commanding tone brought me out of my reverie. "Chloe, I want you to do it now. Don't think about it, do it." The way he commanded that I take the picture, sounded like it was second nature to him. Paul's voice was urgent and demanding.

For the umpteenth time since our conversation

my mouth was dry, and I struggled to swallow my saliva down. Licking my lips, I uncrossed my legs and pulled my feet toward my butt, then splayed them out to the side. Positioning the phone on my heel, I could see myself down there.

Weird how my pussy changed in color with the rush of blood flooding it and the hormones making me feel wired inside, as if it were connected to a million tiny electrodes positioned throughout my body which ignited with the words he was using and the touch of my own hand.

I was barely able to control my shaking hand. The excitement of doing something so intimate with a complete stranger was totally liberating. Sensations rushed through me and my heartbeat raced, pounding wildly in my chest. Sharp electrical pulses deep within in my core seemed to fuel me on.

Conscious of the conflicting feelings and the endless debate going on in my head about what to do, I tussled with Ruby's comments about the mysteries of the one perfect night of sex which swayed my decision and pushed me into action.

Snap. The sound of the camera on my smartphone taking the picture was one thing, being able to send it to Paul, quite another.

"Where is the picture of your pussy, Chloe? I'm waiting. Send it now."

Hearing him order me in that now familiar masterful tone, I sent the picture by text, submitting to his want again. As soon as I did, half of me wanted to hang up, the other half imagining him opening the picture and seeing the part of me only one other man has ever seen.

Excitement and nerves made my heart rate soar even higher, as I waited for him to speak.

Could I admit to that without coming across as easy? What if he got the wrong idea about me and thought I just wanted to have phone sex every five minutes?

"Tell me you want a picture, Chloe, I won't share with you until you demand one from me."

Truly, there was nothing I wanted more. Every fiber in my body was desperate to know what he looked like. Every nerve in my body was aching for sex at that point. A desperate feeling had begun to grow in my core and was starting to surface by radiating to all of my erogenous zones.

My nipples were pebbled with the effects of tingling pulses at the thought of him looking at me, and me looking at him. My flesh crept with excitement and turned my normally silky smooth skin into goose flesh. The sensation of his seductive voice was setting me alight inside. I was so turned on by how he was talking to me, and the demands he was making.

"Show me." Barely recognizing my own voice, I had suddenly demanded the same of him. And immediately following that needy command, in my mind I considered if asking to see his dick made me curious, or was I perverted? Two strangers sharing the most intimate parts of their bodies to each other by text... what were we trying to achieve?

Loud beeping from my phone alerted me to the fact that he'd sent his text. I wasn't sure whether I wanted to look at it, and if I did, what did that mean? Strange how in a matter of minutes everything I thought my boundaries were around sex had imploded, and I had a picture of a naked stranger's penis on my phone.

A moment's quiet between us unsettled me. Was he looking at my picture and what was he thinking? Clearing his throat, Paul spoke in a raspy, uneven voice laced with lust.

"So, Chloe, did you look at me yet?"

I shook my head, because I had still been deliberating about opening the text.

"No, not yet." Shocked about how my lack of confidence came through in my voice, I almost hung up, thinking that the game we were playing had gone far enough, and that we shouldn't continue. I wanted to tell him I'd delete his text without looking, if he'd delete mine. I knew that was a very naïve thought, no guy that was sent a picture like that could resist looking at it.

"Aren't you curious about how my dick looks?" Chloe, I want you to open the text. We'll open them at the same time. Please put me on speaker phone, you are going to need your hands in a few minutes. And I want to talk to you when I open your text picture.

"Okay I'm opening it now."

"Same here," he husked.

Closing my eyes tight, my heart raced and my

hands shook again as a sudden burst of adrenaline hit me from the thought of me doing something so reckless and trusting him with such an intimate image. Paul's gruff tone broke into my thoughts.

"I'm opening the picture you sent me now." There was silence for a couple of seconds and I nearly concluded the call. "Fuck. You have the perfect pussy, Chloe. Thank you for sharing yourself with me." For some reason I was completely elated that he approved. There was silence again then he spoke. "Fuck. Hot dammit. Damn. You described your pussy perfectly, it's... beautiful, honey."

The last two words were almost a broken whisper and then silence hung in the air between us until he hummed like he was thinking and repeated. "Hmm, fuck. Your pussy is beautiful, darlin'." I hadn't known how to respond to that, so I chose that moment to open his text, completely unprepared for the impact that one image would have on my mind and body. Electrical currents fired off in all directions, my eyes widened and strangely, I reached out and stroked my index finger down the screen. A strong pulsing sensation clenched my pussy and for the first time ever, juices escaped my pussy, soaking into the pillow under me. I could actually feel my clitoris become erect.

"Do you want me to tell you what I see, Chloe? What I feel when I see this picture?"

Did I? Weirdly, what he thought really mattered to me. He was the only person apart from Kace to know about that part of me, even if he would never know me intimately.

"I do." Pursing my lips and still staring at his image, I waited for Paul to explain how seeing my pussy had affected him.

"Beautiful. Your pussy is beautiful. Actually, it's perfect." Humming again, he growled and said, "I don't think I've seen a more perfect one." Starting to giggle, I thought he was being facetious and rolled my eyes, embarrassed again about sending it.

"What are you laughing at? There is nothing funny about looking at you. Seeing this part of you makes me feel wild inside. You are beautiful Chloe, and the only thing I can think of when I'm looking at this, is that if I was granted one wish, I'd use it to sink my dick balls deep inside you to see if it feels as amazing as it looks."

Smirking at his reply, I could completely relate. When I saw the photo of his dick, perfect was the word that came to mind, even with that strange metal bar with the silver balls through the head. Emotions and feelings came from somewhere deep inside that were a contradiction to anything I had previously thought about sex.

Nothing about this experience had anything to do with love and romance. It was carnal with a wanton desire, which had an insanity all its own.

"Are you looking at my dick, Chloe?" Paul's seductive voice echoed down the line at me.

"I am, I stated honestly.

"What are you thinking?" Pursing my lips as if to prevent me from disclosing the horny mess I was, I initially said nothing, still trying to get my head around what I was doing. It was so out of character, but he was drunk and I was an emotional wreck so it just seemed right because no one was ever going to know what we were doing.

"Are you shocked by what you are doing, Chloe?" The guy seemed to have a knack for hitting the nail on the head as far as my thoughts were concerned.

"I am – this is the last thing I ever thought I would do, and especially with a stranger," I replied honestly.

"Is that what I am, Chloe – a stranger?" Paul sounded a little surprised by my statement.

"Aren't you?" I was wondering how he saw himself, if not that.

"Honestly, I feel... in my head, that I've known you for a long time, Chloe. I connect with you like no one else. Like you are the girl I should have met when I was seventeen. If I had known you then, I think my life may have gone a bit differently."

Hearing his thoughts scared me. Suddenly I felt prickles in the back of my neck, his disclosure both exciting and frightening me.

"What are you thinking? I'm weird? Some kind of sicko ... maybe I am. Calling my random wrong number and flashing my dick at her in a text while I'm drunk, but you asked and I'm giving you my honest thoughts about you. Tell me, when you see my dick what are you thinking?"

Admiring his candid answer, I felt he should at

least have the same from me. "I'm thinking I'd like to feel your dick and the sensation of it sinking deep inside of me. I'm sure this is a momentary reaction but I think I'd use my one wish to touch your dick, to feel the stretch and burn as you enter me." My voice trailed off and I realized I had just poured my thinking voice down the line and I had gone too far.

"Are you connected enough to allow me to make you come, Chloe?" At that moment he could have asked me to throw myself into the Grand Canyon and I would have agreed.

"Definitely." The confidence in my voice was different from how I had been all through the rest of our conversation.

"Good girl. Are your legs spread open for me?"

Without hesitancy I answered. "They are."

"Good girl. Pull your knees up towards your chest, and then roll your knees outwards." Doing as I was told, I was suddenly focused on the instructions he was giving me, obeying without hesitation.

"Close your eyes." I did and there was silence for a moment, then Paul's low, husky, seductive tone, cooed, "I'm stroking myself, but you are not to touch your pussy, do you understand?"

Bunching my brow, I became frustrated because there was no way I was going to be able to stop giving myself pleasure to find my release. Especially since he had ordered me not to touch myself. Forbidding me from doing that just made me want to do it even more.

"Remember how I told you I'd make you come

just with words, Chloe? You don't believe I can do that? I am about to prove to you it is possible. Just keep your eyes closed and listen."

Paul began talking in the most seductive tones about my body, explaining where his hands and lips would be and how he could make me feel so alive with his fingers and mouth. Where he would suck and lick and caress.

Every part of my body was alert and humming in anticipation at his sexy low southern tone, his words caressing my mind like a warm sensual palm, and making my core pulse with such vibrancy and regularity that the feelings deep in my core began to put me on edge.

Once in a while, he would ask how what he was doing was affecting me. This was usually just before I was tempted to reach down and touch myself, and I guess my breathing kept changing and alerting him to that.

Becoming lost in his words, his descriptive language of what he was doing to me, made me forget that he wasn't in the room with me. The effect of his tone, words, extensive teasing, had a kind of hypnotic effect on me, to the point where I could swear I felt his hot breath on my pussy, his tongue lapping at me and the pulse of him sucking on my clit.

A familiar heat and pleasure sensation built deep in my core and I felt my pussy begin to tighten. Paul told me he was going to fuck me with his tongue and I was going to come over it, he gave a guttural groan into the phone and I felt myself release.

"Stroke your clit, Chloe." I'd never have believed that someone could have had an effect on me to the point where he could make me climax without touching me, until that happened between us.

Quietly, I lay wondering what the hell to say to that. Did I say thank you? Did I ask if he came? Did I dare ask... have you done that before? Would I want to know the answer to that? I knew that he'd told me it was a first for him, but Paul was so authoritative and precise in his direction that I began to doubt that very much.

Another thought struck me, how many women had he done that to, and were all the phone calls we had, a kind of grooming process to get me to this point with him?

All of a sudden, I was Chloe with low self-esteem, not wanting to talk or dissect what had just happened. Mumbling that I needed a bit of time to absorb what had just gone on, I ended the call before Paul had the chance to speak and lay there feeling like another man had taken advantage of me. Sure he'd been drunk but I'd been weak enough to fall for his attention and it was just a sick game.

Paul had been having sex prior to calling me, and then all of that had happened between us. And I'd actively participated in it and there was a picture out there of me like... that. There were so many overwhelming feelings running through my mind. Disgust, confusion, hurt, anger, sadness, loneliness, embarrassment and feeling like I'd been played for a fool and that the whole wrong number had been a preamble to what had happened between us.

He never called me the next day or the one after that. Several days later I was still at a loss for what to think, but even with what had happened I was still checking my phone, waiting for contact from him. With each day that passed I felt it confirmed that what I had felt towards the end of the call was sadly, correct. I'd been groomed for some sicko's pleasure and he now had a picture of my most intimate body part. Thank God he didn't know my last name or where I lived.

CHAPTER 18

CONFUSION

Gibson

Jesus Christ, what did I do? Bad enough I was arranging to meet her and then I get pissed and pull a stunt like that on her? What the fuck is wrong with me? The damage was already done, and I had a few days to get my head straight before coming face to face with her. Then what?

Charlotte and I had already discussed how I would be able to mask my identity. There was only a hint of me on the phone. Everyone commented that I didn't really sound like myself on the phone. Suddenly I wasn't confident on that score. Normally I acted the typical alpha-male asshole, but suddenly I was wavering on my ability to pull the whole ruse off.

Flying up to LA in the Lear Jet from the gig in Arizona took no time at all. I could have done with an extra hour to gather my thoughts about how to deal with Chloe when I saw her. I was wondering how the fuck was I going to look her in the eye after what I'd done on the phone? We hadn't spoken since that night and five days later I was in uncharted territory.

Why did I give a shit about how what we did affected her? I've never cared before about someone's feelings? What the fuck was I doing? Maybe Lennox had it right, and I was putting her on a pedestal. What if I saw her after all that time and thought meh… she's not doing anything for me? Then thought, could I spend a whole weekend with a girl I wasn't into, when I should have been meeting Toby? All I knew was I had too many questions and not one answer coming back at me.

High winds rocked the plane as we were descending to land at LAX. Turbulence shook the plane violently and it seemed to lurch then fall like a small yacht being tossed in high seas before the calm came again. An ache in my fingertips alerted me that I had been clutching the leather arm rests on both sides. Flying never bothered me, but it seemed to affect me that day for some reason. Fuck, I was really restless and on edge.

Finding our way to the hotel, and getting to my room, I'd opened the door and my eyes scanned the pale gold, cream and terracotta colored soft furnishings, which gave the room an opulent feel. Wandering over to the French windows, I opened them wide, letting the warm breeze into the room. Air conditioning was bad for my throat, and I had to sing, so I wanted to make sure I could deliver the best gig I could for Chloe.

Walking over to the bed, I turned and fell backwards, flat on my back. My body sank into the soft silk comforter and my arms stretched out to both sides on the super king-sized bed. It felt like a great bed to sleep in.

Staring up at the ceiling, my mind began to think about everything Chloe described to me on the phone. It was the memory of the sound of her voice, laced with lust, and her seductive sweet tone that made my dick twitch in my pants, suddenly interested in more than what my mind could recall.

Closing my eyes, I conjured up the image of Chloe that was stuck on a loop since I knew she was coming to LA. How much of the girl would still be there, and what changes would I see of the woman she'd become. That phone call made me horny as fuck. God knows what would happen if I actually had her.

A repetitive knocking sound woke me and I realized I had drifted off for a few minutes. Rolling to the side, I sat up and pushed myself to stand, the mattress dipping under my hand as I pushed myself away from it.

Wandering over to the door, I heard Lennox's voice. "He's not in there. He must have gone down already." Remembering we had a press conference in the hotel conference room, I pulled open the door to see Len and Mick walking down the hallway.

"Wait up guys, I fell asleep."

During the conference there were the usual questions, smiles, flirty jokes with female reporters, and I almost yawned, because I was so tired of the same-shit-different-city routine that followed us everywhere we went. In fact, as I looked at the faces in the room, I figured it must be the same for them. There were at least eight reporters I recognized as regulars from all the conferences we had.

Fifteen minutes later, we were heading for the elevators and back to our hotel rooms for a quick shower before going to The Staples Center. When Charlotte made the arrangements she booked Chloe and her guests into four rooms in the Westin-Bonaventure in LA.

Initially, I freaked out about that. Putting her in a hotel that was a different one from us... how the hell was I supposed to get close to her, if she was somewhere else? Charlotte's reasoning was that prize winners never stayed at the same hotel as the band. It was bad protocol, and she should know, she's been doing that stuff for us for almost seven years.

Clever girl put them up at the Westin-Bonaventure because it was right next to the airport. If I was headed in the direction of the airport, that hotel was the last place they would think I was going. So I reeled my neck in and mumbled, "Thanks," to her.

Standing in the shower, I had a familiar feeling in the pit of my stomach and there was only one other time where I had experienced it, and it was that split second before we went onstage. I'd guessed it was nerves, because there was this odd wired feeling going on inside me as well.

Unusual feelings invaded my body. As soon as we got to the venue, we were told there were twenty eight competition winners. By talking to Charlotte, the production and promotion teams, and of course the band, I found we had twenty four winners before the gig this time. Four winners afterwards: Chloe and her three friends.

I had eaten a selection of meats, cheeses and fruit on the plane, I resisted eating more because the prize promised dinner for Chloe and her three friends and if nothing else I'd enjoy dinner.

At the winners' meet and greet, there were a few good guys who were really fans of what we did and had followed us all through our musical transition from amateur to professional musicians. Spending forty minutes with them before the gig calmed my nerves.

Disappointed faces and forced smiles surrounded us as we ended the session, and they were led out. As soon as they disappeared I gargled with some water, and then began to warm my voice getting ready for the gig. Less than twenty minutes since they left we were walking through the maze of corridors again to the stage and an unfamiliar feeling of apprehension rose again.

As Mick struck the first chord and the lights beat down on us onstage, I was conscious that Chloe had me at a disadvantage again. I was in full view of everyone and she was out there being anonymous, able to regard me and free to judge.

The moment I came face to face with her would be different. Would I be able to hide my feelings of the initial impact of seeing her again? And what would that reaction be?

That gig was different to any I had done before. Sure, I was still Gibson Barclay the showman. But there was no female interaction other than engaging the crowd to sing along and me jumping around on stage. I knew that when the show was over I would have to suppress the adrenaline rush that I always got towards the end of the show.

Somehow that made me at my most vulnerable to fuck up, because all I wanted at that point was to have sex. Performing was like foreplay to me, and because of my job, there was always someone there willing to help me out with that last part.

Scanning the audience in the section where I knew she would be, all I could see initially was a sea of heads, but as I started to sing "Inches From Paradise" a blue spotlight fell on the stage, and somehow my eyes roamed to the edge of the light. Part of the spotlight fell on the closest section of the audience, and there she was.

Those unforgettable, huge, inky blue eyes were staring up at me and when mine made contact with hers, Chloe dropped her gaze to the floor. I wondered why she still didn't understand how hot she was. Dressed perfectly in her blue jeans and amber tight fitting top that showed her midriff, she had finished her rock chick look off with a tiny brown leather bomber jacket.

Staring up at the stage, Chloe had a serious look on her face, listening intently to the song I was singing. So, without her really knowing, I focused completely on her as I sang every word I'd written about that one moment we'd shared all those years ago, and how she'd made me feel when she looked into my eyes.

Reaching into her jacket she took out her cell and began taking pictures of me. And fuck, if I hadn't wanted to take mine out and capture her image, to replace the one that had been playing on a loop in my mind.

For the rest of the gig I tried not to keep looking at her and focus on entertaining the masses. Crowds crushed at the edge of the stage but all the time, Chloe remained in her seat, hand fanning through her hair, and I wondered what the hell she was thinking. Yeah… I was still looking at her.

A guy standing next to her leaned in and started speaking to her. Chloe turned to look at him. Flashing a wide smile, she nodded and accepted the hand he held out for her. Together they began weaving through the crowd towards the exit at the back. Where was she going? I knew she wouldn't be leaving but I couldn't make sense of what was going on. Then it clicked.

Fuck! Out of left wing, I was sucker punched. For all my planning, the one thing I never expected her to do was to bring a guy with her. When we had talked on the phone, she was pretty clear that there was no guy. Did she lie about that? Hell, maybe there was a lot more going on with her than she was able to share with me. I was a stranger, after all.

Panicking, I stared at the seating, trying to make sense of what I saw. Marking it all out in my head, I saw four girls in a row, the empty seats of her and the guy she was with, and one guy on the end of the row. *Two guys on the end, Chloe and her friend?* I was concentrating so hard on trying to figure out who was with whom, that I almost missed my cue to sing the next song intro.

Luckily singing was on auto-pilot, because I was too busy formulating a plan in my head for how the hell I was going to deal with her being in front of me and her guy standing next to her. My plan was going to shit. Then it came to me; I was just going to have to use the guys in the band as wingmen to keep her and her boyfriend apart so that I could, at the very least, talk to her.

As soon as the encore was done, I was off the stage and downstairs to the dressing room like a blue assed fly. Adrenaline was coursing through me and I knew what that meant. Impulse. I had to dig deep to fight the horny feelings that the adrenaline rush and being on stage gave me.

Behaving appropriately wasn't so much of an issue for me these days, but when I really got something into my head, it was pretty difficult to reason it back out without having a will of iron. Same if I was drunk. What I wasn't sure of was, after five years of fantasizing about Chloe, whether all the willpower in the world was going to be enough to stop me from fucking it up in her presence.

Lack of supervision as a teenager had made me an obstinate bastard during the first few years on the road, but I was in a different place altogether now and I had learned to control my petulant ways for the most part.

Taking a shower after the gig I was interrupted when Lennox opened the shower door. "What the fuck was that about, Gib? You almost blew the whole fucking gig tonight. Where the hell were you? Two words reversed in one bridge and a whole line missing from another song? If having that girl in the crowd has that effect on you, better you fuck and forget her tonight because I don't want to be out there in amongst that shit again, hear me?"

Giving Lennox a solid stare, I waited until he showed signs of being unnerved, then pushed him back and closed the shower door, calling after him, "Seems I can't even get cleaned up without one of you fuckers trying to get into the shower to ride my ass."

Wrapping a towel around my hips, I padded barefoot back to the dressing room to pick up my stuff and pull on my clothes. Someone had hung them neatly on the back of the door and I hadn't even been able to choose what I wanted to wear.

Thankfully it was just some jeans and an open neck shirt with the sleeves rolled up. As I put my hand in the sleeve I mused who the hell thought to roll my sleeves up for me? Obviously, it was some anal image nut or someone with too much time on their hands.

Buttoning my black and white checked shirt, I wandered back into the communal space in the dressing room to where the others were. I was running my fingers through my hair when I became conscious of Tori, watching me intently. "Keep your fucking eyes to yourself, Tori. There's nothing here for you to see, got it?"

Mick snickered and took a swig from the dark green beer bottle he was holding before lowering it and narrowing his eyes as he regarded her, "Honey, I don't mind if you want to objectify me. I'm far better looking and a much hotter lay than Gibson. I hear his dick has been rubbed so much it's been worn smooth."

Raucous laughter got louder as Lennox and Simon cracked up in the far side of the dressing room, then Len saw that I wasn't seeing the funny side of Tori leering at me and dropped his smile. Clearing his throat, he wandered over and put a foot up to rest on the edge of the chair I was sitting on and addressed everyone.

"Right, y'all, this is an important event for our baby tonight, is that right, Gibson?" Suddenly I felt some griping in my stomach. Maybe that's why I was so frustrated and irritable these past few days. It was as if all of that was due to a culmination of pent up feelings that I really couldn't fathom, and nerves too if I'm honest, because she would finally be face to face with me and I'd be putting a ghost to rest.

Everyone's eyes were on me, waiting for me to

say what I wanted about what was about to happen. "Guys, I know you all think I'm pulling some crazy stunt, doing this. Let me tell you all, as I stand here in front of you, that today is the most important meet and greet any of us, as a band, will ever have." Tori was picking imaginary lint off her black velvet pants and pretending she wasn't listening.

"Just want to reach out to you here, because I'm sticking my neck out and asking for your support with this, 'cause I have a feeling I'm really going to need it. This chick doesn't know who I am anymore. However, we were going to enjoy entertaining a group of four girls, but the reason I was off my game was because I never figured she'd bring a guy along."

Lennox gave me a look of distaste and I knew exactly how he felt. It left a sour taste in my mouth as well. I figured that they could at least manage her time with him while I was around. We may have bitched and fought like dogs sometimes, but the one thing we did amazingly well, other than play together, was have each other's backs. Staring at Tori, her attitude gave me another worry to think about.

CHAPTER 19

HUH

Gibson

Hollow sounds came from the cheap paneled door as someone knocked and Simon made a loud grunting noise as he leaned over and sprung the door handle down, rocking back on the stool he was sitting on. The white paneled door crept open and red hair with flecks of blonde appeared, followed by a nerdy looking guy's head. "All your guests are waiting in the green room when you're ready."

Slight tremors began to surface from deep inside my body and radiated to my arms and legs. It was a weird sensation. Sitting there, I thought about what I had done. It was almost as bad as stalking. Horrible thoughts about her staring at me in disgust all those years ago began to shake my confidence. *What the hell was I thinking about, trying to pull something like this off?*

Funny thing, nerves. I had never suffered with them before that night. However, the main issue I was fighting was how she would react to me. I was sure that as soon as I spoke the game would be up, and then another question entered my head. If she did recognize me, how would she react after how we'd spoken to each other, and what we had shared the last time we spoke.

Fighting a panic inside and the unfamiliar feelings of insecurity engulfing me, I took a final swig of the can of soda I'd been drinking, crushed it and tossed it at the trash can. Then there I was, headed towards the green room about to meet her and say hi like I had no idea who she was.

Snickering, I shook my head at that thought, because Lennox probably thought just talking to a girl was beyond my capability. Until recently, it was.

Normally, meet and greets were second nature, yet the feeling inside me was like the first day of high school. I'd checked myself out in the mirror and was conscious of what I was wearing, and how I was behaving.

Walking toward the meeting room, there was a feeling of despair instead of excitement. It could go either way and at that point, I didn't dare think about her reacting negatively to me. Lennox slapped my shoulder and the rest of the band walked behind us as we made our way to where everyone was waiting.

With every inch the door opened, I could see more into the room. In my mind the door opened painstakingly slowly, yet all of a sudden there she was. Chloe. Stunningly beautiful to look at. She was sitting on the far side of a huge black leather sofa;

same guy sitting next to her, with his arm stretched along the back of her head.

Familiar looking body language between them with his body turned slightly towards her in an almost intimate way, but not. I wondered who he was to her. It was hard to read how close they were.

A tall dark haired girl, who looked vaguely familiar, was perched on the arm of the sofa next to her, and another guy stood facing all of them. Heads turned and all eyes moved toward our direction as we strode further into the room.

At first I tried not to meet her eyes, but when I found the nerve to look at her, hers were trained on her lap. Wondering what that meant, I moved closer, glad in a way that she wasn't looking at me, because it gave me the opportunity to peruse her without embarrassing her.

Moving closer, I found that Chloe was even more beautiful than she had been at eighteen. No doubt about it, she had grown into her own skin and had developed from the gorgeous young girl that she had been, into a very beautiful woman.

Slightly more curvaceous, delicate facial features with those luscious lips, and huge almond shaped inky blue eyes, Chloe had no make-up on whatsoever and her natural flawless beauty almost overwhelmed me.

Throughout my seven years on the road, I had come across many beautiful girls, some beyond my expectations, but no one had ever had this effect on me in the way Chloe had. There was no way to explain what it was that got to me. She was amazing to look at but that wasn't it, it was a feeling that was way different from any other feeling I'd ever known, and after all that time, it had never left me since the last time I saw her.

Charlotte began to speak and with her first words, Chloe looked up and our eyes locked instantly, shocking me. Because the one thing I never expected to see was a sadness that made me so fucking mad, I couldn't find my voice.

What the hell was going on with her? Had she already realized that the guy on the phone was me after hearing me on stage? What had I done to her?

Introducing us, Charlotte chatted easily while Len, Mick and Simon shook hands with each of them. Len spoke to Chloe and the smile she gave him melted my heart. Those beautiful eyes lit up and suddenly she was the girl that had captivated my thoughts for years.

Just watching her smile made the corners of my mouth curl up. She had this innocent charm that captivated me even further. Clearing his throat, I heard Lennox break into my trance. "So, Gib, are you going to stand there and stare or are you going to welcome our guests, dude?"

Instantly showman Gibson took over. "Jeez, Len – can't a guy stare at a beautiful woman in peace?" As soon as I said it, I was kicking my own ass because that was the last thing I wanted her to take away from this trip. Me, objectifying her and getting pleasure from doing it, even if that *was* partly true.

Brushing over my comment I began shaking hands enthusiastically until I came to the dude who was with Chloe. "And you are the winner's boyfriend, Gavin, right?"

Gavin's eyes flicked to Chloe's and hers to his. Their transferring glances were awkward and she blushed and looked a little flustered before looking away. "I wish", he said, looking nervously back at Chloe. "No, not her boyfriend unfortunately, just a friend."

Relief flooded through me. I hadn't realized how tense I had become during that little interlude until I felt my muscles relax, but now my heart raced in my chest, because that meant I'd be able to manufacture some time alone with Chloe.

"Ah, your loss is my gain then Gavin, because that means you won't be jealous when I whisk the winner off for her dinner alone this evening." Smirking, I turned and raised an eyebrow at Charlotte, who gave me a what-the-fuck look, because that wasn't in the plans for the weekend at all. Turning back, panic and something else I couldn't put my finger on was written on Chloe's face.

"Don't look so frightened honey, I don't bite… not unless that's your thing of course, and then maybe I could make an exception in your case."

Gavin's arm reached out and pulled Chloe close to him. "It's okay, honey, he's just messing."

Seeing him excuse my behavior made me so pissed, I almost blew it and threw a punch, but Lennox and Mick had me covered. "Come on guys, let's get some drinks and make ourselves comfortable. We have until late Sunday to party before you go back home again."

Lennox smirked surreptitiously and slapped his hand heavily on Gavin's back. At the same time Mick moved in and threw his arm over the other girls shoulder, I think her name was Ruby. Both started to distract them away from where I was standing. Mick began saying, "Tell me Ruby, I've seen you somewhere before. Do we know each other?"

What Mick was asking was, did I fuck you and can't remember? Beginning to smirk, I caught myself and the smirk dropped, because when I thought about it, maybe I had too. She was familiar, but we'd had so many girls back then, and the only one I was sure I hadn't had a thing with, was right there in the room with me.

Suddenly I was tongue-tied. Reaching out, my hand slipped around her shoulder and I pulled Chloe into a tight hug. Hugging was what I did when I had no words. I felt her slender body tense and tremble slightly when I did. I almost let her go, but she suddenly seemed to relax into the embrace after a second.

From the moment she gave into the hug, her body became all soft curves and my head was filled with this amazing womanly scent. Nothing could have stopped me at that point, and I leaned into her, inhaling her skin deeply.

Holding her like that gave me an incredible feeling of warmth. There had been times when I lost sleep over wondering what she would have felt like in my arms. Feeling myself become aroused, I had no choice but to break out of the hug.

Stepping back, I gave her a soft smile and dipped my knees slightly to capture her gaze in mine and took her hand to soothe her. The way her hand molded into mine felt like a fit. I can't explain it, but I just felt so comfortable holding it, and the touch of her made my dick twitch.

"Hi, honey, congratulations on winning the competition. This is as nerve-racking for me as it is for you I've never done this before either."

Chloe's face instantly brightened and her eyes lit up in appreciation at my gesture. Staring in amazement at the transformation in her, I squeezed her hand and mirrored her wide smile, "Let's just try and have a good time together, no pressure okay?"

Smiling nervously, she bit her lip and tried to hold my gaze and for the briefest moment, I was transported back five years to Matt's office and those same eyes inches from mine. Losing confidence, her eyes lowered in the direction of the floor again, and a pink tinge touched her cheeks.

Reacting without thinking, I placed my forefinger under her chin and raised her head to get eye contact again. "Don't look at the floor. You have the most incredible eyes, I'd like to see them if that's okay."

Not sure what to do with that compliment, she hesitated and I saw her swallow before turning her head away from me. She trained her sights on her friends, maybe for reassurance, but they were being kept busy by the guys.

Tori stared over at us and I instantly knew by the look on her face what she was thinking. Reading her from the first day, I knew she was desperate to get with me and would do anything to fuck up the tenuous connection I was building with Chloe.

Simon was talking to the other dude that was with them and I inclined my head just a fraction in Chloe's direction and directed my eyes pointedly at her. Without a word between us, he knew what to do. Excusing himself from the guy, he wandered over and began chatting with Chloe. Smiling, I excused myself and briefly left the room to chat to Charlotte.

"Romantic and casual I read, so I've asked the jet to be prepared for you. You're taking her to the Casanova restaurant in Carmel-By-The-Sea. I figured the twenty minute flight each way would be a great way of ensuring there were no interruptions or prying eyes, and the restaurant is so romantic that no one would ever think someone like you would be there. So it should make for a pretty private party."

Staring back at Charlotte, I should have been pleased with the effort she had gone to, but the comment about the restaurant and me not fitting in, smarted with me. Who the fuck did she think she was, talking to me like that. Employees seem to overstep just when they do something great. What the fuck was it with that?

"You don't think I can be romantic? You don't think I have it in me to pursue a girl and make her feel like she's the only person alive? That my heart can beat only for her? You know fuck all about me, Charlotte. No one does. Hell, I hardly know myself. Why? Because I've never really been given the chance at a relationship."

My voice sounded harsh and aggressive. I gave her a solid, don't fuck-with-me stare for a moment longer than I'd intended, before I exhaled heavily. On reflection it was probably intimidating.

"No one has ever come close to knowing me. All they've wanted is to fuck a guy in a band. What does that tell you? Is it me, or is this the first time I've found someone I want to give a fuck about? Just do your fucking job, arrange stuff for me, but don't fucking judge, you hear me?"

Charlotte grasped her right upper arm with her left hand and looked nervous. Surprised and shocked because she's used to dealing with cranky and pissed Gibson, but not the genuine anger I'd directed at her. Her defensive pose told me my words had hit home. What did she think I was going to do? Punch her?

Stepping back, I turned on the balls of my feet to walk away; then turned my head over my shoulder to look back at her. "Everyone knows me as Gibson the manwhore, not one person in my life has ever understood me, so why the fuck shouldn't I have done what I wanted to?"

Turning, I headed back to Chloe and Simon. When she came into view, the way she was leaning against the wall talking to Simon was a turn on in itself. Standing with her legs crossed at the ankles, elbow perched on the wall, and her head resting in her hand. She seemed so much more relaxed than when she was looking at me.

When Chloe saw me wandering back, she pushed off of the wall and straightened up in a formal stance. It was me she was uneasy with. I felt sure she had no idea it was me on the phone by then but her conversation on the phone about what kind of person I was still rang in my ears. I wondered if or when she was going to mention her past connection to me. There was a nervous aura about her that I was struggling with. It was a vibe I never got with the girl I was around all those years ago.

Simon made eye contact with me and said, "Okay Gibson, I'm gonna get a beer with the rest of the guys. I'll see you later. Lovely getting to know you a little, Chloe, I'm looking forward to spending the day in your company tomorrow." Patting her arm, Simon nodded at me and headed back to the others to give us a bit of privacy to continue our conversation.

"Alright, are you ready to get this party started honey?" Smiling at her, I expected her to smile back, but again I was met with a strange, almost angry look. Chloe crossed her arms and gave me a solid stare.

"Thank you for your hospitality for me and my friends, but I didn't enter a competition hoping to meet you. That was purely by default after buying a new phone with automatic competition entry."

Grinning at her, but trying to hide the fact that I

had manipulated this whole situation, I replied, "Well, I guess you're not really a fan then, but we'll just have a good time anyway. What do you say?"

Chloe pursed her lips and I could see she was uneasy, sighing heavily she met my gaze. "Gibson, I know you don't remember me, but we've kind of met before. I just want to say a couple of things to you."

Taking a towel off the chair by a small table, she sat down, crossed her legs and clasped her hands in front of her. "Firstly, I am indeed a fan of M3rCy. I have every album you have made, but to be honest, I know what you are doing, trying to lure me away from the others. You may be used to women dropping their panties for you whenever you wanted them to. Please understand I am not a star struck teenager and that won't be happening with me."

Raising my eyebrow, I felt pissed that the legacy of my horny ways was following me at that moment. "Hmm, this is the second time today someone has decided what my intentions are and got it wrong. I really want you to enjoy yourself Chloe, so I'll clear the air. I, Gibson Barclay, am not going to fuck you, so you can relax. All I want to do is take you to dinner. Is that a problem for you?"

CHAPTER 20

EXCITED

Chloe

I suppressed the nerves in my stomach where a knot had formed and had me feeling nauseous. Blood rushed and swirled in my ears while my heartbeat became so wild that I thought my heart was going to detach itself and rise up out of my chest and into my throat.

Sixteen was the last time I had felt that nervous energy; the day I walked into my new high school when we had to move across country. Being at the gig was way different though. I was at a concert, watching a guy I had seen when he was nothing. No... if I was being honest, I never thought Gibson could ever have been described as nothing to anyone. He had too much of an aura about him. The guy had everything. Problem was – he'd also *had* everyone... almost.

Sharp pangs of excitement gave me that wired feeling. Small shocks jolting different parts of my body with each moment that passed from the moment we'd landed at LAX. The anticipation of what was going to happen was making me feel like a teenager waiting for her date to go to the prom all over again.

Knowing there was no way he'd remember me gave me a smug feeling like I had the upper hand. It was the one advantage I had over someone with his status. Hard to believe that it was actually happening, and that five years after I last saw him I was going to face him again. I kept checking the letter containing all the details of what was going to happen that weekend, and I kept having second thoughts about the whole deal.

Not that I expected that much from the band itself, but there was the fact we had a whole day with them, and there was the added stress of not really knowing Gavin and Eddie that well. My one worry about Gibson was Ruby. I had made my mind up to disclose my reservations about her constant need to match make around me.

Waiting for the concert to start, I considered that there was so much that everyone didn't know about me and my whole situation. Ruby hadn't known about the incident with the towels, Gavin and Eddie knew nothing of my fantasy about Gibson, and Eddie hadn't known the whole story about Kace and my abusive past. Obviously, the guys in M3rCy had no idea about anything other than that I had won a competition.

When we took our seats later at the concert my

breathing was shallow and I fought the anxiety I was feeling about our meet and greet. There was something about the psyched anticipation of waiting with a massive crowd that created a special atmosphere. Echoing catcalls and bellows of distant laughter sounded alongside the strange feeling of expectation, all adding to the occasion.

We were seated right at the side of the stage on the first row. Close up and personal with Gibson and his band again and I felt a little freaked out to be so close to someone who had the kind of effect on me he had. And who had intimidated me the last time I saw him singing.

Suddenly the lights fell in the venue, plunging us into semi-darkness a sudden hush descended on the vast space. Twenty thousand people all in one place and it may just have been possible to hear a pin drop for a second. The emcee's official sounding voice broke through the hush with a commanding tone which echoed through the building.

"Fresh from their world tour, The Staples Center proudly presents for your entertainment, M3rCy!" Bass guitar and drums began to play and the loud rumble of their instantly recognizable beat vibrated across the floor and rose up through my body. Goose bumps rippled like a wave across my skin.

A crush formed in front of the stage as people jostled to get nearer to the band. Sitting back in my seat, I scanned the actions on the stage. Gibson was much less overt in his behavior, and even less provocative in his manner. Way different from the guy I remembered at Beltz Bar.

Maturity had made Gibson even more stunning to look at. Mesmerizing actually. Same beautiful even features, plump, really kissable lips, strong jawline, and the one thing that always struck me... his amazingly flawless, satiny, golden tanned skin.

Incredibly fit, toned and strong, his energy seemed boundless. Gibson oozed charm and charisma and there was a defiance about him that made his bad-boy image a magnet for people. No matter how hard I tried, I couldn't watch the rest of the band. They were just grey in comparison to him.

Gibson was bounding around in his full technicolor glory, while his band made noise behind him. That's how it looked to me anyway. Trying to focus on Mick Stanley, I briefly took in a clever riff that he was playing, before my eyes were again trained on Gibson. What was it about him that made the guy so irresistible?

His reputation alone should have made me hate him. He was everything that I usually despised in men. Arrogant, completely comfortable in his own skin, but with an attitude that said he took no prisoners, and from what I knew about him, he danced to his own tune and everyone else did as well.

Watching him do his thing had a pretty powerful effect on me. It was easy to see how everyone fell madly in love with him. Enticing his way into women's hearts all over the world was like shelling peas to a guy like him. I'd never known anyone with the power he appeared to have over men and women alike. Suddenly, I realized my panties were drenched just watching him do his job.

Glancing around at the audience it was fifty/fifty, male and female, although I didn't see any guys throwing their boxer briefs at the stage the way I was seeing the women throwing their thongs up there. Feelings rose up in me that were akin to suffocating. I fought the desire and want inside me and I allowed myself to wonder what it would be like to have that one perfect night of sex with a guy like Gibson. No... not a guy like him... with him.

Realizing I had drifted off and was playing with my hair, Gavin leaned in, "Want to help me get some more drinks?" Watching Gibson had made me thirsty and the last thing I wanted was to drag my eyes away, but I agreed because the air in the room was so thick with the hormones flying around the arena. He had everyone turned on at some level from the whole experience.

When the concert finished, a security guy with a mic taped to his head with invisible tape, and a bluetooth earphone came and ushered us through a small, heavy metal door at the side of the stage.

Striding purposefully in front of us, the security guy took us down a maze of corridors and into the bowels of the stadium somewhere under the stage, leading us to the place where we were meeting the band. I was surprised at the opulence and tasteful decoration of the room.

Soft lilac colored walls with one deep purple

feature wall, housing a massive screen that was still tuned in to the stage, was an unexpected sight. The large room was comfortable and obviously stacked for the pleasure of the particular band that was playing. The one thing that was definitely out of place was the fresh flower arrangement.

Five massive black leather sofas dominated the room. Smoked glass end tables were full of bowls of nibbles and ice buckets with champagne as well as different branded beers on a few of the others.

I wrinkled my nose knowingly when I remembered my dad's lecture on the perils of eating from table snacks. "Never eat anything in a nibbles bowl they are full of other people's germs, think of where their hands could have been." He ruined me for peanut bowls the world over with that single comment.

"Make yourselves comfortable, M3rCy will be with you shortly. Did you all have fun at the concert? Looking expectantly at us, I wasn't sure why he would even ask that question. We weren't going to be at a world famous band's gig and not enjoy it, were we?

Glancing over at Ruby, I nearly peed in my panties when she mouthed, "OH. MY. GOD. Gibson Barclay, Chloe." Nerves gripped me and suddenly I was feeling nauseous and antsy. Gibson Barclay had given me a few of the most heart stopping moments of my life and he wasn't even aware I existed.

Panic started to take over as the irrational side of me began to toy with my thoughts. Would he shake my hand? Try to kiss my cheek? Tease me with his taunts like I had seen him doing to other girls in the past?

Ten more questions ran through my mind in that few minutes as I sat wringing my sweaty hands in my lap and playing with the emerald ring on my middle finger.

Those feelings turned from nerves to panic to dread. I had about forty eight hours in this guy's company to go yet. Butterflies in my stomach turned into crippling wasps that were crawling up and stinging my vocal chords, rendering me speechless, so I sat quietly anticipating the reaction of the guys who were forced to spend time with the prize winners.

It was almost ten in the evening and I was suddenly starving. I hadn't eaten since the plane because we were promised dinner, and the combination of hunger and nerves were making my insides sound like an old boiler gurgling. Either that or my anxieties had turned me into a 'fridge monster' wanting to eat to fill the void of anxious, empty feelings I was having.

When I heard footsteps, my instinct was to examine my hands. I figured if I did that, then I wouldn't have to look at the man who had consumed my thoughts for the past week, since I heard I would be facing him again.

Foolish to say, but I swear the air in the room became thick and I could hardly breathe. By a weird sixth sense, I knew he was there with me long before anyone spoke. Weirdly enough, the band's PA Charlotte... something or other, began to introduce us, and when I looked up it was straight into those amazing grey eyes of his.

If I hadn't known any better, I'd have said there was a look like he was either shocked or that he recognized me. I figured that it was shock, because surely he wouldn't remember me. Either that or he was thinking how the hell had I landed with this lot for a weekend?

Introductions were done by Charlotte, and then the other band members started to converse with us. Gibson stood quietly weighing us up, and his focus on me made me feel really uncomfortable. Offering myself some reassurance, I kept telling myself he was just interested in me because I was the winner.

Lennox, M3rCy's drummer, was a good guy. Sweet and gentle in his manner, he made me relax for the first time since I arrived at the center. Large frame, but not fat, he was a powerful build, with jet black hair and piercing blue eyes, and some amazing ink on his arms.

A few years older than Gibson, Lennox was a very handsome guy, with a warm smile and a gentle voice that was not at all fitting for the mad image of a drummer in a rock band. Aware that Gibson was completely still and staring straight at me, I became self-conscious, wondering if he was sizing me up as a possible post-gig fuck for the night, then and I thought he was going to be disappointed if he thought that of me.

Lennox seemed to notice and drew Gibson into the conversation. Gibson was his usual arrogant self. “Jeez, Len can’t a guy stare at a beautiful woman in peace?” Initially, I tried to stare him out but it didn’t work because I lost my nerve and was about to look away when he began to introduce himself to the group.

Gavin looked uncomfortable when Gibson mistook him for my boyfriend, and I was silently kicking myself that I hadn’t asked Gavin to pretend to be that for the duration of the trip, but I never expected the amount of scrutiny that Gibson was putting me under.

Almost as soon as he established what Gavin was, Gibson began to make his move on me, all charming and charismatic, giving me that charismatic smile that would have melted the panties off of the most frigid of women. He tried to seduce me, suck me in with his warm attention and flirtatious words until I was almost hypnotized.

Unexpectedly, he placed his arm around my shoulder and pulled me in for a hug, which freaked me out. It was the first time a man had done that since Kace, and he was Gibson Barclay.

My body stiffened and I felt myself holding my breath. When his arms held me tightly, the comfort I felt from his strong hug seemed so genuine, I just felt my body involuntarily sag into his warm chest. Gibson’s arms responded to me, by molding around me even more and pulling me tighter into his chest.

Briefly, he inhaled deeply and his chest expanded, pressing harder against mine. The deep draw of his breath was incredibly sensual, focusing on me so much that when he exhaled I was almost completely entranced.

His warm, slow, steady breath fanned across the curve of my neck, sending shivers down my spine while goose-bumps erupted on my skin. It made my pussy pulse and clench tightly with need. Just as I was becoming overwhelmed with the sensation of his embrace, he stepped away again.

Feelings of loss washed over me like a tidal wave and I choked a little, because I wondered if that was my moment with Gibson because I so wanted it again. If it was, I was sure all of my senses hadn't had time to tune in to what we did in that few seconds. Fighting conflicting emotions and trying to decide what that all meant was halted abruptly when he reached out and took my hand in his.

He gave me that beautiful wicked smile. I had never seen him look more attractive. "Hi, honey, congratulations on winning the competition. This is as nerve-racking for me as it is for you. I've never done this before either."

Smiling my first genuine smile, I was relieved at his honesty. It was a pretty weird situation to find myself in, and I was glad that we had that in common at the very least. In response to my smile, he squeezed my hand and his own smile grew even wider. "Let's just try and have a good time together, no pressure okay?"

Still smiling, I tried to meet his gaze with confidence but there was something in the way he looked at me that was too intimate, so I quickly dropped my head down and looked at the floor.

Feelings I knew I would have to fight if he came closer to me were rising fast, and there was no way I could allow myself to fall into the web he spun so well. I'd been unlucky to see that happen so many times in the past, and knew what it meant to him.

Seconds after I looked away, his index finger crooked under my jaw line and he teased my face up to meet his, bending slightly at the knees to look me in the eye. "Don't look at the floor. You have the most incredible eyes, I'd like to see them if that's okay."

Embarrassed by that level of attention I looked away, and almost frantically searched out Ruby to come to my rescue, but she was too involved with Mick Stanley to focus on me.

Luckily, Simon the bass player came over and took the heat out of the moment by chatting about the concert and how we were finding LA. Gibson seemed to take his leave and disappeared out the door altogether.

Relaxing the instant he was out of sight, I welcomed the pleasant conversation of the easy going bass player. Simon was a great looking guy, wiry build, fantastic tattoos, toned, tanned, muzzy hair, and a fabulous smile; M3rCy were a great looking band.

Simon's laugh was infectious and he was really

funny as well. There is just something about a guy who can make a girl laugh that had always been really appealing to me.

After about ten minutes, we'd fallen into easy conversation, but I felt Gibson's presence back in the room before I saw him. Simon broke eye contact to look past me and I just knew Gibson was approaching us again.

Simon seemed to dismiss himself quickly and I wondered how much of the last ten minutes was staged. Did Gibson arrange for Simon to keep me busy? If so, how did that happen?

"Alright, are you ready to get this party started, honey?" He smiled widely at me but I was still trying to figure out what the deal was with Simon and I guess I needed to put Gibson straight on a few things.

"Thank you for your hospitality for me and my friends, but I didn't enter a competition hoping to meet you. That was purely by default after buying a new phone with automatic competition entry."

Gibson managed to look completely unaffected by my admission. "Well, I guess you're not really a fan then, but we'll just have a good time anyway. What do you say?"

Pursing my lips, I knew that I had to warn him off because if I didn't and we got too comfortable goodness knows where I'd find myself with him. I could already feel the fight in me ebbing away in his presence. Breathing out deeply, I tried to keep my voice even and look him square in the eye. "Gibson, I know you don't remember me, but we've kind of met before. I just want to say a couple of things to you."

Looking around for somewhere that created some extra space between us, I sat on the chair by a small table.

"Firstly, I am indeed a fan of M3rCy, I have every album your band have made, but to be honest, I know what you are doing, trying to lure me away from the others. You may be used to women dropping their panties for you whenever you want them to. Please understand I am not a star struck teenager and that won't be happening with me."

Gibson gave me an enquiring look, as if he was surprised by something and a sullen expression took hold.

"Hmm, this is the second time today someone has decided what my intentions are and got it wrong. I really want you to enjoy yourself Chloe, so I'll clear the air. I, Gibson Barclay, am not going to fuck you, so you can relax." He was wagging his finger as he gesticulated at me with his arm and his jaw clenched.

"All I want to do is take you to dinner. Is that a problem for you?" Swallowing hard, there was nothing I could say to that. I felt embarrassed that I'd been stupid enough to presume that I'd be attractive enough for him to hit on. So I shook my head and apologized. "Sorry, that was wrong of me."

CHAPTER 21

EASY

Chloe

Scowling initially at my outburst, Gibson stood staring into my eyes as if challenging me to retort with some kind of clever come back after putting me firmly in my place. As soon as I conceded that I had been presumptuous, his face softened, visibly relaxing. The edges of his lips curved into a soft half smile.

"Shall we start again?" Gibson's eyebrow raised in question and he waited for me to respond. I wasn't being fair to him. He never asked for me to be here and the fact that I was and he was being gracious about taking the winner to dinner, made me feel stupid and judgmental. Trying to push the images of Gibson with all those girls aside, I accepted his valiant attempt at making peace between us, after my mini-rant about knowing him.

Exhaling slowly, I nodded. "I'd like that, I murmured softly. My reward was his wide roguish grin and another firm hug. This time it was brief, but as he drew back, the palms of his hands smoothed down my arms and I wished my jacket sleeves hadn't been in the way of that. As he reached my wrist his right hand wrapped around my left wrist and he held it possessively.

"Come on, let's go. We need to leave now if we're going to have dinner this side of midnight." His off-the-cuff remark went over my head. Everything that had happened from the moment we left The Staples Center until we got on the plane seemed surreal.

One thing really surprised me during the journey to the airport – no flashy limousine. Instead there was an inconspicuous black Chrysler Grand Voyager SUV. Still a big car, but a lot of larger families have those.

Turning behind him, he pulled out a bottle of ice cold champagne and a glass. "For you."

Already corked, he gestured for me to hold the glass and poured it half full with the golden liquid. I watched the bubbles dance in the crystal glass. He twisted his body and reached back behind him. My eyes followed his movements as he replaced the bottle in a silver ice-bucket attached to a built in stand on the floor.

"Are you not having any?" Gibson glanced up at me as he straightened back in his seat, and smiled ruefully.

"No. No alcohol for me today, Chloe. Especially… not today." Puzzled by that response, I wanted to ask why especially not today? Suddenly feeling self-conscious, I figured it must be because he was with me.

What had that meant? He already knew he wasn't going to enjoy our dinner? Of course… he was on duty. This wasn't two people going to dinner, for Gibson it was just another job.

"Tell me something about yourself." God, the way he said it made me think of Paul. He'd asked me that once. And their voices; although not quite the same had the same intonation and pitch. They had the same rich, deep timbre and seductive, slow southern accents.

Thinking of Paul, I blushed and felt a pang of loss that we'd ruined our little daily chats by doing that stupid phone sex thing.

"Not much to tell, really." *Where did I start with someone like him?* Making small talk with someone who oozed sex appeal, was stunning to look at, and had a beguiling way with them wasn't something I was adept at.

Besides, what could I tell him? While you've been off making millions and fucking your way around the world, I was practically kept hostage and beaten in my own home by a man that I thought loved me?

Gibson smirked as if he was humoring me. "Okayyyy, no small talk for now then." Sliding right down in his seat, he folded his arms and closed his eyes, letting his head fall back. "You won't mind if I catch ten minutes' nap then, until we get to where we are going."

Disbelief rocked me. Not that I really expected that much of him, but how rude of him to dismiss me like that and go to sleep when I was sitting right there with him. *Fuck you, Gibson Barclay.*

Staring out the window as the city gave way to scrubland and eventually plunged into darkness as the street lighting ran out, I found myself looking at his reflection in the window. Face completely relaxed and peaceful, lips slightly parted, his long dark eyelashes fanning across the top of his cheek bones and just enough stubble on his chin to hint at the sinful man I knew he was.

Captivated by his features and the incredible magnetism, I turned to face him. Even when Gibson was asleep, he had a presence I'd never experienced with any other person. I couldn't have dragged my eyes away from him for anything.

Allowing my eyes to roam over his body, I could see his solid frame and muscular arms, even though he was covered completely by a black and white checkered shirt. Beautiful strong hands led me to indulge in the memory of his hugs earlier. When he tugged at my wrist earlier, that possessive grip had sent shivers across my body.

Gibson stirred and I jumped in fright like a child would do at being caught with their hand in the cookie jar. Turning my head away quickly again I looked back out the window. Seeing him open his eyes and straighten, I kept my eyes trained on the window.

As I watched I saw him peruse me. His tongue leisurely rounded his lips, making me shiver again at the sight of him doing something so teasing.

"Are you cold?" Gibson noticed and leaned over to produce a small green chenille throw from the back seat.

Shaking my head, I put my hand up to stop him. "No, I'm fine." Shrugging, he tossed it over his shoulder into the back of the car.

"Sorry about that. When I've been on stage I get a huge burst of energy afterwards. If it has nowhere to go, it kind of knocks me out and I have to sleep to recover. Usually, I manage it well but I guess today it caught up with me."

Weird, how he could be so natural around me and able to fall asleep like that... like he was completely comfortable in my presence. There was no way I could ever have fallen asleep around Gibson Barclay – that was for sure.

Leaving the car, Gibson put his hand out to help me down from the SUV. Accepting, I never expected that he would continue to hold it and lead me up the steps of his plane.

"Umm, what's happening? You never said anything about getting on an airplane." Turning to look over his shoulder, his eyes met mine and there was a humorous twinkle of mischief in them.

"Do you want to eat today or not? Because if so we need to take this or it will be too late." Confused, I let him lead me up the steps and into the small cabin of the plane. Large plush leather seats with round padded armrests, grey carpeting and a large sofa with lap restraints were visible immediately.

Sitting down, I noticed that there were a series of buttons on a panel on each chair, which housed a video system and iPads that turned into TV screens. Amongst the various sound and lighting operations, there were controls for the massage facilities, Skype and cell phone charging docks.

Gibson sat facing me, his face hard to read, until he asked me if I was afraid of flying. I wasn't but it was my turn to feel exhausted, planes always seemed to have that effect on me, and I sat back in my chair. "No, but I'm tired."

Gibson looked solemnly at me, and I thought he thought I was one of those nerdy girls that went to bed at 10:00 pm. "God, I'm sorry... it's half past one in the morning for you, isn't it?" Taken aback that he would even know that, I was even more surprised at the genuine concern in his voice.

Raising my eyebrow, I couldn't help but smile in reassurance at him. "It is, but I'm okay. Planes have this effect on me for some reason."

Nodding his head in understanding, he smirked knowingly. "And cars have the same effect on me." Grinning at each other, I realized I actually had something in common with Gibson Barclay. Go figure.

Forgetting myself for a moment, I asked, "Clever of you to remember the time difference we have, your PA briefs you very well, Gibson." I don't know what I said wrong, but his wide smile dropped the moment I'd said it, and his tongue started to play along his top teeth at the side, as if he was hiding something. When he did that, I noticed for the first time that he had a piercing almost in the center of his tongue.

Wondering why I hadn't noticed that before, I figured either it was new, or I had been too shy or too drawn by him to stare for long enough to notice because the pull I felt toward him was so strong. His cabin crew came over to say we would be taking off shortly, and Gibson's cell rang.

Answering it, he unclipped himself, saying he had to take the call and moved to another seat further down the plane for privacy. Once again, I felt I was being put in my place, and knew there would be constant reminders that I was nothing more than a prize winner.

Slumping down into the seat, I closed my eyes and drifted off to sleep. Dull humming began to break into my consciousness and my eyes fluttered open. Gibson was back in his seat and staring intently at me. He had been watching me sleep and that fact embarrassed me. *Had I been drooling, was my mouth gaping? Did I look a mess?*

Slowly his lips curved up at the corners and his eyes became brighter as a smile played on his lips. "Well Chloe, this is a night to remember for sure. We've slept with each other and it has all been totally appropriate."

Gibson's past and his reputation flashed in my mind but I pushed it back and grinned because I really could see the funny side of that after my rant at him earlier. "We'll be touching down in about ten minutes. I'm starving now and I hope you are hungry too. I should have asked, is French food okay with you?"

French food was my first choice if I was going out, Chinese for takeout. "Sounds great, I could eat a horse, I'm so hungry." Gibson frowned and stroked his lips with his thumb and forefinger, pulling his bottom lip out slightly.

"Hmm, not sure if they do horse at that particular restaurant, or bourguignon sauce, you want me to ring ahead and see if they can get some for you?" At first I was going to argue that I had been joking with him and that it was just a figure of speech, but he started laughing at me and I instantly relaxed.

"Very funny. You are such a tease, Gibson."

Gibson's response was instinctive and honest. "Of course I am, it's my second occupation, in fact sometimes it's hard to know what I am more famous for, teasing women or being a singer in a band."

A quiet fell between us as he held my gaze a moment too long and I looked away. When I looked back, he looked pissed about something again. I remember thinking, he was hot and cold. Intense one minute and a flippant couldn't-care-less attitude the next. The fluctuating changes in Gibson's moods were way too complex and sophisticated for me to deal with.

Five minutes of silence made me want to

scream, the uncomfortable quiet gnawing away at the both of us. Gibson had stirred restlessly in his seat several times and made eye contact with me, always appearing as if he was going to say something, but then exhaled and shook his head again.

Picking at my jacket, I felt compelled to say something. "I really didn't mean to offend you when I said that you were a tease. I was just saying..."

Gibson's head snapped up, his eyebrow raised "No? You weren't? And if not you'd be the first, and that wasn't what you said in your school ma'am voice earlier either. I know what people think... and yeah, I suppose it's my own fault, but fuck, can't a guy grow up without having a legacy that follows him like a fucking cancer when he's just trying to have a normal day?"

Strange, but I never thought I'd see the day when I'd feel pity for Gibson, but suddenly I had. Although, from what I knew of him before, it could have been part of his game plan. Previously, he wasn't beyond using pity as a way of flirting with girls, and it had paid dividends.

Unsure of what to say, I stared back at his beautiful but angry face, wondering if I should continue with this whole thing. However, I was sitting at God knows how many feet high in his jet, and I had no clue where I even was. Once I thought about that, I had to fight the panic again that I was being controlled by a guy who would do whatever he wanted to get his own way.

Three muffled dings on a bell broke the silence and the stewardess appeared and strapped herself into a drop down seat right at the front of the plane. Elegant and leggy, she crossed and uncrossed her legs, puffing her chest and pulling her jacket down, all flirtatious and all the while smiling at Gibson, who glanced over and gave her a bright smile.

She then turned her attention to me, eyeing me from head to toe. She met my glance and gave me a sarcastic looking sneer.

"I know what you're thinking, I'm not fucking him so you can stop thinking that I'm his next easy lay you hear me?" Reacting badly and I shocked myself with my outburst. I had felt embarrassed that she might think that was why I was with Gibson.

After the way Kace had made me feel about myself I felt sure that she would think that's why I was with him. Gibson looked at the stewardess and scowled. "Enough of the attitude, Laney. Who the fuck do you think you are?"

Laney's facial expression changed immediately to one of worry, knowing that she'd overstepped her position. Gibson turned to me and I'm sure he saw how angry I was, but I guess he wasn't used to women rejecting him. He reacted to the way I was looking at him by laughing.

"What? What are you laughing at?" Folding my arms across my chest, I continued, "I'm glad you think it's funny, because I definitely don't."

Throwing me a knowing smirk, Gibson ran his hands through his hair and looked first at me, then at the stewardess before giving her his full attention. "She's right Laney, I'm definitely not fucking her." Gibson's tone sounded harsh.

Just like that, Gibson Barclay had humiliated me for the third time in my life. And this time I couldn't run and hide.

CHAPTER 22

TRUCE

Chloe

Bristling in my seat like my pants were on fire, I really didn't care how I was getting home. I had already decided I was getting away from him as soon the plane touched down. Gibson may have been able to do whatever he wanted with most women, but I was not 'most women.'

Thinking we couldn't have gone far, because it had only been forty minutes since we'd taken off, I thought it couldn't be that difficult to get back to Ruby and the others at the hotel.

When I realized I only had my driver's license and virtually no cash with me, I felt gutted that I had let my guard down and left myself in such a vulnerable position. What was I thinking going with him into the unknown like a lamb to the slaughter? I decided I was going to ring Ruby when I got to the airport, and ask her to hire a car to come get me.

Closing my eyes, I could feel my ears popping

and stomach lurch with the plane's descent and my stomach was already feeling acidic from the lack of food. The exchange between Gibson and the cabin crew girl made me feel so... jealous? And I wondered if Gibson had been with her before. Stupid really, of course he had. That hadn't mattered because he had humiliated me by putting me down and that had made me feel stupid.

Swallowing hard, I fought back the feeling of being inadequate to Gibson. Mainly because of the way that Kace had conditioned me and how he made me feel so undesirable over the past year. My gut twisted and the threat of tears choked me, making my throat close. I struggled following that to keep my composure.

Still sitting with my eyes closed when the plane landed, I wished that he would just leave and I could save face and slip away quietly. Reality told me that was definitely not an option, but I had managed to get my feelings in check before I opened my eyes and was relieved to see that the stewardess had gone.

Gibson was still sitting with one leg crossed with his ankle resting on his knee, his face with a grim expression on it. His elbow was resting on the plane window, and his head resting in his hand. The lap belt buckle was undone and the arm rest nearest the aisle was pushed up.

Before he could speak, I got in first. "Don't say a word. Just tell me how to get home. I think you've done your job and I don't want to be here anymore than you want me to be, so let us stop the pretense and just let me go home. All I need is to call Ruby to come and get me or someone can drop me at a bus station and I'll make my way back. Where the hell am I anyway?"

Sounding much more assertive than I felt, I tried to stare at him, but I lost my nerve and turned away from him to look at the window on the opposite side of the plane. Inside my body was trembling and I had to dig so deep to suppress the panic that was rising inside me.

Gibson dropped his knee and pushed himself up straight in the leather seat. Leaning forward he placed his elbows on his knees and his hands together between his open knees. Lifting my head, I was met with his face close to mine, staring intensely, his eyes searched my face.

"Fuck, Chloe, that came out wrong, but I could see how upset you were so I wasn't going to take it back while you were starting to get emotional about it. I figured you wouldn't believe me and I'd just succeed in hurting you more."

Pursing my lips, it was a good argument but he was always so plausible when he wanted to win people over. Gibson obviously didn't know just *how* much I knew about him. My confidence was growing more the angrier I got at him.

"Seriously? You expect me to believe that crock of shit? I saw that smirk and the venom you used to put me down in front of that Barbie doll of a woman."

Suddenly he began to laugh loudly at me, and I

lashed out angry that he was so insensitive, but my seatbelt held me firmly in my seat. Fumbling with the buckle, I eventually managed to break free from my chair and lurched forward at him, fists clenched.

Gibson's reactions were like lightening and he grabbed both of my wrists, pulling me onto his lap. "Whoa! STOP. What are you doing? Where is this violence coming from?" Strong arms engulfed me and held me firmly on his lap.

Stopping instantly, I was ashamed that I had lashed out, but his behavior was reminiscent of how Kace had made me feel sometimes. Whenever I had expressed a concern or needed reassurance, he would do something just like that to keep me off kilter.

As soon as I stopped struggling, I expected Gibson to relax his hold on me. Instead, he held me firmly and all at once it felt comforting. There was no way I could hold back after that. A sob caught in my throat as I began to cry. Of all the things I expected to happen at that point, what Gibson did was the last thing I'd have expected from someone like him.

Shifting me slightly on his lap, he cradled me in his arms and began to rock me back and forth. Dipping his head to mine, he brushed my hair tenderly from my temple and kissed it gently. It wasn't a sexual kiss but one of comfort. "Chloe, you don't need to do anything honey. Take all the time you need. I'm here. I got you."

Normally if Gibson, or any guy like him, had said something like that to me, I'd have run a mile, wondering what 'I got you, darlin'' entailed, but the feeling he gave me was one that I hadn't felt before, even in the early days with Kace. Safe.

Wrapped in his arms, his soothing embrace cocooned me and an emotion I had been missing began to surface. Shaking my head, I tried to sit up because it was a feeling of trust, and at that point I had almost forgotten what Gibson was all about. Clever, how he was just exactly what I needed, yet the whole sorry episode had started because of his horrible words.

Initially, he was reluctant to let me move, then I felt him relax his grip and I moved off his lap. Before there was any awkward exchange, Gibson stood up and hugged me close to his chest again. My cheek landed between his strong pectoral muscles, right over his heart. There was no way I could ever explain how I felt when I stood there listening to his strong, steady heartbeat.

Overwhelming emotions washed over me, my senses becoming aware of just how amazing Gibson was, physically. His touch, when his hand splayed on the small of my back, was exquisite, softly; yet firmly caressing it with just the right amount of pressure to make me feel safe. The faint scent of body wash and his manly scent was an addictive combination. Gibson's body was attacking my hormones, giving me a mixture of emotions to deal with. Setting alarm bells off and inciting intense feelings of lust.

Feelings that were vaguely familiar; I had experienced only once before, when I had shared myself with Paul on the phone the night when he had been drinking. I could feel the heat rise to my cheeks, recalling the most intimate parts of that call as I thought about Paul but being touched by Gibson.

After a short while Gibson started to talk and his low timbre rumbled in his chest, vibrating against my cheek. "You okay? I want to take you for some food. You must be starving, honey."

Pushing me at arms-length and stepping back to look at me, he made eye contact and we were locked in a moment, each of us unable to tear our eyes off the other until I lost my nerve and looked down at his chest.

"And while we're here I want to clear the air again. The reason I sounded so pissed about what I said to Laney? It wasn't because I didn't want to do that to you. I was pissed because there was nothing I wanted more, than to be with you that way."

Dropping his hands from me altogether, he smiled softly. "Sorry, I know that's probably the last thing you wanted to hear or expected me to admit to. I'm a lot of things Chloe, and there is a lot that is written about me that isn't strictly true, but... I am an honest man. Sometimes that honesty pisses people off. And the reason I was laughing was because of the Barbie doll comment. You wouldn't know about this but my best buddy Toby calls her that as well."

I wasn't sure that I believed him but I was smart enough to figure that it was better to be on speaking terms until I got back to the others, so I gave him a half smile.

"Truce?" Gibson gave me a small smile, his concerned eyes searching my face for approval. When I nodded, I saw his shoulders drop in relief and his smile stretched wider. "Good girl. Let's go get some food, I'm hungry."

Leaving the aircraft, a dark grey metallic Mercedes was sitting on the tarmac, with no driver. "You're driving?" Everything he did threw me. Maybe I had been reading too many rock star gossip columns, but the way Gibson's team had handled his travel arrangements, how he lived and all the other stuff, made me wonder what other surprises I was going to come across.

Smirking knowingly, Gibson walked over and opened the passenger door. "I am. Is there a problem with that?" Looking around I wondered where everyone else had gone. We were the only ones out there. Gesturing at the plane with the door flap steps still down, I asked, "Aren't you going to lock that?" Gibson chuckled mischievously and shook his head.

Puzzled, I slipped into the passenger seat and he closed the door softly once I was in. Wandering around to his side, he opened the door and connected a call he made on his cell at the same time. "She's all yours, dude."

Hitting the call end button Gibson turned and looked at me, then crooked his fore and middle fingers under my chin, raising my head so that my eyes met his again. "The guy with the keys to the bird," he said, gesturing at the cell sitting in the cradle on the dashboard. Exhaling heavily, Gibson gave me a slow smile. "I promised you dinner. I hope you have a big appetite, because I'm ready to eat the table as well as the food on it."

Part of me was scared to be in the car with him, partially in terms of my proximity to him, but mainly because of the feelings he was bringing out in me. The Gibson Barclay I remembered did everything with an extreme attitude. So it wasn't surprising that I was nervous sitting next to him when he was behind the wheel of a powerful machine.

After about mile, I had to take my prejudged idea about his driving back. Gibson was extremely attentive to the roads and drove at a steady forty miles per hour. "Do you mind some music?" When he asked that, I really welcomed those words because the silence between us was becoming awkward and I was racking my brain for something to say.

Tuning in to a station, "Superheroes" by The Script was playing. The song was about people going through hard times and learning to deal with that, and it was completely right for me, but looking at Gibson, I had no idea if he even knew what a hard time was.

I pulled out my cell to text Ruby to tell her where I was, but I'd used up the battery taking pictures at the concert and it was now flat. I considered asking Gibson to use his, but I remembered that I didn't know Ruby's cell off by heart.

Seeing the road sign for Carmel-By-The-Sea, I

realized we were about three hours from LA by car. There was no way I could ask Ruby to drive that far anyway and I doubted there would be any buses at this time of night back to LA, so I resigned myself to making the most of dinner and getting the hell out of LA as soon as we got back.

"If the directions are correct, we should be there in five minutes." Gibson's head turned briefly to address me, and then turned back to the road. I had naturally turned my head to look at him. I continued to watch him even after he looked back at the road.

"What are you thinking, Chloe?" Gibson's head turned giving me brief eye contact then looked ahead again.

Biting my lip, I just said exactly what I was thinking. "You look incredible." Once I had said it, I blushed. "I mean, you are a good looking man."

Before I could say anything else, we'd pulled by the sidewalk outside a quirky, cute looking restaurant. All of the outside tables were empty. Soft yellow lighting glowed on the rustic looking restaurant front, making it look idyllic. Old weathered bench seating and flagstone flooring with wrought iron ornamental lamp lights and arched paneled windows gave it curb-side appeal.

The heavily weathered wooden door was a truly welcome sight to us as hungry travelers, but my feelings of anticipation were back and I wondered if we were going to be told we were too late for dinner.

Inside the door there was a polished wooden

desk with a smartly dressed female maître d'. Smiling, she addressed Gibson in a seductive tone with a thick French accent. "Ah, Monsieur Barclay, you arrive! Welcome! We are so 'appy to 'ave you 'ere. Please come an' sit. Wine, yes? Your food ezz prepared already."

Walking in front of us with her catwalk posture and slender long lines, it was difficult to see how I could be remotely appealing when someone like her was around. She was the whole package. Her accent was sexy as hell and she looked so sophisticated and chic. Once I had made the mistake of comparing her to how I viewed myself, I felt myself shrink in her presence.

Confused at what was happening, I slowly sat down on the chair Gibson pulled out for me, taking in all my surroundings as I did, falling in love with the gorgeous scene of this very intimate restaurant. Fairytale rope lighting was wrapped around pillars and there was a massive wooden trellis with ivy and grape vines growing up it in various places.

At the center of the outside area there was a huge tree, again covered in the string lighting. Between the twinkling lights, Gibson's presence and the aroma of herbs and spices, I felt like I had walked into paradise.

"Pierre will be your waiter for z'night. Please let 'im know what you desire and we will do our best to make your eating experience with us memorable." Turning on her heel, she sashayed away in the direction of the desk again.

Briefly watching her walk away, I turned to look across the table at Gibson once she was in her seat again. Serious grey eyes met mine and Gibson ran his tongue over his bottom lip. "Are you okay now? Are we okay now?"

Apart from his brief sleep and his outburst on the plane to 'Barbie,' he had actually been great. No, he'd been amazing, and really, I had to accept some responsibility for his temper in regards to what he said. I had been less than kind back at the venue.

Putting everything into perspective, I'd won a competition. Who was I to go laying the law down at him like that without just cause? He'd never asked me for anything.

"Sure, I'm happy to start again, if you are." My response was rewarded with his sinfully sexy smile. It made my heart flutter and melt. I'd seen Gibson smile many times, but there was something about that particular one that made him look genuinely happy.

CHAPTER 23

UNWELCOME FEELINGS

Chloe

Dinner was beautiful. The setting, the food, the wine… the man. All perfect, except for the way Gibson looked at me sometimes. From looking like he wasn't into me or my type, to focusing intensely on me.

Everything that had happened in my life during the past six weeks seemed so unbelievable. Being beaten badly by Kace, my inheritance, running away to a new life and the wrong phone calls from a guy named Paul.

The most ridiculous and incomprehensible thing of all that happened to me; winning a competition that led me to be sitting across the table having dinner with Gibson Barclay. There was my fantasy guy who was larger than life, stunningly handsome and smiling at me… it was all just so insane.

There were times during the meal when he unnerved me, and times when I could almost forget his past. Those charming and charismatic skills of his were out in force with me in that romantic setting. Gibson had said he wasn't drinking but relented with the French red wine. Two and a half bottles of wine later between us and I was more than a little woozy.

Finishing the last mouthful on his plate, he placed his knife and fork neatly on his plate as he licked his lips, hummed sexily and sat back in his seat with his hand over his abdomen. The guy even managed to make appreciating his food look and sound deeply erotic. Just watching him made me have thoughts that had no business in my mind in regards to what I would do to him.

Sitting back casually, Gibson raised his glass to his mouth and he was definitely checking me out over the rim of it. Hooded, dark eyes ticked over my body and I couldn't help but feel as if he were sizing me up as dessert. Occasionally, as he perused me, he would lick his lips and at one point he dragged his tongue piercing past his top front teeth.

"Why did you do that to your tongue?" It seemed strange that a singer would do something which could affect their speech or the way they sang.

Gibson sat looking completely relaxed, but bit his lip as he thought about how to answer. During that time he never broke eye contact with me. After a couple of minutes, he gave me a knowing smirk. "It's a way of expressing myself… and for both mine and my woman's gratification… that is when I'm having sex with someone.

Thinking he was saying it to shock and

embarrass me, I tried not to react but felt myself stiffen slightly and in my effort to cover this up, threw another question. "How so?" As soon as I said it I chided myself, annoyed that he'd thrown me some bait and how quickly I had taken it.

"Maybe I should show you sometime, it's kinda hard to explain." Juice suddenly soaked my panties at Gibson Barclay suggesting he should go down on me. His eye contact was heated as he looked directly at me while a small smile curved his lips. I'd wanted to sigh but I choked it back determined not to be seduced by him.

"I know when I've had oral from a girl with one, it's an awesome feeling. That little change in texture when I'm being sucked off feels off-the-charts hot." Smirking, I could see he was biting back a grin and I felt my cheeks burn. I could have kicked myself because as brave as I was trying to be, I couldn't bring myself to hold his gaze.

Why the hell had I asked him that? Why didn't I know about piercings? I'd never been around people with tattoos and piercings – except for the two bands I'd known. The one that Ruby's ex was in and M3rCy.

Feeling pretty stupid I had set myself up like that, I was lost for words. Really, I just wanted a time machine or a time portal or whatever to appear in the restaurant that I could step into. I wondered how I would have been able to act normally around him from that point.

"Oh," was all I could manage in reply to his explicit explanation. What else could I have said? So I sat twirling my wine glass by the stem between my fingers, suddenly fascinated by the red wine licking around the curve of the glass like tiny red waves.

When I had recovered my composure enough to look back at him, Gibson gave me a soft smile and leaned forward in his seat. Reaching over, he took my hand in his and held my nervous gaze. His eyes were sympathetic and he bit his bottom lip.

"Seriously Chloe, I'm sorry. I can see by your reaction it was a genuine question. I called it wrong. When you asked me that, I thought it was an opening for something. I am so used to people wanting to talk sex and flirting suggestively with me. Asking me intimate questions like that. Honestly? It isn't often I find someone who is asking because they care about me and want to know Gibson Barclay the guy, and not Gibson the possession."

Squeezing my hand gently, he continued to hold it as he began to explain to me why he had them and what they meant for him. "My piercings are hidden. I love piercings and ink, but in moderation. They are an extension of me, imperfect and wounded. They are my way of controlling something in my world. So much in my life is controlled by other people who try to tell me what to say, what to wear and who to speak to. That gets fucking tiring after a while. My tongue piercing was done a long time ago and although it's not advisable to take it out, I don't wear it when I'm working. Usually, it's saved for my private time and I put it straight back after a gig. My other one, well... let's just say that doesn't come out and it was also an intimate decision."

Puzzled, I wondered where the other piercing was. Gibson began to laugh, "Your face is a picture." Laughing louder and heartily at me, he lifted his hand from mine and held my chin, his thumb brushing my cheek. "Chloe, you are my breath of fresh air. Innocent but not, feisty but not, challenging but not, very contradictory and very, very intriguing."

Unnerved by his sudden scrutiny, I bit my lip. My heart was beating so fast it made me light headed and I wasn't sure what all of that meant exactly until it fluttered in my chest. I inhaled heavily trying to get it under control. Most women would have fainted at his feet if he had given them the look that he'd given me at that moment. But, in the back of my mind, was Gibson with all those girls.

All I asked was why a tongue piercing, but as soon as he made that intimate move, his smile dropped and his gaze became intense. Those smoky grey eyes became hooded and lust filled and Gibson's eyes dropped to my lips.

For a moment I thought he was going to kiss me, and in that split second I had made my mind up that if he did, I was going to let it happen.

One kiss. Who would have blamed me? More would think I had been crazy to pass up the opportunity to kiss him. And, there was a table between us so it wouldn't have been able to get too out of hand.

Swallowing hard, I tried with everything I had in me to find the courage to keep my eyes trained on his, but the longer he looked at me, the more I melted. Feeling horny as hell and frustrated that he hadn't kissed me, my confidence waned.

Part of me thought I obviously wasn't attractive to him; the Gibson Barclay I knew had always taken what he wanted. So the more I thought about it, the less confident I became, until once again I averted my eyes.

Gibson let out a long shuddery breath and let go of my hands. Placing his palms on the table, he pushed himself out of the seat and stood up. Walking behind my chair, he placed his hands on the back rest and bent down close to my ear. His closeness made my body hum in anticipation of what he would do next.

"Come on Chloe, we need air." As I began to stand he drew the chair back from me and waited for me to step clear.

Inclining his head and smiling at the maître d' he opened the door and held it for me to walk through. When I hesitated, he smiled softly, "I told you already Chloe, I don't bite." Smirking, he winked at me playfully.

Once outside, I expected to go back to the plane, although, I had already decided I wasn't getting in a car with him after the amount of alcohol he'd drunk.

Preparing to have another stand off about how we were getting back to the airport, Gibson caught my wrist and pulled me gently toward him, holding me close, but not intimately. His face was serious. "Chloe, I've had too much to drink darlin', I can't drive back."

Gibson had said that I was contrary, but my expectations of him were constantly being challenged. There was a maturity in him that I never expected and part of me was wondering if it was because I really wanted to see good things in him.

If so, maybe that was because he had awakened feelings in me, that I thought weren't possible without a high level of trust. Especially after what I had gone through with Kace.

Suddenly Gibson slung his arm around my shoulder, his fingers skimming over my bare arm and sparking a shiver of pleasure that ran down my spine. Leading me forward with the pressure of his hip, he headed in the direction of his car.

"Are we sleeping in the car?" My voice sounded more highly pitched than I wanted it to. Stopping abruptly, Gibson leaned back to look at my face and I turned my body toward him. Grinning wickedly he raised an eyebrow, "Well, I suppose we could, I had my money on the beach, but the car works just as well, although it is a little too exposed here."

Shaking my head, I turned my body away and tried to free myself of his hold, but he stood firm. "I'm not sleeping with you, Gibson." After everything I had said, the argument on the plane in particular, he seemed to be back to that again.

Gibson frowned at me and his jaw twitched in annoyance. "Well fuck Chloe, you can stay awake all night if you want, but I need some rest. One of us was working earlier and it's..." Gibson squinted at his platinum Rolex, "fucking one-thirty in the morning."

Looking over at the car, then back at me, his mouth made a silent 'O'.

"Jeez, Chloe. God, no. I didn't mean we were having sex in the car. What I meant was, if I fell asleep in there, someone might recognize me. I'm much less likely to be discovered lying asleep on the beach than I would in a car by the sidewalk.

"Come on, we're going to the beach." Walking over to the car, he pressed the car fob and the trunk sprung open. Gibson leaned in and busied himself moving stuff around, before pulling out a rucksack, a sun shield and a blanket. Turning to look at me, it would have been difficult for him to miss my raised eyebrow.

"You're thinking that I do this all the time aren't you?" I must admit I was thinking how would someone know exactly what to put in the trunk of a hired car for him? When I didn't respond he smirked and shook his head. "Damn that low opinion, and you have it all wrong." Without waiting for him to say anything else, I responded.

"Only from what I've seen and know of you, Gibson. You may not remember me, but I certainly remember how you operate." I was feeling tired, and I really didn't want to have any more confrontations with him, but I wasn't going to pussyfoot around what I knew about him.

"Alright Ms. Fucking Marple. What the fuck am I doing with a backpack, a sun shield and a blanket?" Putting his hand up to stop me from replying he continued, "Don't. We'll be here all fucking night. I'll let you in on the scoop. This backpack contains a bottle of wine and some chips. Two bottles of water. A toothbrush and paste, a spare cell battery and phone, a battery operated razor, a flashlight, passport, driving license, a roll of dollars, credit card, a cap and a long sleeved t-shirt."

Gibson pushed the fob again and began to walk across the road with the contents before the trunk had closed, leaving me to scurry after him. Spinning around he made eye contact again, his eyes blazing with his fiery temper.

"Don't, I'll answer why as well. That *was* your next question wasn't it? I have all this shit around because I am Gibson fucking Barclay and I am not anonymous. This is an emergency kit packed in such a way that it helps me to slip away from the media. As I have used it to do on several occasions. There are a lot of perks to being me, but there are a lot of risks as well. So, what you think you know –from when you *thought* you knew me; to what you *actually* know about me, isn't worth shit, understand?"

Looking extremely disheartened and suddenly weary, he turned and threw over his shoulder, "Do what you want, I'm getting my head down, I've had enough of being polite and having everything I do and say analyzed by you for one day."

Gibson began striding along the sidewalk away from me, and I realized he was hurt. Setting off after him, I was about four paces behind him; half walking, half running trying to keep up with him. Still a little unfocused and heady from the wine, my reactions were slower than usual.

Reaching the beach, I saw the first of Gibson's 'bag contents.' A small, but powerful torch lit our way over to a secluded rock formation. Gibson pulled out the sun shelter and popped it up, then lay the blanket down inside. Tying the torch to one of the straps, he then had his hands free to delve into the backpack.

Incredible really, what was inside of it, all vacuum packed to save space, the t-shirt and cap were minute in the packaging. Everything else had been packed with precision. Taking the wine out, Gibson kicked off his shoes and sat barefooted on the blanket. Standing helpless and awkward at the edge of the sun shelter, I waited for him to speak.

"Come here, sit," he commanded, patting the blanket beside him. I was too tired to argue any further, so I did. Gibson handed me a plastic beaker and poured red wine into it. "Drink it. It will help you sleep. We'll be fine here. It's a warm night and the soft sand here tells me the tide will come nowhere near us."

Feeling altogether too close to Gibson, I sipped at the wine a little too quickly and before I knew it, I had drained the beaker. Gibson finished the bottle by emptying the rest of the wine equally, then reached up and turned off the torch.

We weren't fortunate enough to have a full moon, but what we did have was an amazing view of the stars. Gibson lay down on one side, perched on his elbow facing me. I could make out his outline in the dark but little else. "I remember you, Chloe."

I had just closed my eyes for a second and for some reason thought I might have dreamed that Gibson had said that. Either that or that he had said something else, and I heard what I wanted to hear. When I recapped and convinced myself he had, I wondered if he thought he had slept with me previously and I was angry about that.

"You didn't hook up with me when I was at college, Gibson, you can relax." I sat up long enough to drain the wine from my glass and lay down again. My nerves were becoming an issue in the dark beside him and I sounded bitter.

Gibson snickered, then reached out and stroked down my forearm. "I know, I would definitely have remembered if I had. Are you going to sit at a ninety degree angle all night or are you going to lie down beside me?"

How many women had dreamed Gibson Barclay would ask them that? Not sure if it was the wine or my inner conscience tempting me, or if I wanted that one fantasy night with him, but whatever it was, I lay down flat on my back beside him.

As soon as I did, Gibson shuffled his body nearer to mine. Feeling his hot breath on my neck and the smell of the red wine on his breath gave me feelings that had my body buzzing with excitement.

Between the effects of the wine, his presence, his touch and my lack of vision in the dark, lying there next to him like that was highly intoxicating.

"Are you drunk enough to kiss me Chloe?" Gibson's seductive tone whispered close to my ear, sending shivers down my spine and a rash of goose bumps across my whole body, putting my hormones on full alert.

Honestly? I was absolutely desperate to kiss him. Half of me couldn't believe I was there with him and half hadn't wanted to be for fear of doing something with him I knew I'd regret later.

Gibson's hand reached out in the dark and he stroked my hair. "Chloe this isn't the wine that's making me react to you like this." Warned by observing many of my friends in similar situations previously, when a guy had been drinking and said that, I would have guessed it was the wine.

"You are the most beautiful girl I have ever seen." And there he was spinning me a line. Thinking what he really had meant was, suddenly I was the flavor of the month; in the absence of any other females on the beach in Carmel-By-The-Sea, at what must have been two in the morning by that time.

Determined not to be intimidated by that, I felt as if I may as well go into this with my eyes open and not be fooled by his charming ways, but I had still shocked myself when I closed the space between us and kissed him tentatively on his closed mouth.

It was supposed to be a peck on the lips and nothing more, but within a couple of seconds, Gibson responded and had pinned me to the blanket by the wrists with my hands above my head.

With the swiftness of his action and his face inches from mine, my heart had leapt from an excited beat to racing beats that thudded wildly in my chest, making my body tremble at the effect. He had aroused me instantly with the possessive hold he had on me. My reaction was more intense than any foreplay Kace and I had ever had. And strangely, I wasn't afraid of Gibson at all. I felt a stirring, a need deep inside me and some pretty strong, passionate feelings which were threatening to rise to the surface.

Gibson's upper body was across mine and he was taking his weight on his elbows, but his presence was all around me and it felt powerful and assertive.

"Thank you. You have no idea how long I've waited for you to do that. Now that you've plucked up the courage to kiss me, Chloe, I'm going to kiss you back."

CHAPTER 24

COMPASSION

Chloe

Words hung in the air between us that stopped my heart beating. Catching my breath, I gasped for air. Gibson thought he was leaning too heavily on me and adjusted himself slightly. One hand left my wrist, and he moved it towards his other hand where he then took both of my wrists in one hand still above my head.

"Am I turning you on, Chloe? I think you like it when I pin you down. When I take charge. Do you want to know what else I can do that you will like?"

My first thought had been, HELL, YES! My second, Fuck, no. My third, what magic trick did he have up his sleeve? The girls I had always seen him with seemed to be doing things to him. Apart from when he was sticking it to them that is. Was I scared? You bet, but the worst had already happened to me with Kace and with Gibson it was raw passion not malice.

"Be brave, Chloe. Tell me what you like. What turns you on?" Staring up at the black silhouette, his outline was visible but devoid of any visible features. I briefly thought he could be anyone. Then smirked in the dark because I thought there was no one I knew like Gibson, so even in the dark, he became visible, even if it was only in my mind's eye.

Swallowing hard and noisily I then sighed deeply. Overcome in the moment, my voice was barely a whisper. "What do you want to do?"

Without another word, Gibson's freehand wrapped gently around my neck, sending shockwaves of electricity straight to my core as his mouth claimed mine, his hot tongue poking passionately through my lips, demanding entry.

Dancing tongues, soft moans, and wanton sighs passed between us. Gibson's kiss was everything I knew it would be and more. Tingling feelings left my scalp crawling in reaction to his mouth on mine. His piercing clicked now and then against my teeth. I liked that.

Trailing his hand down my neck, over my breast and down my side, his hand cupped my ass as he turned my body in toward his. Sparks of electricity burst like bubbles over each erogenous zone he hit with his expert touch. All the time he had been stroking me I could feel him handle me with care, but his hold was possessive.

Pressing his palm against my butt, he pushed me further into him and I could feel how hard he was for me. Feeling his arousal made me feel both elated and confused. Gibson Barclay didn't just kiss someone. This was a preamble to a much more energetic activity for him. Was I a willing participant or was I being manipulated? None of this made any sense to me.

"Every sexual fantasy I've ever thought of, everything I've ever done, everything I've yet to do. You have no idea how much I want you, Chloe." Gibson's voice was a raspy, low murmur. From the fly of his jeans, it was evident how much he wanted me so I did have an idea about that. Well, that he wanted to get laid anyway.

Gibson released my hands and rolled onto his back, pulling me on top of him. There was no mistaking just how hard he was. I could feel the outline of his dick as he adjusted me comfortably over his hips. We were perfectly lined up, my pussy and his hard dick. Both hands were now on my ass pulling me tightly into his groin, his hips undulating in suggestion of what he needed to do next.

Growling, he began tracing my neck with his flat tongue, his piercing adding to the excitement of the sensations he was evoking in me. Expertly positioning me, he parted my legs and lifted his knees, putting his feet flat. Suddenly I was completely astride him.

Pulling back, I tried to sit up and as I did, his hands slid from my hips up pushing my t-shirt and up as they glided over my rib cage, his thumbs pushed my bra above my breasts. Again his hot tongue followed, leaving a rash of goose flesh. It lit a trail of fire in the wake of his mouth, until his hand cupped my breast and his mouth claimed it.

Gibson wasn't gentle with me but not rough either, when he sucked my breast it was deep and kind of possessive. His constant sucking rhythm and the sudden pleasured pain sensation had my pussy clenching almost in time with his mouth. The ball of his tongue piercing adding to the mixture of feelings I had.

Tracing his hands down my belly again, his hands connected with my hips and he thrust his pelvis at me, rolling me over his erection. He felt huge and the way he moved his hips and rocked me on him hinted at how powerful a lover he would be.

Gibson's hand slid over my ass and in between my legs from behind, his hand making a sawing motion as he rubbed my pussy through my jeans. Part of me wished my jeans weren't there.

Instinctively, my hips rocked on his hand and in response a soft moan escaped from my throat. He was driving me crazy with want. Pulling me down across his body, He rolled me till he leaned over me again.

"Fuck. Chloe, these feelings are insane. You have no idea what you do to me." I did, if the feeling pressing into my pubic bone was anything to go by. Then again, I remembered all the girls seemed to be able to achieve that with him.

Tremors of anticipation made me crazy with lust. Part of me was glad he couldn't see me clearly, because the shameful thoughts that were running through my mind about what I wanted him to do would have crippled my senses if I had to face him. Conflicting feelings of Kace tried to rise but I'd kept pushing them down because Gibson made me feel what Kace said I wasn't—desirable.

Gibson was nibbling at my neck, drawing the tip of his tongue down the curve, his hands weaving through my hair then down across my breasts.

I heard myself ask, "Tell me what I do to you." I figured if it was really me he was thinking about and not just being inside a girl, he'd be able to answer that.

Still writhing around, hands all over me, licking and sucking gently on my neck he murmured, "Can't you feel it? Can't you understand this connection between us? Chloe, I can't explain it, you just totally do it for me."

The stark reality of that statement for me was that he could have said that to a hundred girls before and every last one of them would have believed it, because that's what they needed to hear. Just like I needed to hear him say it. So I pushed for more.

"Do it? Gibson what exactly is 'it'" Taking my head between the palms of his hands, his forearms close to my head, he bent forward until his mouth was a hairsbreadth from my face. When he started to speak I could actually feel the words leaving his mouth and fanning my face at the same time as I heard them.

"No one has ever made me feel what I feel for you. Of all the girls I've met, all the girls I've fucked, all the girls that have been around me, no one has the effect you have on me. I mean it, Chloe. This isn't me trying to get laid. I told you, I'm not fucking you. If I ever get the chance with you, our first time isn't going to be a half drunken grope in a sun shelter on a beach after a dinner in a restaurant called fucking... Casanova that I didn't choose."

Placing his hands either side of my body, Gibson straightened his legs and pushed himself to stand. Sighing heavily, I watched as his silhouette stretched, his elbows coming up as if he was running his hands through his hair.

"Don't freak out, okay? I need to tell you something and when I do, promise me you'll hear me out. Okay?"

The whole crazy experience seemed to be going from one extreme to another and I sat thinking, what the hell would he have to tell me that had anything to do with me?

"Can you just tell me you'll listen and not judge me straight off the bat?" Sitting up, I hugged my chest to my knees and nodded, then realized when he said nothing that he probably hadn't seen it in the dark.

"Okay."

Gibson dropped down to his knees in front of me and although we could only make out the outline of each other, we were face to face.

"I'm your wrong number, Chloe." Confused, I thought he was telling me he wasn't right for me, and although he liked me I shouldn't get involved. I was waiting for more until he eventually said, "For Christ's sake, say something."

"Gibson, I know you aren't really interested, you don't need to let me down gently." As I said it, I realized when he said 'wrong number' something had clicked with his voice in my mind, he sounded like Paul when he said it, but he didn't know Paul, so that wouldn't have anything to do with him.

"Chloe, I'm Paul." Closing my eyes, I was overwhelmed and my brain wouldn't compute how Gibson Barclay and Paul could actually be the same person? And, how the hell I was in the situation where I'd had phone sex with him and then won a competition to see him in concert.

Racking my brain, I tried to think if Ruby had somehow told one of the band members about my wrong number sounding like Gibson and they passed the information forward to him.

"Okay. I need to explain a few things. It was me who called your phone. I'm wrong number guy, Paul. My full name is Gibson Lesley Paul Barclay. No way will I ever call myself Lesley, it was my dad's name – Lesley Paul Barclay, but I'm actually named after an amazing guitar. Orville Gibson was a genius guitar maker. My dad played in a band and saved his pay checks until he could own a second hand one.

"Meeting my mom put paid to him playing in a band. And my dad wasn't good enough to make any money at it. Anyway, they fell pregnant with me when my mom was nineteen, so my dad had to sell the Gibson to help pay for the deposit on the rental they secured.

"When I was born, my dad figured as he had to sell his prized possession to pay for the house for me, I should be named after the guitar he lost." Gibson huffed heavily, and leaned into the backpack, then I heard what sounded like a water bottle cap snap.

Hearing him suck on the water and swallow it down in the dark was incredible. He never seemed to do anything half measure. I could just make out that he wiped his mouth with the back of his hand and a cool plastic bottle hit my leg. Taking it, I started to drink from the bottle where his mouth had just been as he began to talk again.

"Paul Lesley is the name I use when I need privacy. I fly under that name, book hotels, cars and stuff. What I'm saying — I have a lot of explaining to do, Chloe. Please don't be mad at me but I had to meet you after fate or whatever shit threw us together again."

Conscious Gibson's mouth had been on the bottle again, I sipped the water, still confused saying, "I'm really not following any of this." Feeling embarrassed as well because if he really was Paul then he knew me intimately already, and I knew him. I should have been wild with anger, but I was too stunned to think. The old Chloe would have smacked him around the head and been out of there in a shot.

"Towels. The rain, Beltz Bar, you, me, that moment. And then you were gone. Chloe, the look in your eyes that day... I've never been able to forget you. We connected and you ran scared. I had made up my mind that night in the bar to go after you, but I knew you would never get with someone like me. I know what I was then and I can't undo those things you saw, but fuck, since the moment I saw you, you've been in here ever since." His elbow was at ninety degrees again and I think he was pointing at his head.

Everything he was saying began to overwhelm me. I had thought I was safe from being manipulated and controlled and Gibson had been doing the same with those phone calls. Tears began to roll down my face. I was stuck on a beach with a guy who I had thought was one thing, but by then I knew the whole situation, and had turned out to be someone else who had taken advantage of me in my vulnerable state.

Rising to my feet, I stepped past him and began walking, needing to make some space between us. Gibson was on his feet and caught my hand before I'd gone ten yards.

"Stop. It isn't what you think. I wanted to tell you, not at the beginning, but I did want to tell you. Please, Chloe. Please let me finish explaining."

Something in his voice screamed to me that no one seemed to allow Gibson to be heard. It was a desperation that made me stop. Sure everyone listened to Gibson the showman, but who were his confidants?

Standing still, I closed my eyes, and he surprised me by pulling me into another hug. His strong arms around me should have made me panic, but they didn't. Once again, I felt safe... a feeling in contradiction to the situation before me and in my personal experience.

"When I called you, I was calling Toby Francis from Gamete. You had no idea who I was and I never knew it was you, and Chloe, you have no clue what that did for me. Someone talking to me who treated me like a normal person instead of a piece of meat or a cash cow. With you I got to be *me*. For that few minutes a day. I got to be myself. You know you are the only person ever to hang up on me?"

Listening to him explain how he felt was really an eye opener. Leaning against his chest, his voice was rumbling in his throat, right before the words impacted on me, and it was awesome. His voice was even and soothing, even though he was telling me things that I should have been so freaked out about. I wanted to feel angry and for the warning bells to sound but they just wouldn't come with him holding me like that.

"Chloe, when I heard our music play and you said all that stuff about me, I was ashamed. I could have stayed on the line with you that day, but I ran away because you were the one person that affected my conscience about how I had been living my life back when you were at college. No one gave a shit about me, least of all me, but I've never forgotten the girl with no name and the eyes that could see into my soul. There has not been a day that has passed that I haven't had two images of the way you looked at me in my head. One, the night I was getting laid in the staff room at Beltz and the other in Matt's office."

Snickering softly, Gibson squeezed me a little tighter then let go. "I'm sorry that I was drunk and called you in the middle of the night Chloe, but I'm not sorry we had the conversation we had. Five years is a long time to fantasize and dream about a girl, and then by some freak of fate or whatever, I find her at the other end of my cell phone. Come on, what are the odds on that? Chloe, you and I may never have met again, if it weren't for me being famous. And it was only because I am that I could orchestrate meeting you."

"Gibson save it. You haven't changed or did you never notice your phone called mine while you were having sex one night? It may have been a crazy fluke you getting my number, but now you're saying what you think you need to because I won a competition to meet you and you've run out of options."

Stepping back away from me, he held onto me by my upper arms. "Chloe, the competition you won had one entrant. You. I have to put my hands up to that, because I really couldn't wait any more to see how this panned out between us. I'm petulant and impulsive and I had to know if what I had been harboring for the past five years had some substance to it, and I wasn't driving myself crazy over some fantasy. In actual fact Chloe, when I kissed you tonight, all my suspicions were confirmed. I am absolutely smitten by you."

Twenty one hours of insanity had started at nine in the morning at JFK airport, and had continued to unfold in an unbelievable turn of events. Events that hurt my head to think about. It was all too incredible to be real.

There was only one thing I knew for sure – I needed space and time to think. But there was no way I could have a coherent thought while Gibson was setting my senses alight with his touch.

My instinct was to run. Run like hell. It felt like I was playing with a grenade with no pin and I was scared. For the previous six weeks I had been fighting my inner demons as I tried to shake off all the negative experiences I had at the hands of Kace. No matter how scared I was feeling, I had to be strong and face my past and live my future or else I was merely existing, but was Gibson the person to exorcise those demons?

CHAPTER 25

CONFESSIONS

Gibson

Ludicrous arguments were keeping me from getting to know Chloe. So little time together and I was fucking everything up left, right and center. Thinking initially that I was the damaged one, I had been trying to do everything my way instead of doing things properly and confessing from the beginning that I knew who she was.

Chloe's comments on the phone about me stung. Apart from that, face to face she was so sensitive and defensive to any comment I made. Plus she was judging me all the fucking time and second guessing what I was about. Strange, I never got that vibe about her at Beltz. She seemed like a girl with her head screwed on the right way.

Sure, I'd noticed her before, who the hell wouldn't have? She was sweet as fuck and dressed so understated that she was sinfully appealing, wearing little cute tank tops that would have looked great hanging on my bedroom chair and jeans that were cut like they were made for her ass alone.

One thing that struck me about her was that she was oblivious to my charms. Not once did I ever get eye contact with her on an even footing. Every time I'd seen her previously, I was kinda busy with other girls.

Charlotte had pissed me off as well. I thought about what she knew about the situation? She knew it all. Bad enough that I had to confide in her about Chloe to get her help, she threw a spanner into the works by picking a restaurant with a name that suggests the kind of lifestyle I was trying to detach myself from.

The feelings Chloe gave me made me want to do things properly with her. Five years since I'd seen her, yet her face had never left me. Five fucking years. Either I was mentally deficient or that meant something significant. I was banking on the significant part because she was the only person who ever managed to impact me in any shape or form.

Having her with me was more difficult than I thought. Surprising really, how right she felt in my arms and how hard our communication was. *What does that say? I'm attracted to her but she pisses me off? No that's wrong, she doesn't do that. It's that she doesn't trust me and I know why. And she's so damned defensive.* I get that, really I do.

Chloe unnerves me because she's not that responsive to me. I've never known anyone like that before. Of all the girls I've ever met, she seemed to be the one I couldn't fully figure out. That made me wonder why and then I decided it would be better not to try.

Seeing her cry the way she did on the plane broke my heart, especially because she was crying over something that I had said. Well, she'd said it first, but it was the way I had said it and that it seemed insensitive, like I was humiliating her. When really it came out like that because there was nothing I would have loved to do more.

She had consumed most of my waking thoughts after that phone sex session. I knew it would probably hurt her that I hadn't rung back, but I couldn't risk that with it being so near to her coming face to face with me for the show. I wasn't sure I was going to tell her. Maybe that's why I wanted her to forget what I sounded like.

Being honest with her hadn't worked much in my favor so far, but tonight there were times when she looked at me and I thought yeah... there is definitely something between us, and then her suspicious mind took over again. She was always assuming the worst about me and never considered that there may have been a logical explanation for how things were being done in a certain way.

Instinct kept telling me she was different. Chloe didn't react to me like everyone else and she just got me. Yet when it came down to it... since we'd been face to face, she was making the same assumptions about me that everyone else did.

Normally, if someone had treated me the way

she did; when she ranted she knew me and what I was, I would have quietly walked away and that person would never have interacted with me again, but I couldn't do it with her. Chloe was under my skin and had been for five years.

I'd been semi-hard all night just watching her. The delicate way she picked at her food, the way her eyes rolled with pleasure when she found a taste that she connected with. She was unaware that when she moaned in response to the taste, the sounds she made had made me want to sink myself balls deep in her just to hear it again.

Oh! But when she kissed me, FUCK! That little peck on my lips was worth all the rides any girl had ever had on me and it sent a message straight to my dick. That tiny little signal from her made me feel like I'd struck gold. If I hadn't been lying down, she'd have knocked me off my feet. Not with the kiss itself, just that she wanted me for that one moment. And, jeez I wanted her back – badly.

From that point I almost lost control. I was used to taking charge, taking what I wanted, but I never did anything that a girl hadn't wanted me to do. With the wine and all the emotional shit that she was showing me, I knew I couldn't just steam ahead and get all hot and horny with her.

With that first roll, when I felt her weight on top of me, I'm telling you, there has been no better feeling inside of me – ever. I'll admit I cupped her ass in my palms, then slid them to her hips, and pressed her closer, my hips rocking up to meet her sweet spot. What I was doing was teenage boy's stuff, but sweet Jesus I almost creamed my pants at the sensation of her heat right on top of mine when I dry humped her.

I'd taken advantage of her on the phone and that was a bad call, because I knew who she was, and she had no idea that I knew. Since all of that was still hanging between us, and with my blunt oral sex suggestion, all I was achieving was to push her further away from me.

Chloe had layers going on with her feelings, and I had the feeling she liked me, but there were parts of her that seemed closed off. Hearing what she thought of me on the phone those few times made me feel that she'd never believe what I had to say about her, and I doubted whether I was someone she would ever want to get close to her.

Chloe reacting like that on the plane was awkward, because I'd never had someone I cared about have a meltdown to the point where I felt so fucking helpless that I couldn't speak. All I could do was hold her tightly and try to remember not to get hard doing it.

Being there with her on the beach, I had to reach out to her and tell her the truth about me being the one who had been calling her. She needed my honesty if she was going to learn to trust me.

Strange, but she had nothing much to say about what happened on the phone at that point, but I was learning that still waters ran deep and she seemed to mull things over before she was ready to speak her mind about anything. With that in my own mind, I knew there was a powder keg with a fuse waiting to be lit sometime soon.

Staring at her silhouette in the dark and wondering when that particular minefield would come up, the beach no longer seemed a good idea. "Come on, we're getting out of here. I could easily have called someone to come and get us. Gibson Barclay the rock star can make people do whatever the fuck he wants, Chloe. The reason I didn't was because I wanted to spend some time with you."

Taking her by the hand I strode back to the sun shelter and closed the hamper. Picking it up, I slipped into my shoes and began walking back to the car with her.

"Aren't you going to get the blanket and stuff?" She asked, surprised that I wasn't packing everything up.

"Nah, someone will be glad of that when the sun comes up. This wasn't how tonight was supposed to go, Chloe. I didn't mean to drink all that wine. I guess I just felt relaxed enough to do what came naturally."

Stepping onto the long boardwalk from the beach, Chloe's face became visible with the walkway lighting. "And I know what comes naturally to you, Gibson, that's the part that worries me about you."

Shaking my head at her, I was so damn pissed that she thought I just wanted to get laid and that was all I thought about. Maybe that was true from what she remembered, but that was when I was nineteen.

"We could have gone to a hotel to sleep Chloe, but I figured you'd think I had expectations of you that I didn't. No matter what I did from the time I was drinking the wine, you would have seen it as a precursor to sex, am I right?"

Watching Chloe's reaction intensely, I saw her swallow, embarrassed at her assumption. "Sorry, I just thought..."

"Well, don't! Quit second guessing me, it's fucking tiresome."

I didn't mean to sound so forceful but she was frustrating the fuck out of me. All I had wanted to do was meet her, take her to dinner and get to know her. The result of that was that I couldn't even manage to make it past that point, without her thinking that everything I did was laced with seduction so that I'd get her to lie down and open her legs wide for me.

Pulling my cell out of my pocket, I flicked through the contacts and connected to Johnny the co-pilot and my security. He was asked to stand down earlier and leave us to have a normal night for once.

Going to Carmel-By-The–Sea at 11:00pm, it was very unlikely I'd be mobbed or harassed by anyone unless it was a girl I'd once had. Then again, with my odds lately maybe I shouldn't have been too complacent.

"Johnny, it's me, we're still at the restaurant and I've had too much to drink. We'll wait in the car." Swiping my phone, I shoved it deep into my jeans pocket and stared at Chloe, wondering what she was going to say next.

Unlocking the car, I said, "Get in." Seeing the hurt in Chloe's eyes and a hint of fear, I spoke much softer to her, even though my temper was flaring.

"You're not giving me a fair crack of the whip, Chloe. The way I got you here with me was all kinds of wrong but fuck I'm not a bad person, I've just done some bad things."

Chloe turned to face me, her eyes locking in on mine. "I know that. And I'm sorry, it's ju... it's just that I've been though some stuff and it has made my views a bit skeptical where relationships are concerned."

I jumped straight in on her point of view. "Is that what we're doing Chloe, having a relationship? Because it feels like I'm under interrogation instead of having a night out with a beautiful woman."

Instead of answering me back she just got into the car with me and looked at me for the longest time. Looking but not seeing and I wondered if she was lost thinking and didn't realize we were still facing each other.

"Why did you do that? The phone calls, the... words... the picture. Talking to me, the flirting, the phone sex..." Chloe's voice sounded like she might cry and I thought *oh crap* because I wasn't sure I could cope with a meltdown like that in such a confined space as the front of the car.

Sighing heavily, I placed my hand on her cheek and amazingly enough, she leaned into my palm and held my eye contact. Her small action made me connect with her instantly and I felt less angry.

"I'm really sorry I started that. I was horny and drunk and you sounded so incredible on the phone. Really, I wanted to touch you more than anything during that call. Actually, I wanted to hold you in my arms and just love you. There was a vulnerable sound to your voice but fuck, Chloe I think you seduced me more than I did you that night. I was the drunk one, remember?"

Warm heat stained her cheeks and a slight curve to her mouth told me that she had accepted her part in what we did. It had pained her to do it, but it was pretty courageous given who I was. And that wasn't meant from an inflated stand point, just that I had a reputation, and she'd stood up to that.

Chloe's eyes lowered for a second then glanced back up to look at me. "I'm sorry too, Gibson. Really, what you did to meet me would have been romantic had I not known about you before. So it's poor judgment on my part. I've only seen those snapshots of you as a teenager and read gossip in the local rags and mags."

Suddenly she was the one with her hands either side of my face and a half smile on her lips. "I've ruined what you tried to do for me tonight. I'm sorry Gibson, and I really appreciate the sentiment of it all. I'm just not in a place where I'm ready to have fun, you know? If I am honest it isn't all you, it's me as well. History shapes us Gibson, yours and mine."

Chloe's eyes dipped to look at my lips, and she

licked her own. "May I?" Asking permission to kiss me just about blew me away. Fans grabbed my face and tried to stick their tongues down my throat all day long and my little Chloe asks, may I? Fuck me. Definitely a first.

Shaking my head, I smiled wickedly, as I closed the distance between us, "Oh, I'd be sorely disappointed now if you didn't." My body was already on full alert and was humming to be closer to her, and I had been fighting all my habitual, skewed tendencies to pounce on her and do everything I'd ever imagined doing to her.

Soft full lips pressed against mine and she surprised me by being the one to trace the seam of my lips with her warm wet tongue, my lips parting to accept whatever she was willing to give me. She stroked my teeth with her tongue, then probed deeper into my mouth.

Desperate to go at her pace, I could feel her trying but it wasn't a spontaneous kiss. My hand slipped up her arm from between us and tangled in her long silky hair. Grasping a handful of it at the nape of her neck, I pushed our heads closer together, deepening the kiss.

Chloe's body began to shake slightly and she broke the kiss, her fingers trembling as they stroked her lips where mine had just been. "I'm sorry, Gibson, I'm just not that… good at this sort of thing right now."

Confused, I understood that she may be a little nervous about us being intimately close, it had been a lot to take in, but I could feel something else blocking her from relaxing around me. The only time she fully relaxed was when she was asleep on the plane. Her face had a whole different appearance, more like the younger version of Chloe that I was still in my head.

CHAPTER 26

FRESH START

Chloe

Soft tapping on the car window distracted Gibson and he turned to face a guy who I had seen climbing out of the cockpit of the plane last night. Gibson turned back to look at me, smiled slowly then cleared his throat as he turned and opened the door.

The car rocked slightly as Gibson got out, making his side suddenly lighter. Closing the door softly, he had a brief muffled conversation with the guy before he got in the back of the car and the guy from the plane slipped in beside me. It was only then that I noticed another car do a U turn and drive past us.

"Johnny, I want you to meet Chloe. Chloe, this is Johnny, he's my security detail and a close friend."

Raising my hand in a half-hearted wave I said, "Hi Johnny, pleased to meet you." My smile was genuine because I was glad that Gibson had someone keeping him safe. Some of his fans at the gig appeared insane.

"So… did you guys have a nice dinner?" The dinner itself was amazing, but I knew that in guy language he meant something completely different and this was confirmed when Gibson snickered and huffed a forced breath from his lungs.

"The food was good, everything else until a couple of minutes ago was debatable. Your timing was impeccable as always, Johnny."

As soon as Johnny started to laugh, I knew that he must have interrupted Gibson from getting to the 'fun part' of the night on many occasions. Feeling my face flush again for some reason, I felt that the joke was on me. No one said anything so maybe my low self-esteem had just made me feel that way.

"What's the plan for today, Gib?"

Good question. I glanced at my watch it was 4:00 am Gibson stretched out and I heard him adjust in the back.

"First up, Chloe and I are going to bed."

My head snapped in Gibson's direction in the back. "In your dreams, Gibson."

Johnny began to laugh heartily, and then turned and stared at me a moment too long for someone who was meant to be driving, before turning back to look at the road. "Crashed and burned there, my friend. Chloe, have I told you how smoking hot you look?"

"Enough. That's not fucking funny Johnny, Chloe isn't a groupie. Remember your fucking manners, buddy." Feeling awkward at their exchange, I stared down at my hands and prayed silently that we'd get to the plane soon.

"Sorry if that made you feel uncomfortable, Chloe. Johnny is worse than me when it comes to women. He's had so many it's a wonder his dick still knows up from down."

It was Gibson that was embarrassing me at that point, saying things like that about Johnny to me, and especially in front of him. I think he just forgot himself for a moment.

Arriving at the gate, the plane was already lit up and the cabin crew were on board. Within seconds the door was open and Gibson had taken me by the hand and was running up the stairs to the cabin. His hand felt strong and his assertive grip gave me the same safe, warm feeling I'd had a few hours earlier when he had taken my hand at the meet and greet.

Barbie was gone and a tall, handsome guy called Marvin was our cabin crew for the flight back. I almost commented on this but decided she didn't deserve another moment of my time.

Feeling much more relaxed this time, than I had on the way out, I wondered if that was because Gibson and I were kind of co-existing, or our relationship had taken a little turn from what we had learned about each other... or if it had been due to the hot little kisses we had shared. The whole atmosphere felt different at the beginning of the journey back, compared to the flight out and dare I say a comfortable silence had developed between us.

Grabbing some headphones, I put them on and

the noise reduction quality was amazing. Selecting an album from the touch screen on the iPad panel, "All Fall Down" by One Republic played and I laid back and closed my eyes, letting Ryan Tedder's dulcet tones lull me into a semi-conscious state.

Gibson slid down in his seat and flicked the foot rest out. Stretching out his long muscular legs along the leather, his feet reached over to my foot rest and skimmed the skin on my ankle. That's when I noticed he was still barefooted.

Opening my eyes, that first flick to his foot had sent a tiny pulse of electricity through my body with his skin on skin contact. Glancing up at his face, his eyes were watching me, twinkling and they had a touch of mischief in them.

A slow smile began to form on my mouth, and I could feel the corners of my lips curl up almost involuntarily. I was done fighting for that moment. Gibson's smile was much more instant when he saw mine and that roguish grin that melted so many hearts, wrapped itself around mine.

"That's much better Chloe, I love your eyes when you smile, they are so... luminous and bright." I didn't exactly hear it because of the headphones, I'd been lip reading and thought I'd read what I'd like him to say, not thinking Gibson would say something so... flowery, so I leaned forward and removed one headphone. Excuse me?"

Shaking his head, he took his feet down and unclipped his belt and knelt on the floor beside my chair. Tilting my chin towards him his breath fanned across my face. "Chloe, when you smile you light up the room, light up my heart, but mostly your eyes become so luminous and vibrant they make me feel breathless. When I see them like that my heart stops momentarily, while I lose myself in them."

His statement stunned me, because who would have thought Gibson Barclay could describe eyes and what they do to him in such a romantic way? The Gibson Barclay I knew back then would have said something like, *'Nice eyes, want to fuck with me?'* I was listening to Ryan Tedder, as he stared intensely at me. And I thought, this could be my moment, the moment that defines whether I am strong enough to face my future, whatever that may be.

I was still scared and partly broken from all the hurt I'd experienced before, and that had happened with a guy that had been dependable. I wondered how much worse it could be with a guy like Gibson. So for a moment I sat, like I was perched on a tightrope and one false move would be the end of me.

That may sound dramatic, but I was staring at Gibson Barclay and the risks of being hurt by him were colossal. Comparing the risk of what could happen with Gibson, to the risk of Kace becoming an abuser, was mind numbing. However, if someone like Kace could turn out like that, what were the chances of Gibson being the opposite of his public image?

Does a leopard change its spots? Then again, Kace changed. Caught between a heaven and possibly another nightmare situation with Gibson, I was so frightened to trust any man again. But I put on a brave face and fought the feelings of nausea as I stared at Gibson and tried not to allow myself to slide back to the meek, timid behavior I had been displaying before I left Kace.

Mostly, if I was being honest, I just wanted to stay home, safe in my bed in the little apartment I had made my sanctuary. Safe in my own space with no one to control me, no one to place any demands on me and no one to have to place my trust in. I could rely on me.

When I moved to New York I wanted safety and anonymity but I knew I couldn't live that way forever, alone and without love. To do that would be giving in to Kace's abuse and whether I was with him or not, he'd still be controlling every aspect of my life, except it would have been from a distance.

Maybe Gibson and Ruby were right. Maybe I needed to look at sex and relationships from a different angle. Maybe I needed to have a fling, a fun-fuck just for the sport of it and to see if I viewed my life the same afterwards.

Part of me would have loved to throw caution to the wind and try to have fun, but when the man tempting me to do just that was someone like Gibson, how did I deal with that and what did I do with it, afterwards?

"Penny for them." Gibson's voice brought me out of my reverie and I sighed heavily, realizing I had spaced out for a while. I'd been distracted with all of those thoughts about him, Kace, Ruby, and the little devil on my left shoulder poking me with that fork saying 'go on you will regret it if you don't.' Gibson reached out and brushed some hair from my forehead that was hanging down from the headset I was wearing, just as I had that thought.

"Have you always looked perfect, Chloe? Was there an ugly duckling stage or were you just this amazing looking as a child? Has anyone ever told you how even and beautiful your features are? You are an incredibly beautiful woman. If I had to choose someone that I wanted to represent what a woman should look like, I'd choose you."

Smirking, I thought, *damn he's smooth*. Bending forward I puckered my lips and kissed the end of his nose. Gibson rewarded me with that sexy, mischievous smile of his.

"Thank you for that sweet line you gave me, but I'm a little long in the tooth to fall for that one." Gibson's smile dissolved and he frowned with a confused expression on his face. Sitting back on his heels, his hands rested on the armrest of my chair and he shook his head.

"What makes you think it's a line, Chloe? You think I would embarrass myself by saying something like that to a groupie?" Sitting to the side on one hip he began to get up, looking hurt.

"I get it Chloe, you think I'm out to get into your panties and that isn't going to happen no matter how hard I try. Well, I have news for you honey, I've never had to beg before and I'm certainly not about to. So you can rest assured, your message has been received loud and clear."

Leaving me staring at his back, Gibson walked over to the other side of the plane, his cell appearing out of his right pocket and he was calling someone. Strapping himself into the furthest seat of the plane, he was as far away from me as he could get.

Continuing to listen to music, I tried to pretend that our newest spat hadn't bothered me, but it had. A lot. More than I expected it to. I was hurt and confused by the new feelings because they were about him, and how he had rejected me and left me sitting captive in a plane while he shunned me in the same space.

It was such a short flight, but it suddenly dragged with every minute that ticked by, adding to the agony of being there with him. Glancing over, Gibson was sitting with one foot up perched against one of the tiny windows on the side of the plane, chatting and smiling. I was in headphone misery with Tom O'Dell singing "Another Love."

Three bell sounds on the airplane intercom broke into the music and Marvin appeared to do his final checks. Signaling to me, he asked that I remove the headset and stow it for landing. Gibson didn't return to the seat opposite me and when I looked across he was sitting upright, buckled in with his eyes closed.

Feeling confused and hurt at the mess the whole experience between us had become, I just wanted to go home. Trying to spend another day in his company with this constant conflict was something I neither welcomed, nor wanted.

Thousands of women would have loved to be in my shoes and have Gibson play the attentive suitor but as far as I was concerned, he probably only wanted me because I had said no.

Thinking that made me worry and I was so tired of games and men with manipulative ways, that I had no heart left in me for that kind of torture.

Closing my eyes was the best way of trying to shut everything and everyone out. Last night should have been one of the highlights of my life, having dinner with a rock star. It wasn't. Examining all the facts, the one I came up with as the least favorite thing that happened, was that I had kissed Gibson Barclay and he had kissed me back – twice.

Why was it my least favorite part? Because I had enjoyed it? Because I had felt things I had no business feeling with him? Because he manipulated me? Because he was contrary to what I knew about him? Because he was charming? Because I felt what I did to him? Because I felt what he did to me? I guess it was because of all of those reasons.

Hearing movement around me, I opened my eyes and they immediately sought out where Gibson was sitting. Except he wasn't any more. The plane door was open and he had left the plane.

Giving me a sympathetic smile, Marvin turned and reached up to get my purse from the overhead locker. I wondered if Gibson was just going to leave me there to fend for myself. An overwhelming feeling of panic and hurt hit me. I wasn't sure what to do next.

Marvin caught my elbow and told me that Gibson was waiting in the SUV on the tarmac for me. Embarrassed that I was going to have to face him after he'd obviously dismissed me, yet had felt he owed me a ride to my hotel, had made me feel like I should walk past the car and find my own way back.

Again, I couldn't do that because I was in a strange place and the money issue was still burning with me for not being fully equipped to deal with emergencies. We can't all be Gibson Barclay with someone packing a backpack for us.

Reaching for the handle to open the SUV door, it slid back automatically and I stepped inside. Gibson was sitting up front with the driver, leaving me sitting alone in the back. Talk about feeling ostracized! Tears welled in my eyes. Given my lack of sleep, feeling emotionally fragile and rejected, it all suddenly seemed to engulf me.

I began bawling in the back like a two year old. Sounds I didn't even recognize were coming from my throat and were clearly audible. Seeing the top half of Gibson's body twist as he turned to look at me was mortifying but I just couldn't stop myself.

"Oh jeez, Chloe. Don't cry." Gibson's voice sounded so sympathetic which made me cry even more. The SUV stopped by the side of the road and Gibson got out and climbed into the back beside me. Once again, he scooped me up and cradled me in his arms, speaking so low and gently to me, that I had no option but to stop crying just so I could hear what he was saying.

Wiping my tears with his thumbs was becoming almost a full time occupation for him. I was making more than he was clearing up. Eventually, Gibson shrugged out of his jacket and put his hand behind his head, tugging his t-shirt off over it. He then used the hem end of it to wipe my tears away.

Kissing my temple and cradling my head against his chest Gibson whispered, his lips moving against my temple. "I wish you would tell me what's going on in there." Briefly, I lifted my head and stared at him, then put my head back to his warm bare chest again and was soothed by his regular, strong, slow, heartbeat and his hand smoothing down my hair again. "It's okay Chloe, I got you, darlin'."

CHAPTER 27

DIFFERENT SIDE

Chloe

Embarrassing how I just gave in to my feelings in the back of the car on the way to my hotel, pouring out a years' worth of pent-up sadness, anger and hurt. Gibson initially told Johnny to take us to the Hilton where he was staying, but I insisted on being taken to my own space because I needed to be alone.

Johnny took me to my door, leaving Gibson in the back of the car because he didn't want Gibson to attract attention to himself. That would have meant having to deal with the usual flock of people that gathered whenever he showed up anywhere. And it would have drawn attention to me as well, as a prize winner of his competition. That meant potential discovery of my whereabouts by Kace.

As I turned to get out of the back door Gibson grabbed my wrist and pulled me back slightly.

Turning to face him, I noticed how tired he was, but his stubble and disheveled look gave him an even hotter appearance, and he just oozed sex appeal.

A fresh wave of grief washed over me. He had really tried to be a good host. It was all the shit that Kace had put me through that stopped me from just being myself and having fun with him. I felt really sorry about that.

Looking tired, Gibson gave me a half smile but it was a sad one. "Please Chloe... sleep, meet me later, we'll talk, okay?" His hand reached out and stroked my hair tenderly before he placed it against my cheek. I immediately felt comforted by his small gesture.

Staring at him for a moment, his concerned eyes looked back at mine and I felt guilty that I'd been so hard on him. I smiled softly before I responded. I owed him that much, so I agreed to meet with him later that morning.

Gibson's smile widened, reaching his eyes at that. "Great, I'll call you later, Chloe." Lifting my hand to his mouth he kissed it tenderly and I smiled back and turned to leave the car.

Johnny surprised me when he put his arm around me and pulled me into a hug as we walked into the hotel. Where I would have normally flinched at this action had Kace done that, Johnny's embrace made me feel protected.

"Gib is a great guy, Chloe. He's not all about music, gigs and getting laid. Not many people know Gibson the man. People don't get to see how special he is. Sensitive, compassionate and generous to a fault, he does stuff that no one ever sees. They won't publicize it in case it damages his image. I'd die protecting him not only because it's my job, but because I love him like a brother. Anyone fucks with him, they fuck with me."

Arriving at my black, shiny, hotel room door Johnny took my key card from my hand and swiped it swiftly down the entry pad. The door latch clicked and I pushed the door open. Managing a weak smile, I turned to say thank you to him for seeing me back safely.

Placing his hand on my shoulder, Johnny squeezed it slightly which gave him my full attention. Addressing me with a serious look on his face, he let out deep sigh.

"Gib really likes you, Chloe. You are all I've heard about for weeks, and the only girl I've ever heard him talk about in the six years I've worked with him. Give him the chance to show you who he is. That's all I'm asking for – a fair chance to see him for himself, not the 'rock star' version of Gibson. He fucks up every now and again, but it isn't intentional. He has a good heart honey, and he's hard to stay mad at. So get to know him better before you write him off, okay?"

Wondering what it was that Gibson did that no one saw, I stored the question at the back of my mind to ask later because I was so drained at that point, I just wanted to crawl into bed and sleep.

Nodding at him, I said nothing in response, just stepped inside. I kind of expected to see Johnny still standing there as I closed the door but he was already heading back to take care of Gibson.

I was a real mess. Sweaty, with grains of sand stuck in my hair and between my toes, a tear stained face and a headache from hell from all the crying, not to mention the wine which had made me feel light headed and confused. I knew I wouldn't even find the energy to have a shower. It felt like I was grief stricken. Anything and everything at that point was too much of an effort. I was completely washed out.

Sweat drenched me as sat up with a start. I had been having a bad dream that Kace had somehow found me on the beach in Carmel and was dragging me through the sand by my hair. Sitting up suddenly, my heart was pounding in my chest and I had a really uneasy feeling from my dream which I still couldn't shake by the time I had run myself a bath.

Checking out the luxury bath pack that Charlotte had brought to replace the usual hotel standard bath pack, I opened and smelled the small attractive bottle of pearly orange bubble bath.

'Oriental Mandarin', it had stated on the bottle. The smell of the liquid was immediately uplifting and I wondered if I could order a bucket of the stuff to help me drown out all the negative feelings that were constantly plaguing me and preventing me from moving forward with my life.

Beginning to strip out of my underwear that I'd slept in, I was interrupted by a knock on the door. "Chloe, are you in there?" Ruby was on her way in and I knew that would mean there was an interrogation coming with every question imaginable. Grabbing the bath robe from behind the bathroom door, I pulled it on and padded barefooted to let her into the room.

Ruby looked fresh faced and bright eyed, and her smile was too bright for whatever time of day it was. "Where have you been? I was worried about you. I tried to call but your cell voicemail kept kicking in. Damn girl, look at you, heavy night, huh?" Throwing me a knowing smirk, she elbowed my rib. "Details honey, right now." When I didn't reply, she became more forceful. "Come on, Chloe, dish the dirt and don't leave anything out!"

Wandering back into the bathroom without answering her, I placed the robe on the commode and slipped into the bath, lying back with my eyes closed.

"Damn... that good, huh? I can see you're worn smooth. What did I tell you about fun sex? It's insane right?" Snapping open my eyes, I stared darkly at Ruby for assuming I looked like I did because of a night of debauchery with Gibson. I rolled my head from side to side never losing contact with the back of the bath.

"Wrong Ruby. You are way off. I never slept with him."

Snickering, Ruby's voice sounded convinced "I betcha didn't." Ruby waggled her eyebrows at me and sat down on the commode, crossed her legs and waited for me to disclose more to her. My immediate feelings about that were that she was going to be disappointed in me because I hadn't just allowed myself to be as free as most girls would have been with their love when faced with Gibson.

Exhausted from earlier, I really hadn't wanted to rake over the coals and stir feelings that would make me feel guilty, inadequate or hurt from what had gone down between Gibson and me. So I gave her a big enough picture of what happened but the 'CliffNotes' version of events.

By the time I finished I had fat tears running down my face again and Ruby's face had softened. Sliding off the commode she knelt beside the bath and hugged me tightly. "Chloe, you have got to try to put what happened with Kace behind you. I know it's easier said than done, but what he did to you was a one-off.

"One day, Chloe. You have one day here, to have a once- in-a-lifetime experience, and this is it! Today. Not next month when you feel you can cope, not next year when you are stronger. Today. Please, Chloe. I'm begging you, take it. Do insane things, have the time of your life. Live today like it's your last day on earth."

Ruby's lecture was interrupted by my cell ringing on the nightstand. Ruby went to answer it as I pushed myself to stand and stepped out of the bath. I was reaching for the towels hanging on the towel rack as Ruby walked back into the bathroom. I turned my head and pulled the towel against my front. "Yup she's right here, standing buck-naked, dripping wet, slippery and covered in bubbles, Gibson."

Dropping my jaw I was stunned at the smug smirk which turned into a grin because Ruby thought she'd achieved something clever. Snatching the phone away from her I put it to my ear. "Oh, Fuck. You're killing me. What I would do to swap places with you right now."

"It's me Gibson, Ruby was being ridiculous." My face flushed immediately when he said that and my heart was racing. I could hardly hold the phone, secretly pleased about the swapping places comment, but even more pleased by the lust and want in how he said it.

Ruby's advice may not be welcome but she was right on two counts. I couldn't keep blaming other people for Kace's behavior and I did only have one whole day left in Gibson's company. We were due to fly home Sunday evening.

The weirdest feeling came over me because I had heard his voice on the phone for the first time since our phone sex session and he really did sound different. He was Paul on the phone and not Gibson. Telling him how different he sounded, Gibson continued to flirt with me.

"Hmm and what exactly was it that you liked about Paul so much?"

No idea why but I just blurted out, "Well there were a couple of attributes Paul had that I haven't seen of Gibson." Cringing as soon as I said it, of everything I could have said, I had said THAT! Ruby's jaw dropped, and then she smirked and sat on the toilet.

My heart was thumping so wildly in my chest, I could feel the vibrations in my mouth and I had a naughty smirk on my face that registered with me when I saw myself in the mirror. Gibson chuckled.

"Damn Chloe keep talking like that and I might just have you check if I measure up."

By this time I was feeling so horny from his comment I was almost fanning myself. "Gibson, I thought we were all meeting with the band today, we'll be surrounded by people, if you do that you might just find yourself having your picture taken down at the local cop precinct."

Gibson laughed loudly and I found myself laughing as well. Ruby was communicating silently by mouthing to me. "What is he saying?" I was gesticulating for her to go away but there was no abating her. Waving frantically at me she was telling me to keep it going by moving her hand in a continuous winding motion.

"You did bring a bathing suit right? We're going surfing water-tubing and water skiing with Toby, his band as well as mine, and then we're having a sand bar party." I knew what a sand bar party was.

Growing up in Florida we used to have them all the time when I was in high school. Taking a boat out to an expanse of land surrounded by water was awesome. The water was shallow enough to paddle in and we could make as much noise as we liked at the sandbar.

Still feeling nervous about being around Gibson, I knew it wasn't going to be simple to move us forward but something that Johnny said made me feel that I should at least reserve judgment on Gibson's intentions and throw myself into the day as wholeheartedly as I could.

A blacked-out SUV came to collect us from the hotel and drove us for about forty five minutes. Seeing signs for Malibu Beach, it gave us a hint of where we were headed. Gavin grinned at Ruby, "Are we seriously doing this? Going frigging surfing with Toby Francis and Gibson Barclay?"

Eddie shook his head. "I know I'm gonna piss you all off but my cell has been on charge all night and I'm gonna be taking tons of pictures. Not one, but two of my top music idols in swimmers on a beach in Malibu and me partying with them, what the fuck is that about?"

Delight and disbelief in Eddie turned him into a teen-fan and he sat quoting fact after fact about his two music idols, which both informed me and gave me a sense of exactly what Gibson had managed to achieve in the years since I'd last seen him.

"It's a shame really, that no one ever discusses the humanitarian work he does every year. Did you know that twenty-five percent of his royalties go to different projects he sponsors every year? The guy has provided schools, hospital equipment, health program funding, plus food and water projects for thousands of people."

Pushing myself upright in my seat, I thought I

had been hearing things. "What did you say Eddie? Who were you talking about?" Eddie took off his sunglasses and placed them carefully over his brown wavy hair then concentrated his gaze back on me.

"Gibson. Beats me why they try to hide that stuff. He's so fucking cool anyway and I think people would like him even more but his management exploit the bad-boy image that he had when he was younger… that and his manwhoring ways."

Feeling myself scowl, I gave Eddie an angry look. "Eddie what Gibson did when he was a teenager and what he does now are completely different. I knew him back then, or at least I witnessed a lot of what was going on, and after spending last night in his company, I didn't see any of that 'teenager' in him when he was with me."

Eddie snickered and said, "Well maybe you weren't his type although I can't really see it. Chloe, you're a total babe but from what I know of Gibson Barclay, any woman still moving and with a pulse seems to be his type."

Ruby elbowed Eddie and threw him a look that said shut up, but without actually saying anything. Eddie shrugged and glanced at Gavin and his eyes widened warning Eddie not to push it. I remember thinking a day in Gibson's company wasn't going to be as easy as I thought after that.

The atmosphere in the SUV was one of anticipation because there were two famous bands to hang out with, not one. Gametes and M3rCy were possibly two of the top ten bands in the world and that brought expectations of what these wild men of rock did on their down time.

CHAPTER 28

PARTYING HARD

Chloe

Just visible on the far side of the beach was a group of what looked like normal Californian beach boys. Sun kissed hair and golden tans, surf boards and wetsuits that were on but stripped to the waist, the sleeves hanging down.

The closer we got the more Gibson seemed to stand out. I wasn't sure whether that was because he was the one I most wanted to see or the one that was the most difficult not to think about.

Standing side on with just his profile showing he gave me the chance to observe his amazing form. His long and lean but muscular frame captivated me. Strong thighs, arms and from what I could see, a back rippled with hard muscle.

As if sensing I was there, Gibson's torso twisted in my direction and his eyes connected with mine. Instantly, his face was glowing and he smiled widely. Striding across the sand towards me his hand came up in a wave.

"Hey. You made it. How are you feeling?" Smiling warmly at me, Gibson could have been any regular guy greeting a friend. The way he was attentive and open made me feel more relaxed than I had before I saw him. "Come sit, we're just checking we've got everything before we head out. Did they set you up with a wetsuit yet?"

Nodding, I looked in the direction of the two guys that had brought us to the beach. They were carrying them over their arms along with two body boards. Gavin and Eddie were already in theirs. Eddie was standing staring at Toby Francis like he was some kind of apparition.

I hadn't spoken at all since I arrived but Gibson hadn't seemed to notice and was nervous, which was something I hadn't really experienced with him before. "I'm really glad you're here, Chloe.

"Today is about having fun, darlin'. Toby and I have been friends since we were kids and we haven't seen each other for fourteen months. I was going to blow him out because you were here, but I figured that we would do better in a group and we've only got one day. Are you okay with this?"

Again, Gibson had somehow outdone any thoughts that I may have had about him trying to get me alone. He had obviously considered my feelings and was trying to arrange something that didn't put our relationship, thus far, under any more pressure. I wasn't really sure how I felt about that because part of me was kind of at the point where I was ready to test the water and try it Ruby's way.

Splitting into two boats, myself, Gibson, Toby, Jill, Ruby, Mick, Gavin and Eddie were on one boat and the other had Lennox and Simon from M3rCy and Hugh and Denis, from Gametes, with what I assumed were their girlfriends.

Like everything else Gibson did, he water skied with an expertise that made me wonder if he had ever gone to school in his life. I mean, he must have spent all his time on the beach to have learned the tricks he could do.

My heart was in my mouth as the boat sped along at 45 knots and he was cutting across the wake we were leaving and zigzagging left and right, doing somersaults and leaping through the air as if he were born to do it.

Tubing was a lot of fun even though I was always scared to try it. The speed of the boat made the tube feel out of control at times and I was scared of the beasts in the sea. Manatees were freaky looking creatures, like big dollops of moving blubber, and sharks... well they had teeth and they snuck up on you. That was the only information I needed to know to feel frightened about the ocean.

After some coaxing, I was persuaded to tube on my own. Butterflies in my tummy danced like there were too many of them all jostling for position. Accelerating away from me, the boat got smaller, then suddenly the rope was taut and I was being dragged at speed behind the boat.

Gibson was smiling, standing at the back with his

arms on his hips; enjoying watching me being bounced around by the white foamy wake the boat was leaving as it cut through the water.

Hitting a wave wrongly, my tire bounced high in the air and as much as I tried to hang on, my wet fingers slipped free and I was coasting in mid-air with a feeling of fear gripping me that my stunt had somehow gone terribly wrong.

Sharp pain stung my belly as I hit the water in a belly flop, then I seemed to be tumbling downwards through the dark, freezing, salty water. Holding my breath, I was trying not to panic but I knew I wasn't a strong swimmer and the undercurrent was quite strong. After what seemed like a few seconds I could feel my lungs begin to burn and I knew I was in trouble.

Panic began to take hold just as a pair of strong arms encircled my waist and began to pull me to the surface. Sharp gasps of air re-inflated my lungs with fresh oxygen as I sputtered and spat, my arms fighting the hold on me.

"Stop!" The voice from behind me was Gibson. "I got you, Chloe. Don't fight me, lean back into my shoulder." Gibson was under me and I was lying with my upper back on his chest, his hand under my chin, keeping me afloat.

"Don't panic honey, you're okay, I got you." Gibson swam confidently towards the boat and passed me by my underarms to Gavin and Eddie who pulled me aboard. Gibson pulled himself up on the back board then up into the boat. "Okay, she's alright, everyone back off and leave her to me. I got her."

Without any hesitation he pulled me on his lap and hugged me tight. "Fuck Chloe, tell me you're okay. I'm sorry, I shouldn't have pushed you into doing that." I'd had a fright, no doubt about that, but Gibson had got to me before any damage was done and he was taking the blame for me being in the water.

Both of our chests were still rising and falling from the effort of getting back to the boat safely, but it was his eyes I was focusing on. They were full of concern and hurt that I had been in a tumble.

Smiling softly, I wanted to reassure Gibson it was an accident and I didn't blame anyone. "I'm fine, I was figuring out the tubing thing, it was fun, it's the falling off I think I need practice with."

Gibson's face immediately relaxed and he kissed my forehead. "Damn, Chloe. You are banned from tubing. That was agony for me to watch. You have no idea the feelings that ran through me when I watched you being tossed up in the air like that. You must have been thrown about fifteen feet before hitting the water and coming down flat on your front like that." Shaking his head, his voice trailed off like he was traumatized by the event and didn't want to recount it.

Seeing the way Gibson was affected by what had happened to me warmed my heart. I couldn't remember the last time anyone had shown that level of personal concern for me. Taking his cold cheek in my hand, I lifted my face to his and placed a soft, slow kiss on his lips. "Thank you for saving me. So I need to add 'hero' to the titles you hold now, huh?"

Gibson smirked. "Nah, it was a no brainer going to get you. There isn't another fish in the sea like you." As soon as he said that, I started giggling and he pretended to look injured. "What? What did I say?"

"Jeez Gibson you need to get better lines. I thought you wrote lyrics? And that was the best you could come up with?" I said, glancing over at Ruby, I smiled reassuringly at her worried face and saw it relax. She turned and began to speak to the others and I heard her tell them I was fine.

Chuckling heartily Gibson squeezed me to his chest. His laughter vibrated against my body. "Corny, cheesy... call it what you want, it's true. I'm smitten with you, what can I say?" Still chuckling he was stroking his thumb up and down my arm, and his smiling eyes turning more intense by the second.

"I'm not messing with you, Chloe. You give me feelings I've never had before. I don't know what the fuck to do with them. All I know is when you are near me it's like... like someone has stuffed a helium-filled balloon inside me. Like a floating feeling but inside my chest."

His explanation had me giggling and he started laughing again. "Just don't ask me to write a song about you because it will be shit. If this is the kind of line you bring out in me. I don't think I'll ever have a hit with the stuff that's going on in my head about you."

Becoming conscious that there was a group of people around us, I looked away from Gibson to see Toby staring at me, shaking his head and smiling. I don't know why but it gave me the feeling that he was reading how Gibson was flirting with me, and that made me think that maybe, he was somehow playing me.

Pushing myself away from him, I rose off his lap and stood up. As soon as I did I could see the confusion on his face. He hadn't done anything wrong, and I wanted to believe that what had happened between us was a genuine exchange, but when I had seen Toby's reaction I wasn't sure anymore.

Maybe if Gibson had been just a guy, and Toby just a guy, I wouldn't have felt the way I did, but these two rock stars were in the news almost daily about their conquests, so I did have some scope for feeling the way I did.

Walking across to the starboard side of the boat I balanced myself against the edge and began to pull off the wetsuit. My mood lifted with the warmth of the sun on my skin when I pulled the suit free of my body, my skin instantly drying with the searing sun.

Ruby came over and leaned against the edge of the boat, one foot up on the soft leather seating beside me. "Damn girl, I thought he was going to lay you out on the deck and have his way with you for a second there. The way you were looking at each other took me right back to Beltz Bar all those years ago."

Ruby wasn't the quietest of speakers and Gavin turned to look at the both of us. "Guess I don't stand a chance after that huh, Chloe?" Again Gavin had made a reference to us being more than friends. When I made eye contact with him there was a look in his eyes that said he wasn't joking either.

I really liked Gavin, he had been a good friend and I was kinda attracted to him, but I wasn't interested in having him as a boyfriend. I wasn't in the right frame of mind for a relationship with anyone. Or so I thought until this stuff that's been going on with Gibson.

Now, him I was extremely attracted to. Actually from what Gibson was saying, I was the magnet and he was the shiny metal. I was drawing him toward me and he was starting to stick. I was scared to think about him in those terms, because I would start to believe that something more than a one night stand could happen between us.

Magnets attract and repel, because they have lines of force that enter their south pole and exit the north. Opposite poles attract each other while similar ones repel. With that reasoning I could concede that Gibson and I were definitely opposites.

Ignoring Gavin's comment Ruby covered the awkward moment for me by starting to chat with him and I turned to scan the horizon. Glancing at the beautiful scenery of the ocean and distant shoreline I realized my conflicting emotions.

Emotionally, I was fragile. Trust was going to be

really difficult for me because of Kace but my feelings were telling me that Gibson deserved a chance, just like Johnny had said to me. Sliding a hand gently around my waist Gibson pulled me into his warm smooth chest again and I turned my head to the side to see him standing half behind me.

"What just went down, Chloe? You're confusing the fuck out of me. One minute you're smiling and relaxed the next it's like someone stuck a poker up your ass and you jump away from me like I'm on fire."

Swallowing hard, I knew my behavior must be frustrating. The hot and cold feelings were something I desperately needed to work on. Girls that did that were given names like 'prick tease' and that wasn't my idea of how I wanted to be known, especially to Gibson, his band and his friends.

"I'm sorry, Gibson. Delayed shock of what happened?" Despite his candid disclosures about how he felt towards me I found myself lying. We had one day, like Ruby said, and I wasn't going to spend it talking about something as depressing and traumatizing to me as Kace.

Bending so that his mouth was near my ear, he whispered seductively, "You have to forgive me Chloe, I'm struggling to keep my hands to myself with you today. If I could have one wish it would be to be alone with you." Gibson's warm breath fanned across my ear and sent shivers down my spine.

When he confessed what he wanted my mind flitted back to the wish we had both shared from our phone call, when we'd been desperate for more than words. I felt my nipples pebble as my body reacted to his touch and the slow, seductive timbre in his voice and the memory of our mutual want.

Long fingers closed slightly, gripping a little firmer on my bare flesh exposed by my tankini swim suit. Turning me to face him, Gibson shuffled backwards with me until I was leaning on the back of one of the chairs and he glanced down to my chest. His eyes briefly fell to my breasts, my nipples clearly protruding under the thin unpadded material, he then slowly looked up to meet my eyes.

"Fuck, Chloe. You have no idea how much I want to hold those in the palms of my hands." Right at that moment, if we had been alone I was sure I would have encouraged that. Instead I said nothing, and just stared back at him.

Conscious there was another six people on the boat, I looked past him to see who was looking at us but they were all turned in the opposite direction, watching the antics of the guys in the other boat.

Stretching up on my tiptoes, I took the initiative again; not asking for permission this time, and kissed him slowly, my lips light on his. Gibson's hand worked up to my ribs from my waist and his other wrapped around my shoulders. He murmured seductively to me, but his lips never left mine, and his voice was thick with lust. "Chloe, please trust me. We have one day, please... let's just do this. Let me in."

CHAPTER 29

PRYING EYES

Chloe

Gibson pressed his body against me and I felt myself melt into his chest. Gently and tentatively his mouth pressed against mine; handling me with care, moving at a speed that was so slow it was increasing my need for more than what was happening.

His unhurried cultivation of the kiss between us made me so needy that when he suddenly pierced my mouth with his hot tongue and claimed it almost forcefully, the shock of it only heightened my desperation for him.

When he broke the kiss, he let out a shuddery breath, his mouth trailing down my neck and into the crease of it beside my collar bone. Trailing his tongue flat up my neck again towards my ear, he whispered sexily, “Good girl, Chloe. Relax. Feel how I feel for you. I got you.”

Between his sexy whispering that made me tremble, his low raspy voice, his touch and the way he demanded my attention with his kiss, he pushed my limits of what I felt safe doing, increasing his overall effect on me.

Breathless, our chests heaving with the effort of controlling ourselves, we both drew back from each other at the same time. Gibson grinned wickedly at me and murmured in a low gravelly voice, "Fuck, Chloe. You're killing me… slowly, but you're doing it nevertheless."

Smirking wickedly at me, he leaned in and pressed his lips to my forehead brushing a few strands of hair from my shoulder at the same time before bending his head and peppering my neck and shoulder with little kisses again.

Stepping back, Gibson's hand trailed from the back of my head down my arm until he grasped my hand in his. "Pity we have to be appropriate around these assholes Chloe, because I have the feeling if we'd been alone right now that kiss would have gone much further."

Something about the sexy way he said it had me nodding my head slowly, then I felt my face flush and I had to break eye contact with him because my pussy was pulsating with a need I hadn't felt before and there was an ever increasing damp patch forming between my legs.

Gibson turned on his heel and clapped his hands together. "Right that's enough of this kind of exercise for a while. Sand bar time." Toby fired up the engine and we powered at speed around a couple of small islands until we came to an expanse of soft white sand with crystal clear waters.

Killing the engine, Toby coasted closer to the sand bar then he threw the small anchor in as everyone began to get off. Gibson jumped into the water and turned with his hands up to face me. Smiling warmly he gestured for me to jump into them. "I almost lost you once today. I'm taking no chances this time."

Smirking at him, I was delighted that he wanted to keep me safe. Nervous, I was wondering how I should jump down into his arms without hurting either of us. I figured I might as well just launch myself and trust him to get a hold of me. Something I reflected on afterwards, because if that had been Kace I know there would have been a lot of debate about me doing that.

The cool water was just above his thighs and as he caught me I wrapped my arms tightly around his neck, while his hands moved quickly from under my arms to under my butt cheeks to haul me up his body and get a firm hold.

During this, his thumb went between my legs and his head snapped back, his eyes connecting with mine. Worry changed his appearance and his brow furrowed. I could tell it was an accident but I figured he might think I thought he'd done it on purpose.

"Sorry." Strange seeing how awkward he looked when that happened because the Gibson who had been at Beltz Bar would have been delighted that he'd copped a feel of me. I tried to ignore it but I couldn't ignore when he slowly moved one hand up my back and pulled me even closer before sliding me down his front.

Sliding past his hips, there was no mistaking how Gibson was feeling about holding me close to him. Fortunately it was easier for me to hide what I had been feeling. The sensation when his thumb skimmed my core between my legs was incredible.

Just one swift movement with that thumb but it just about set me alight. Immediately after that I felt the way he handled my butt and there were a couple of little squeezes that he passed off as general positioning, but he didn't fool me.

Once he had placed me on my feet in the water, his hand snaked around my waist so that he was holding me firmly against him. Glancing up at him, his eyes were already on mine and a slow smile tugged at the edge of his lips. "Not a very dignified exit from the boat there, Chloe. You and boats definitely have issues, you do know that right?"

Gibson kissed the top of my head and said, "Luckily for you I like you so I'll just have to go on being your hero for the rest of the day since we've got to get back on the boat again later." Smirking with a glint in his eye, he took my hand and led me out of the water and on to the soft sand.

I had to admit to myself that as a teenager, when I had been swooning over my favorite pop star, I had dreamed of just such a scenario; meeting him and that he fell in love with me.

Fact is stranger than fiction in this case, not that I was as naïve as to think that Gibson was in love with me. Facing facts; if I could fantasize about meeting a pop star, who's to say that Gibson wasn't living out that particular fantasy in reverse, by meeting a fan and getting me to fall in love with him. Not that I was... in lust, definitely, I'd admit to that.

The others had all set about bringing equipment out of the boat and setting it up. I was amazed at what they had brought. Two huge cool boxes full of beer, ready mixed cocktails and wine. Steaks, burgers, buns, salad and even the dressing. Chips and dips, and a sound system that ran on solar power. When I saw exactly how much they had brought I figured we were going to be here for quite a while.

Gibson must have had a thing for pop up sun shelters because there were eight of them and two massive multi-colored beach parasols that somehow screwed into the sand. Fold out beach chairs and a few beach mats completed the whole deal.

Jill sat beside me, smiling warmly and flicked sand off her legs. "Hey, Chloe, we've not had a chance to talk today. Gibson's been kind of monopolizing you." Naturally suspicious because of the look from Toby earlier, I waited to see what she wanted to say.

"Glad you took the prize and went to see Gibson, he looks happy honey. I've heard him talking to Toby about you. Who would have thought you two would cross paths again like that." She smiled slowly at me. I figured that Jill was just a girl like me, who found herself in a situation where she was in strange circumstances because of the guy she happened to be with.

"Well it's only one day, Jill. We fly back tomorrow night. I'm just going to have fun today, I like him, I mean, who doesn't? But I'm not going to fool myself that there is more to this. Gibson is only excited because he sees me as a challenge. Once I'm gone he'll move on."

Shaking her head, Jill said, "Not so sure, Chloe. I've known Gibson for three years. I've never seen him go after a girl before. So this is a new one for me." I smiled nervously and little butterflies fluttered in my stomach at what she had said.

Looking over at where Toby and Gibson were, I saw them in deep conversation until Gibson pulled out a plastic airtight bag, took his cell out, and started talking to someone. Jill followed my gaze and cocked her chin up in their direction when I looked back at her.

"Those guys are incredible together but dangerous at the same time. Both magnets for women and dripping with pure unadulterated sex appeal. I always get nervous when they are together because I never know what they are going to do next."

Intrigued by the word dangerous, I was about to quiz her when Gibson and Ruby both came over and sat down beside us. Ruby leaned in and spoke softly to Gibson, "So... which girl is Mick's?" Gibson was taking the top off a bottle of beer and stopped mid action to glance over at the group of girls from the other boat.

"None of those are Mick's." I could see Ruby do the math, then said, "Who's that one on the end with the barely there bikini?" Gibson's jaw twitched and his eyes got darker like he was annoyed with Ruby. "Tori. Not a girlfriend, a band member."

Looking over at the girls, I realized she was the keyboard player that was with the band but I thought that she had been a sessional musician, because she played some songs at the gigs but not all. And I hadn't known they had a new band member she wasn't at the meet and greet.

Tori seemed to sense we were talking about her and looked directly at us. Jill turned to Gibson and asked, "So... when did that happen."

Gibson shook his head, "She's on trial we don't know if we're keeping her yet." Gibson rose up off the blanket quickly and reached over for my hand.

"Come, I want to show you something." Ruby made a high pitched 'ohhh' noise and attracted the attention of the others, teasing me because someone like Gibson wanted to "Show me something."

Starting to blush, I glanced nervously at Gibson again who pulled me into his chest while responding to Ruby, "Go fuck yourself."

Ruby wasn't fazed by Gibson's brush off and looked at Mick. "Hmm I might just have to do that if there isn't anyone man enough to do it for me around here," she retorted with a salacious smile playing on her lips.

"Seriously, Chloe, your friend has a smart mouth

on her." Gibson scowled and I wondered what it was about Ruby that was off putting to him. I'd seen her smile at him pleasantly and that was met by furrowed brows as well.

Leading me by my hand, he wandered down to the edge of the shore and began paddling with me into the cool ocean. He stopped when he had taken us far enough away from the others not to be heard. Gibson began moving his foot slowly back and forth through the crystal water, making tiny ripples, and gave me a sideward glance.

"I didn't really want to show you something, I just wanted you to myself. Are you feeling okay? I mean after... after last night?" I was kind of wishing for last night again, after this morning. I nodded and my face became heated when I remembered my behavior at times.

"I'm really sorry, Gibson, I never really gave you a chance did I? There was no cause for me to behave the way I did toward you. Like I told you before, it isn't you, it's me. I'm the one with the problem."

Gibson turned to face me and took my face in his hands, his eyes searching mine intensely. That concerned look from earlier was back. "What is going on in that pretty little head of yours, Chloe? Why are you so afraid in my company? Am I really that intimidating? I told you before, I don't bite and I'm never going to push you to do anything you don't want to happen."

Holding his gaze, I swallowed audibly and tried to answer him honestly. "You have to understand,

Gibson. I'm not used to being out there, having casual dates and doing things on the fly. My life has been… very structured in the past few years. Especially, during this past year."

Drawing me close to him, Gibson gave me another tight hug. The kind of hug that left no question that it was genuine. When he didn't break away from me, I stayed there with my cheek against his bare chest, and suddenly became emotional. Holding me that way was what Kace should have been doing for me, not kicking and punching me.

Dropping his head forward he kissed my neck which sent shivers radiating out from my core and down my spine. A soft gasp escaped my lips. "Oh."

Gibson held me tighter, his hand sliding down to cup my ass and he growled into my neck. "Fuck, what you do to me, Chloe." His voice was shaky and sounded urgent. "Come on, I want to be alone with you." I grinned at him and shook my head, because the sand bar was a single strip of land about a hundred yards long and there were sixteen of us on it. How we were meant to achieve that, I had no idea.

Gibson dropped my hand and strode back over to the group who were all kind of milling around together by then, instead of the two group divide that we'd left. Some were sitting down relaxing and the music was on. Maroon 5's "Love Somebody" was playing and Gibson turned and smirked before addressing his bandmates. "Can you both get up for a minute?"

Tori and Lennox stood up and Gibson swiped the mat that they were sitting on. "Thanks, I need this." Throwing the mat over his forearm, amid protests about flying sand and being a selfish bastard, he then went over to the cooler and pulled out a bottle of wine and a small pack of plastic cups.

From where I was standing Gibson looked like he was on a mission, his alpha-male persona out in force for everyone to see. I was still confused about how we were going to be alone and amused to see what he was going to do with the mat, chuckling softly to myself when I thought he may throw the mat over the top of us and pretend no one was there.

Once 'caveman' Gibson had done his hunting and gathering routine, he twisted his upper torso to check on me and then turned back. Leaning in he said something to Toby, who shook his head and threw his head back in raucous laughter. Gibson turned back with a dark look on his face, Toby's reaction obviously displeasing him.

"Stay here." Gibson strode past me holding the mat and wine above his head and began wading into the water. At first I wondered what the heck he was doing, but quickly realized he was taking me on the boat that was moored about fifty yards out.

Tossing the mat on board, and placing the wine on the back board, Gibson pulled himself up on it with one strong fluid movement, stood and lifted the wine, placing it inside the boat before diving back in the water and swimming strongly towards me in about six strokes.

"Don't look so worried, Chloe, I just want to have you to myself, is that such a bad thing?" My heart raced and something in the way he said it made my hormones leap into action. It wasn't the 'having me to himself' that was worrying me, it was what he was going to do when he had me to himself that was making me sweat.

Gibson lifted me out of the water in a fireman's lift much to the delight of those on shore who were catcalling and whistling. Mortified, I felt a bit like a sacrifice being held up just before the kill. Wading with me to the back board, he spun me from his shoulder and around his neck to place me feet first on the board.

He must have seen the confusion on my face, because he inclined his head, "If we're going to sit on the boat I figured you would be uncomfortable if you're, suit was wet." Once again, Gibson stunned me with his thoughtful gesture.

I must admit when we got on board, I was apprehensive and shaking slightly because I wasn't sure what was happening and if something was going to happen, did I want it to? Or was Gibson tired of waiting? Was he going to do whatever he could get away with because time was running out? I might have won a prize but I couldn't help but get the feeling it was coming at a price.

Suddenly this felt different, I was feeling vulnerable again because someone was taking control without asking me, making me feel wary. The other night when he had taken charge, I'd coped, but I found it hard to try and shake off the feelings from my past and suddenly being there with Gibson gave me the feeling I was jumping out of the frying pan and into the fire.

Men will say whatever they need to in order to get laid. My mom said something like that when I was fourteen. A true man won't take you until he knows you are ready, so if one pushes and you don't feel it's right, then stand your ground. Question was did I want to be 'taken' by Gibson?

Gibson left the mat rolled up and I was confused about why he'd taken it when there were leather seats everywhere and nowhere to spread it. "Please, Chloe, sit down I'll explain what we are doing in a minute. Actually, just a sec..." Gibson pulled his airtight bag out of his pocket and answered his vibrating cell, "Good five, okay."

Swiping his phone off again, poking it back into its waterproof packaging and stuffed it back in his pocket. Moving to the control panel, he turned a key and pressed a couple of buttons.

Powerful vibrations rocked the boat as the engine fired up and Gibson walked to the bow and leaned over. I realized he was checking the automatic anchor lift had done the job. Turning his head Gibson said, "Stay sitting down and hold on."

I dropped to a seat and lifting my legs, crossed them in front of me, wondering what all the mystery was about. Gibson pushed the throttle to open, and the boat immediately accelerated with quite a kick.

We sped away from the sand bar for about a minute to much deeper water and then he killed the engine again. Hearing the automatic winder lower the anchor, I lifted my head to see that he'd taken us about half a mile off shore.

CHAPTER 30

SUPERMAN

Gibson

Chloe gave me the fright of my life, tumbling through the air when she came off the tube. When I saw her being thrown like a rag doll and land flat on her belly, it made me feel sick. The force she hit the water with made me so worried that she had somehow been badly injured.

Without hesitation, I was in after her and briefly heard Toby telling me to wait. Fuck that – there was no way I was hanging around for another second when every single one counted in making sure she was safe. I swam frantically towards where she had entered the water, breathing steadily and trying not to let the panic take over. *Clear head Gibson, she'll be okay. You'll find her.*

At first I couldn't find her and dived down twice in quick succession, rising to the surface again for air, spinning around to check she hadn't surfaced on her own, feeling my anxiety levels rising with each time she hadn't. Luckily, I found her about twenty feet down, on my third attempt.

Eyes wide with fear and with bubbles of air beginning to escape told me that she was close to taking in water. Grabbing her under her arms, I paddled my legs rapidly to get us to the surface as she tried to fight me off. Controlling her enough to bring her to air was so damn difficult.

When we broke through the surface she panicked, gasping for air and continued to fight me. My lungs were burning, bursting in my chest and my heart pounded hard then fluttered in an arrhythmic beat like it might have stopped at any second. Gasping and spluttering, coughing and struggling, Chloe had become disorientated because her brain had become starved of oxygen and was instinctively fighting me off like a wildcat.

I raised my voice to get her attention and she stopped and stared at me, then I spoke softly and gently to gain her trust to get her back to safety. It was either that or I slapped her. I was a lot of things but there was no way I could ever have contemplated hitting any woman, never mind Chloe. Eventually I handed her to Gavin and Eddie and breathed a sigh of relief that she was safe.

Once I got her back in the boat I had to hold her. No. I needed desperately to hold her after that. My stupid coercion had almost cost her, her life. Gibson the big shot pushing her to do it when she had already told me she was scared of it. If anything had happened to her I'd never have forgiven myself.

When Chloe was cradled in my arms on my lap, she looked up at me and smiled. The relief I felt was immense when she did that. Staring at her with all that emotion running through me, I definitely fell a bit deeper for her. Until the accident we had been making progress and I was in no hurry to let her go.

One minute I was gazing into her eyes and then I'm not sure what the hell happened, but she was suddenly off my lap like I was on fire. My eyes followed her, trying to figure out what the hell was going on? I'd been trying to tell her how I felt but I'll admit the way it had come out sounded like I was spinning her a line. It was just that I couldn't really explain the feelings I had going on inside.

Anger festered in my gut at the thought that she was upset. I couldn't figure out what the deal was and what had changed in that few seconds. So I wondered how the hell I was supposed to earn trust from someone like her in one day with a whole fucking group of people around me.

Even on a boat with everyone present, I couldn't keep my eyes off her. She was just mesmerizing. Strong feelings that I needed to be close to her and to touch her were almost overwhelming at times. It physically hurt for me not to be able put my hands on her when I could see her.

Toby winked at me and snuck me an okay sign with his fingers to show his approval of her and when I turned to see where she was again, she was stripping out of her wetsuit. *Fuck.*

Arranging for Toby and the other guys to come

for a sand bar party had been Johnny's idea. Personally I had felt it was a waste of the time I had because I wanted her to myself, but he insisted I'd only scare her off.

On the way back after dropping Chloe at her hotel, Johnny said that the only chance I had to get closer was to be myself, and the best way to do that was to hang out in a natural way. So he thought the sand bar with friends shouldn't have been too stressful for her. That was before the fucking tubing incident and feeling like I was losing any ground I had made on the phone that morning.

Standing with her back to me gave me a fantastic view of her beautiful tight body. She was all soft womanly curves, slender but not skinny, long legged but not tall, classically beautiful not trendy. Chloe was definitely not the average pretty girl and she made me hard just to look at her. No one had done that apart from her since I was about fifteen.

Rising from my seat, I padded over to her and slid my hand around her waist, drawing her nearer to me. She felt perfect in my hands and I leaned over her shoulder from behind to speak to her, asking what had happened for her to suddenly bolt away from me like she'd been told I had leprosy or something.

Tilting her face up to me, she had told me she had delayed shock and it had just hit her, so she wanted to take a moment. I could accept that, but my hands felt too good on her and I didn't want to let her go, so I blurted out that I was having trouble not touching her.

Chloe blushed when I said my wish was to have her alone, her eyes widening in recognition of when we said that to each other during our impromptu phone sex session. That was fucking hot. When she didn't object to my hands being on her I turned her around and walked backwards until I had pinned her against the back of the leather co-pilot seat.

Chloe sighed deeply, making my eyes drop to the rise and fall of her pert breasts. The 'tankini' latex material covering them left very little to the imagination. Her nipples were erect and my fingers and mouth were itching to be on them. Smiling seductively, I told Chloe that as well.

By now my dick was stretched to capacity in my swimmers and there was no way I could hide the effect she was having on me. Nervously, Chloe glanced past my shoulder, then rose on tiptoe to plant a soft kiss on my closed lips.

Once she did that there was never going to be any chance of her walking away and leaving me to deal with the feelings going on inside of me. Feelings and emotions that I wanted to share with her because I couldn't put them into words adequately.

So I pressed my body against hers and gave her my undivided attention, taking her mouth in a slow, smoldering and tender kiss. Fighting my instincts to devour her, I kissed her gently for as long as I could before the passion began to take over and my tongue had to penetrate into her mouth deeply.

Fighting to control my instincts, I broke the kiss,

both of us panting breathlessly. I could feel that she was still tentative so I asked her not to block herself from getting to know me. "Chloe, please trust me. We have one day please... let's just do this. Let me in."

Getting her ashore was interesting and I almost let myself down when I accidently brushed against her pussy with my thumb. Luckily, Chloe saw it for what it was and didn't make a big deal out of it. I'll admit I did have a little fondle of that peachy ass of hers though... having it in my hands was incredible.

I think that was the point when I thought, *fuck Johnny and his buddy party I need to get this girl out of here.* The clock was ticking and I was not going to miss the opportunity to see if we could be something more than a 'competition' together. I had put a Plan B into place with Johnny on standby, just in case his group event wasn't panning out.

After seeing me with Chloe, Toby thought I had lost it. "All the pussy you've seen and done and you are chasing one that's reluctant? What's gotten into you, Gib? You're going soft in your old age." Toby then smirked at his own reference to a flaccid dick.

When he heard what I had arranged, he was stunned. But I wasn't hanging around with them another minute, friends or not. This was my chance to make an impact on Chloe. When I told him I'd leave the boat and Lennox could take him to bring it back, he thought I'd gone mad.

"Get her drunk, take her in the water if she's shy, fuck her brains out and forget her, Gib. I've watched her. She's nothing like my Jill. She's the kind that wants babies and the white picket fence, dude. And we both know you're never gonna be able to stick with that."

Believe me, if she hadn't been watching my every move at that point I'd have given him a piece of my mind. Instead I ditched them, grabbed the girl I wanted to spend time with and took her to his boat.

Chloe looked worried with every step from me grabbing what I needed to lifting her, putting her in the boat and steering us out to deep water. When I killed the engine and turned to look at her she looked terrified.

"Stop. Whatever is going on in your head, stop. I have less than a day with you now, Chloe. I want to spend it alone with you. No pressures or expectations just... us, okay?" Slowly Chloe nodded and bit her bottom lip and fuck... when she did that, she looked so innocent and appealing I went hard so I sat down to try to hide that fact.

"Listen, here is my plan. Sitting on a strip of sand with some hairy assed guys that I see every day isn't my idea of a day off. Plus I figure everything we think we know about each other is bullshit. Give me ten minutes and we'll spend some time just talking okay?

"Talking, Chloe. Nothing else. No expectations except to spend some time together. Is that okay with you, because if it isn't say right now and I'll take us back over there to your friends."

Chloe gave me a weak smile and I was determined to eliminate that fucking legacy of being nineteen, horny, and promiscuous. Powerful engine sounds got nearer and then the chartered motor yacht with Johnny on board came into sight. I'd planned my own afternoon in the event the one Johnny suggested didn't feel right and it definitely didn't feel right the moment Chloe came off that fucking tube.

Chloe's eyes were wide and her chest was heaving, excited and apprehensive at the same time by the sight of the huge yacht now blocking the horizon. Fuck, I was excited. Of all the stuff I'd done, I'd never taken the time for anything this frivolous with any other girl.

I was going to dump Johnny somewhere and pick him up later. There was no way he was playing spy on the boat with us. Anything we said or did was going to be completely private. So I came up with a better idea than my original plan for dumping him with a mat and a bottle of wine somewhere.

Johnny ended up in Toby's boat and took that back to the sand bar to join the others, leaving one steward, the pilot, Chloe and me on board. Once Johnny left we were like two normal kids finding ourselves letting loose on something so spectacular we couldn't help squealing with delight. Yeah fuck, even me.

After twenty minutes of excited chatter and exploring the yacht, the steward appeared and asked what we would like to drink. Chloe shrugged and I asked if she would be willing for me to choose something for her. She shrugged again.

"Do you like ginger beer?"

Smiling slowly she nodded again, "Yeah, it's really nice with ice isn't it?"

"Well, I was thinking more like a cocktail. We're on a fucking yacht Chloe, not a picnic." Giggling, Chloe agreed to try a Moscow Mule. Vodka, Ginger Beer, and lime cordial.

By the time the steward arrived with a jug of the stuff, Chloe and I were relaxing on sun loungers on the deck by the Jacuzzi that we were filling up. My eyes were perusing her body whenever I could sneak longer glances. We were like two kids, but with alcohol. Visibly, Chloe was more relaxed and her chatter was much more spontaneous.

I waved the steward over when I saw him darting between the main cabin and the pilot's chair with a sandwich. "Can we have some sounds? Nothing too loud just something to give us some background noise."

A few minutes later, "Waiting for Superman" by Daughtry began to play. She giggled and leaned over to stroke my arm. "Oh, this song is about you. For your act of bravery today. You know, this is the second time I've heard this song in relation to you. It was playing on my playlist that day I was sitting in the park when you called me. I'll be telling my grandkids about the day Gibson Barclay saved my life in the Pacific Ocean."

Chloe's comment stopped me in my tracks. One day she'd be a grandma. I didn't know what to think about that. Crazy but it stirred feelings in me that made me pissed. We hardly knew each other, yet I didn't want her to be a grandma to kids that I may not know.

Sitting with my legs on the side of the lounger, I had just sat down from pouring more drinks. "Grandkids? I can't imagine you ever being a grandmother, Chloe. You're way too hot."

Snickering at me she said, "Well it's not as absurd as you being a granddaddy." Almost choking when I heard her childish name for a grandfather I laughed loudly and Chloe leaned over and swiped at my arm then placed her hands on my pec muscles and tried to push me back against the lounger's head rest.

Instinct made me grab her arm and pull her as I fell backwards and Chloe landed full frontal over me. All sound ceased at that moment – the soundtrack finished and the laughter was frozen on her lips as her gorgeous blue eyes found mine.

CHAPTER 31

EXPECTATIONS

Chloe

Sharing a joke with him had been great. I was feeling relaxed and everything seemed really normal between us. Well, as normal as it could be given the situation. Gibson acted like a really regular guy.

No airs or graces, no macho bull and no trying to impress – if you excused the yacht. To be honest I think that was more about privacy and comfort than trying to impress me, given his boyish reaction to the chartered boat when we climbed on board.

There had been only one slightly awkward moment and that was when we went exploring and kept finding huge beds everywhere. Gibson's smirks turned into cheeky grins by the third super king-sized bed we found in the berths.

When we got back on deck I commented that we had a tub like the Jacuzzi that was on the deck at home, and my friends and I used to sit out in it at night time watching the stars and sharing secrets.

Ruby, Sarah, Mira and I, used to get told off regularly by my parents for waking half the street with our loud laughter.

Gibson frowned and said he never had an experience like that and asked if he could do that with me. I started to say that it wouldn't be dark for a while and reminded him we would have to get back to the others. Pulling gently on my wrist to stop me, Gibson placed his forefinger to my lips.

"Please Chloe, I just want to share that experience with someone and I can't think of anyone more beautiful I could do that with."

Obviously, I wanted to believe that and it wasn't just Gibson just wanting to get in a hot tub with a fan, so I nodded cautiously and wondered how I would deal with being in there with him when the time came.

So from that point on we fell into an easy co-existence lying on deck loungers, drinking cocktails and talking about regular things. Gibson talked about life on the road and from what he was telling me, his band seemed to work twenty four seven doing interviews, public and television appearances, events and gigs, and that was only to promote the work they did in the studio.

I was exhausted listening to him, and there were times when I sympathized with his lifestyle of 'any port in a storm' with women. Gibson asked the steward to put some music on. I was pleased about that, because I was used to my music on all day in the background and had begun to miss that connection with it.

"Waiting for Superman" by Daughtry came on and it was the perfect song for what had happened earlier in the day. I pointed that out to Gibson and that it was the second time it had played while he was talking to me. Once in the park when he called me I was listening to it. Coincidence that it should be the first song being played on the boat, was there a message in that?

We began joking about him being a hero and that led me to tell him I'd tell my grandchildren about being saved by a rock star. Gibson teased me and I got a bit animated and pushed him backwards on his lounger. Gibson lost his balance and grabbed my wrist but still fell backwards and I landed flat on top of him anyway.

Still smiling, I stared into his gorgeous grey eyes. Those twinkling eyes held the hint of a smile and I could have stared into them all day long. Silver grey with dark circles around the iris and set against possibly the whitest sclera I've ever seen. For someone who was a rock star living life on the edge, his eyes made him look the picture of health. Not to mention how seductive and sexy looking they were.

Pretty weird watching the emotions that flashed over Gibson's face when I was lying on top of him. Surprise, worry, confusion, indecision, delight and finally lust. Gibson's hands slapped at my butt cheeks to keep me in place and as soon as he did, a smirk played on his lips.

"You think that fate is trying to tell us

something, Chloe?" Not sure what to say, I just continued to lie there and stare into his eyes. Gibson continued to stare into mine until his hand moved from my butt up my back and grasped the nape of my neck.

Skin that was silky smooth turned to goose flesh. Gibson's also responded the same when I drew the back of my fingers along his ribs past his shoulders to nestle in his hair. His physical response was to rise up and lick my neck suddenly then growl into it as his hips arched up to grind on my pubic bone. The unrestricted movement of his swimmers and my small flimsy swimming bottoms meant there was very little between us.

Instantly Gibson's lips were on mine, moving slowly. His open eyes never left mine, intensely watching to gauge my reaction. Mine doing the same to him. His hips were undulating in time with his lips and tiny explosions were going off all over my body as his hand opened and closed against butt and my scalp. Deep guttural growls rose up from his throat and he shifted us down a little.

One of my legs slid off the lounger and Gibson raised his knee, bringing my heat closer to his. Suddenly the passion built in our kiss and his tongue was lashing against mine, our lips meshing together like our mouths were made just to kiss each other.

I moaned softly and Gibson drew back and gasped shakily, his eyes full of fire and desire. Something about the way he looked at me made me want to climb inside him. And my heart flip-flopped in my chest.

Before I knew what was happening, Gibson had hooked the back of my knee in the crook of his elbow and he was grinding himself desperately against me. I found myself meeting him with the same action.

Gibson shuffled around until I was fully astride him, pulling my body down flat against his chest, his arms locking across my back in a possessive hold. His lips left mine and he buried them in my neck, nibbling and kissing it the whole time. I had never been so turned on by anything Kace had done, like I was when he did that. The way he was holding me so tightly made me feel safe. Even when he was doing simple movements like holding me firmly, it was setting me alight.

Inside I was thinking that I might be wrong to do this. Allowing someone like Gibson to take control and being drawn to him like that was a huge risk for someone like me. Then thinking if I let myself have that one time with him it would put the ghost of Kace and what he did to me to rest. Another thought made my heart sink… that if we did have sex and it was great and it was only once, it might ruin my expectations for other relationships with men in the future.

Then I thought maybe I was thinking too much, maybe I just needed not to think and just do it. Go with my feelings. My head was telling me Gibson was wrong for me. My body telling me even if it was, it felt so right. How does doing the wrong thing suddenly feel so right to someone like me with a damaged past?

"What's going on in there, Chloe?" Gibson had stopped kissing my neck and moving and I realized I had been distracted by my fears. I wondered whether to tell him that or not when he started talking again. "Did I take a liberty? Your reaction felt like you wanted me to do that. And by my reaction to yours we both know I definitely wanted to do that and more with you. Sweet Jesus, much more."

"I do too. I mean I did… react… and it was good. *Really* good –amazing actually." I swallowed hard and watched his lust filled eyes searching my face, waiting for the 'however' to come.

Pushing myself off of him, I stood up. "I'm not that girl, Gibson. I'm not the kind of girl that gets fucked by a rock star and gets on with her life. Too much has happened to me to allow myself to fall for your charm. God knows, I'm digging deep. Believe me if I was that kind you wouldn't be here with me now, because you'd have already done me and moved on. But I did react and you are so tempting, *believe* me but I can't."

"Why? What the fuck happened to you? What do you mean I wouldn't be here with you now? How the fuck does everyone get the right to second guess me and tell me what I'd be doing all the fucking time? It makes me angry that everyone seems to know me better than I know myself." Gibson let out a huge heavy sigh.

"I like sex. Does that make me sick? Does that give everyone the right to judge me? What the fuck does my past have to do with what is going on in here between us?" Gibson tapped his temple with his forefinger, "Or in here?" He slammed his palm hard on his chest and the sound of it made me think it must have hurt.

Shaking his head, he continued. "No one knows me like I know me. No one knows what the fuck is going on in my head. No one has the 'skinny' on my fucking feelings Chloe, you know why? Because they are fucking *mine*. So don't tell me what I'm thinking or what I'm going to do because only I know that. Get to know me. Gibson Barclay without the fucking rock star tag. I'm a person first. Gibson and M3rCy are two different entities. I happen to sing to millions for a living, that's what I do not who I *am*."

Gibson's face softened, his jaw twitching as he tried to get himself back in check and I'll admit to feeling a bit scared at how angry he had become. There must have been some recognition that he scared me because he stood up and pulled me against him again, stroking my arm.

"Sorry, I'm just tired that my mistakes from years ago still plague me. We were doing so well and I go and fuck it up by getting frisky when I can't help feeling the way I do when I touch you. When I saw you responding like that to me, I figured you were consenting to a bit more. I obviously read something wrong but your body was opening up to me."

Gibson was right, I was being contradictory. Hot and cold, sugar and spice, and that wasn't fair. Hell, I didn't know what I wanted. That's wrong... I really did know what I wanted in my heart. It was my head that was fighting for the upper hand.

"I'm sorry. I know I'm giving you mixed messages, Gibson. I really don't mean to do that. You are amazing..." I stepped back a foot and he dropped his arms.

Gibson huffed out a breath in exasperation and held his arms out at his sides. "If I am so amazing, why are you resisting this? Why won't you give me a chance? Let me prove myself to you? Chloe, you think you know me. You can 'know' someone a lifetime and never really know them. Few people bother to hang around to see what's under the surface. Can't you just think, fuck the risk, I want to fly off the edge? I'm gonna do this and so what? I might fall on my ass but I'll know I tried and it was fun at the time?"

As he stared at me I watched him search my face, his gaze intensifying and then he licked his lips. "Fuck it," Gibson stated, pulling me close to his chest and I thought for a second I should have pushed him back but his embrace was so comforting and again, I was giving him a mixed message but his hug was sooo good.

"Damn, I don't want to fight with you. We have one day and you are frustrating the fuck out of me, Chloe. Every time I think you're beginning to get to know me something drags your mind back to those girls at Beltz, am I right?"

Of course he was right. I have never forgotten those images that made such an impact on me. Not that I could have picked any of the girls out, it was Gibson's expressions which were in my memories, and what he was doing. He was right I was judging him and letting all my negative stuff with Kace get in the way.

The question I had to ask myself was; if I stripped back my knowledge of old regarding Gibson and how I was treated by Kace, could I allow myself a day free from guilt just to be with him? When I removed those barriers the answer was yes. Gibson deserved me to see him for how he had been since I met him.

Pushing myself away from him slightly, I tilted my head to look up at him. "Okay, Gibson, from now on I'm going to try to give in to having fun instead of worrying about everything." No sooner were the words out than Gibson grabbed me up against his body and walked backwards with me to the lounger again.

Initially, I thought damn this is it, the moment when I get to experience what all those other girls raved about. Gibson surprised me when he sat me down gently and walked over to the jug with the cocktail mix in it, picked it up and signaled to the steward by shaking the jug from his wrist that we needed something else.

"Can we have 'Tequila Sunrise,' cocktails this time?" Spinning to face me, he smiled and raised an eyebrow at me. "You come from Florida. You dig orange juice right?" Nodding, I smirked. Being brought up on the stuff, I used to drink it by the gallon until I found out how much sugar was in it. Nowadays it was a treat instead of a habit.

When the steward returned it was with two long cocktail glasses with red liquid at the bottom, orange juice and I could smell the tequila as I moved the cocktail umbrella with the maraschino cherry to sip at the drink.

"Mmm," I said, licking my lips and rolling my eyes. Glancing at Gibson to see how he was doing, he was staring again. "Damn, Chloe… don't you do anything that doesn't sound erotic?" Snickering, he then teased, "Do it again." After that we kind of fell into an easy chat and after two more cocktails I was feeling pretty free in my mind.

Gibson took my hand and pulled me up. "I think we need a walk to clear our heads." Slinging his arm over my shoulder casually, he began to walk over to the middle of the boat. Damn that meshy thing looks pretty inviting. I bet it's cool to lie on.

Gibson was referring to the trampoline between the catamaran section of the boat when stated that. There was this thick material stretched between the two sections. "Fuck, it's a trampoline." He stated smiling mischievously. Can we get on that thing?"

The steward nodded, replying, "Guests use it to sunbathe and fish from sometimes." Without another word Gibson pulled me on to it and we both staggered on the bouncy surface trying to get our balance, before I collapsed in a heap and he did the same right beside me.

We were both rolling around, bouncing slightly,

giggling at how ridiculously uncoordinated we were at walking on it. Between the motion of the boat on the waves and our alcohol intake, we sucked. Gibson rolled on his side facing me and tried to get up on one elbow before rolling back on his back.

"Jeez, Chloe help me out here, you have to come to me." Rolling on my side, I managed to get on my elbow to face him. Gibson reached up and brushed some strands of hair away from my face, tucking it behind my ear.

"You have the sexiest laugh, the sexiest smile and the sexiest body I've ever seen." I wasn't sure what to say but he smiled and brushed my nose with his index finger. "And you still have an issue with boats."

CHAPTER 32

BREAKING DOWN

Chloe

Glancing down Gibson's body, I couldn't help but notice he was erect. Then I couldn't help noticing it again and again. Worse thing was; Gibson caught me doing it.

"Do you want to see it in the flesh? Or did the picture I sent you traumatize you?"

Hitching my breath at his blunt question, I expected to see a grin or at the very least a smirk. Gibson's face was serious, his eyes hooded seductively and staring hard. He was waiting for me to say something, but before I could answer we heard the steward clear his throat.

"Towels, sir."

Gibson twisted his body and head to look up at him, raising his hand to block the sun, squinted up at him with one eye. "Throw them down then go take a break, dude."

Two huge fluffy white bath sheets slid down and

landed where the weight of us made the trampoline dip.

"Well now that the after care is ready, back to my question. Are we doing a show and tell? I'm not shy, Chloe. Whatever you want, darlin'."

Thinking that Gibson was calling my bluff, I swallowed as best as I could with my very dry throat. My heart pounded excitedly against my breast bone and I mustered up the courage to look him square in the eye. "Go on then… or did you want an emcee to announce it? That's usually how you start your performances isn't it?"

Expecting Gibson to laugh and the sexual tension to pass, I smirked for effect and licked my dry lips. Not for effect, just because they were dry. Before the smirk was able to die on my lips, Gibson dug in with his heels and hauled his swimmers to his knees.

Once I had taken in what he did my eyes went wide and I kind of averted them. "Fuck, Chloe, take a proper look at it. My dick has been in agony since I saw you this morning. Semi to hard all day long so far and right now it feels like it's gonna explode." Gibson took his thick length in his hand and began to stroke it slowly while he spoke to me.

"Does it scare you, Chloe? Sex? Are you afraid to have sex? What is wrong with doing something so natural? It's free… it's wild, it's sensual, it's energetic. Lowering his tone and talking in a seductive whisper, he said, "It's dirty and you can have it however you want it darlin'."

"Touch me. Go on, take me in your hand. Show

me you're not afraid of me. That it isn't that you have a problem with sex and me."

I didn't take up his offer and shook my head, "I don't have a problem with you, Gibson."

"No? You could have fooled me darlin', you have teased and tested me since yesterday. On the beach last night, on the boat today, on the sand bar earlier, on the deck? And you act like I'm the one that can't be trusted? I'm here – naked, honest as the day I was born and you are still playing fucking games with me."

Gibson reached out and grabbed me by the back of my head, turning me over and hovered over the top of me. I can't explain it but his action excited me, instead of feeling frightened as I would have been if Kace had done that.

"Tell me not to kiss you right now. Fucking say you don't want this and this boat can go back to the dock and you can leave." When Gibson raised his voice I jumped, my nerves getting the better of me, because I was terrified when Kace shouted at me.

By then Gibson was really scaring me but what was happening was my own fault, I had pushed his patience and he was at his limit. Did I want to get out of there and let Kace's treatment toward me affect me to the point where every relationship from then would be tainted? No. Did I want Gibson to kiss me to release me from the hold my abusive relationship had on me? Yes.

"So what do you want to do?" Gibson continued as he hovered above me, his arms locked straight.

His face was etched with impatience and frustration. "How do you want this to go?" Gibson bounced the material either side of me and I flinched.

"Jesus Christ, Chloe, why did you do that? Never be scared of me. I'm pissed but there is no way I'd ever hurt a hair on your head darlin'." Gibson's eyes searched my face and I felt it was a now or never moment for us... for me to rid myself of my past.

"Kiss me." My voice was quiet, almost too quiet.

"What if I do? Are you going to get me all riled up and push me away again? Are we going to fool around, Chloe, or are we gonna stop playing games? Because I'm okay with you not wanting to be with me, but I'm getting pretty tired of being with someone that's dry humping me one minute and shying away the next."

"Yes."

"Yes what? Tell me what you want. You need to tell me what it is you want me to do."

"I want you to kiss me. I don't want to play games. I never have. It's just..."

"Yeah I know it's not me it's you. You told me that shit already." Gibson continued to hover over me for a minute then he let out a deep sigh, and his face seemed to relax. Whatever he had been thinking, he let it go.

Bending forward, his lips touched mine in a soft, almost closed-mouthed kiss, followed by a brush with his nose on mine. Staring intensely into my eyes, his became cloudy with lust again. Lowering his body down to mine again, he shifted his weight to the side.

"Can I touch you?" Gibson's eyes searched my face again and I nodded, I wanted that.

"Yes." Gibson growled with frustration and heaved a huge deep breath into his lungs. "Fuck Chloe. Where? Where do you want me to touch you?" Gibson's tone was impatient, his voice deep and husky as he continued to stare at my body unabashedly, waiting for me to answer.

"Everywhere." My voice sounded confident for the first time since the conversation began and Gibson didn't miss that. Less than a heartbeat later, his mouth was on mine, taking me in a kiss that turned me inside out. Moaning, my back arched up and his hand slid across my belly to grasp at my waist.

Sliding his hand up the inside of my tankini top, Gibson cupped my breast and groaned low and long before whispering, "Chloe." Feeling him tremble with want as he palmed my breast with such tenderness and rolling my nipple between his fingers was indescribable.

Soft breathy moans rose up from my throat and Gibson responded by groaning into my mouth while he rolled his hips on top of me. Breaking the kiss, Gibson shot me a quick glance and smiled slowly, before shuffling down and leaning to the side to pull my top up.

At the sight of my full firm breast Gibson hitched his breath and his mouth engulfed my erect nipple. While sucking slowly and squeezing the other breast in his hand gently, I could feel a tremble between us, like our bodies were communicating silently and that all of this was anticipation; a preamble, to something much bigger.

Drawing his head back, he murmured softly in a gruff voice, "Are you alright?" Nodding, I smiled slowly at him not trusting myself to speak for fear he'd hear how turned on I was, just like I had heard in his voice.

Gibson saw me twist my head up in the direction of the bridge and anticipated my concern that the captain or the steward may be watching. Gibson followed my gaze then looked back at me.

"I need to take you somewhere more private, Chloe. Tell me to stop and I will but I just don't want to be where there is the potential for prying eyes." Stunned at the change in him, I'm sure my eyes went wide at that. The Gibson I knew was an anywhere, anytime kinda guy.

Gibson pulled me to my feet after standing precariously on the trampoline material and hauling his swimmers up over his butt. Helping me pull my swimming top down, he then led me back onto the deck. Placing a protective hand on the small of my back, he led me back towards the bar area.

Reaching into a small display fridge he pulled out a bottle of Cristal and grabbed two glasses, a tray of fruit and a bucket of ice. Smirking at him gathering things again, I thought about his comment about us being on a yacht not a picnic. It was beginning to look like a picnic was in the offing after all.

Gibson tucked the bottle of champagne under his arm and winced with the cold before chuckling and holding my hand. He began to lead me through to one of the cabins striding confidently as we walked. I was tagging behind thinking, *shit, this is really happening? Can it happen? Will I be able to do this?* But at the same time, wanting to do it more than anything.

Gibson wandered over to the small table at the bottom of the bed and placed all his finds there. Turning, his delighted smiling face changed to a concerned look. I realized I'd been hovering in the doorway and smiled to reassure him I hadn't changed my mind about being in the room with him.

Two strides and his arms were around me. "Come here darlin'." Suddenly Gibson lifted me off the ground and wrapped my legs around his waist. Striding over to the bed he turned and sat down on it, tucking the top of my feet back over his thighs so that I was astride him but my legs weren't obstructing him from pulling me nearer to him.

Flopping backward on the bed, he took me with him and suddenly I was on top of him again. Without hesitation Gibson was asserting himself as alpha male, master in the relationship between us.

Hungry, desperate kisses full of passion and want made my head swim as he took me over. Our passion rose to the point where we were both writhing on each other, until he rolled over and lay on top of me.

My legs uncurled and wrapped around his back

as I lost myself to the whole Gibson experience. "Fuck." He growled raggedly and pushed himself off the bed.

In one fluid swoop his swimmers were on the floor and he stepped out of them. He smiled devilishly as his dick bounced as it sprung free and he crawled back over me like he was stalking his prey.

Gibson curled his fingers into my bikini bottoms and smirked. "May I?" His request was completely out of the blue and made me giggle nervously. I felt so damned horny by that time, caution was gone, replaced with desire and a desperate want to be filled by him overtaking anything to do with reason.

Nodding slowly, our gaze was fixed but Gibson furrowed his brow.

"Say it. Tell me to take them down." His command really turned me on and I mimicked his words.

"Take them down." I was amazed at how assertive I sounded.

"Good girl." Gibson looked delighted with my response and tightened his fingers and thumbs around the small briefs, smiling slowly. I expected him to rip them off but instead his slow unveiling was sensational.

Removing his hands from the waistband he placed both of his palms between my legs at the knees then slid his hands tantalizingly slowly up my inner thighs, but without parting my legs any further. Eyes darting up to mine he made sure that I was consenting to what he was doing.

Slipping his hands under the elastic when he reached my pussy, he drew his fingers outwards before turning them over and hooking his long fingers at the waistband and teasing them downwards. I dug my heels in and he pulled them past my butt, then down my slightly trembling legs.

Gibson's eyes glinted with pleasure as he stared lustily at my heat, sucking in a long breath of air as he focused first on my shaved pussy, then on the task he was doing, but growled loudly again and shook his head. I loved the effect I had on him and I had never seen this amount of attention given to any other girl he'd been with. What he had been doing with them was purely perfunctory.

Gibson stopped short of taking my panties all the way off, leaving my bikini bottoms at my ankles. "Chloe, you have to want this. It's your call to take them off. If you take them off, that means I am not solely responsible for anything else that may happen between us." Staring back at him, I couldn't believe that he would torture himself by asking me to consider again at this point.

"I've taken them down to this point because I think you've wanted this since that day when you gave me the towels but there is something holding you back." Gibson's eyes looked down again at my half naked frame and he licked his lips and swallowed hard. "And I don't think this has anything to do with the promiscuous legacy that follows me."

Gibson sat back on his heels and ran his hands through his hair. "I felt you lacked courage to let yourself do this and that's why I've gone this far. Deciding to take them off or not Chloe, that's your call."

We had one day, that's all. Gibson, my fantasy guy since I was eighteen, was letting me choose whether or not I should get with him, whether I should live out my fantasy. It was clear that I was one of his.

I was sitting on the edge like he had said. Could I fly off like Gibson wanted me to, like I wanted to and not to fall for him at the same time? Although I desperately wanted to let myself go and be intimate with him, I knew another bout of heartache would follow. I knew what heartache felt like, but I didn't know the pleasure I felt we could give each other even if it was only once.

Slowly I bent my leg and allowed one ankle to slip out of the leg of the bottoms, then using my toes I removed the rest with my foot. Gibson was smiling and shaking his head as I trembled and waited for what was going to happen next.

I suppose I was expecting him to lie down beside me but instead he slid his hands under my butt and lifted me up off the bed and stood, nudging me up his body. Sitting down, he tipped me back, freeing my legs and placing them over his shoulders. He moved himself to sit upright on the edge of the bed with my pussy in his face.

"Oh, Chloe. I'm going to take really good care of you and make you feel so fuckin' good darlin'. I hope you're paying attention." Swallowing hard, I shivered and shuddered at the sexy way he said that to me, his statement was so full of intent.

Gibson stared at my pussy and then glanced up at me, desperately lusting after what was right in front of his eyes. I stared back at him and felt myself tremble at the slow deliberate way he was savoring the moment. When his eyes flicked back to my heat he dipped his head forward and kissed one thigh and then the other.

When he did that, one last glance up at me as he licked his lips in preparation to taste me, it almost pushed me to my limit. My pussy was soaking wet, coated in my juices and my heartbeat was in overdrive. In that split second before he acted my body hummed while I waited for him to make his move. One thing for sure, the way he was holding me, I knew that I would remember that day for the rest of my life.

CHAPTER 33

FIERCE

Gibson

Lifting Chloe up, I placed her back on my knees and lifted her legs over my shoulders then sat her up again so that her pussy was level with my mouth. I inhaled her feminine scent deeply and kissed both thighs before I glanced up, watching her, watch what I was doing. Chloe was looking down at me, biting her lip in anticipation of what I was going to do.

When I kissed her thighs I heard her breath hitch and felt her legs begin to tremble slightly. She placed her hands either side of my head to steady herself and tiny shockwaves ran from my scalp to my fingertips.

Chloe's touch and mine transferring between each other had us both erupting in a rash of goose bumps. The sexual tension hanging in the air between us was so thick it made me feel like I was suffocating. She was nervous, her whole body shaking slightly and her nerves were actually affecting me.

I took a really good long look at her pussy. She had described herself perfectly, even with her legs astride me it was only slightly open and glistening, hinting at the pleasure I'd feel when I tasted her. She was beautiful.

Swallowing hard, I was a little overwhelmed to have her where I could finally do some of the things I'd been desperate to do with her – to her, but for some reason I was treating her like she was too fragile.

I'll admit I hesitated and looked up at her again; she was staring down at me and looking so vulnerable and nervous, looking both petrified and excited and I knew that whatever else I did I had to make this right for her. Show her just *how* special I regarded her.

With that thought there was this sudden pressure I'd never felt having sex. Handling her like she was this priceless, rare, fragile possession, but wanting to convey the confidence of a man who knew how to treat her well.

Already I was missing Chloe and I hadn't touched her yet. I knew that she'd be gone soon and thought that if this was a one-time thing maybe it would be better never to have known what she felt like, what she tasted like.

Fleeting thoughts went through my mind of how many girls might have felt like that about me? How many girls had I hurt, behaving like I did back in my 'horny boy phase?'

Shaking the thought off, I focused on the beautiful gift in front of me and I was lost. Convincing myself this was only the beginning for us, I dipped my head between her legs and applied a gentle pressure on her ass as I drew her towards me to drink from her.

Smelling her scent was intoxicating and I drew my tongue up her seam lightly just the once. Chloe gasped in reaction to the sensation she felt when I licked her pussy for the first time. My tongue was coated with her juices and I pulled back slightly to stare up at her, gauging the expression on her face. How I never threw her on the bed and fucked her brains out when I tasted her, I'll never know.

Lips slightly parted, neck extended to the side, her hair flopping over her shoulder, Chloe looked like a rag doll for that split second, then her head rolled forward and we had this intense moment where our eyes locked and I could hardly breathe at how amazing she was in my arms.

Passion took over and I moved in on her again, giving her languishingly slow licks, soft and hard sucks, nibbling and flicking her clit. Chloe moaned softly and murmured, "Oh God, Gibson," in a husky low voice. Exploring her with my mouth, I sucked her clit in quick and slow pulsing motions and continued teasing her until I felt that slight tremor a woman's body does right before she comes.

I swear I could feel her pussy clench on my tongue as she started to come. When she did, Chloe's insides bore down so hard that when I stuck my tongue inside her I could feel the pressure from the intensity of her climax as she came all around it.

Chloe's reaction was to clamp her legs on my head and try to push me away, but I growled long and loud and hung on like a leech. No way was I missing a drop of her juices and I wasn't nearly done tasting her.

When Chloe screamed, "Oh, Gibson," and when I heard my name on her lips like that, I felt everything I never knew I could when the person that said it meant so much. My heart swelled. Eventually, when her climax ebbed, I stood up, securing her back in my arms, turned us around and gently laid her flat on the bed.

Watching her chest rise and fall, still heaving from the pleasure I had given her, was incredible. Chloe smiled lazily at me and I felt my lips curl up in a satisfied smile. I finally had her here with me and we seemed to be on the same wavelength. Crawling alongside her, I leaned over to take her jaw in my hand and poured all the tenderness I was feeling about her into our warm wet smoldering kiss.

I wanted her to enjoy the taste of herself on my lips and I needed to enjoy the taste of her on her lips as well. Feeling like I wanted to keep her there forever, I wrapped my other arm around her head and held her tightly in place beside me. When I did, a strong emotional wave washed over me. Most definitely a feeling of emotional well-being, which was completely different to anything I'd had with any other girl before.

Breaking the kiss, Chloe began to shuffle down until her head was at my hips. Tugging her hair slightly for her attention, I shook my head. "You don't have to do anything, Chloe. If you do it, do it because you want to do it, not because you feel you should or it's what I expect of you, okay?"

A part of me was satisfied with what she allowed me to do. Another part of me was dreading the pain in my dick if she accepted my statement and didn't want to do any more.

Small, delicate, trembling fingers wrapped around my dick and she briefly glanced up to me to gauge how I was reacting before she closed her hand around my shaft. The sensation I felt when she held me like that, the intimacy, was something I still find hard to describe in words. I was a guy who had had sex with hundreds, if not thousands of girls and I had almost creamed myself at her touch.

Crouching on her knees, her butt at her heels, she bent down and kissed the head of my dick. "Fuck." The word fell out of my mouth and my dick wanted to ride hers. She took a moment from her initial reaction to taking me into her mouth and I growled loudly with pleasure. It was fucking incredible.

I found myself gasping and between the both of us the noises were an amazing aphrodisiac in itself, but I couldn't stay still and was raising my hips, my dick sliding further and further into her mouth as I tried to lose control and ride it.

Who would have thought this kinda quiet girl

could give head the way she did? She was working with my body so well, I became much more vocal than normal. "Oh damn." Shifting up onto my elbows to watch, I was so fucking mesmerized by what she was doing to me. "Mmm, fuck yeah, like that... damn."

Chloe's stimulation had me so turned on, I wanted to taste her again as well as her blowing me so I positioned her sixty-nine style with her hips over my face so that my mouth could work on her as well. Within a couple of minutes she was gone, grinding in my face, moaning around my dick, and the urge to be inside her overtook any pleasure I'd been getting with her mouth.

I had to be sure she was signing up for this because I knew that once I got started she was going to have to commit to what I was going to do to her. Sure I'd try to be tender, but I feared my inner animal would be unleashed purely because she'd been my fantasy girl for so long.

Repositioning myself to place her on her back again I stared at her intensely, as she stared back at me. When she still looked relaxed I shook my head not quite believing we had actually arrived at us finally committing to exploring the feelings we had about each other.

Bending down between her thighs again, I licked her a few times to make sure she was wet enough to receive me, then cupped my palm over her pussy possessively and stared at her, fascinated that she was so receptive when she was relaxed.

Chloe's eyes were gone. Drunk and filled with lust and a wanton look on her face, she was ready for me. "Chloe, holding you here… in the palm of my hand… it feels right. More right than anything I've ever felt in my life. Do you want me inside, Chloe?" Several expressions flashed over her face, fear, nervousness and she looked worried and swallowed hard, so I kissed her again to give her time to decide what came next.

"Yes I do." She murmured around my lips in a breathy half whisper.

Breaking the kiss, I rolled away from her and hoped that Johnny had left some condoms in the nightstand. Thankful and relieved when I saw that he had, because the last thing I wanted to do was assume that she'd have unprotected sex with me.

Chloe's reaction was fierce as she struggled to sit up. "How did you…?" She shuffled to the end of the bed, became extremely pissed and started to pull her bathing suit on again.

"Wait, Chloe. Fuck. *No.* It isn't what you think." Tears were rolling down her cheek as she pulled the bikini bottoms up over her ass and I was watching all our efforts at being together going to shit.

"No? You get me alone on a fucking boat, ply me with alcohol then take me to a cabin to seduce me – and ohhhhhh you are so fucking good at that. Then you reach over to a drawer on a boat you've never been on, because this is supposed to be a spontaneous gesture, and there just happens to be a box of condoms in the drawer?"

Putting my hands up I stood naked on the plush cream carpet preparing to defend myself. "Chloe, Fuck, I knew the condoms were there because Johnny put them there. If you go to any of those rooms I bet there is a box in all of them. I have them in my glove compartment, my plane cabin, every hotel and dressing room I have ever been in. Johnny does it, I don't ask him to it's just what he does."

Beginning to put her tank top on and flicking her hair back, she gave me a solid stare and that disgusted sneer that was locked in my mind from way back. "What? So that makes everything okay? You use protection?"

Chloe felt it was all planned, but it was just something that Johnny did. He's convinced I'd die of syphilis or some other venereal disease, so I reasoned that it was Johnny's way of protecting me, but she was livid and continued to pull her tank over her breasts, getting the wrong idea about that as well. Like I thought I should be applauded for wrapping my dick up before it got wet or that I might have caught something from her.

Slowly, I tried to reach out to take her by the arm. I had wanted to explain about the condoms but she flinched like she was seconds from being beaten. What the hell did she think I was? I was shocked and feeling completely misunderstood by her reaction. She was behaving like she was bipolar, upbeat one minute and freaking out or depressed the next.

"What the fuck? Will you stop doing that? The last thing I ever want to do is to hurt you. What the fuck has you doing that? You think I've ever had to take a girl by force? You think because I play in a rock band I don't know how to be tender? For fuck sake Chloe, have I given you any cause to feel that?"

For the second time in as many hours, Chloe had responded like I was someone to be afraid of. In fact it pissed me off so badly I called her on that because nothing I had done would have suggested I'd ever be anything but gentle with her.

When she started crying again, I got frustrated and knocked the bucket of ice I'd taken in with us to chill the champagne, but hadn't because my attention was on her.

Who knows we could have gotten a little kinky with the ice as well, but I ended up using it to vent on, knocking it off the table and fuck if she hadn't flinched again and cried all the more.

Cutting quite a pathetic picture, Chloe crouched down beside the bed and continued to cry without making a sound. That was when it dawned on me. All the full-on-full-off behavior –Chloe had been subjected to some kind of abuse.

I found myself placating her and pointed to the bed before sitting on it. I was trying to be careful not to rock her fragile state any further, telling her that I would never harm her, that I was definitely not the kind of guy who found it cool to hit women. Reaching over, I picked up my swimmers and shucked myself into them before kneeling down a couple of feet in front of her.

Again, I tried to reassure her about me, then

asked if I could hug her. All the while I was watching her, it became more apparent she'd been hurt badly by someone and that thought made me so fucking mad, but I had to contain it or else I'd frighten her again.

When Chloe didn't answer me, I figured she was in shock because she was staring blankly at me and shivering, so I bunched the comforter in my fist and dragged it off the bed, wrapping it around her.

Pulling her gently against my chest on the floor, I began to rock her, speaking in a low even tone in my effort to soothe her. I told her I'd take care of her now and not to worry about anything.

We sat in silence, perhaps because I was so pissed; anything I had to say would have been unhelpful. My legs and back began to ache from the position we were in on the floor. "Darlin', I'm just going to move you and cover you up, you're cold." Once I had warned her of my intention, I moved slowly to my feet and helped her onto hers, then lay her on the bed.

Chloe was completely passive when I moved her but she lay as stiff as a board on the bed, before she curled up suddenly into a ball on the edge.

Desperate to protect her, I climbed on the bed and lay behind her, hugging her firmly, but not intimately. By the time I did this, I was shivering as well. The air conditioning in the cabin had made the air in the room cold, so I covered the both of us with the comforter and draped my arm over her.

CHAPTER 34

RECLAIMING

Gibson

"Tell me. Who the fuck did this to you?" I needed to know because I wanted to kill the bastard who took my sweet girl's smile and her sunny disposition. I may never have spoken to her but she always had a smile on her lips then.

"You weren't the only one watching back then, Chloe. You were definitely in my sights, but I'd never have come after you. I'm glad you were with someone then because I didn't deserve to know you at that time and I'd have ruined trying to get to know you now."

I wanted her to know that I wasn't spinning her one of my famous chat up lines and that I really had noticed her and she wasn't the only one with images in her head from our time at Beltz Bar. Although, all the images I had of her were mostly inappropriate ones.

She surprised me by turning to face me, flatly

saying, "Kace." Pulling my head away from her to look at her, I waited for some recognition to kick in – did I know him? I was sure I didn't. "Who's he?" For the following hour she told me about her life since I'd last seen her and it left me feeling sick.

By the time she was done I made a mental note to speak to Johnny. I wanted that fucker found and dealt with, but in a clever way. She was mine now and I was going to make sure that Kace stayed out of the picture.

When she mentioned Ruby, my heart sank because I still wasn't sure about her. I couldn't exactly ask her if I had fucked her but I was going to have to have Lennox do that for me, because she made me feel uncomfortable.

Also, if I had then it would suck to have to come clean to Chloe that her friend had been with me and not told her. Right at that moment, that was immaterial. My task was to make Chloe feel safe with me. So I stored it at the back of my mind to address at a later date.

"I got you, darlin'. Trust me, no one is ever going to harm you while I'm around. That bastard is a poor excuse for a man. Where is he now?" Chloe shook her head, then lowered it so that I couldn't see her face, so I just held her close to me again and we both fell asleep.

Darkness bathed the room when I woke to the feel of Chloe pulling away from me. My hold around her waist immediately tightened and I was fully alert.

I would have liked to have laid there in the dark

holding her, but I felt I should say something. "Hey. How are you feeling? I guess we both passed out."

Sitting up, for me to see her, she faced me and I heard her swallow audibly. Chloe was sitting in the perfect position for me to see her by the light of the moon. She was sitting back on her heels on the bed facing me. Bright moonlight illuminated her small frame, but everything around her was dark.

Speaking softly, she apologized for her behavior around me, but I didn't want to hear it. None of how she had been behaving was her fault. She was ashamed and blamed herself for some of her situation and I think that made me more pissed that she seemed to make excuses for how he got to the point of hitting her. He had done a real number on her. Chloe had become a victim in what sounded like a slowly progressive situation that took her self-worth.

It was my turn to apologize because had I known what she had been through, there is no way I'd have taken a chance to get her in front of me the way I had. I'd have done things very differently had I known all this then. I couldn't conclude our conversation without asking her to give me a chance to know me.

"Why?" Chloe's voice was small in the room, and the lull of the engine almost swallowed it up.

"What do you mean?" Why couldn't she get that I thought she was amazing?

"Why me? What did I do that you are so fixated on me? Do you see me as a challenge?"

"Fuck no. I never saw you in that way. Besides, I wasn't into challenges when there was so much pussy it didn't matter if someone wasn't into me. Hell if they weren't, I never noticed anyway." I looked sheepishly at my raw reaction and the way I'd explained it but I am what I am, so trying to dress it up would have given her less cause to trust me.

"Chloe, I noticed you because you weren't the same. All those other girls in the room were. Dressed similar, pretty and flirty in the most obvious of ways." I could see immediately she thought I thought she was plain.

"You weren't pretty, Chloe. You were like a fucking distress flare in comparison to all of those girls. Completely unassuming, completely unaware of how you drew my eye and kept it on you. Those little tank tops you wore to work drove me wild. Without doing anything *you* had my attention."

Chloe leaned forward and kissed my closed mouth. I was scared to touch her because even in the dark I could see she was trying to find a way back to a better emotional place than she had been for the past couple of hours apart from when she was asleep.

"Should we be getting back to the others?" When she asked that question my heart sank. It cemented the fact we were running out of time and I couldn't do a damn thing about it.

"Do you want to go back and find them?" The thought of her slipping away from me gave me such a feeling of dread. Inside I was screaming to hold her again. My body physically ached to keep her beside me, but I was trying to resign myself to the fact that our time alone was probably over.

Convincing myself I had to do whatever she needed because her past dictated that patience from me, I mentally prepared for us to leave when Chloe answered.

"No."

Damn, she was so fucking frustrating with those one word answers.

"No?" It was my turn to ask her to express herself without pushing her in either direction, so I just mirrored her answer.

Chloe cleared her throat and sat upright, her body looking more confident with her new posture.

"No, Gibson. I don't want to go back. I want to stay right here and finish what we started earlier. I've never taken a risk and always tried to do the right thing. This feels like the wrong thing – to have sex with you… in my head I mean, but my body is telling me I'd be missing out on something pretty mind blowing. I'm hurting anyway, so if this is what I think it is, at least I'll know what it is like for a man to really want my body."

So, the Gibson legacy had reared its ugly head again and I was faced with a woman I'd wanted for years who was now willing, but had already decided, probably because of the condoms, I just wanted to screw her like all the rest.

Thinking I would cut my nose off to spite my face if I told her I wasn't fucking her, I wasn't stupid enough to go down that route. This was my chance to be able to show her that it was more than that between us, but there was no way I was going to be her consolation fuck either.

She frustrated me to no end, but at least there was a reason why she was behaving how she was. Fear and hurt were all there. Now that she'd told me about her past, it was written all over her. How she held herself, how she tried to be invisible, how she blended rather than shone these days.

"So that's it? You want to have mindless sex with me, Chloe? For me to treat you like I treated all those other girls, you want me to fuck you like a rock star? You want me to throw you down on the floor and fuck you until you can't see or walk straight and your pussy is aching and sore for days, because I might like some rough sex? Is that what you want from me? Is that *all* that you want from me?"

Chloe climbed off the bed and went into the bathroom while I swung around and sat on the edge of the bed nearest the bathroom door, waiting for her to come back. I thought I had struggled to contain my temper around her comments about how having sex with me would be wrong for her. If we were going to progress, I needed to change tactics because we were just about at the end of the road.

Suddenly it dawned on me that she'd gone to make space between us. I'd scared her and now she was going to regress again. I was just about to get off of the bed to go after her when she walked back, wrapped in a towel.

"I believe the tub will be full now and you wanted to watch the stars. Are you coming?" Fuck, with the feelings I had when she said she wanted to be in the tub with me, I may well have been near to doing just that.

Chloe turned to look over her shoulder. "You better bring that box of condoms with you, I have a feeling we'll find use for them." Smirking, she turned and walked out the door with a confidence that confused me.

Somewhere inside my heart cracked at the courage she was showing, because what she'd just done had to be a front, especially when I had seen how broken she was a few hours earlier. Fragile but courageous.

With her clear expectations of me came the dilemma that if I didn't fuck her because I wanted to show her this was more, she'd feel rejected. The conflict in my mind must have been similar to hers. Now I was feeling like I shouldn't but was desperate to and she was telling me she wanted me to but for what reason?

By the time I followed her out she was sitting in the tub, bubbles erupting around her collar bone, her hair in a messy knot that she'd tied with her own hair. Smiling sexily at me with genuine warmth, she asked, "Okay, rock star? Think you can be a regular guy for the next hour or so and sit watching the stars with me?"

Drawing her hand out of the water, she beckoned me to get in beside her. As I stood on the steps she pointed at my swimmers and shook her head. "Umm ... the swimmers need to go. This is a skinny dipping star-gazing session."

My carnal thoughts must have registered on my face because she gave me a naughty smile, undid the knot, letting her hair drop before dipping her head back to wet it.

I was focusing and thinking how hot the action of dropping her hair was when she arched her back and her breasts came out of the water as beads of water ran in little rivulets across them. The force of the jets making them bounce on the surface. As soon as I saw that, my palms were itching to hold them again.

Shrugging myself out of my swimmers, I climbed gingerly into the tub beside her. My dick stood proud and I didn't miss her eyes noting that. The steward, who had introduced himself a few times during the day, but whose name still escaped me, was lurking in the shadows. "Dude, come here." I didn't give him the chance to speak.

"Crystal, two glasses, lights off and cabin, understand?" He nodded and headed over to the bar, while I turned my attention to Chloe. "So teach me. What star groups are you going to show me?"

Chloe snickered and leaned in a little. "You mean what constellations? Didn't you do any astronomy in school, Gibson?"

I shook my head, "Must have been during the time I was learning to play the drums." Chloe turned her head and extended her neck so that her face was looking up at the sky and damn, I wanted to lick her neck so badly. The crew guy turned up with the champagne and killed the lights on his way back to the door leading to the cabins.

When I glanced back at Chloe she was truly a vision of beauty, her moonlit skin, eyes wide, her naked frame so near to me yet so far. I poured and handed the ivory colored champagne and leaned back.

"You see that star there?" Chloe was pointing at the sky that was absolutely riddled with stars.

"Yes… I'm sure I do." Meeting her gaze, I couldn't help but smirk. Well, I could see the funny side of it anyway. "Can we just look at them? Or is there going to be a test at the end?

Chloe grinned and said, "Whatever you want, Gibson."

What I wanted was to kiss her, so I thought I'd shoot for that. "Anything I want?" Chloe's face was a picture. She was excited but embarrassed and I could see she liked where this was going.

"Sure, we have one day, Mr. Barclay. Tell me what you want. Say it."

Almost not believing what I heard, I asked her again and she told me to quit stalling and tell her what I wanted. So I did. This was not the same Chloe that I'd been dealing with in the cabin. This one was confident and assertive and much, much hotter.

"Alright. I'll tell you. What I want is you sitting astride me right here, right now. My dick buried deep between your legs in your fabulous little pussy.

I want your ass in my hands, your teeth in my neck and your nails clawing my back while you ride me as if your life depended on it. Then... I want you to come screaming my name with your head thrown back in ecstasy. How does that sound?"

"Do it." Fuck, two words, I suppose it was an improvement, which was my initial thought, and then I realized it was actually a command.

Reaching over, I grasped her by her wrists and pulled her over to me through the water and she immediately straddled me. I couldn't believe my luck and I was so fucking high from the feel of her warm satiny skin on mine.

My hands skimmed the length of her back, smoothing over and resting on the globes of her ass. Stroking, caressing, testing and teasing until the passion built between us, our hands and kisses becoming frantic with each other.

Peppering kisses up her neck, my mouth rested near her ear and she rubbed her cheek against it. "Chloe, we ... we need a... condom." All the while I was trying to speak she was rubbing herself back and forth on my length and her body felt so fucking good in my hands I could hardly think.

Grinding her pussy against my length again, Chloe moaned and nuzzled my neck taking the skin gently between her teeth. "Fuck, Chloe, what you're doing to me... this... feeling is insane, I'm gonna lose control... condom."

"No! No condom. Kace never used a one. I want him erased from my body. I'm claiming it back right now. You want me, you take me bareback. I've never taken a risk in my life until now."

For me, I hadn't had sex without a condom since I was sixteen. Being hooked on sex was one thing, but I was definitely scared enough of becoming a dad or having to visit a genital/urinary ward, not to use one until that moment.

"You're not going to regret that after the fact? It is me, after all." This time it was me that was quoting my own legacy to her. From the look on her face, she knew exactly what I was talking about. I wanted her to think about the chance she was about to take. Not that I was diseased. I was talking about her taking a risk with my reputation and history.

Watching for any signs that she was being brave and not really committed to doing more, I was surprised to see her relaxed expression, she had wide lust-filled eyes and the way she was holding her head was definitely flirtatious.

Chloe gave me the sexiest smile, smoothed her wet hands through my hair and took my face in her hands. "Gibson, what better way to rid my body of my past than to have mind blowing sex with a man I like, who is supposed to be quite an expert at it? You have shown me more tenderness in twenty four hours, than I've had in the past few years with the man that was supposed to love me. You want a condom put it on, but I'd really prefer to feel you inside me without one."

I was stunned by her reply, considering she'd seen me having sex with different girls. Closing the space between us, I kissed her hard, meeting her soft, plump lips. Hot wet kisses, tongues swirling and dueling against one another's. Our passion built again quickly until we were both incredibly horny and needing more.

Chloe reached down and took my thick, hard length in her hand and rising up on her toes positioned the tip of my dick at her entrance. Leaning forward, she dipped her head to bury her face in my neck and began to lower herself onto me.

CHAPTER 35

DESERTED

Chloe

Telling myself it was then or never to reclaim my life back made me more determined to give myself that one night with Gibson. Once I made that decision, I knew that I wasn't going to do it half-heartedly. So what if I got my heart broken? It already had been broken once – how much more broken could it be?

Thinking nothing could be worse than what I had lived through during that past year, I reasoned it was better to have that one time with someone like Gibson, than never to have known an intense sexual experience with someone that knew exactly what they were doing.

Watching me intensely with a serious look on his face, Gibson gave me his full attention as I lowered myself onto him. Nerves were threatening to overtake what I was trying to do. I was scared and excited at the same time.

Making a deliberate decision rather than doing something spontaneously, I nudged the head of him inside my entrance. Swallowing hard I began to edge my way down his long thick length, my tight slick walls stretching to accommodate him.

Feeling the burn when his thick dick stretched my walls as every inch more of him entered me was exquisite. At one point he readjusted and pushed himself further in, a little quicker than the pace I'd been setting, my breath hitching in my throat. "Ohhh God." I moaned and crouched forward, my head on his forehead, then sat up again. Gibson's brows bunched in concern, his eyes searching my face for what to do next.

With every inch deeper that Gibson penetrated me, I could see the changes in his posture and facial expressions

When I saw his eyes roll and the way he tried to continue to focus back on me, I knew he was committing to the whole experience with me, not just using my body.

I didn't miss the way he bit his lip or the way his sculpted muscles pumped and relaxed as his body initially steeled then sagged in the water, or his jaw dropping slightly when I took him inside me. The soft, "Ohh," that escaped his lips was like an exhale of relief to finally take me.

Unsure what to expect, I was glad when Gibson held me firmly by the hips, rolling his groin slowly under me, but allowing me to control the slow languishing way I was rocking on him. I needed that time to adjust, to accommodate his size and to give myself time to feel okay about what I was doing. Gibson instinctively had the patience to let me have that time.

When he sank to the hilt, Gibson gave me a guttural groan and I could feel him in my abdomen. After a few minutes I relaxed and lost some of my inhibitions, soon becoming lost in him. Gibson grasped my jaw and kissed me sensually, his tongue exploring my mouth in a restrained but hungry way that was making me shudder.

His hand slid from my hip to my breast and he squeezed it gently, but possessively at the same time. Breaking the kiss, he dipped his head to take my breast in his mouth, flicking my hard nipple with his tongue then closing his mouth around the hard peak teasing it out with his teeth.

Wired sensations ran throughout my body, taking little messages from one nerve ending to the next, making me lose rational thought until the only thing I could think about was the delicious way he was teasing my body to the brink of insane pleasure.

Hands moved expertly over my body making me feel alive and with each movement he sent tiny electric shocks to my core, making my pussy clench and release, making me ride him all the more vigorously. Suddenly I could feel myself begin to tremble and Gibson clasped his arms around my body, holding me tightly. For the first time since we'd started, he became more active in our union.

Initially, I almost freaked out because of the

strength in his control, but when I came it was everything I understood I'd been missing... and none of what I'd ever experienced before with Kace.

Collapsing forward in my orgasm, my head fell on Gibson's shoulder and I buried my face in his neck with my teeth nipping at his skin. Strong, sharp, clenching pulses of pure pleasure radiated from my core and sent tingles and tremors all the way down my legs and all the way up into my brain, giving me a light headed feeling.

Screaming Gibson's name was completely involuntary, but the thing that really affected me was how he had been able to make me feel completely safe by holding me like that while I was so vulnerable. It was like he instinctively knew what I needed him to do, even though I never knew what that was. Staring intensely at me after my orgasm, his eyes still sparkled with pure lust.

Tears welled in my eyes. Not because I was upset, but because I felt it was a significant moment for me. As if it released me from some of the negative thoughts that I had about myself. Gibson pushed me away from him to look clearly at me, his expression at first was one of concern, but then it changed to one of understanding.

Pulling me back into him, he closed the space between our faces and kissed me again very slowly. "I got you darlin'," he whispered protectively as his lips met mine. His low, sexy, dominant tone made me shiver at how sensual he'd sounded and it made me believe, at least for that moment, that he did.

Surprisingly, I'd been losing control again and grinding myself against him when Gibson broke the kiss. That time he exhaled heavily and held my hips still. When his lips curled up at me in a slow sexy smile, he murmured, "Slowly now darlin'… I want you to ride me slowly. I've waited a long time for this and I'm damned if it's going to be over in a few minutes for us."

Water bubbled around us as we sat joined together in the dark, but I could still see his face, his eyes scrutinizing my expressions. Gazing back at him, I wanted to know exactly what he was thinking and then thought maybe I didn't. I didn't want anything to ruin our moment together. And I kept reminding myself that's all it would ever be… a moment between us.

Gibson Barclay was world famous, used to having any woman he wanted, any time he wanted. What was happening wasn't a forever thing for him. It was all a fascination for him. What the hell was fascinating about me, I had no idea.

Then I got to wondering how the hell this was happening at all. That extraordinary fluke that had brought us together again was a ridiculous chance event and what was happening now still felt like a dream. But I already had a feeling I'd miss him when our time was over.

It had been a hot day, and there was no release from that with nightfall. Humid night air and the heat from the water in the tub seemed to make our crazy, hot scene even more intense.

The moonlight shone on areas of Gibson's taut, shiny skin, highlighting some of the sculpted muscle groups on his arms, chest and shoulders. Transfixed as I was by the definition on his strong shoulders and biceps, he had me in awe.

Gibson was a rock star in every sense of the word. Incredible to look at, attentive and caring – even if it was his charismatic way of getting laid – and charming... too charming for someone like me. I consoled myself that his combination of attributes were impossible for any woman to resist.

Powerful and strong, sexy and charismatic, Gibson was definitely someone that people could never ignore. Staring at him almost hurt because he mesmerized me and I knew that each time I looked at him it was one less look until he was gone from me.

Pushing aside the fact that I was leaving the next day, I stroked his lips with my finger. Gibson immediately took it into his mouth and sucked it hard. My pussy squeezed his hard length, still deep inside me and released it, kissed the tip and smiled slowly.

Being uncertain at the beginning that night, I had tried to control the situation by taking the role of the dominant partner in the act. But I really wanted Gibson to take over, because I had no real clue how to please a man like him and mostly because I really needed him to show me that sex wasn't just about men helping themselves to a woman's body, the way Kace had done with me.

Placing my mouth near Gibson's ear I whispered softly, "Show me." Gibson leaned away from me and stopped moving. He stared questioningly at me in the moonlight, looking for a sign I hadn't just asked him that.

Gibson massaged his lips together, then moved in to kiss my lips softly before moving his mouth across my cheek to my ear. Gripping a small handful of my hair he asked, "Trust me?" His voice was raspy and low, almost a whisper, when he asked if I would submit my body to him to show me what sex was about.

"Yes." Instantly Gibson's mouth trailed down my neck and the sensation was electric. Sliding his hand from the middle of my back down between the crease of my butt, his finger began to tease around the entrance of my ass.

Soft moans escaped from the both of us and the effect he was having on me with his expert touch sent shivers all over my body. Shaking slightly, my body was humming in anticipation. But I was also feeling something new... fear. However, it was fear and excitement and I was wondering what I had just agreed to.

"Tell me what you want, Chloe. What do you like? How do you like it?" Gibson was moving inside me again, undulating, but he'd begun to take charge, lifting and lowering me, pushing and pulling my ass cheeks to help me ride his dick. He took my hand, then my weight in his strong arms and handled me like I was a feather. The water lapped around us and

I was vaguely aware of it making more noise with Gibson's more urgent and bigger movements.

"I want you to do what makes you feel good. If it makes you feel good it will do the same for me." Gibson took my mouth in another kiss, a fierce hungry one and began to move his hips more, lifting and lowering me a little faster than before and within five thrusts of his hips, I was clinging to him. Gibson's face in my neck barely nibbled a piece of my skin as if he was trying to control himself from more. Growling low and desperately, he broke away to look at me.

"Damn, Chloe, what the fuck are you doing to me? You're like a fucking drug."

Standing up, Gibson crushed me against his chest and managed to edge us out of the tub without pulling out. Knocking the soft, padded tub cover to the floor, he placed his hands on my butt cheeks and lowered us on to it. Lifting my legs upward and outward he crawled nearer to me, pushing himself deeper inside. "Oh, Gibson."

"Fuck. Chloe, I'm fighting to stay in control with you darlin'. I've never wanted *anyone* so badly." Feeling Gibson tremble slightly, the heightened awareness of his sheer physical size and strength made me stare back at him again, awestruck. He had swooping curves and chiseled muscle groups in his arms, pecs, and abs, making me literally want to lick him.

Taking my wrists in one hand he placed them together above my head. "Don't touch me, keep your hands there," he ordered. "Clasp them, no matter what, you keep your hands there, okay?"

My face must have registered my alarm because Gibson immediately held my face tenderly, crouching over to kiss me. In a low soothing voice full of emotion he said, "I got you, Chloe. Trust me." Something in the way he said it, made me relax.

Knowing what I had been through and how he responded when I told him, helped me to put my faith in him. Gibson began to rock into me, never taking his eyes off of me, his hands trailing both sides of my ribs, up over my breasts and shoulders and down my arms. My body was erupting with pleasure in the wake of each wave of sweeping movements he made. It was tender and attentive. I'd never known this level of adulation from Kace.

Again, I could feel tears choking my throat with emotion at how considerate and selfless he was being with me because every time I'd ever seen him with a girl, he was pounding her hard.

Watching him stare like that was sucking my soul from me so I closed my eyes. Gibson's mouth kissed my neck and he whispered, "Please Chloe, open your eyes, I want to see what I do to you, how I make you feel and for you to see how you make me feel."

How I was making him feel? When he said that, I was pretty confused. I was the one with my hands above my head, it was Gibson that was doing all the stimulating. I was so aroused and drunk with desire that a few moments later I began to lose it again and was stunned when I heard myself say, "Fuck me,

Gibson. Please fuck me."

Gibson continued to rock into me, keeping me on the edge and he gave me the sexiest smirk I've ever seen in my entire life. All my senses were on high alert, especially since I wasn't able to use my hands or bring my arms down.

"Good girl, you're learning to respond to your own body but you are going to have to convince me you really want me," He said smiling at me, but I'm sure he had been trying to sound stern. For a guy with his reputation, his self-control was amazing and not like the guy I remembered at all.

"I need you to show me, Gibson. Please show me what I do to you." Sexual tension radiated from his body, then Gibson's eyelids drooped seductively and he growled into my neck. "Fuck Chloe, I could easily lose control with you darlin'. Don't test me."

"Don't worry Gibson, there is no test at the end," I threw back at him, quoting again from conversations we'd had on the phone. Giving me a grin, it quickly dropped to an intense silent pause before he swept his hands under my back and rolled me on top of him.

Without warning, Gibson bunched a handful of my hair in his hand and held it close to my head. With his other strong hand on my butt cheek he began to move it up and down on him, pushing himself in and out of me deep and fast. Overwhelming feelings of pleasure and an emotional rush prevented me from being scared about this new experience.

Again, his face was inches from mine and he brought my forehead down to rest on his murmuring, "Let yourself go, Chloe, I got you. You're safe with me." At that point we both lost control, my nails digging into his hips, both of his arms holding me against his chest tightly as he did before when I started to come.

"Do it. Come. Don't hold back." Reading my body perfectly, Gibson could feel my muscles tighten, suddenly squeezing his dick tightly and drawing him deeper into me as my pussy clenched with my release.

Euphoric waves of ecstasy washed over me forcing me to bear down inside. Sharp, jerky muscle spasms lifted my head off the tub cover. "Beautiful Chloe, I got you, I got you." As hard as I tried to keep looking at him, my brain was in meltdown from the desire and being sated by the guy who definitely lived up to his reputation of a sex god, as well as a rock god.

Growling with need, Gibson held my butt cheeks in both his hands and rode me much harder for about a minute, pushing and pulling to ride him at his pace, thrusting rapidly from underneath. I'd never been fucked that hard or fast before and I heard myself say, "Don't stop that feels... sooo good."

I felt myself rise in orgasm again and so did he. "Do it, fuck, do it, I'm coming, yes, oh fuck yes, oh yeah... shit. Damn." His hot cum spurted inside me, his dick pulsing, his body stiffening then jerking in time with mine.

Gibson surprised me when he didn't slip out of me, but rolled me on my side and spooned with me. Turning my head, he cupped my chin and kissed me hard. "That was about you, Chloe. The next time, it's for me. Next time, we're doing it to my tune, darlin'. You'll feel the difference."

Lying in silence, I wondered what that meant. I felt like I'd been horse riding on a three day trek with a lot of saddle time. I had no idea how I would manage a 'next time' in the next few hours. We were due to leave in less than twelve.

"Almost five years." I frowned and searched his face when he spoke, then met his gaze and stroked down his arm that was across me, waiting for him to speak again. Gibson brushed some strands of wet hair away from my face and neck then licked his lips.

"Chloe, of all the girls I've kissed, your kiss has been the sweetest. Your lips have been the softest, your tongue the most teasing. Hell, you make me hard by kissing me – did you know that? I should apologize for all those other women but if I hadn't been with them, I'd never have known exactly what you do for me... to me."

Perplexed by his continued attention, I lay there staring at him, wondering why he was continuing to say all those things to me when he'd already got what he'd set out to have. Gibson had no reason to continue with his pretense.

He'd set his sights on me like every other woman who had ever swooped past him in life, I'd given him what he expected. In the process he had changed my view, in that Gibson Barclay wasn't just the two dimensional rock star manwhore I had thought he was.

CHAPTER 36

STARGAZING

Chloe

Gibson rolled onto his back and stared up at the dark sky. Sliding his arm under my neck, he drew my head into his chest. "So come on, educate me. Explain what's up there." He turned to look at me and I tilted my head up to meet his gaze.

The way he was smiling at me was so sexy. My heart did another flip-flop before I answered him. "Beats me, I'm not a star gazer, Gibson."

Gibson's brow furrowed and he shook his head. "That isn't what you said before." Smirking knowingly, I shook my head back at him, rubbing my cheek on his smooth hard chest.

"No, I said we looked at the stars. Not that we knew anything about them." I began to giggle and he tickled my ribs, which made me wriggle around at the side of him, then he kissed the top of my head and sighed deeply.

His affectionate gesture was so unexpected and

took me by surprise. I stared up at him mesmerized by the gorgeous man lying beside me, holding me and again, my heart squeezed. We both lay quietly for a few minutes until Gibson's cell phone rang again.

Looking at me, he exhaled deeply, then he shifted and got up off the floor to pick up his swimmers to retrieve his cell phone. With his withdrawal, I became very aware that I was still naked and lying on the floor, but as if Gibson sensed what I needed, he disappeared in the direction of the en-suite and brought me back a soft white bathrobe. Gibson listened to the caller and I didn't hear what was said while he had gone below deck to do that. When he hung up he looked worried.

Initially I had felt he was going to dismiss me, but he led me into the bathroom and leaned into the shower, turning the faucet on. I was feeling a little tender after our sex session and it must have shown on my face, because when he turned to face me again, his brow was creased in concern.

"Are you okay, Chloe? Did I hurt you?"

I was a little sore because of Gibson's size, but it was a reminder that I had let what happened with Kace go. I'd happily have chosen that kind of pain over the agony of being emotionally and physically beaten.

Smiling, I reassured him it was only through lack of any action recently and made a little joke out of it. I stepped into the shower and the water was so soothing. Gibson pulled a flannel from the side and soaked it under the shower then folded it and placed it between my legs. "Does that help?" It did, I wasn't used to that level of care.

I half expected Gibson to stay in the shower with me, but he didn't. Wandering through to the cabin bedroom, he disappeared out of sight. Tears threatened again and stung in my throat and I thought that was it. My reckless moment with Gibson Barclay.

This is where we went our separate ways. Then I was completely embarrassed because all I had to wear was my tankini and I really didn't want to sit around displaying my body after what had happened between us.

Pulling on the bathrobe again, I shook my hair out as best as I could and towel dried it. Making my way back into the bedroom, I saw Gibson lying on the bed talking on the phone in what looked like a serious conversation. When he looked up and caught my gaze he concluded his call abruptly. "Gotta go. Yeah, five minutes... got it."

Gibson edged his way to the end of the bed and stood up. You done? I'm just going to get in real quick. Johnny is coming with Toby's boat in five to take us back."

Gibson walked past me without looking at me and carried on through to the bathroom. There was no way I was taking that robe off again after that reception from him. True to his word, he was back in less than the five minutes and dressed in his swimmers again.

"Come on," he said, taking me by the hand and leading me back up on deck. Bombarded with a range of feelings, I followed but didn't speak. His contrary actions weren't working in my favor for being able to read what he was thinking.

Almost too intimate with the cloth in the shower, Gibson demonstrated a level of care I'd never experienced before – and then he had kind of dismissed me and left the bathroom. He'd arranged for Johnny to come as had gotten what he set out for with me, but yet taking my hand and being attentive while we waited for him. When Johnny arrived, I was feeling mortified because he probably saw me as just another groupie. Hell, maybe I was.

Again, while transferring into Toby's boat from the yacht Gibson was there, anticipating what I needed. "I got you, Chloe. Let go." Asserting his command, he placed his strong hands on my hips and hugged me tightly to him when I did.

Arriving back on dry land, I felt pretty stupid in my bath robe. Especially as it was about eighty eight degrees and directly opposite the flood lit jetty was a restaurant full of people, staring out the window at us.

Johnny drove us to our hotels and dropped Gibson off first at his before taking me back. I was feeling pretty choked up, as well as cheap, when Gibson kissed me hungrily, then gave me the, 'I'll call you' line before he got out.

Sitting in silence on the way back to my hotel, I fought back tears and thought that was it. My fantasy day with Gibson was over and I was desperate to be in the privacy of my room so that I could have my breakdown.

Johnny pulled up in front of the entrance and got out to open the door, but I had already opened the other side and was making my way out in the stupid bathrobe and my bare feet. At that point, I didn't care what I looked like and I didn't want to give him the satisfaction of becoming a mess and he and Gibson possibly having a discussion about me later.

Unfortunately, I wasn't quick enough and Johnny grabbed me by my arm, almost pulling me off my feet. "Sorry honey, I always get the rough end of the stick with this stuff. I'm sure if he said he'll call you, he will."

Feeling a sob trapped at the back of my throat, I turned on my heel, fled through the hotel foyer and into the elevator. Once I was in there I realized I had no key to open my door, so I headed to Ruby's room.

My luck had run out as she wasn't in there so I found myself at Gavin's door, but by that time everything had become too much for me, and I was distressed and sobbing. Gavin opened the door and as soon as he saw me, his arms engulfed me and he pulled me inside his room and into his chest.

Once again all the history I'd been fighting against came rushing back, making me feel like a victim and making me feel a combination of easy, angry, stupid, weak and cheap.

What I'd done with Gibson was amazing, and

he'd shown me more courtesy than he had with the other girls I'd seen him with. The fact remained that he'd set out to have a girl, 'bagged me,' and discarded me.

Gavin placed me on his bed and went to get me a glass of water. When he came back his jaw ticked with anger and he looked agitated. Showing a lot of consideration for my history, Gavin was gentle in his probing about what had happened to me.

"You don't have to talk about it if you don't want to, Chloe. Just tell me one thing. Did he hurt you?" He had, but not in the way that Gavin was thinking. Gibson had been considerate and attentive all day, but the way he reacted as soon as we'd had sex had made me feel he had used me, like he had no further use for me.

"You're staying here tonight, Chloe. I can't let you go back to your room in this state. I don't want you to be alone."

I nodded in agreement because I had no choice. I had only my tankini and the bathrobe from the yacht. My phone was in my bag that I took to the beach and left on the sand bar. I was so stupid – why didn't I think about keeping myself safe around Gibson? I lost all ability to protect myself, and really didn't want to be alone after today. Instinctively, I knew that Gavin was only telling me I was staying for him to look after me.

Gavin asked me to call the concierge and tell them that I left my key and that Gavin was going to collect it from them to bring me some things from my room. When Gavin left the room I was feeling so exhausted that I stripped everything and crawled into his bed. I knew it was stupid to do, but I needed to get out of the swimsuit. Besides, I was such a teary mess and feeling so low, that I didn't really care what happened to me at that point.

My mind was blocking everything that had gone on from the point where Gibson took me on to Toby's boat. I knew it was protecting me from further distress because my brain wouldn't let me think about what had happened during the day. Each time I even tried to recall something I had a tense knot in my stomach and my head and heart hurt.

I never heard Gavin coming back, but when I woke it was morning and he was lying next to me, staring at my face. "Sorry, I didn't know what to do for the best, Chloe." Initially, my brow creased, confused at what he meant, but then realized that the comforter was only covering my legs.

Alarmed, I clutched at a sheet and pulled it over me to protect my modesty, not that there was anything left to the imagination by the time I was awake.

Rolling over and standing up off the bed, Gavin ran his hand through his hair and sighed heavily before he sat with his back to me on the bed. Dressed in his jeans but naked from the waist up. I'd had mixed feelings about him lying beside me during the night.

It was his bed, but he had been lying facing me while I slept naked. There was a lot wrong with that picture. I'd taken him with me to see a guy who was a mega rock star, who had orchestrated meeting me and then took me on a boat to have sex, dropped me off and now I was lying naked in the bed of the guy I'd brought with me. What made it ten times worse was that he knew I was asleep but still lay beside me while I was exposed.

"Jeez, Chloe... I'm sorry, I wasn't deliberately looking at you. When I came back last night, you were sound asleep. My first thought was to go and sleep in your bed. Then I figured that Ruby may come and get the wrong idea if she found me there, so I stayed here and tried to sleep on the chair. I was so uncomfortable that when I woke my back was in a spasm, so I just took my shirt off and lay on the bed. Chloe, I swear I never touched you and with what you told me, I was careful not to do anything.

"When I woke, which was about a minute before you, I was still trying to figure my shit out about how to get off the bed without waking you. If I'd covered you, I was worried you'd think the opposite and that I was trying to take it off."

Actually, he was right. Although I wasn't happy about him seeing me naked, he hadn't asked for any of what had gone on. He was just a friend giving me somewhere to sleep for the night. Gavin nodded his head and his eyes flicked over to the second chair that was in the hotel room by the small coffee table.

There was my toiletry bag, some lingerie, flip flops, jeans, shorts, and my favorite blue and cream t-shirt. Gavin had even coordinated my underwear with my outfit. Just as I was about to get out of the bed, there was a knock at the door. Gavin looked at me and innocently went to answer the door, while I repositioned the sheet.

I was stunned when I heard Gibson's voice asking if Gavin knew where he could find me. In the mirror I could see Gavin's back with the door open slightly, but Gibson wasn't visible to me.

"Sorry dude, no, I thought she was with you." Gavin was covering and I wasn't sure whether I wanted that or not, but after seeing how I was the previous night, I guess he thought he was protecting me.

"Can I come for in a minute?" My heart, which had been pounding in my chest that he was there at all stopped when I heard him ask that, but Gibson didn't wait for an answer and pushed his way in before Gavin had the chance to object or react.

Two strides past the mirror, and I was visible but I think he had caught sight of my reflection before he came face to face with me.

"You gotta be fucking kidding me, darlin,'" Gibson's face was scowling when he glanced at Gavin and his thunderous look quickly turned nasty. Gritting his teeth, his mouth twisted with one lip curled up, and I could see he was seething about the scenario he thought he was facing.

Before either Gavin or I could speak, Gibson spoke in a low threatening tone. "My security guy made me feel like shit because he said I'd hurt her last night. Guess you were there to comfort her, did you fuck her to make her feel better?"

I was appalled he could even think that after everything I had told him, but I was too scared by his aggression to speak up for myself at that point.

"Dude..." Gavin started to talk, but Gibson grabbed him both by the throat and the crotch and squeezed. Gavin yelped but couldn't speak because Gibson had him by the throat and his face was getting redder by the second.

"Do your nuts hurt? I fucking hope so, I should cut your dick off. You're a fucking asshole, you know that? What the fuck, dude? Ain't you got no shame, taking my sloppy seconds? Couldn't fucking resist her even though you knew she had been with me?"

Looking at me over his shoulder Gibson threw another insult, "You fucking let him bone you, when you'd been with me only a few hours before? Spinning me the sweet victim act? Damn you, Chloe... it fucking worked, I believed you."

Gibson gave Gavin his attention again. "I saw the way you looked at her. Did you make her come the way I did?" He pushed Gavin back by the throat and he knocked over a bottle of whisky that Gavin had opened on the side.

Amber liquid flowed from the dressing table onto the carpet, soaking into it silently until it was so saturated it made a patting sound, as the rest dripped from the bottle. A strong odor filled the room and Gibson twisted his body quickly to stare at me, still sitting in the bed.

"You're fucking good. I'll give you that. You had

me fooled for sure. All that crying and shit, I really believed your sob story. My instincts were to fuck you hard, but I took care of you. Did you enjoy taking me for a ride? Thought it would be cool to give me a taste of what it feels like to be used?"

As Gibson turned to address Gavin once again, I wasn't frightened for myself but for Gavin. There was no way I was going to allow Gibson to continue to target him like that.

"STOP!" I bounced off of the bed and was standing naked in front of both of them, my hands up to stop Gibson from continuing his assault. Glancing over at Gavin, he was still struggling to get himself together and clutching his throat. The agony on his face told me that Gibson hadn't held back on his handling of him. Poor guy had done me a favor and ended up on the wrong end of Gibson Barclay's raw side.

The both of them stopped to look at me and I almost cringed because of my naked state but I stood firm. This wasn't about what I looked like naked. It was about someone damaging my reputation. He may be Gibson Barclay but I was damned if I was going to be tarnished with the same brush because I had been with him.

CHAPTER 37

READ WRONG

Gibson

"Devastated." When I had asked Johnny how Chloe was when he dropped her off, he gave me that one word answer. There wasn't time to explain what was going on. I just had to deal with it before it got so out of hand she never spoke to me again.

The steward on the yacht, who I knew now was Wallace Price, had taken some pretty damning pictures of the two of us on deck and named his price. Three major US newspapers and two gossip magazines had picked up the story and my legal team were on it, but I wanted to oversee it myself.

One headline read, "*Gibson Gropes Gorgeous Groupie*" The article went on... "*Gibson Barclay scores a home run with yet another stunning female. Grooming her in style, the ever promiscuous Gibson meticulously planned his seduction of innocent unsophisticated competition winner, Chloe Jenner, of New York City, yesterday. Hiring a luxury yacht for the day, Gibson moved in on the curvaceous Chloe after plying the unassuming blonde haired beauty with cocktails. Their day had begun with a day out frolicking on the waves with best mate Toby Francis and his band mates, the rest of M3rCy and Chloe's friends. According to Price, a steward in attendance on board the yacht, the couple weren't shy about their alfresco session. Gibson and his latest squeeze arrived on the boat wearing only swimwear which was quickly discarded. In true Gibson style, Price stated, that as soon as Barclay achieved his goal and the smoking hot scene with the pretty fan was over, the date came to an abrupt end. Jenner won a recent competition to meet her idol and fell under 'the Gibson effect', resulting in the not so private sex session. Chloe Jenner was conspicuously missing from her hotel room late last night, so was unavailable for comment."*

Fuck. Usually, I laughed when I read how interested the paparazzi were about me getting my rocks off., but this time, the one time I wanted to keep everything private, and had gone to lengths to make sure we were alone, I'd blown it.

Legally, Price had abused my trust and lost his job and my lawyers stated they were going to sue for invasion of privacy. However, that didn't help me or protect Chloe from the media bashing or the crazy fans that would target her for being with me.

Strong, almost primal instincts to protect Chloe from everyone hadn't panned out, and she was facing a potential shit storm that I could neither make go away, nor offer her the anonymity she needed. The press and fans would hound her.

The only way forward was if I kept her with me. That thought excited the hell out of me. However, reading the headlines I doubted my capacity to make her see that my intentions weren't what the media were portraying, so the chances of keeping her close to me until this blew over were almost non-existent.

While we were heading over to her hotel, Johnny complained the whole time, telling me that this was not the way to make things better, showing up at her room when the media were already fueling a story and spinning it to slant in the direction they thought would sell more copies.

Overwhelmed with crazy mad emotions, I could see Johnny was worried that some of the paparazzi might challenge me and I'd throw a punch. As for me, the way I was feeling I was kinda hoping someone would, so that I could feel justified in doing just that.

Chloe's hotel foyer was swarming with media parasites, cameras flashing everywhere as soon as I walked through the door, rushing at me like flies on shit. My mood was so fucking black that I was biting my lip in my attempt to reach the elevator lobby without saying anything that made it worse for her. Johnny was talking for me, stating that I had nothing to say, and then he pushed two guys back that got too near.

"No fucking comment dudes, back off, Johnny barked, as two hotel security guys pushed forward and threatened to call the police if they didn't move out of the way. Just then, the elevator arrived and we both stepped inside. Some photographers were still trying to take shots and one reporter squeezed under the security guy's arm in an effort to get to us, but the door closed and insanity instantly stopped.

Sagging back against the wall, I ran my hand through my hair and stared darkly at Johnny. "Fuck, what a cluster fuck. How the fuck am I going to convince her that yesterday wasn't what they are saying it is?"

Johnny folded his arms and crossed a leg over his other one, leaning sideways on the wall to face me. Snickering, he commented, "Gibson, if anyone can talk her round, it's you. This is where all your lines and seductive ways get to join forces, dude. Plus, she's a chick. I've never known one yet that can stay mad at you for more than five minutes."

All those women I'd ever spun a line, teased or flirted with in the past were haunting me. Johnny's words were exactly why I'd have trouble convincing Chloe to believe that yesterday wasn't just staged to ensure I got laid.

Charlotte had already established that Chloe wasn't in her room and that Gavin had picked up a key for her last night. So we headed directly to his room which would give me a couple of precious minutes to establish where she was before someone from the press caught up with us, because they would think I was heading straight to hers.

When Gavin opened the door, there was

something in the way he held the door that told me there was a chick in there with him. I'm not stupid, I've stood the same way on many occasions. "Hey, dude, sorry to interrupt you. Do you know where I can find Chloe?"

Being a guilty man all too often, I recognized the look he was giving me and before he spoke, I was already realizing that Chloe was in there with him. My heart began to thud fast in my chest because she was hiding from me.

"Sorry dude, no, I thought she was with you." As soon as he lied my temper went from zero to sixty and I fought to keep it under control.

"Can I come in for a minute?" Not waiting for Gavin to answer, I pushed him back and strode into the room, expecting to see Chloe sitting there. Instead, I saw her reflection in the mirror; a shocked look on her face, sitting naked in the dude's bed.

Taking in the scene and that Gavin was half naked, I assumed he'd probably pulled on his jeans to answer the door. Feeling so fucking hurt by her being with him, I wondered who was playing who? I thought she'd left my bed and jumped straight into his. "You gotta be fucking kidding me, darlin'."

Thunderous thoughts that she'd gone to him for help and the dude had taken advantage of her vulnerability made me want to kill him.

Addressing Gavin, "My security guy made me feel like shit because he said I'd hurt her last night. Guess you were there to comfort her and fuck her to make her feel better, right?"

Gavin tried to speak, "Dude..." Reacting to my seething thoughts, I grabbed Gavin by the windpipe and his nuts because I was done being reasonable. Gavin yelped and I honestly didn't give a fuck how much pain he was in, it could never be as bad as I was feeling about giving myself to someone, opening up my feelings and getting them trampled upon.

Glancing at her in the mirror, sitting there holding a sheet over her to cover up what was already etched into my mind, I felt betrayed by the one person I had thought might be the reason why my life had had such a void until now. The one void that might have been my true purpose in life, who meant more than making music and hanging out in the fucked up world I had sold into.

"Do your nuts hurt? I fucking hope so, I should cut your dick off. You're a fucking asshole. What is it with you, dude? You got no shame taking my sloppy seconds? Couldn't fucking resist her even though you knew she had been with me?"

Deep down in my conscience, my rational side kept telling me to stop; that there must be a logical explanation for her being there, but seeing how he behaved at the door and her sitting naked in his bed... it just seemed to add up to a lot more.

So I threw a few more insults around, accused her of getting with him after me. In fact, I almost lost it altogether and really went for it about how she'd played me, then it got to the point where I was so fucking annoyed I was going around in circles.

Suddenly, Chloe got off the bed and stood in

front of us naked. Gavin looked away and I could see he was thinking about her modesty, but I was transfixed. She had guts, knowing everything I knew about her and seeing the look on her face, I knew instantly I had called their scene wrongly.

When she started to attack me with words like hypocrite and defending Gavin, getting in between us, I was done. I'd come to protect her and she was turning what had happened between us into a fucking hook up.

"Just who the hell do you think you are, Gibson? It's okay for you to fuck around and no one else, right? Or, you behave that way and think everyone else behaves like a dog as well? Fuck you, Gibson Barclay."

Chloe walked over to a chair and began to dress in the cutest blue lingerie and I was mad we were arguing because I'd have loved to have laid my hands on her cute ass in those blue lacy boy shorts she was pulling over the globes of her ass.

She pointed to Gavin who was still looking at the ground. "This guy right here –take a good look Gibson, because this is the guy who took care of me last night when you discarded me. He never slept with me and he never touched me. Gavin was the perfect gentleman. Unlike you, who performed your famous 'done and run' routine on me."

Drawing breath to come back at her, it caught in my throat and I stopped dead in my tracks and gave her a stunned look because that was the last thing I wanted her to feel.

"Is that what you think happened? I used you? Did nothing I said yesterday sink in to that skull of yours? You have no fucking idea how I feel or what I do, or why I left you with Johnny. For one day... just one day I wish people wouldn't think the worst of me."

Glancing over at Gavin, he looked as if he were still in pain and I felt sorry for him because by then I had realized he had done my job for me and taken care of Chloe. I should have been thanking him. But I still wasn't feeling very benevolent toward anyone so I just nodded and said, "Do you mind dude. I want to speak with Chloe alone."

Gavin raised his brow and turned to Chloe. "Well, what does Chloe think about that, Gibson? Anyone dismisses me, it's her. For the record, because of how you took care of her yesterday the paparazzi were all over her room last night. She was safer with me than she was with your provision. Also, I owe you nothing and you're lucky that I know Chloe's history and have more self-control than you do, because if you want to come at me like that again, best your bodyguard is on the same side of the door. Ever grab me by the balls again, and I'll break your fucking fingers."

Gavin wasn't a pushover I could see that, but I knew if he fucked with my chances with Chloe, I'd fuck with any part of his anatomy I saw fit to. Staring him down, the altercation could have gone either way, but I had a bigger issue to deal with so I let what he said wash over me. "Chloe?"

Exchanging glances with Gavin then me, Chloe nodded at Gavin and he went over and held her by the arms, speaking to her like she was one of his children. “Any problems I’m outside in the corridor honey, okay?” Chloe smiled weakly at him and Gavin limped toward the door. Striding past him I pulled it open and signaled to Johnny to keep him busy.

Once we were alone, I explained my reason for leaving the yacht so abruptly. When I broke the news about the pictures to Chloe she was devastated, as I knew she would be. Her first thought was about the ex-boyfriend coming after her.

“Chloe, the way I figure this is, you can be a victim or you can adopt the so-fucking-what attitude. Personally, I think it has worked well for me, too well really, because no one believes I can do anything honorable anymore.

However, my take on this is that shit happens and after several years of getting pissed and wanting to get even I was beginning to develop an ulcer, so now I have the so-what-nobody-died attitude and that gets me through most things.”

Seeing how devastated she looked, I stepped forward and pulled her against my chest. I remembered the first time I hugged her; how tense she had been. There was no difference in that hug to my effort to comfort her at that point but I held her tightly and after a few seconds felt the sag of her body against mine as she became relaxed, her arms snaking around me and clinging to the back of my t-shirt.

Pushing away from me, Chloe's head tilted upwards, her eyes meeting mine, tears were welling in hers. "What am I going to do? What if Kace finds me? What if these people follow me home?"

Biting her lip, Chloe looked terrified and I thought about everything she had told me the day before and how difficult the situation would have been for the most emotionally sound of people. Add domestic violence to being stalked by the media, and it could push her to a breakdown.

"You don't have to be anywhere, do you? I mean, when you go back to New York you don't have a schedule to follow or anything?" Chloe's brow bunched and I could see she had no idea what I was thinking.

"No, I'm trying to write, I told you that. So..."

There was only one answer to this. "Okay, settled. The best way to keep you safe and get the media off your back is for you to stay with me. You're coming to Rio with me."

Chloe immediately tried to free herself from me, but I held her tight and began to reason with her, talking quickly to stop her from shutting down on me.

"Listen, wait, whoa! Those guys won't let up on us unless we do this my way, I guarantee it. The best way to get rid of them is for me to deal with this with my team behind us. We'll face this head on. So we issue a statement that we don't care who knows we've had sex, that's what couples do, right?"

I could see that Chloe was about to protest

about the couples reference and I was concerned that she wouldn't go for it, but fuck I wanted her with me not just because of the press, but because I needed more time with her.

"Okay, we make a statement about us being old friends turned lovers, and that we don't care who knows we had sex because we're finally together. I mean, it's not a complete lie is it? We had met before. Once the press see us together, their 'groupie' tag will be dropped and they'll go find someone else to stalk."

Staring at me, Chloe looked visibly distressed as she tried to explain her feelings and come to grips with what the pictures meant for her.

"Kace is going to know exactly where I am if I'm with you, Gibson."

"So he might, but who better to deal with a guy like him than Johnny?"

I could see her mull over what I said. Chloe knew I was right about that.

"How many more days do I have to spend with you for the story to die down? How do I, plain old Chloe Jenner, recover from all of that attention, Gibson? I'll be known as the groupie girl who won a competition and got to fuck Gibson Barclay, forever."

When she said that, I really felt for her and wondered what I had done by bringing her into that circus? Chloe's face was ashen and set in a grave expression and I prayed I'd be able to talk her around to coming with me.

CHAPTER 38

PASSPORT

Chloe

Shaking my head in disbelief as I inspected my newly acquired passport, I was impressed at the way Gibson's name could produce it for me in an afternoon. I was more than a little frightened and feeling intimidated about the situation I had found myself in.

Knowing that Kace would have found out exactly where I was as soon as the story broke, I was petrified that he'd find me before I got out of there, so I had agreed without much forethought to accompanying Gibson and M3rCy to Rio. So much for my secret new life.

There was no doubt about it, the media articles would have alerted him about my whereabouts, and if I knew Kace the way I thought I did, he'd have been on his way to LA as soon as the story broke. We had unfinished business and my instincts told me he would be coming after me with a vengeance.

Biting my lip, I pondered at how ridiculous my situation was. For most girls, being linked to Gibson Barclay would have been a dream come true, but for me, it was beginning to become a traumatic event.

All the press coverage that Gibson talked about made me think that there may be weeks of the same scrutiny, not to mention my reputation and how that would look to my parents and the scandal they would have to endure at home.

Apart from that, whatever story Kace had been spinning about me would gain more credence for my apparently off-the-rails tryst with Gibson. Behaving like a star struck teenager was the most likely gossip, or I'd had a breakdown. I could almost hear what they'd be spreading and I was stuck; standing with my head bowed in shame with my hands in my pockets looking guilty, metaphorically speaking.

Every combination I thought about for dealing with the news, lead me nowhere. Gibson was right. Staying with him was the only way to deal with the media and keep me safe from Kace until I could formulate a new plan to get away from him again.

At least Gibson was doing the right thing and not just casting me out to deal with all the attention on my own. It was bugging me that he was going to spin it like we were a couple, because in a few weeks when I was no longer there, I would still have to face everything at some point and maybe I could never go back to my apartment, now that Kace and Gibson's fans had wind of where I was.

Being with Gibson hadn't been ideal but it gave

me a way forward. After having sex with him it was weird, but I felt like I was free of Kace's control. However, with the media attention it was critical that I focus on the bigger picture and gain strength from the progress I had made so far.

"Alright. I'll come." Gibson's smile beamed widely then he was hugging me tightly and I felt him exhale as his arms tightened in a small squeeze. "Good girl. I got you, Chloe. No one is going to fuck with you as long as I'm around."

Hearing him say that made my heart swell. Being near him made me feel heady, although thinking about him taking me on tour to another country gave me a bout of nerves that almost made me turn and run. *Am I insane?*

Before Kace, I had always been a strong girl. It would have taken a lot to break me. It *had* taken a lot to break me, so right at that moment I had to reclaim myself from falling back into the role of the beaten, timid and scared young woman that Kace had molded me into.

Within a matter of hours, I'd been smuggled through the hotel kitchen and into a plumber's truck, like a kidnap scene from a movie. Afterwards, I was driven to the airport and stowed aboard Gibson's plane. I was thanking my lucky stars that 'Barbie Doll' was absent.

I found myself sitting on the plane alone and was suddenly overwhelmed with everything that had happened in the past twenty-four hours. Silent tears rolled down my face. I tried to convince myself once again, that I had made the right decision to accompany Gibson Barclay on tour to Rio.

Gavin and Ruby arranged to collect my stuff from the hotel and were taking it home. Because of the risk of the press getting to me, I could only to say goodbye to Ruby by phone. After she explained that the media were going nuts about me, I knew I'd made the right choice to stay with Gibson.

Kace had already been in touch with her because he saw her picture in another newspaper, which described her as Mick Connor's hook up. An accusation she never denied. I made a mental note to come back to that with her, once I knew I was safe.

About forty five minutes later Gibson and his band arrived and took their seats. Gibson sat alongside me and there were three seats left once the guys in the band sat down. Tori, the keyboard player, took the seat opposite me.

My initial feeling was one of relief that she was going to be friendly, but her facial expression told me that she was feeling anything but that and she was staring at me hard.

"Find another seat." Gibson scowled at Tori and her eyes flicked to mine, but she didn't move. Gibson huffed heavily and said it again. "I said find another seat, I want some privacy."

Tori looked at me, and commented, "You heard the man, Chloe, Gibson wants me alone."

Gibson leaned forward and spoke in a low voice to her. "Not fucking funny, now get your ass out of that seat before I do it for you."

Tori snickered and stared at him, her lips curving upwards in a smug smile. "Gibson, not clever to talk about touching my ass while you have your little... whatever, with you." She shook her head and Gibson unbuckled his belt and stood up.

"Move it. Get the fuck out of that seat." Within seconds Lennox was by Gibson's side.

"Tori, are you making mischief with the boss again? Move your ass over beside me and leave him alone. You know full well you're pissing him off and he wants to spend some time with Chloe."

Lennox took her hand and she slowly stood up, leaning her breasts in toward Gibson and she whispered something in his ear. Gibson's mouth curled up in a snarl and he bit his anger back. His jaw muscle twitched several times as he became agitated and his whole posture seemed aggressive.

Flopping back down on the chair, Gibson's elbow landed on the armrest and his index finger ran across his lips while he exhaled heavily again. "Sorry Chloe, band stuff."

Jeez, I got some insight into why Gibson acted the way he did but the guy was a blatant liar... there was more going on between those two than I knew. Glancing across at Tori, I could see she was annoyed about me being on the plane with them and looked back in time to see Gibson staring darkly, shaking his head with pursed lips at her.

Tori leaned over and flicked the music newspaper that Lennox was reading with the back of her hand. Lennox pulled the paper down and gave her a hard stare before shaking the paper out in her direction. She was a good looking girl but her attitude made her ugly.

Tori inclined her head in Gibson's direction but spoke to Lennox. "What the fuck is wrong with you, Gibson? Someone bite your ass?" She turned and smirked at Gibson, who was seething. Then smiled sarcastically at me and commented, "Don't worry, Chloe, we know it wasn't you. You're way too submissive and vanilla to do anything kinky."

Gibson unbuckled his seatbelt again and got out of his seat. That made me nervous because the plane had begun to taxi along the runway and the cabin crew girl, Lexa, called out from her seat for him to sit back down again.

Gibson threw his arm back in her direction and walked over to Tori. Bending forward he said, "Watch your fucking mouth, lady. You play the fucking keyboard and piano – not me, got it? If you have a problem with that tell me right now, 'cause the way I'm feeling about you, there is only a door between you and that tarmac out there. You got me?"

Seeing the smirk drop from Tori's face as Gibson's words hit home was strange. One minute she was all assertive and cock-sure of herself, the next she was looking pretty stupid and not nearly as smart mouthed as she had been a few seconds before.

Gibson came back and sat down heavily in his

seat, reaching for the buckle and clipping himself in securely, only just making it as the plane left the ground. Exhaling heavily, he threw her another dark look and muttered almost to himself, "Fucking bitch, she'd better watch that smart mouth of hers."

Being in between them like that was difficult and I felt really uneasy about having to be there at all. Apart from the hugs when I agreed to stay with him, he hadn't shown any other obvious affection toward me and I figured I was there because I needed to be, not because that was what he wanted.

We were all pretty exhausted from the day before and for most of the flight we slept or the guys had some discussions about their set order and promotional stuff. Charlotte had sent a wad of photographs for the band to sign and a ton of other small tasks that kept them busy until we arrived in Rio.

M3rCy was playing at Rock in Rio, a massive festival with hundreds of thousands of music fans, and as usual they had top billing on the last night on the main stage. From the moment we got off the plane, there was an entourage of people, all vying for the attention of the band members.

Luckily Charlotte was already there and ushered me to the side where she introduced me to a tall, brick built guy called Jerry. At first I thought he looked really familiar, like I'd seen him somewhere and then realized he was the spitting image of Mark Wahlberg.

Jerry grabbed my bag and walked me to the

SUV. He placed my red, hard bodied suitcase in the back as I got into the SUV. Gibson was still standing on a platform in front of the media on the tarmac.

My initial thought was that poor Jerry was going to be the one keeping me company until it was time for me to go home. Panic struck when I thought about that, because I no longer felt safe from Kace by being in New York.

Sliding into the back seat of the car I glanced over and expected to see Gibson still being swallowed up by the crowd of people on the runway, but instead he was only about ten feet from the car and heading in our direction.

Jerry opened the door and Gibson slid in beside me as the sound of the door closing clunked with a finality that registered with me. Gibson grinned but it wasn't like the smiles he'd given me the day before, it was his sexy rock star, glittery image that I'd seen a million times on posters, album covers, and on T.V. "Sorry about that darlin', sometimes we're treated like fucking circus freaks when we arrive in town."

That day I'd been travelling with him and his band for about ten hours altogether, but I'd only spoken about five sentences in total. Gibson hadn't seemed to notice because he was involved in band meetings on the plane and media stuff.

Watching the band meeting had been interesting, mainly because Gibson's 'alpha male' persona was out in force as he dealt with decisions in a curt, almost dismissive manner, especially with Tori.

Also, the odd altercation between him and her had him seriously ticked off because after his initial exchange with her, he had sat in an angry silence. From what I saw of her, I knew I didn't like her, but if that was always how Gibson treated her then I wasn't surprised by her behavior toward him.

"Chloe, we're heading to the hotel now and you're going to be staying with me. I won't be able to sleep if I don't know you are safe." So far I had been swept along with his plans, mostly because I was afraid of Kace finding me, and partly because there was no way I wanted to face the media and fans about sleeping with Gibson, but I refused to be a burden to him.

What was clear was his language. There was nothing reassuring for me and he hadn't said he wanted to keep *me* safe. It seemed that I was only there so that his mind was at rest. With that, a wave of emotion threatened to engulf me. On the one hand, he had treated me like I was the only girl in the world for him, and on the other he did exactly what he wanted, in true Gibson form.

With that thought I felt like I was going to break down again and I had told myself I was done with doing that, so taking a deep shaky breath, I knew I had to find the courage to walk away and somehow sort that mess out for myself.

Embarrassment about being a burden made me feel more than a little angry. Anger is a great emotion for making impulse decisions and I knew I was taking a leap in the dark, but there was no way I was going to stay in that ludicrous situation with someone of his magnitude out of some strange sense of duty.

Realizing I had allowed him to take on the problem because the effort of dealing with it – the consequences of the pictures and Kace – scared me. I was afraid of the outcome and also realized that relying on someone like Gibson wasn't the answer. Easy solutions required that I think outside of the box, so I figured the best answer was for me to get lost abroad for a while.

Glancing up at Gibson, I managed to smile even though looking at him had begun to break my heart. In the short time I'd been with him, I had fallen under the Gibson effect. Heartbreakingly handsome and with a personality that sucked me in like a vacuum, I had allowed myself to think for the briefest time that everything he'd said to me was genuine.

After observing him on the plane, and how harsh he was with Tori, the headlines about Gibson rang true. In his own setting he seemed self-indulgent and I wasn't sure whether his behavior around his band was complete self-assurance or arrogance.

Gibson slid his arm around me and tried to pull me into his chest, but I lifted my hand and pressed it against his firm pectorals to stop him from completing the move. Gibson looked at me with a puzzled expression. It was going to be hard to walk away, but this was going nowhere and my heart was already aching at the loss.

"Listen Gibson, I'm really grateful for all you've done to take me away from those people, but I don't expect anything else from you. I'm not sure that allowing people to believe I am attached to you is such a good idea for me right now. More lies won't solve the attention I've had. Thank you for helping me to steer clear of those people and Kace, but I've got it from here."

Gibson looked visibly shaken by my response and removed his arm from around me. "You think that's the only reason I brought you? That I only brought you with me for that? That my people wouldn't know how to hide you? Fuck Chloe, what do I have to do to make you understand? I like you... fuck... I *really* like you. Jeez, girl, you think I'd have wanted to soothe someone who's freaking out around me all the time for fun? What do I have to do to make you understand I want you here?"

CHAPTER 39

SOMETHING I NEED

Gibson

Sitting up straight in the car seat, I lifted my arm clear of her and placed my now fisted hand hand down on my knee. My knuckles were white and I could feel the tension in my neck from the tight muscles flexing. I felt agitated and pretty pissed off that she'd gone along with my plan and come all that way with me, only to jump as soon as we'd got there.

"You think the media and your dumb fuck of an ex are the only reasons I brought you here? That I only brought you with me for that?" I began rubbing my hands up and down my jeans because if they weren't busy I think I'd have punched the window out. No matter what I did, people judged me on my past conduct and also with their own suspicious minds.

Turning to face her but careful not to touch, I noted the crease in her brow and the worried look she had, and I tried to soften the way I was speaking to her, but fuck that wasn't easy. I was tired of people not being straight with me or thinking that I didn't have any feelings because I was this big shot rock star who everyone knew or thought they knew all of my business.

"You think that my people wouldn't know how to give the media the slip and hide you from that fucking excuse for a man you had? Fuck Chloe, what do I have to do to make you understand? I like you... fuck... I *really* like you. Jeez, girl, you think I'd have cared for you like I did if I'd been toying with you?"

Jerry had the radio on in the front and I could just make out, "Something I Need" by One Republic and the line, "In this world full of people there's one killing me..." and I thought *no joke. I knew once I'd met her I needed her in my life, but never figured on all the shit she'd been through.*

We arrived at the hotel, and I was done trying to be amenable. I'd had a fucking long day and she was staying. Five years I had thought about her and I had wondered since I'd found her on the phone, if there was something in that feeling I'd been harboring. Once I had spent time with her I was more convinced than ever that she had all kinds of possibilities for my future.

I took her by the hand, there was no way I was giving her time to think about what I was doing. Jerry stopped the car and I wasn't giving her a second to come up with yet another rejection line. "We need to talk about it upstairs. It isn't safe for me here. Come on, we need to go, now."

That wasn't exactly a lie. There were hundreds of girls who already had wind that we were around and were camped out in front of the hotel door. Not to mention those with money that had snagged themselves a room in the hotel. A year ago, one of those may well have made it into my bed if they'd been inventive enough at getting my attention.

Over the years I'd witnessed all sorts of antics in order to get with me and yeah... sometimes when I was younger they had worked, but I was mostly past that behavior now, except when I was drunk, but I was working on it.

Jerry was always ahead of the game and he'd pulled down the alleyway. I knew this hotel layout well because I'd stayed there several times before. The security guys always gave me a dry run of where the emergency rooms were to take sanctuary in, in the event someone prevented me from making it to my own.

From past experiences, I knew that my fans could get a little, or a lot crazy. And, some had pretty fucked up fantasies, mainly that if only I could spend time with a particular girl they all hoped I'd learn that she was 'the one.'

Jerry ushered us into the elevator after making sure it was clear of fans and the three of us rode up to our suite in silence. Johnny was already at the hotel, and was waiting outside when we arrived on our floor. Walking ahead of us, Johnny led us down the narrow red carpeted corridor, until he arrived at the double doors of the penthouse suite. Swiping the key card he pushed the door open to our room, then handed me one.

Being with Chloe the day before had made me want to be a better person. The sex hadn't been perfect, because I'd had to hold back all my crazy pent up feelings about her. The last thing I had wanted to do was scare her, and I could tell she hadn't been very adventurous and didn't have a great deal of experience before.

Circumstances around our first time had made me feel annoyed that I had moved in on her despite what had gone on before, but I'd had little control after waiting all those years to explore the possibility of real relationship with her.

Feeling her in my arms and finally touching her amazing warm, satiny skin was an incredible feeling. Chloe showed me her strong side because despite everything that had happened that day before we got down to it, she had taken the lead.

That must have taken her a lot of guts, especially because she was recovering from a shitty relationship and she knew all about my reputation. All things considered, I had thought we definitely had a lot of potential.

Oh, but fuck, could she give head! That part had been perfect and despite everything there was still a great connection between us. She never even blinked at the fact I had an Apa and I wondered if her ex had been pierced when she made no comment.

In my mind there was definitely going to be a next time and the one after that featuring in my plans, because I really wanted to get to know her and explore the chemistry going on between us. My thoughts about us were that there could very well be some very explosive sex in the mix.

Understanding was what I felt Chloe needed and I hoped I could help her with that. Not to forget her past, but to live with it. Maybe if I did that for her, she'd concentrate on what was going on between us.

Like all the other penthouses across the world, the one at this hotel had the standard luxurious soft furnishings and heavy drapes with huge tie backs and fancy window dressings. The neutral, cream colored, deep pile carpet and velvet furniture and shiny, walnut hardwood end tables were obviously expensive. For me though, they all looked the same. The only thing that ever changed was the direction of the bedroom and the bed.

Funny how those rooms used to intimidate me, yet it was only décor, but when I glanced at Chloe standing over by a console table with a huge display of fresh flowers, I could see that's exactly what was going on with her as well.

Chloe was wearing a soft, loose, electric blue, sleeveless silk blouse and a mid-thigh length straight skirt and stiletto shoes. Height-wise her head fitted perfectly into my neck. Her soft, golden, silky blonde hair was to die for and smelled so incredible that I seemed to inhale involuntarily every time I came into contact with her.

Looking younger than her age, she seemed tiny standing next to the massive flower display and large gold gilt edged mirror. She had one arm across her waist hugging herself was biting her lip. My instinct was to go and hug her to make her feel safe.

Taking her in my arms, she was tense again, struggling to deal with whatever was going on with her thoughts. "Chloe, despite what you think, I really want you here with me." As soon as I spoke, I felt her body sag against mine and she relaxed into my arms so I kept going, but my dick grew hard and strained against the buttons of my jeans, and I tried my best to ignore it and focus on her.

"This isn't a chore for me being with you, Chloe. It feels effortless most of the time." Chloe leaned back and stared up at me.

"When I'm not drowning, crying or having a meltdown you mean?"

Delivered with a straight face, Chloe's irony cracked me up and I began to laugh loudly. "Oh honey, those were the most effortless moments of the whole deal. I love the fact that you did what you thought you had to do to get my attention."

Chloe's lips curved into her gorgeous smile as she gave me a small infectious chuckle. Her smile lit up her eyes and I couldn't help but dip my head and kiss her softly on her lips. Both of our smiles dropped as we gazed into each other's eyes, which soon became an intense stare. I'd never seen her look as beautiful as she did at that moment.

Nothing could have stopped me from kissing her again and when I did I couldn't hold back my desire any longer. As soon as my tongue penetrated her mouth and hers began to play with mine, the passion I'd been reigning in began to unleash.

Holding her even closer, my hands snuck under her blouse and skimmed over the smooth skin on her back. We both erupted in goose bumps, still kissing her hungrily, I dipped slightly and lifted her up into my arms, briefly breaking the kiss. Chloe's arms encircled my head and her mouth found mine again.

Confident that she wanted me as much as I wanted her, I walked her over toward the super king bed and gently lowered her onto her back. As soon as her head hit the pillow, I lowered myself fully onto her my lower body lying heavily against hers, but taking my upper body weight on my elbows. When I did, I couldn't resist grinding my hard, aching dick against her pubic bone.

Chloe sighed softly against my neck and gave me the sweetest moan I'd ever heard. That sound unleashed all of the pent up feelings about her I'd been trying to keep a wrap on. Lust and want flooded my veins and my desire to have her overwhelmed me.

Looking into Chloe's eyes, they were cloudy with lust as well, her sclera turning from pure white to having that pink tinge that said she wanted more than we were doing.

Suddenly our hands were all over each other. Rolling us on our sides, our hands ran through each other's hair, mine clasping hers against her neck, pulling her face nearer to me and taking her mouth in a hungry passionate kiss. I was in danger of losing control so I pulled back and paused to look at her.

Her lips were already bruised from our passionate kiss and her breasts were heaving because our kiss had left her breathless. "Are you okay, Chloe?" Chloe stared at me, then smirked and nodded, her face a little flushed with how much she had been letting herself go as well.

Taking the hem of her blouse in my hands, I began to tug it up and she surprised me when she sat up for me to remove it. Discarding it on the floor, my hands slid up to cup her breasts as she rolled onto her back. All of that seemed to become one fluid movement in my mind. It probably wasn't like that at all but that's how it felt.

At the same time, Chloe fisted of my t-shirt and began to haul it up my back, silently telling me she didn't want the material barrier between us either. Quickly removing it for her, Chloe's hands ran over my back and around to my ribs and the sensation made me shudder. Her touch was electric and I could feel pre-cum escape from my aching dick that was pressing hard against my soaked boxer briefs.

Within seconds we were naked, her tugging at my belt buckle and me ripping her lacy panties, then suddenly she was on top of me, sixty-nine position, with my head buried between her legs and my dick in her mouth. Chloe was stroking and sucking my shaft, making soft moans and slurping noises with her mouth, and my tongue was lapping around her pussy like a man dying of thirst.

"Fuck me, Gibson." I stopped dead, thinking my

mind made it up, that she'd just said that to me, but then she said it again. "Please fuck me, Gibson." Believe me, it registered the second time.

Flipping Chloe onto her back, I held myself back for a moment, delivering warm, wet kisses all over her neck and breasts, but Chloe was wriggling and her wet heat was hard to ignore as she'd wrapped herself around one of my legs and was leaving a trail of her sweet juice all over it.

"You know, when I get inside you this time I'm not going to be able to be as gentle as the last?"

Chloe smiled sexily at me, her eyes hinting at the promise of her own sinful thoughts and laughed softly. "I'm banking on that."

Damn, those words made me desperate to have her. Lifting her thigh over my arm, I spread her legs wide with the other hand and leaned forward to kiss her. "Hang on, Chloe, I intend to enjoy every single second of being inside your body. You showed me your version of star gazing darlin' it's my turn to show you mine."

Yeah, I know it sounded corny. I was joking with her, wanting to ease any last tension she was having right out of her body before I put it right back there for her, but mine was going to be sexual.

Lining my dick up, I drew my fingers down her entrance again, and felt them being coated in her slick, sweet, nectar. I knew we were on. Drawing one finger over her lips I bent in and kissed her hard, letting her taste herself on me.

Pulling away slightly, I rested my forehead on

hers and stared deeply into her eyes. She held my gaze intensely as I began to slide my dick slowly inside her. Chloe's eyes initially widened, as did mine I think, she was so fucking tight but she was dripping wet, so I pushed myself balls deep and stayed still for a moment.

Chloe swallowed hard and I kissed her mouth passionately then bent to take a breast in my mouth. A soft moan and a long sigh escaped from her lips and I growled deeply. I was so turned on I was fighting not to just take her as hard and fast as I could.

Sucking her nipple a few times, I felt her pussy clench back, pulsing and squeezing my dick tightly, telling me what I was doing was affecting her to her core. Glancing up at her face, she smiled down at me and I knew she really wanted whatever I was about to give her, so I began to fuck her. Hard.

Pure passion and desire was poured out in that bed toward her. Nothing tame or caring in what I was doing. I just showed her my pure unadulterated lust for her and she took everything I could give her.

Changing position several times, Chloe came over and over. Smiling and moaning softly, it was clear she was handling my vigorous pounding of her sweet pussy and loving every minute of it. "Oh Gibson, you feel so good... right there... don't stop."

Two hours later, we'd both had a very thorough workout resulting in countless orgasms for her and three of my own. We lay breathless and panting, soaked in sweat, and she started laughing loudly. I'd licked, sucked and fucked about every inch of her as she did the same to me, and I was already desperate for more of her.

Smoking wasn't the word for the chemistry between us, it was more like a fucking forest fire. She must have been sore, because the end of my dick was raw. All that she'd been through and she reacted to me like that. *Damn.*

I nearly choked at how free she was during our session, knowing her history. Nails scraping and clawing my back and the little wildcat bit my neck and gave me a hickey, which I never noticed until I was a few minutes from going on stage later that night. I'd have given her one back but for what had happened to her with Kace. I hadn't wanted to do anything that frightened her.

The strangest thing about being with Chloe was there was no question about me doing a 'done and run' with her. Pulling her close, we lay quietly while I stroked her hair and her belly, cupped her breast and when she turned and laid her head on my chest and sighed heavily, it had been the best feeling in the world.

I knew there was still all the shit with Kace to deal with, and I still had to get to the bottom of the feeling I had about her friend, Ruby. Tori was going to be a problem as well, I could see that already. Whatever was coming, my priority had to be trying to make Chloe trust me and give her the confidence to make her resilient enough to deal with whatever we faced.

CHAPTER 40

REARING UP

Chloe

Sitting in the tub thinking about what had happened between Gibson and me a couple of hours before had my head in a strange place. Something had shifted in the both of us – between the both of us. Feeling confused and elated, I remembered Ruby's comment about sex being fun, then tried to reason what I'd just done with him and what it meant for me.

There was no way I could say there was no emotion in what had happened between us. Not for me anyway. It was weird, Gibson had this reputation, yet I had placed more trust in him in the previous couple of days than I had in the whole time I'd been in my long-term relationship. What did that mean? Were my defenses completely shot to hell after Kace?

Climbing out of the bath was a slow process for me. I was feeling really tender after sex with Gibson.

He hadn't held back and he all but demolished me during that couple of hours. Although, instead of Gibson's alpha-male-aura scaring me, he seemed to empower me sexually.

Gibson's strong handling and confident skill, along with his expert understanding of a woman's body, gave me a sexual experience I could never have imagined was possible.

Again, he'd confused me because of all the encounters I'd ever witnessed. I had been used to seeing Gibson thank the woman then disappear like some genie from a lamp. Yet, after sex with me, he stayed there hugging and caressing me. There was no hint he wanted to be anywhere else, but it was his room so he couldn't exactly disappear from there either.

A soft knock on the bathroom door, then Gibson strode in and sat on the toilet. "How are you feeling?" *He was interested in how I was feeling?* "Are you sore after..."

I wondered why he was still being considerate toward me. What had happened had been my choice as well as his. "Yeah, I'm fine thanks, you?" Gibson smirked and shook his head.

"Damn, Chloe *my* dick is tender. That's a first." I blushed pink and he stood up and bent over to place his hand on the back of my head, kissing me softly then straightened his stance again.

"I'm going to have to head to the festival, Chloe. Stay here and take your time. Jerry is going to bring you when you are ready. I've punched his number in your cell phone, it's on the night stand."

Without another word, Gibson walked through the door and a few moments later I heard the suite door latch click shut. Twenty minutes after that, I had dried my hair and pulled on some jeans and a figure hugging red top. It was dressy but not over the top. Stepping into my black Jimmy Choo Stilettos, I was as ready as I'd ever be to face the public with Gibson.

While I stood quietly in the elevator, I had a chance to reflect on something that Gibson had said that made me scared and excited about what I was doing. I had taken a chance when I left Kace, and that chance in some weird way had led me to Gibson. And now I was taking another to be with him.

We'd talked just before I went into the bath and decided we'd announce we were indeed a couple. Then he said something that my mind wouldn't compute the consequences of.

"Chloe, you are my last score... my fucking symphony." Gibson smiled warmly and kissed my nose when he saw my puzzled face. "You don't get that? A symphony is usually made up of four different elements that come together to make this amazing music, Chloe. A masterpiece. You bring warmth to my heart, fierce feelings to protect you, you make me horny and affectionate beyond reason and those four things bring light to my soul and make me happier than I've ever felt before."

Recalling his words brought a smile to my lips. When I stepped out of the elevator, Jerry was waiting and gave me a tight smile back as he strode toward me. It was then I became aware that the foyer was full of women and a tall, leggy, red headed girl wearing a t-shirt with Gibson's face on it was running toward me.

"Whore." She spat. Reaching out, her hand barely skimmed my hair as she tried to grab it. Looking stunned for a second. I could hardly move as Jerry spun her away with one hand and ushered me at speed towards the door.

Half running and half being dragged, my heart was beating wildly in my chest, pulsating in my neck and I was shocked at what had just happened. The reality of the situation I was in hit me and I was scared that someone who never even knew me wanted to hurt me that badly.

Flashes of Kace coming at me raced through my mind and as Jerry secured me and started to drive I fought back tears and wondered again, what the hell I was doing there at all. Jerry was talking rapidly to me but I wasn't taking anything in. It was all just noise, because the sound of blood swishing in my ears and my panicked state were preventing me from processing anything else that was going on.

Jerry stopped the car and came into the back seat. "Jeez, Chloe, you need to toughen up, girl. That's going to be a regular feature if you hang around the main man. Crazy chicks are hard core in this industry and if he's boning you they won't like it that much. You just gotta suck it up and deal, hon. It's the way of the world."

Staring back at him, I was thinking it might be the way of Gibson's world, but it hasn't been mine. If being that close to danger was a regular event then it was doubtful that I could stay in that environment. I was just beginning to find myself again, and there was no way I wanted to be placed in a situation that meant I was going to be subjected to more violence by anyone.

Still shaking by the time we arrived at the festival, I was petrified to get out of the car. Jerry was telling me how it was going to go and then suddenly the door was open and there were four burly security guys; two either side of me, arms outstretched, ushering me into the backstage area. There were a lot of people milling around, although this was the artists entrance we'd driven into.

Jerry caught up with me, explaining that Gibson also had fans who were celebrities so they weren't taking any chances with me. That comment made me even more worried about being associated with Gibson Barclay.

Once inside, Jerry told me we could relax and began to walk me towards a series of doors with various well known bands, and solo artists' names on the doors. M3rCy was right at the end and Jerry explained it was so that no one disturbed them when they were resting before the gig.

Pushing the door open, the first person I saw was Tori, who threw me a look that could have killed then put her head down shaking it like she was disappointed. Placing her palms on the dressing table she pushed herself to stand and walked past me.

"Go home, little girl – you're going to be eaten alive." It was said in almost a whisper, but the tone of her voice told me in no uncertain terms it was a threat.

Gibson had begun to stand when I went in and was smiling when he saw me, his lips stretching to form a grin until the altercation with Tori. "What the fuck did she just say to you?"

Gibson's face was dark and I was not about to upset the applecart when he was about to go on stage. "Welcome to the madhouse honey," I replied.

Gibson's face relaxed and he strode over and pulled me into a hug. "Damn, girl, you look good enough to eat." Smirking, he bent his head, placing his lips close to my ears. "Oh, but I did that already, right? I'll just have to work up an appetite on stage so that I can fit those seconds in I guess." Leaning back, he grinned wickedly and came back in for a hungry kiss.

Normally I'd have been embarrassed, but the way that Tori had behaved made me want to show her that she was toying with the wrong girl. Just because I hadn't said much didn't mean I wasn't capable of taking care of myself, so I kissed Gibson back, allowing my hands to snake up his t-shirt and run across his belly and back.

Gibson pushed back and stared at me with hungry eyes, cloudy with lust and he shivered more than once when I'd stroked my hands over him. He had certainly been getting aroused and his hands slipped to cup my ass and pull me against him.

"Fuck, Chloe. I can't do this now. You've gone and made me hard in these skinny jeans. You need to keep those magic hands of yours in your pockets pre-gigs, darlin'." The beaming smile on his face made his eyes twinkle and my heart fluttered in my chest at the way he was looking at me.

Someone coughed at the side of us and Gibson turned his head. My eyes followed his and we saw Lennox smirking and shaking his head. "Hmm... definitely a first. Get your horny ass over with the rest of us and put her down. You can play with her later."

Gibson punched Lennox on the shoulder. "No one plays with Chloe. Not even me, and fuckers, y'all are gonna give her respect, y'all hear me?" Simon made a snorting noise and Mick and Lennox started laughing. Mick came over and put his arm around me. Gibson scowled and he put his hands up and backed away from me.

"Jeez, Gib, I was only going to welcome her into the fold, dude." Mick turned to face me, "Seriously Chloe, it's great to have someone to keep this dumb fuck in his place. Anyone that can control his dick is an asset to us all, right guys?"

Gibson's jaw twitched and he threw a fuck-you look at Mick and his smile dropped like Gibson had slapped him. "Joking aside, glad to have you with us, Chloe. I'm sure Tori will be happy for the female company." Glancing at Tori, she gave me a sarcastic smile and then went back to reading her Kindle.

Initially, I hated standing there being judged by all of them, wondering what they thought about me, and maybe taking bets about how long I'd last. After a few minutes though, they were chatting easily and asking my opinion about stuff and I really felt accepted by them. Well... all but their female band member.

Rapid knocking and the ten minute call came from a muffled voice outside the door. Everyone in the room immediately got on their feet and I suddenly realized how conditioned these guys were. It may have been the same routine they did week in week out, but they were all extremely disciplined and professional as soon as it came time for them to go to work.

Staring out from the side of the stage was a surreal experience. Watching the thousands of heads, the nearest with faces so clear, their expressions were priceless. Looking back further I couldn't even ascertain the hair coloring.

Monotonous low murmurs of noise from the sea of heads echoed in the stadium until they killed the lights, then there was an instant silence. I was in awe at how the flick of a switch could control that many people.

Once that initial act had sunk in, the anticipation of the crowd to the band coming on stage had begun to grip them and there was a low buzz of conversation. I stood waiting with them and for the inevitable roar of appreciation from them when Gibson and the rest of M3rCy were visible on stage.

I was extremely excited at being given the privilege of seeing M3rCy perform at such close quarters, and like the crowd, I was buzzing as well, especially since I knew Gibson intimately by then. I was still getting my head around that thought when the bass boomed out of the amp next to me, and I almost jumped out of my skin with fright.

Stunned, then shocked to the core by the sudden noise and the pace their performance moved at, it took me a couple of minutes to focus at what was going down on stage. Gibson was Gibson at his best, flirting with all the women, but he never touched anyone, not like in the old days when he was being dragged off of female fans at Beltz.

That performer had been a boy. The version I was looking at in front of me right then was very much a man. A man who could do and have whatever he wanted. Girl after girl threw numbers on stage and Gibson played into that by picking them up and putting them in his pockets.

Tori came off stage during a song where there were no keyboards and stood beside me. Folding her arms she said, "I give you a week." Inclining her head at Gibson she said, "Baby girl, he's way too hard for you to handle. Trust me. That right there is a *lot* of man. He can play rough."

I had already made my mind up about her. Anything she said I was going to suck it up even if I didn't like it. Turning to look at her, she was giving me a smirk, and I could see that she looked smug.

Tori had a trump card; I'd seen that look before

and there was no way I was giving that girl the satisfaction of seeing me running scared. "And you'd be the one to know that how?"

Snickering she said, "Well, he almost cut me in two when he made me come. And he's rough. So..." Eyeing me up and down, she took a towel down from her shoulder and dried sweat from her arm then placed it back there again with a smug smirk on her face.

Her words demolished me and as I looked up at Gibson I almost faltered in my resolve, but he was doing an acoustic set of "Inches From Paradise" sitting at my side of the stage with a single set of blue spotlights shining on him.

I stopped thinking and started listening, mesmerized. When he finished the song, it was as if he sensed I needed him and turned, smiling over at me. However, when he saw Tori speaking to me, his face became dark and he began to stride across the stage in my direction. As soon as I saw his reaction, I was sure she had been telling me the truth.

Overwhelming emotions of jealousy, loss and hopelessness threatened to cripple me as I stood there for a moment, my eyes flicking between Gibson and Tori, then out to the crowd that were predominately women at the front. I then wondered how I was supposed go forward with everything I knew about him? All that temptation day after day, staring him in the face.

Before Gibson could get to me Tori stated, "Day one, Chloe. That's when he made me come. He's a one and done kind of guy. You want to try to tame that dick? Good luck girl, but if I were you I'd get that shiny little luggage bag of yours and get out of Dodge. He'll break your heart and you don't look like the kind of girl that can deal with the shit that's gonna be slung in your direction."

Swallowing hard, I knew that if Tori hadn't delivered her last few sentences in the way she had, in all probability I'd have made the decision to cut and run, but when I saw the look on Gibson's face, I knew that someone had to place their trust in him.

Against all the odds of us meeting again, against everything my head was telling me, I was still standing right there in front of him. Someone had to place their trust in him sometime, and he'd asked that it be me.

Smiling at Gibson, I blew him a kiss and his concerned, furrowed brow seemed to disappear with the impact of it. A wide smile spread and he winked sexily at me, making my panties instantly wet.

Confident for the moment I was making the right choice, I turned back to Tori stating, "Yeah, maybe that's the difference between you and me. There's a huge difference between five years and five minutes, honey. Maybe if you hadn't been so blatant and easy, you would have had more success."

I gave her an intentional smug smirk and looked her up and down. "Then again… maybe not. By the way, I'm not the pushover you think I am. And, for your information, I fight dirty. So bring it on Tori, because Gibson wants me and you just made my mind up for me. So... I guess I'm definitely staying, unless you stop having designs honey, my guess is your card is marked."

Shaking inside, I was impressed at how confident I'd sounded when I delivered my warning. My epic performance with Tori, the first class bitch, was almost as good as the one Gibson had just finished on stage. I felt that whatever was going on was between me and Gibson and what came out of it may be something and nothing, but for that moment I'd made up my mind to be with him.

Gibson came off stage and scooped me up in his arms, my legs wrapping around his waist as his hands slid under my ass in support like a well-practised routine. Backing me up against the wall, his sweaty face was inches from mine.

As we walked away from the stage, the lights came on and the crowd began to leave. "Love Runs Out" by One Republic played on the Tannoy and Gibson hummed the tune for a moment, then turned and looked at me again.

"Are we okay?" Smiling, I nodded and his mouth crushed mine in a devastatingly, mind blowing kiss and my heart raced as my senses went into overdrive. When he drew back to look at me he gave me a knowing smirk. "Promise you won't laugh?" Furrowing my brow, I nodded again.

"Chloe... right here, at this moment you give me reason." I almost asked him what he meant, but something inside told me that what he had said was a big deal for him so I just smiled slowly and shook my head bashfully, then dropped my gaze. Gibson's finger crooked under my chin and he lifted my head to fix my gaze again. "So Chloe Jenner, are we going to do this? Are you ready to trust me?"

No way was I ready to give Gibson an all-access pass to my feelings and fully commit to anything, but I was happy to be with him until he gave me reason not to be. "Trust is somewhere in the future for me, Gibson. If you can accept that, then I'm here. Whatever else happens is up to you."

Gibson nodded and pulled me in for a hug, and I knew then that it was really the beginning of something between us. The odds of us ever even coming across one another again had been an almost infinite number, so I figured as long as I had one rule, if he raised his voice in anger to me or I felt threatened by him, then that would be my cue to leave.

The odds were definitely stacked against me with Gibson and I knew I was choosing a dangerous path to go down, but I had played it safe with Kace and look how that turned out. Gibson had said we get one life and that I was different. I had barely existed for the previous year with Kace, but with Gibson I felt I had lived a year in a day when I was with him... and he made me feel safe.

There was definitely some rough times in our future with the constant fear of what Kace's next move would be and how the media would deal with us as a couple. And I'd be hated by Gibson's fans. Those thoughts petrified me, but I knew I wanted to be with him, so I had to trust the team of people working with him to keep me safe.

"You can be with someone a lifetime and not know them," Gibson had once said to me. That was certainly true about Kace, I thought I knew him well and being with Gibson and seeing how he was in public and private, in one day I felt I had a better insight into him than I ever had with Kace.

All it had taken was a few days for Gibson to rock my world as I knew it. I was thinking about Gibson's legacy and what that meant for his former reputation as a womanizer. Could I change that? I was up for the challenge.

I was scared as hell about trying to fit in to his future, but he'd chosen me and gone to lengths for us to get that far, so I figured it was time for me to meet him half way.

To be continued

OTHER TITLES BY K.L. SHANDWICK

Lily's story (The Everything Trilogy)

Book 1 Enough Isn't Everything

Book 2 Everything She Needs

Book 3 Everything I Want

Love With Every Beat (Alfie's POV on music, fame and love).

just Jack (Jack from the Everything series).

The Last Score Series

Gibson's Legacy

Trusting Gibson

ABOUT K.L. SHANDWICK

K. L. Shandwick lives on the outskirts of London. She started writing after a challenge by a friend when she commented on a book she read. The result of this was "The Everything Trilogy." Her background has been mainly in the health and social care sector in the U.K. She is still currently a freelance or self-employed professional in this field. Her books tend to focus on the relationships of the main characters. Writing is a form of escapism for her and she is just as excited to find out where her characters take her as she is when she reads another author's work.

Website:
http://www.klshandwick.com/
Facebook:
https://www.facebook.com/kl.shandwick
Twitter:
https://twitter.com/klshandwick

CPSIA information can be obtained
at www.ICGtesting.com
Printed in the USA
LVOW04s1742180117
521395LV00015B/1379/P